The Breakdown Lane

The Breakdown Lane

Jacquelyn Mitchard

HarperCollins*Publishers*

HarperCollins books may be purchased for educational, business, or sales promotional use. For information, please write: Special Markets Department, HarperCollins Publishers Inc., 10 East 53rd Street, New York, NY 10022.

FIRST EDITION

Designed by Joseph Rutt

Printed on acid-free paper

Library of Congress Cataloging-in-Publication Data

Mitchard, Jacquelyn.

The breakdown lane / Jacquelyn Mitchard–1st ed.

p. cm.

ISBN 0-06-058724-5 (alk. paper)

1. Multiple sclerosis—Patients—fiction. 2. Mother and child—Fiction. I. Title.

PS3563.I7358B74 2005

813'.54—dc22

2004042375

05 06 07 08 09   ❖/RRD   10 9 8 7 6 5 4 3 2 1

For Patty and Patti,
One mom, one mainstay,
And for Jeanine, forever pal and body double

Acknowledgments

———~———

Though this story is entirely a product of my imagination, and any errors of fact my own, multiple sclerosis is a real and vicious disease, a thief that each year randomly robs strength from 50 percent more women than men in the prime of their lives. For helping me understand its ravages, I thank Rebecca Johnson, Bob Engel, Sara Derosa, and Sarah Meltzer. Linda Lerman gave me advice on advice. Dan Jackson helped me understand dance. I thank the Ragdale Foundation in Lake Forest, Illinois, without which no book of mine ever would have been written, and where portions of this one were written in spring of 2004. Grazie to Roberta, Ed, Steve, and John for their candor on the subject of breaking up and to the three kind women who told me of the hopeful and sometimes vexing world of alternative communities. Good buddy Kathleen graciously looked at Julieanne's poems. My friend and editor, Marjorie Braman, with her piano tuner's ear for words and phrases, the divine Miss Kelly, who has made every book a cause for celebration, the finest publisher I know, HarperCollins, and my cherished agent, Jane Gelfman, for twenty-two years my reliable tether to reality, deserve Purple Hearts all around for putting up with me. I owe much to Pamela English, my assistant, my heart, and part of my own intentional community, and send love also to Franny, Jill, Karen, Kitt, Joyce, Stacy, Gillian, Karen T., Laurie, Bri and Jan, Clarice, Emily, Cathy G., Mary Clarke, and Esa. My magnificent sons and daughters and my gentle husband, Chris, you are all the center of the center of my heart.

But for D.C.B.A., my own "Gabe," this one is especially for you.

But, when the days of golden dreams had perished,
And even Despair was powerless to destroy;
Then did I learn how existence could be cherished,
Strengthened, and fed without the aid of joy.

—Emily Brontë,
"Remembrance"

The
Breakdown
Lane

Genesis

EXCESS BAGGAGE
by J. A. Gillis
The Sheboygan News-Clarion

Dear J.,

*I'm getting married next summer, to a man of another
nationality. Both families are very happy, but there is a
problem. His many female relatives—aunts, grandmothers, and
sisters—must sit in the front row, as is their right. As
descendants of the Masai in Africa, they are very tall. My
family is Japanese-American. We are small—in number and in
size. My father is only five feet four, my sisters less than five feet.
The wedding will take place in a hotel ballroom with chairs set
up in rows. We did not want to have a "bride's" side and a
"groom's" side, because we want this to be a true blending of
families. However, I know that the women in my fiancé's family
are going to wear large, decorative hats (I don't mean
ceremonial headdresses, as these are African AMERICANS of
many generations, but what my fiancé refers to as "church-lady"
hats, which are the size of our wedding cake). This will make
them even taller, and so no one except my mother and father
will be able to see me during the ceremony. I don't want to
suggest that they "move to the back of the bus" for my family. So
how can we avoid slighting anyone on our special day? Given*

the disparity of heights, the wedding dance will also be very awkward.

Nervous in Knudson

Dear Nervous,

   This is a matter of some sensitivity, since tensions on a wedding day can leave a bitter taste that can linger for years. But nerves? You've already probably got the once-in-a-lifetime jitters every bride endures. Don't add this small opportunity for creativity to your checklist of stress. With the same joy of life you've already demonstrated by your beautifully bold choice to mingle cultures, craft a circle of joy. Ask the staff at the hotel to place the wedding chairs in a wide circle with the first row reserved for the principal members of both families and the rest of the chairs in staggered rows behind, so that each person, regardless of heights, will enjoy a wonderful view. Guests will be escorted through a small opening, the same place your groom will enter with his parents, a few moments before you enter with yours. Make the altar or other ceremonial platform in the center "a round," also—perhaps exchanging your vows facing in one direction, conducting the ceremonies of rings or candles facing the other, with the transitions gracefully made to instrumental music or song. As for the dance! No one feels awkward at such a happy affair! Think of all the aunts and grandmas you've seen dancing the polka in groups of five!

J.

Let's begin at the end of the beginning. The first moment of the second act of our lives.

It was ballet class. It was the second class of the week, made up of dance combinations and mat Pilates. Steady on the studio floor, I was ready to begin my final stretches. I remember that, a wonderful feeling. I was spent, but pleasurably, my hips not so much aching as aware they'd been asked for something strenuous. This class, and my weight training were the times during my week I felt freed from strain, just shy of pure.

I extended my right leg along the floor in its customary turnout—posturally correct, erect on my sitz bones, a little bit smug, but trying not to glance around me to observe that other women, even younger women, noticed the way my flexibility still came easily—and leaned forward for the hamstring stretch.

What I saw when I looked down horrified me so much that my mind scrabbled away from me, across the birchy floor.

What was it?

Numb shard of bone? Foot clawed birdlike, in spasm?

Worse. It was . . . nothing.

Nothing was different than what I'd seen when I sat down five seconds earlier. It was only my leg, my ordinary leg in the unsoiled glove of my unitard (the silver one my youngest daughter used to call my "mermaid clothes") still bent in a forty-five-degree angle at the knee, my pointed toe nestled against my thigh.

Doesn't sound like much, does it?

You have a right to expect more of terrors. Sharp, single shriek on a silent street. Pea-sized lump your finger grazes as you soap your breast. Tang of smoke in the still air, footsteps' rhythm matching your own, in the dusk of an empty parking lot. A shadow that jumps against a wall in a room in which you know you are alone.

But think! A thing so huge it will dismember your world can be invisible. It can be a germ. A scent. It can be an absence.

You see, I had *felt* my leg open smoothly, like a knife with a well-balanced mechanism. But it had not.

A cascade of thoughts, like the fountain from a child's sparkler, showered over me: the phantom limb phenomenon, the precursor to a stroke, a paralysis caused by some virus. My first instinct was to scream. Instead, like any sane person, I tried again.

My leg refused.

Metallic, icy sweat burst from my pores, bathing my face and neck, painting gleaming half-moons under my breasts. I dampened like a true mermaid in my "mermaid's clothes." From the corner of my eye, I glanced at my friend, Cathy, who took the class with me, as her arms branched and she arched down over her own leg. Her eyes, closed in concentration, suddenly flipped up, like one of those old venetian blinds, as if she'd heard a crack, a clap, as if I truly *had* screamed. She looked at me, quizzically, one eyebrow a beckoning finger. I grinned. I had just thought of it! My leg had gone to sleep. That was the matter! It happened to people. I grinned at her again. She smiled back.

I concentrated harder, and then watched my leg extend, slowly, creeping along the floor. But no longer like a part of my body. It felt like a robotic arm that I was operating for the first time. The outer edge of my thigh tingled, feeling like what I remembered of an acupuncture treatment I'd once had, to allay cramps. Somehow, I finished the stretches, no one but me noticing anything odd.

I kissed the air in Cath's general direction, skipped coffee, and went home.

My husband, Leo, was lying on the floor, his back propped over his spine-alignment device, his laptop balanced on his belly—at that point, a trifle convex, since he'd gained a little weight. At such times, Leo never seemed overjoyed to see me come in, flushed and refreshed from class. It must have felt like a reproach.

"Lee," I said, "my leg feels funny. It did something in class."

He lowered his John Lennon readers. "It did something?"

"I can't explain it, but yeah."

"You're too old for that class, Julie. Why you have to contort yourself, what you're trying to prove . . . I've said this a hundred times. . . ."

"No, it's not that!" I protested, "Margot Fonteyn danced professionally into her fifties. Leslie Caron—"

"You're not Margot Fonteyn," Leo said, "and you're not Leslie Caron." But then, before I exploded and told him to go to hell, he went and Leotized me, just as he'd done for almost twenty years. "I always saw you more as the Cyd Charisse type, da legs and de attitude, too, a midwestern gun moll with a checkered past. You know?"

"Shut up," I told him, already charmed.

I looked over his head, outside to our neat and rustic yard with its boulders and perennials, to where my son Gabe, then—what?—thirteen? Anyhow, too old to be doing what he was doing, hanging upside down from a branch, swinging dreamily like some daylight bat, the smile on his face so rapturous it stopped short of goofy. He was wearing thirty-dollar Dockers, special-occasion pants, the kind of clothes a kid would wear to church if we were the kind of family who went to church regularly. There was no reason for him to be wearing them; he had only one pair, and it was late spring. They simply must have been the first thing Gabe saw. He was ruining them. Back and forth, he swung, lithe and odd as a lemur. Something about Gabe, out there, alone in his solitary but never lonesome-seeming world, suddenly felt so precious but fragile.

"Leo," I all but whimpered, "Leo, if I get the arnica, will you help me rub this? I can't quite reach where it hurts. It doesn't exactly hurt, really, so much as . . ."

He said no.

He said, "*No*, Jules. Come on. You keep on pretending you're twenty, you're going to pull a hamstring. You can rub your own leg. I'm busy."

"Leo!" I said. "Get over it! I need your help here."

"Julie," Leo-my-husband murmured softly, "what you need to work on more is salvaging the inside of yourself rather than the outside. People are so damned shallow. I think that every time I read another one of these"— he gestured at his screen—"complaints about a professor grabbing a graduate student's butt."

"We're talking about *my* butt, Leo! Also my cardiovascular health. And stress relief. How the hell does my exercising get in *your* way? Ballet and Pilates are very inexpensive forms of therapy for my *insides*." I added, "What, do you think the outside's a lost cause? If you loved me, you'd carry me into the bedroom!"

"If I carried you into the bedroom, you'd have to carry me to the chiropractor," he said, slipping his glasses back up into their proper position. Later on I would realize that not one but *two* cherce pieces of evidence had been offered to me on the same day, on a silver platter (and yes, here, the question, did a house have to fall on you, does apply). Something was amiss in my nervous system and in the ecosystem of my marriage. And I ignored them.

Now, English major that I am, I could suggest that if Nathaniel Hawthorne were writing this, he might have done a switcheroo: *Gentle reader, we may now slip unobserved behind the back of our suddenly and unpredictably taciturn, nay may we say even hostile Goodman Steiner, and cast our own eyes upon that which absorbed his attention so fully, so attenuated his concentration away from the predicament faced by his woeful spouse . . .* you get the drift: We could have seen whether Leo was really reading a sexual harassment complaint or, *with secret and concealed passions,* writing to *AN INTIMATE.*

An INTIMATE.

Mine would be another word.

Slut springs to mind. Somebody who made Hester Prynne look like a Benedictine nun.

Perhaps Young Goodman Steiner was writing: "Julie's just home; she's finally hurt her leg badly in her ridiculous ballet class, and I'm sorry I can't be more sympathetic. But $75 a week on exercise?" The reply would have come some minutes later (because true e-simul-chat was not ubiquitous back then). It might have read this way: "Oh Leo, and doesn't she know that for that kind of money, she could save lives? Doesn't she know babies are dying in Rhodesia?" (She, *the intimate,* wouldn't have known it isn't called Rhodesia anymore, because she's so fucking dumb. Ignore that last statement, jury. It's not only way too soon in the story for me to have

known this, it was unkind. She's not that dumb. She's smart enough
to . . . well . . . follow package directions.)

But, who can say what Leo was really doing?

Perhaps Leo *was* reading a sexual-harassment complaint.

Still, whatever the reason, he was acting weird. He was not the kind of
petty bastard who would refuse to help a limping wife. Looking back, I
can see that the way he behaved toward me that afternoon was the domestic equivalent of my thigh tingling in class. It was the trumpet call
outside the gates from the enemy, signaling they would take no prisoners.
And yet, how could I have known that?

What I did know was that *my* Leo would have shaken his head, and
bitched a little bit more about my obsession with keeping up some vestige
of my ancient girlish dancer's fitness, and then gone into the kitchen and
gotten the arnica. He'd have rubbed my leg, trying but unable to sustain
his grouchiness, begun to enjoy the clefts, the topography of the muscles
in my girl places, gradually giving in to a rueful, half-hitched Leo smile.
He'd maybe even have flirted a little, though it would have been the middle of the afternoon, rubbed my butt until I pushed him away—but not
too far away.

And so, I didn't say, *Leo, what's wrong?*

I didn't plop down my things and snipe, You little shit. What are you,
jealous that I can still do the splits and you sit around so much you can't
even bend at the waist?

Instead, I went into my room and, wobbling, removed my clothing,
showered, rubbed the arnica on myself, and lay on my bed with my own
laptop, opening my latest batch of letters, asking for advice, because giving advice is what I did for a living.

Isn't that rich?

I gave people advice on their personal lives.

Me. The poster princess for willful self-delusion.

But I was Julieanne Ambrose Gillis. And as a Gillis, denial was my
birthright.

My parents could drink themselves cross-eyed on a Saturday night and serenely check the waffles for just the right golden skin not six hours later, while a maid quietly and without expression emptied into a plastic sack bloated cigarette butts from highball glasses and splashed club soda onto the wine stains on the carpet. The maid would ignore the waffles and the stains, and we, my little sister Jane and I, would ignore the maid—although, most days of the week, she was our after-school friend and confidante. A post-Cheever Sunday morning was observed, however, with cathedral silence. My father, after all, had bearing. He was A. Bartlett Gillis, popular, bestselling, and yet grudgingly respected novelist, once chair of the fiction jury for the National Book Awards, an aside he managed to slip into three-quarters of his conversations, possibly because his books were historical and featured a serial character, and he wasn't entirely comfortable with that. My mother was, like him, a nightly tippler and a weekend binger. But hadn't they raised two lovely and accomplished daughters? Didn't they regularly receive invitations on paper with a deckled edge? Hadn't they met the queen of England, who confessed a delicious appetite for my dad's books? Almost single-handedly, by dint of publicity and connections, had my mom not saved the Malpole Library with its collection of Hopper drawings? What were a few carpet burns and a ginny stench that could be banished by throwing open the windows, along with the occasional bout of audible predawn retching, set against these achievements? Better just to proceed with breakfast.

Years later, when Panicked in Prairie du Sac would write to me, desperate because the half-dozen weeklong biking trips that Panicked's *sister* kept taking with Panicked's *husband* turned out not to have been a shared interest in sport but *an affair*, I would wonder how this woman had behaved before her lobotomy.

How, I would marvel, could anybody *not know*?

But you can. It's possible. You *can* choose not to know anything you want not to know, if you want badly enough not to know it. And if you have a little help. A husband who lies, for example, not only next to you in bed, but through his teeth.

Why did Leo get sick of me, our family, our food, our spir-it-u-al-ity-lacking life? It wasn't because I spent too much money on makeup or ballet.

I think he turned forty-nine and realized he was going to die, and wanted to negotiate this with the universe. I think he started to see his job as handholding instead of a quest for justice. I think the cuckoos who sent him literature like *Beneficent Bounty,* a cheesy magazine about sustainable agriculture and other great things a person could do to simultaneously rescue earth and soul, which he left lying all over the house, convinced him he was a hopeless bourgeois.

I know this because the one thing I learned from my parents' marriage was that it took work to stay together, and it was essential to remember what you loved instead of what drove you nuts, and to idealize your spouse. Maybe being a drunk helped.

And I did. I tried very hard.

And Leo did, too. He at one time brought me green tea every morning before he left for work (I worked from home by then). He made his one dish, bacon ravioli, which we all loved though it sounds putrid, every Friday night.

See me for a moment as I once was, before I got too sick to wash my own hair. See us.

Leo's cousin once told Leo, "Julie's pretty enough to be a second wife." (I didn't even like Leo's cousin, Jeremy. It's pitiful how much that comment still matters to me.)

I was a wife who left notes on the pillow. Funny cards. For our twentieth anniversary, a new ring with a J and L so cleverly intertwined in white gold that no one but someone who was really looking for it could see it wasn't just an abstract design. And Leo, Leo gave me a moose wearing ballet shoes, with a box holding diamond earrings tied to one paw, after letting me stomp around all day thinking he'd forgotten. I never went to bed without a pretty nightgown and brushed teeth. He never failed to carry in the grocery bags. I always wore something to the chancellor's picnic just unusual enough to gather approving comments but not arched stares, size ten, loose, Katharine Hepburn slacks, crisp, man-tailored shirt. I kept my mane when my contemporaries gave up and got those sheared little flat-bottomed ice-skater bobs, finger-tossing it wild, or looping it into my dancer's knot at the nape. See. A mother who never missed a play, a field trip, a game, a chess meet, or an excruciating band concert, who read *Charlotte's Web* and each of the Little House books aloud three times over the course of ten years, and got a karaoke machine for the kids instead of a Hotbox or whatever they call those hideous, violent video-game machines. Got (way) involved in school. Was gainfully, if not particularly profoundly, employed. Planned the vacations. Wrapped the packages. Still played quotes and strip Scrabble with Leo in bed, as we had when we were newlyweds.

And yes, I was conceited. Doesn't that make sense? Even in a yuck way? I thought I was an interesting wife. A cut above. I lived in Wisconsin, but I was clearly *of* the Upper West Side. I thought it was, well, grace and an aura of self-possession that kept me from disappearing when the clock struck forty. Vigilance and not blind, dumb luck that kept my kids safe and accomplished. And yes, I *did* think the outsides mattered. (Sonofabitch, given what happened, I have no reason to think otherwise.)

I was in fine shape.

Fine shape.

Not one single pound over the exact middle of the middle range of the actuarial tables.

Not one gray hair. Okay, a few gray hairs, a tiny thicket at one temple, which Teresa used her hairstylist's art to make resemble a small and perfect platinum fan.

Cholesterol, 188.

Yes, I got flanked—as one of the Civil War cavaliers in the books my father wrote would have said. Foes from within. Foes from without. Assassins' stealth.

And yes, I was the perfect medium, the well-prepared agar for this virus. Hominidus Gillis Julieannus, I could ignore, as a guy once said, the plank in my own eye even as I searched for the sliver in another's. *Your in-*

stincts are always right, I would tell people forty-seven times a year. Listen to them, no matter how lonely it feels, or whom you may think it might hurt.

The irony of that. It kills me.

It burns me.

And I haven't even gotten to what this really is about.

How can I write about that?

What this really is about is not me at all.

It's about the willful trashing of three great kids.

I can barely think about it.

That's why I babble about slacks and rings and picnics.

I can't stomach telling you about their burden. What they went through that I know about, and worse, what they went through that I don't. Gabe, Caroline, Aury. My rock, my lost angel, and my baby.

I'm so sorry.

Not that it makes a difference, but I'm so sorry.

"My conscience or my vanity appalled."—Yeats.

"What a maroon!"—Bugs Bunny.

When I consider the extremes to which my illness and Leo's defection drove my older children, I cringe. When I think of Aury's contorted, tearful, lost little face . . . I loathe myself.

In my column, I told people every single Sunday that they weren't allowed to feel guilty about things they didn't cause. But the kids couldn't help it, and neither can I. I feel more guilt about what I did to them, and it wasn't deliberate, than about what Leo did to all of us. I could imagine *other people's* children suffering the pangs and pains of guilt, the fallout of their parents' misdeeds and misfortunes. But not mine!

And yet.

The old adage says that every police officer, turned coin-side over, would be an outlaw; every psychiatrist, daft; every judge, a scoundrel. This said, how many of those who dispense wisdom possess it to any special degree? Or do they really, unawares, need it most of all?

All those warnings.

Still. Most suspected infernos really do turn out to be a toaster on stuck. Most stalkers in the covered parking lots are . . . just shoppers.

But sometimes they aren't.

Two equal and opposite things can happen simultaneously. You can make a living as a mountaineer and fracture your skull tripping over a curb.

Once upon a time, not so long ago, I thought of myself as the woman least likely to be served a big, bitter dose of my own medicine, the least likely actually to champion that old sauce I ladled out to my readers in a dozen different ways a dozen times a year—whatever doesn't kill you makes you stronger!—figuring that the least these poor mopes deserved was some kind of life raft.

Did I ever really believe it?

Nah.

Well, I was wrong.

End of story.

Beginning of story.

Everything truly interesting happens in the middle, don't you think?

TWO

Numbers

~~~~~~~~~~~~

EXCESS BAGGAGE
By J. A. Gillis
The Sheboygan News-Clarion

Dear J.,

I dated one man for 17 years, since the first day of freshman year of college. It was the perfect relationship. He told me all the secrets of his soul. I felt beautiful when I was with him. We had a ton of friends in common. When he moved to Arizona, because of the climate and a job, our bond continued, and I was sure that one day, he would ask me to marry him. I would not hear from him for a month or two, but then I would get a letter telling me he was going to visit, and it was as if we'd never been apart. Then, last spring, he wrote to say he'd fallen in love, with someone he met through his work, and that he never realized that what we had was a great friendship, not love of the marrying kind. I was crushed, but I forgave him. He invited me to his wedding, and I went happily. Now, though we have talked a few times, his wife is uncomfortable with our friendship. He says I need to stop calling except on special occasions, and get on with my life. But I'm 38 now, and I wonder if I'll ever find anyone who'll know me as he did, especially since most men want children and I'm getting to the age where that's a problem, and even more, if someone I loved so much could forget me so

easily, I must be pretty forgettable. I feel such a great gap in my
own heart, all the places he filled, that I can't seem to get past it.
Do you think counseling would help?

Regretful in Rheinville

Dear Regretful,

I do think counseling would help. It's possible that you saw
this relationship in a very different way from the way your
sweetheart did. It was clearly the center of your emotional life
and the periphery of his. As wounded as you feel, he is right
when he says that you need to get on with your life. It's rare
that two people who have been in love can preserve a friendship,
at least until a great deal of time has passed. Your focus needs to
change. You can still have a full and wonderful relationship,
and as a woman who had a child at 42, I know even that is
possible. Dwelling on the past, even though it was a long and
important past, is only going to take you around in circles
leading back to self-doubt. This was not your fault. Find a
counselor who specializes in women's relationship issues, and
do move on.

J.

In the beginning, there was Leo.

The end product of a family who'd built their heritage on four hundred years of hard work, cruel bigotry, and absolute loyalty, he had character. In other words, he had no excuse.

In the other corner, me.

You know all about me.

Leo and Julieanne, cut from different bolts, decided to stitch together a garment called marriage.

The simple history of us came what seems like thousands of years before my final diagnosis, before about eighty doctors told me I had everything from chronic fatigue syndrome to parasites to locomotor ataxia caused by a brain hemorrhage to catatonic depression.

But any woman can be dumped, although it is unusual for the dumper to describe a carefully planned path as "accidental." And "nothing to be ashamed of."

It's not unusual for a woman—angel, harridan, sickly, or snooty—to be royally dumped. It is a cliché, not original enough even for one more country-western song. The great ones have all been written. Dolly Parton did a terrific job in two minutes and thirty seconds in "Jolene." Or if your brow is higher, you can read all about the betrayal of a haughty beauty unjustly brought low in *The House of Mirth*.

What makes this story different from those is this: Since those things were written, a whole lot of things are supposed to have *changed* between men and women.

Take the acceptance of aging. Men are supposed to accept the changes that go along with a woman's getting older, just as they accept the changes in their own bodies. Breasts that no longer leap to attention at an even slightly carnal glance, well, those are still good breasts. They are the breasts that perhaps have nurtured children. They may have cradled a man's head as he confessed his grief or frustration, as he could to no other person on earth. When the frantic oscillation of early passion has slowed to a gently swinging pendulum, that's supposed to be okay now, because the sacredness of a long and honest partnership outlasts even the delicious scrimmage of new sex.

This shift in manners and values is, however, bullshit.

For nothing has changed—only, as Alice might have said as she climbed back through the looking glass, the names of what those things are *called*.

· · ·

We loved each other like crazy, Leo and I.

We also sort of wanted to spite our parents—who expected Leo to marry Shaina Frankel. My parents expected me to marry . . . up.

It began at college.

Mother and Father (okay, that *was* what we called them) had gone to NYU. For them, there was no point in any institution of higher learning unreachable by the A line. I rebelled. Their very best little girl *rebelled*. I chose the University of Colorado in Boulder. "Why would you want to sequester yourself on some dusty mountaintop?" my father asked, picturing Boulder as an outpost on the Pony Express with teepees for classrooms and tumbleweed blowing through the dusty track between storefront saloons. I explained that I wanted to scale peaks and wear blue jeans and dance in scarves and leg warmers under the tutelage of Rita Lionella, the legendary modern-dance instructor who had returned from New York to her birthplace and who headed the dance department there. This trilling fell on the deaf ears of a man who could fly to London as if he were taking the crosstown bus, but considered driving to Provincetown equivalent to traveling through the Cumberland Gap in a Conestoga wagon. Father believed climbing the steps of the West Side Y to the tennis courts was all the elevation a normal person needed.

I won, although I already knew I was not going to be a "real" dancer. The ABT and even the Winnipeg Ballet were dreams I'd left behind when I hit five eight and a hundred and thirty pounds. A practical girl, I wasn't willing to live on cigarettes and pepper vodka to dance for three years in the corps of the Houston Ballet, which I did manage, for one summer. Still, I wanted someday to do local theater, perhaps teach dance or teach English at a small college, English lit being for me a medium as familiar as water to a gill-breathing creature.

So one day, I came out of the backstage, after the winter recital. I had done a solo turn to *Afternoon of a Faun,* and I was furious because I had been good. I had been good, and my parents had been in Switzerland. They'd sent roses, all of which I had given to the other girls, who thought of me as a benevolent princess. My hair was still painfully drawn back, my eyes still painted into golden almonds with kohl and gilt. And there was this boy. A boy in a black leather jacket, with what looked to be black leather curls and a reluctant one-sided smile.

"Hi," he said, "you were great," and then, as if he thought I might walk away after thanking him, he added, "You know, I was the only male in there who wasn't a boyfriend or a father."

"You like ballet?" I asked, wondering if this cute guy was either gay or a fellow New Yorker.

"No, I sweep here," he said. I thought he had a speech impediment and starting walking. I was a little pig.

It turned out that he knew this.

"I sweep the *floor*," Leo added, breaking into a trot to catch up with me. "All round here. Outside all the rehearsal halls."

"Do you wait tables at sororities, too?" I asked. I knew scholarship students did. Belatedly, I was considering joining one, though I already had enough credits to be a junior. I lived in a crummy apartment and had learned that divine independence was really having to make new pudding every time one of your roommates got stoned and ate all four servings.

"I'd rather sweep, frankly," Leo said.

"Why? Waiters get free meals."

"I'm not that fond of stuck-up bitches. And I don't think anybody whose first name is Spenser deserves to be waited on."

I studied him. "I'm a stuck-up bitch," I said, allowing one strap of my leotard to slip.

"No," he said, again with that fishhook smile, "you can be stuck up and still not be a bitch."

"Who says I'm stuck up?"

"I know people. I know you name-drop. I know your dad has Kurt Vonnegut over to his house. . . ."

"That's just because they're the same age and he lives down the street—"

"It's still name-dropping."

"Oh, well," I tossed back at him, "thanks for coming to my recital to preach moral hygiene to me. Happy, uh, sweeping."

"Let me sweep you off your feet," Leo said.

I winced at the line, "Ouch!"

"Well, I can do better. Listen. I came because it was the only time I could watch you dance without pretending to work. You're . . . so beautiful it hurts to look at you."

"James Jones," I said.

"Close enough," said Leo.

"Who's stuck up?" I countered.

"Oh, I'm stuck up in a different sense. I have a high IQ. My parents are poor but proud. My mother is a Holocaust survivor. She was two, and her whole family escaped, but it still counts."

"You're a *reverse* snob, then."

"Exactly. And that's ever so much better, moral-superiority-wise."

"Jack Lemmon."

"Well, Billy Wilder."

"So what's your major?"

"Not dance."

"Neither is mine. I love it, but I'll end up forcing kids to read Nell Harper."

"Known to the world as Harper Lee."

"Shut *up!*" I told him, laughing, "I'm not used to guys I can't fool."

He wanted to be a poet. He was majoring in business administration.

We went to the Kafé Kafka for sticky buns and tea. Never made it to the table.

We *fell* into bed. The tea with milk we'd taken away in paper cups grew a gelid overcoat through the long, long night. I was as eager to be devirginized as I was to learn to rappel down a real mountain. (We ended up doing both those things together, for the first time. Leo said *that night* he'd been around the block, but later confessed he'd stopped at the crosswalk.) We tried ably to coach each other, and the morning after my recital, neither of us could walk without pain. I personally wanted to stand up in English 303 (Swift, Pope, and Fielding) to cry out, *I'm changed!* It took a week for the scabby irritation (we called it 'kissing chin') to clear up.

Two months into our affair, a word we never would have used to describe what we felt, which was Love Everlasting, Leo wrote,

Julieanne, with one hand
Dismisses my brown, brown study,
Replaces me, a sloping boy, with a rain-drenched man,
Upright, clean, open to violent blue, purple, ruddy hue
Unused to passion, fearful and yet true,
With one offhand hand, waved by
Julieanne.

Has anyone past college age ever used the word *hue?*

Well, good God, how could I fail to fall in love with a boy who was not only assured of earning a good living, but had also already formally designated me his muse? Business management was transparent, if uninspiring, to Leo. He understood and committed things to memory that were impenetrable to his classmates. And he already had a decent business going, ghostwriting term papers.

On fire, burning through the racks of Trojans, we waited until the following fall, enduring a hideous summer apart. Then, with our parents' bemused permission, I married the boy who described himself as "the only Jew from Sheboygan, Wisconsin."

I was twenty. Leo, who'd had to take fewer class hours to have time to earn out his scholarship, was nearly twenty-five. Think of that. Twenty. Barely. Had our life been normal, I don't know if I'd have let my son Gabe go to Florida on a *road trip* at twenty, much less get *married.* Well, maybe a road trip to Florida. But why did our parents permit this? Were they nuts? Was it a more innocent or perhaps not so tarnished time of the world?

Were we just so evidently right for each other?

The comedy of our parents' meeting was rich.

Hannah and Gabe Steiner Sr., funereally attired in black wool, in the month of June, came to dinner. They were as properly impressed with Ambrose and Julia Gillis as my parents' *droit de seigneur* required. They gazed around my parents' tenth-floor (of ten), ten-room flat at the Venecia, overlooking Central Park West, with the affect of people who feared they might at any moment be arrested. But after three glasses of champagne, my father grew historically and histrionically teary over Hannah's simple description of the disappearance of her entire family into the maw of Buchenwald, their rescue, at the eleventh hour, arranged by the wealthy family of a German priest who'd been a boyhood pal of Hannah's father so captured Dad with its poignancy that I was terrified he would get up and start singing "Sunrise, Sunset."

"I've always admired the chosen people," Father intoned, as Leo and I tried to fold ourselves into a corner of a loveseat.

"We keep hoping the Lord will admire the Lutherans," Gabe Senior told him. They exchanged cigars.

The Steiners' adoration of their beloved, excellent, and only boy was extravagant. My parents clearly considered me a pearl beyond price. My sister, Janey, thought Leo delectably ethnic, though he truly was anything but. He said he'd never even owned a yarmulke. Despite their antecedents, the Steiners were the most casual of Jews, my parents the merest literary Episcopalians, fond of quoting Saint Luke at Christmas. For holiday fare, both families preferred Chinese food. There was no question of a clash of values. In short, we went from dinner to a match. Six weeks later, at Thanksgiving break, we left my parents' apartment for a six-day sail in the Seychelles—my parents' wedding gift—and then set up housekeeping in a crummy apartment of our own, but with good towels and wineglasses.

We didn't let our parents down and ruin our educations. We *were* a good girl and boy. Much as we craved to dispense with the rubbers and mingle chromosomes, we dutifully withheld. When a concoction of the Pill that didn't make me blotchy and fat came along, we got better at pleasing each other's bodies. There never was a question about pleasing each other's minds. Leo and I played Bartlett's in bed, and he could match me quote for quote. We saved our nickels and backpacked in Greece, swam naked in the Aegean. Leo held and looked at the circle of my white breasts, in the surrounding topography of brown and blondest blonde, as though he'd discovered uranium. I felt ever so . . . beyond the other little girls on campus. I wasn't *pinned*. I was *married*.

Leo's first job was at a huge insurance firm in Chicago. I sat smiling blondly as Leo sucked down the indignity of juniority at American Liability Trust. But Leo was a comer.

"It's a six-day week, of course, son," said Mr. Warren, aged by then approximately one hundred and ten, as Leo was promoted from amanuensis to human being within the firm's hierarchy. "And the occasional Sunday. We pride ourselves on being a gentler firm. We know people have family lives. Everyone is out the door by eight every night, latest."

I got work copyediting at the *Sun-Times*, the graveyard shift, reserved for the desperate, the daylight drunk, and the constitutionally bizarre. And so Leo worked fourteen-hour days, and I worked fourteen-hour nights.

Neither of us was the perfect mate. Leo slept like the dead until three in the afternoon on Saturdays while I sat around and carped that we never went to the Art Institute. He asked his *parents* along on our vacation to the firm's condo at Disney World, and gave *them* the master bedroom. We went from being bunnies who could wiggle on any horizontal space in Colorado to the world's youngest celibates. I was mad at Leo for loving fucking insurance settlements instead of fucking the loving me. I got eyes for a golf writer. Once, during one of Leo's business jaunts, I let the writer sit in my car and kiss me, the transgression strictly above the waist and outside the blouse. But it scared me. It was a sign that Leo and I were ready to get on with the next step.

I still loved the rain-drenched man.

There are times, and I would never tell Gabe this, that I still do.

In any case, I wanted a life that felt more substantial. Sheboygan provided that through a double whammy, luck in disguise. Even now, I don't regret it.

Leo's parents were still running the five-and-dime on Pine Street when Grandpa Steiner got prostate cancer. Despite the hopeful prognosis, Grandma Steiner was dumbstruck with fear. Steiner's Sundries went to hell. Grandpa's treatments wore him transparent. It was time for Leo to act like the knight in armor on his company's letterhead. For his family, *Leo* was the insurance policy. But he had to sell me on Wisconsin: the quality of the schools, the beauty of the north woods a few hours away, the cost of living well, the chance to put Leo's degree to work for *us,* not for Mr. Warren. The Steiners were willing to do anything to save the store—the equivalent, to them, of Tara.

Just before we made the decision to move, we spent our tenth anniversary in St. Lucia. I came home dive certified, second-degree burned, and certifiably pregnant. That sealed the deal. There was the chance for the embryo we began to call A. Gabriel Steiner (Ambrose for my father, a nod we'd never use as a name) to grow up safe and clean, near his nicer grandparents. In Chicago, it would have been a major catastrophe, this being a time in the world when firing a pregnant woman was not considered an outrage but common sense. In Wisconsin, where we could live on more for less, I could help out as Leo phased out the racks of kite strings and boxes of checkers and phased in a picture-framing section, more Hallmark-type collectibles, and classier local crafts—making a store into a "shoppe."

The new arrival was a congenial part of the general game plan. I felt more part of a family than I ever had at home. Always having liked Hannah and Gabe, I grew to love them.

Grandpa got well. Business soared. Gabe was born. The Steiners were all but ready to host a ticker-tape parade.

But, then, I lost my mind.

Staying home with your baby wasn't "done" then, by women such as I. After giving him a good start, I was expected to turn Gabe over to the kindly moonbeams at someplace called the Red Giraffe or the Little Caboose. What I hadn't counted on was the volcanic quality of love that would overawe me when he finally emerged, limp and gray as a wet muskrat, after thirty hours of mind-altering back labor. In the early 1980s, people gave the slant eye to anyone who required a whole aspirin during labor; they'd see your one-inch episiotomy and raise you one. I was spent, and so was Gabe, barely able to mewl. When the big, brusque Swedish nurses slapped an oxygen mask over his face, I roared like a reverse Medea at their offhand treatment of my morsel, the only being on earth who needed only me. I never wanted to leave him, never wanted him to grow up. By the time he was two months old, I was already able to make myself cry at the thought of missing him for eight hours, and so I hadn't done a thing about the Little Caboose. Grandma Hannah, though her eyesight was poor, was as strong as a mustang. She stepped in gratis, while I churned out a couple of successful (but theoretical) magazine articles on getting in shape after pregnancy, the importance of being in shape *before* pregnancy, and the ease of delivery afforded by . . . guess what? Being in shape during pregnancy.

Leo, however, was wondering, and finally asking, why are we eating variations on rice pilaf every night, Jules? Why are we not the two-income household we planned—as in the kind of people who could buy a house? Still, life remained mostly genial. Gabe Senior and Hannah bought a (modest but cute) cottage in Door County, where we often went on weekends, and "went in" on a condo in Sarasota with their best friends, Leo's godparents.

Then, quite suddenly, the Steiners' "shoppe" went belly up, victim to creeping strip-mallism.

Instantly, Leo took advantage of the prime location and sold it. Shocked at the worth of their property, the Steiners retired, Gabe Senior (never idle) began to fool with a little stock-marketeering. They virtuously shared their profits with us so we could, as Hannah liked to say, "put something by."

Leo was still a genius.

We put a down payment on a postwar two-flat so huge it was actually two complete houses, slapped one on top of the other. We had four nice bedrooms and a little corner that Leo and I used as an office. We immediately rented the upper floor to a Danish couple, Liesel and Klaus, professors in the Department of Entomology at Wisconsin State, who so often flew off to this or that bug-infested paradise they were practically benign ghosts who paid our mortgage. They had three big bedrooms— one of which they used as a lab. Leo often said he was glad they studied bugs instead of tropical diseases.

Then, Leo decided to spring one on me. He was going to use part of what we'd "put by" to go to law school at Marquette. Unemployed and hoping to stay that way, I wanted to kick him in the knee, but he quite rightly pointed out that, with a law degree and an MBA, he'd be even more marketable.

"Jules," he added, "now you *have* to get some kind of job. We're not going to be able to afford his checkups."

"You know," I'd respond, "did you ever think that with both the degrees you're going to have, you could probably be an FBI agent?"

"Jules," he'd steer me back, but sweetly, "I know you don't want to leave him."

"I don't want to leave him. I think I should nurse him at least a year, and—"

"Even a job share with somebody would help. Get partial benefits."

"We can go to the student health service."

"It's in *Milwaukee*, Julie. It's thirty miles away."

I knew he was right. If it hadn't been for Liesel and Klaus, and the scholarship Leo got, we'd have been living on the rice without the peas.

I became a temp. The less said about this, the better. Leo went to the expedited program for grad students with previous advanced degrees, nights and right through the summers.

And then.

I was nursing and, of course, impregnable.

Theoretically.

The Packers were in the playoffs. Everyone in town went crazy, and so did we.

Hannah Caroline was the extra point.

Two infants did have the effect of making me long for any extended conversation that didn't include bowel movements. I tried to nurse them both, fighting to keep my weight up with lots of beer and cheese curds, nevertheless eventually looking like a lumpy and yet malnourished alcoholic. And though Leo did finally get his degree (summa, of course), the importance of my getting a job was real-life necessity, well beyond political theory.

A law student Leo met brought her two-year-old to our house and took over so I could get outside work. Caro was only six months old, and I've always thought this was why she never seemed to like me as well as Gabe did. Smacking together a résumé, with my stint at the *Chicago Sun-Times* in boldface, I headed down to the *News-Clarion*. Leo bought me a Donna Karan skirt and sweater for my job interview, coral-colored, and the first new thing except underwear I'd owned for two years. (My folks, ever pragmatic, had that Christmas given me a fox-and-leather jacket, which we sold to fix our Subaru.)

I started out editing copy, and, gradually, I made it over to the features department, where the advice columnist, Marie Winton, had written "Winona Understands" for forty years, and had to be eighty-five if a day. I edited her column and, once in a while, when it was too cold for anyone else, got to write the occasional fifteen inches on the ice-sculpting derby.

Marie was still answering letters about whether printed instead of handwritten thank-you cards were ever appropriate. The department's secretary, Stella Lorenzo, the Hot Lips of the newsroom, and I were assigned to copy down numbers of emergency organizations from Al-Anon to Parents' Respite and send them off on cards stamped, "With best hopes, Winona," for every letter we got that didn't involve etiquette.

"It doesn't seem fair," I would whisper to Stella, "she's basically ignoring the real cries for help."

"Tell me about it," Stella replied, rolling her huge, Annette Funicello eyes and lofting her big pile of corkscrew hair with a pencil. "I open letters every day from people who ask her whether their children might not be better off without them. Mother of Mercy, Julie, these women are thinking of killing themselves. I don't know what to do."

Gathering my courage, I asked Marie, who wore a hat to work each day (ceremonially placing it on its stand before she sat down to her Smith Corona), "Are we doing enough for people who are in crisis, Miss Winton? Sending them a phone number doesn't seem to be enough."

"I don't deal with such nasty, personal matters, dear," Marie told me. "My readers aren't all that concerned with those kinds of things." It was only my third or fourth month in the department, but, on the quiet, I started to answer a few of Winona's worst-case correspondents, calling on Cathy Gleason, a friend and family therapist I'd met in a community production of *Oklahoma!* I became obsessed with the letters. The more I read, the more patterns emerged. All humans had their heads on backward. Bank tellers and brick layers. Secretaries and surgeons. I would despair, as I read, at how adults, with jobs and driver's licenses, could exhibit such a stunning dearth of self-awareness. I started wondering how *anybody* ever stayed married or raised a kid or worked for ten years for bosses whose personalities strongly resembled Dr. Mengele's.

The whole phenomenon of writing a total stranger to ask for advice seemed, at first, eerie but deeply, overpoweringly poignant. But really, it's not very different from pouring out your soul to a stranger on a plane. It's a potent temptation. You'll never have to eat your words.

One day, Miss Winton went into the ladies' room and never came out—well, not as Winona Understands. An hour later, one of the general-assignment reporters found her sitting properly, her smile melted, on the pot nearest the door. Ambulance summoned. Miss Winton carried off to Sheboygan Mercy, then to The Oaks. (We went to see her, Stella and I, bringing her handfuls of letters, and *she answered* them, although you couldn't read what she wrote. We smilingly assured her we'd get them into the mail. The next time, we brought Stella's Kmart coupons, and Miss Winton answered those, too.) The snappy new editor, Steve Cathcart, found out via Stella what I'd been up to. One morning, he stepped up to my gray metal desk, planted his feet Colossus-fashion before me, and said, "Gillis. I know you've been tinkering. We need to spice up the advice. Can you do that? Okay. Done. We'll call it 'Tell Julie.'"

"No," I said to him, stunned that I'd dared to contradict an editor, a *new* editor whom I barely knew. "It's not about me, a person. I want to call it . . . 'Excess Baggage.' After all, that's what these letters are, stuff people haul around that's breaking their backs."

He liked it!

Not even one anniversary at the paper and I was a columnist!

I didn't know then, but I do now, that this line of work is one everyone drifts into. I thought Cathcart was impressed by my sense and sensibility. He later told me he figured that since I was a girl, I'd have empathy, and since I was my father's daughter, I'd be able to write an English sentence. We are almost *all* women, except the MDs. And yet I never met an "agony aunt" (yes, we were called that fifty years ago and still are) who, at age twelve, said to herself, you know what I want to be when I grow up? I want to be the next Dear Abby. Dear Abby probably didn't even think that. Most of us were on our way to a psychology practice or some other kind of writing when we were caught and held by the sheer power of being *asked and believed.* There now are advisers for the young, the aged, for every affectional preference, for politicos, pet lovers, quilters, and gardeners. But we're the foremothers, offering comfort over the faithless lover, the thankless child. Most of us have no more credentials than I did. And everyone has a pocket psychologist, like an ace in the hole, to help out. Cathy's a family therapist whose own family, at that time, consisted only of her and her dill pickle of an Irish mother but she knew the ropes of loss and adjustment too. Cathy was gay, and I met her and her then sweetheart, Saren, and we instantly bonded. Cath *loved* the notion of spreading her gospel on sensitive relationship topics while hidden behind my semi-serious column photo. She once said advice columnists should have a 900-number: 1-900-AW-HONEY. When she and Saren parted—because Saren fell in love with a guy—I was that hotline for Cath, and we grew closer, spending long nights with red licorice, red wine, and the Joni Mitchell *Blue* album, the universal soundtrack to women's grief. I questioned, naively, how Cath could so utterly fall apart, gain weight, and spend whole Saturdays in bed, given that she had advanced degrees in knowing how to take care of herself in a period of mourning. "Don't ever let anyone tell you," she said to me once, "that knowing how you should be reacting to a loss has anything to do with how you react when it's your loss."

Leo and Cathy got along famously, at first, and we sort of made extended family of her and her mom, Connie, alternating Thanksgiving dinners at each other's houses and such. He balked when I wanted to make Cathy the kids' legal guardian, in the event that Leo and I should die; but finally saw that she would certainly be a better substitute for us than my sister, Janey, and her husband, or than his own parents. Heck, she was more a sister to me than my sister, in reality.

Just as Leo graduated, a job opened up as legal counsel to the chancellor at Wisconsin State. The money was ever so right, and Leo grabbed it. Soon enough, he was handling legal issues, problems not so different from the ones in my letters. We got raises. I hired someone to landscape the front of the house. I found a school for Gabe where ignorant plate-heads didn't suggest he was autistic because he couldn't name his colors but could make the pencil sharpener run on solar energy. I knew then that there was something different about Gabe, just as I knew there was something different about me when I was little, though they didn't have a name for it then. I wasn't "hot-headed" or "too chatty," I had what would now be called an attention deficit disorder and hyperactivity. Gabe had something else. He could express the hell out of himself verbally, but his writing still looked like a kindergarten child's. He read like a house on fire, but couldn't spell the words he'd just read. But he was so bright and wonderful! I thought I could smite down whatever it was that was off about him—just as, through force of will and a couple of minicourses, Leo and I had become the kind of swing and ballroom dancers who could clear the floor at weddings.

We lived well.

People marveled that we'd been married for so many years. We marveled that we'd been married for so many years, slipping out to skinny-dip in Door County when the parents and the children were asleep. A neighbor once told me she walked past our house and saw all of us on the lawn, trying to teach Caro to stand on her hands; and that turned out to be the night she told her boyfriend that her answer was yes. She wanted a family like ours.

Anyone would have. Anyone except Leo. Leo holds himself blameless for "the turn of events," as he calls it, as if the space that opened between him and me was caused by weather or new tax laws. He tends to hold himself blameless in most things—I guess he always did. Now, if I let myself be the one doing the looking back, I see that Leo may have had one foot out the door before I ever suspected it—that his odd behavior was a detail of a larger picture, of which I could see only one corner.

What he did was, I *thought,* sort of have a breakdown. He began to fall apart from stress, and he let me believe it was largely my fault, or my fault and the kids' fault, or the simple fact of his own clarity muddied by the chaos of our culture. He didn't say in so many words that he was Leo Steiner, victim, but if he'd shouted the implication through a bullhorn, it could not have been clearer.

He began with odd, uncharacteristic complaints. He observed that the organic chicken at the co-op wasn't . . . organic enough. We all needed better nutrition, Leo told us, whole-er food and potions. Our immune systems would collapse otherwise. The extra responsibility of Aury, yet another child to outlive, as he once bizarrely explained it, combined with the strain of work, and the very unkindness of the air we breathed, pushed him to ill health.

We ended up going to this free-range farm where the chickens were actually beheaded, a *forty-five*-minute drive, and driving home with sinister-looking bloody bags in the back of the Volvo. Leo soon began to talk about our raising a few of our own, though I put my foot down, sure that kids who had to eat their acquaintances might need analysis.

But which came first really, the chicken or . . . well, the egg that became my youngest daughter?

I don't think I'm ever going to know that.

I don't think Leo entirely knows that.

If you do, you know where to write to me. Letters still come.

Judges

EXCESS BAGGAGE
By J. A. Gillis
The Sheboygan News-Clarion

Dear J.,

That I keep a boa constrictor as an affectionate pet alarms my roommates. Hercules is seven feet of pure muscle, clean and beautiful, and he has never escaped his cage, nor has he molested any guest in any way. He is allowed out only in my room, with the door closed, for exercise and play. My roommates say that even knowing that Hercules must eat live mice (which I also keep in my room, in a cage) is reason enough for them to detest the living situation. They demand that I either move or get rid of Hercules, but since I am the leaseholder, and my ad specifically said I had an unusual but mild-mannered and hypoallergenic pet, I think they have no case. They are threatening to leave, and by doing so, desert me with a rent payment far larger than I can manage. What can I do?

Annoyed in Appleton

Dear Annoyed,

Though you clearly are the right owner for Hercules, you cannot blame your roommates for feeling a bit alarmed at sharing their home with seven feet of pure muscle that also eats live mice. Think of it from their point of view—when they responded to your ad, they probably thought you had a ferret. I would give your roommates a specific length of time to find other accommodations so they don't feel ripped off, and then advertise for other roommates, making it clear that your pet is a BIG reptile. Studies have shown that snakes are one of the animals that people associate with danger and horror. Good luck. P.S. Have you ever wondered why you consider a boa constrictor an "affectionate pet" and considered something that was, perhaps, warm-blooded? Like, the mice?

J.

It has occurred to me ten or a thousand times that I was punished for looking down on them. My readers. For feeling disdain.

When I would read my letters aloud to Cathy (the myth of confidentiality among doctors, lawyers, and journalists being just that, although it never went outside the house), we would fall against each other's shoulders in helpless laughter. There was the snake man. And the plumber who wanted to start a sheep-shearing business and wondered if he could make a go of it in an urban setting. ("In Brisbane!" Cathy hooted.) The woman who wondered why her two beaux objected when she asked to review their past two years' tax records to decide which she would marry. Even as the landscape of my own life was being shredded, people were asking my counsel, and I was giving it blithely, from a position of strength I either thought I had or actually had, depending on your view in retrospect.

I think Caroline was maybe still in grade school and Gabe just starting middle school when Leo started the worrying about his health. Leo. The same man who had not so long before chided me for "making a religion of sit-ups." He started with his sleep issues, his obsessions with all he hadn't done to ensure his longevity. I could sense his resentment of me, and what

I had done. I would come in from walking a couple of miles and see him give me the kind of baleful look you reserve for people who come over for dinner and bring Newfoundland dogs.

I'd catch him stopping to take his pulse a couple of times every day. He began giving me studies to read about people who lived to the age of one hundred and five on coffee and vitamin C. Leo began driving across town to take yoga in a totally dark and windowless room in somebody's house. He used to sound like his own father when he'd say, "Look. I only run when someone's chasing me. I don't smoke. I don't do drugs. My parents are in their eighties. Everybody dies." I thought his new passion was . . . like a minor case of food poisoning that would burn its way through my husband's system. A little humor was the best antidote, I thought. Saltines for the soul.

I felt sorry for the poor bastard. And a part of me actually thought it was great, something we could share.

"Vikram Leo!" I said, and began to applaud, the first time he limped into the house, so sweat-soaked he looked as though he'd been caught in a downpour, after an hour of contortions. Every few years, Leo would purchase a new pair of expensive running shoes, run twice through the neighborhood, then give the shoes to our tenant, Klaus. But no more. Days went by. Months. It began to seem like the real thing.

As I virtuously rubbed arnica into *his* legs, he asked if I might not like to try it, too. "I don't know if you could do it, though," he said, "given the ballet. Ballet makes you stiff."

I did get . . . stiff, then, with indignation, and rubbed a little harder than was strictly necessary. But I forced a constipated little chuckle. "I, um, I'm actually pretty flexible, Leo. I think the two disciplines have a lot in common. So sure," I told him, "I'll come along. . . ."

"One works against nature and one with it, Julie. You should see people in this class, Jules. Women your age who lift a leg, standing, into an entirely straight plane, like a split standing up."

"I could probably do that. Uh, not."

"Not is right. And I never will. They've been doing a daily practice for years."

"You may be onto something. Everybody swears by it now. Even movie stars. I just can't imagine the sitting-still part."

"That's the big challenge. Just being in one place with yourself. I don't know if you could concentrate enough. You're Julie, my human jumping bean. Remember when you tried the self-hypnosis for labor?"

"I remember that you were the one who got hypnotized."

"Well, I can concentrate."

"Leo, I can concentrate," I hurrumphed. This was a lie. I can never think of fewer than four things at once. "I just can't go into a coma. Remember before you went to law school? And I had the idea right after college I might go to law school, when you were still going to be a merchant prince? I did better on the LSATs than you did." This was a sore point, still, and Leo bristled.

"The LSATs are different from actual *law school*. Anyhow, ballet never led anyone to any kind of spiritual enlightenment."

"Neither did law school. And I was *twenty-one* when I took the law boards, Leo. You were thirty-five. And lots of religions use dance in their rituals and the stories dance tells."

"It's the breathing, Jules. I feel as though I've taken my first real breaths since I was a kid."

"Well, all those monks just got head trips by hyperventilating. But, hey. I've always wanted you to work out with me. We can get long muscles and spir-it-u-al enlightenment together."

"Don't mock it, Jules," Leo said. "We've failed our kids in that area. They have no concept of Judaism or Christianity. . . ."

"They're good Democrats, though," I pointed out.

"Oh, Julie," Leo said with a sigh.

But we *had* been relying on Mark Twain, Robert Frost, and Meredith Willson as the foundation of our kids' moral development. Church just seemed to require such a big . . . effort. Still, we began to attend the Unitarian Meeting House in Sheboygan when Gabe was in about seventh grade and Caro in sixth. I liked it. I loved the Mozart, the old hymns such as "Simple Gifts," the fiery political sermons. For Gabe, who couldn't sit still, they had a Sunday school class for kids through ninth grade, in which they learned why early man worshipped fire and how to build one from nothing but a little dandelion fluff, and why planting trees for reforestation, which they did about every other week, was holy; and one for Caro about how the myths we consider fairy tales really were the basis of religions (Gabe called Caroline's class the gospel according to Walt Disney). But during the silent prayers, Leo looked as though he were trying to take a shit. I think he was concentrating on all the sins he'd failed to repent, all the people at work he'd failed to forgive on the day Jews forgive people every year, for the thirty years since his bar mitzvah. (I'd come to find out he did have a bar mitzvah, and once *had* owned a yarmulke, for about six months. He confessed his was the shortest Torah portion ever, the equivalent in Psalms of "Jesus wept.")

But Unitarian thought, with its B.Y.O.T. (Bring Your Own Theology, as Cathy called it), wasn't enough. Leo kept morphing. He took his first solo vacation, ten days, to photograph petroglyphs. He nearly taught all of us hypnosis with a full hour's carousel of slides of scrapings on rocks that might have been deer, or moons shining, but especially of a human figure Gabe called *Homo muchas erectus*, a fertility god apparently for some ancient Hopis or Zunis. He got them on a disc and rented a TV and a DVD player to show them to us. The kids looked at it as if he'd bought a Harley.

Then, for Christmas, Leo gave Caro a sewing machine and some patterns for wrap skirts for her to sew her own clothes.

She came to me in tears. "Mom," she said, "Daddy wants me to look like I'm Amish."

He gave Gabe a table saw instead of the camera hookup to the computer he'd wanted so badly. Gabe was, however, game. They made a worktable, which Gabe still has, and which is, I admit, beautifully joined, not a nail in it. He gave me a pair of Adirondack chairs (from the Adirondacks, no less) to squeeze in next to the tomato tubs in place of our big chaise longues. This was apparently so we could watch the tomatoes grow and view the neighbors grilling bratwurst while we grilled Little Bear veggie burgers. I kept wondering, sitting uneasily in my easy chair, what would come next?

What came next was that Leo bought a pair of barbering scissors and a book on haircutting, and spent a whole Sunday trying to get near Caroline's head, with her dodging and warning him, "I'll hit you, Dad. I've never done anything that bad and I don't want to, but if you touch my hair, I'll hit you." We could afford Caroline's haircuts, and he knew how much it meant to a young girl to have her hair look downtown instead of downriver. But Leo said he didn't like seeing a twelve-year-old girl spend twenty-two dollars on a haircut. People could do things . . . themselves. To keep peace, Gabe gave in, and went to school looking like someone who had been mowed. Leo praised him for helping us become more "self-sufficient." (Gabe comforted me later, telling me that his hair would grow back, and his peers thought he sort of resembled someone from the Goo Goo Dolls.)

But I was peeved.

Why, I thought, didn't Leo just remodel himself? Or install some solar panels or something?

He went after my makeup next, *uncomfortable* seeing me use one moisturizer in the morning and another at night. He asked me to give up wearing makeup and start using Sloan's soap on my hair and Kiss My Face lotion (you can imagine what we call this lotion now) instead of Clarins on my neck and forehead. And to give up eyeliner.

"Leo," I told him, "you haven't seen a woman who was awake and not wearing makeup since you were in eighth grade."

"That's not at all true. Many women prefer the natural look. They don't mind looking the way women were meant to look as they age. Plus. Do you know *Caroline* wears mascara?" He said this in the same tone he might have used had he accused her of freebasing.

"So what? She only wears it for rec night at the teen center."

"She's not even a teen! She's completely caught up in a whole consumer thing—"

"She is not. She's about half as thing-conscious as Marissa or Justine or any other of her friends, especially that one . . . that girl who's a model now." I was flustered. We didn't need the money I spent on goddamn moisturizer. It wasn't going to change the fate of Third World nations.

"It's just all those jars, sculpted glass, blue bottles, all that packaging. That's what you're paying for. You could have the same effect with vitamin C and petroleum jelly, Julie."

"When did you become a cosmetician?"

"It's globally gratuitous, to spend thirty-five bucks on something your skin can't even really absorb."

"Well, it's locally ludicrous to complain about such a dumb thing. Why don't you get a bicycle instead of driving the Volvo, Leo?"

"I would, but I can't get to work fast enough in rush-hour traffic."

"Rush hour lasts about five minutes here, Leo. . . ."

We let the matter drop. And I began buying Yonka—even more expensive than Clarins, and yes, packaged with the salty joy of passive aggressiveness.

Then one day, Leo told me, "I've been thinking that I may take early retirement at fifty-two, because I know there are going to be cutbacks. What I hear is that everybody who'll do it voluntarily is going to get the full benefits package and pension, plus some salary. I thought, we'll sell this place. Maybe get a cabin. Just a one-room cabin. Maybe up near Wild Rose or someplace nice, when the kids are off to college."

"Have a ball," I told him, "and visit often. I'm not living in a one-room cabin, Leo." I didn't bother to look up from sewing patches on Caro's jeans—for decoration, I might add, not to cover holes. "I have enough trouble with the spiderwebs in the bedroom rafters in Door County."

"Or upstate New York," he went on, ignoring what I'd said. "I'm thinking of going there, just for a photography weekend. I've met some people online up there who are doing some amazing things with small-space gardening."

"More fertile tubs? Tomato prayers?" I asked.

"No, smart ass. I mean, they've turned their yards, if you want to call them that, into a combination of prairie and garden. It's gorgeous."

"Show me a picture."

"I . . . I don't have one," Leo said.

"Then how do you know they're gorgeous?"

"I . . . read about them."

"Leo, Caroline isn't even in high school yet."

"But she will be soon."

"We're talking five years or more from now, Leo."

"But we could buy the land—"

"*Leo!* What about *my* job?"

"You could retire, too."

"And the kids? Do you expect them to put themselves through school and sleep on the earthen floor during summer vacations?"

"I put myself through school; and your dad left them trust funds so they could take out loans and pay them back later."

"That's true, but they expected to see that," I told Leo, my eyes smarting with tears.

He relented. "Forget about it for now. I'm sorry, Jules."

My parents had died the summer before last.

Though they'd rarely come to see us, we'd gone to New York every year to see them. They weren't a presence in our daily lives, as the Steiners were. But when they died in a plane crash in Scotland, guest of some laird, the effect on me was devastating. In a foolish homage, I reduced the space in our bedroom by a third to install my father's mahogany desk, with photos cemented by time under its glass top. Photos of him as a young man, laughing with E. B. White and Truman Capote, neither my father nor any of the others absent a cocktail glass. Leo bored a hole in the back for my computer cords, and I worked there, surrounded by the tweedy presence of my father's loving, offhand protection. I had my sister, Janey, but she was in the mold of Mother and Father—she and her architect husband giving "little parties" for fifty, hanging around the Hamptons with sons and daughters of famous writers with names like Bo and Razzie.

My only real world was Leo and the kids. I wasn't going to have it pulled out from under me like a worn-out rug on a whim.

"I'm not ready to be retired, Leo," I told him severely. "I'm not ready to become *your* parents. And I won't be in five years. I'm a medium-density housing person. I need human friends, not just cybers."

"You could telecommute. They let you do it now whenever you want to." This was true. Steve Cathcart didn't care where I was when I wrote my column. I rarely went into the office except to collect mail.

"This is going to be a log cabin with high-speed cable? What would we *do*? Just living alone?" You're supposed to be charmed at the idea of a loaf of bread, a jug of wine, and thy spouse beside thee in the wilderness of Wild Rose; and I wondered why I wasn't. It made it hard for me to swallow.

"We'd do all the things we never got the chance to do. We'd live. We're in a rut, Julieanne. And we call it life. What do we ever do for anyone? Pound nails for Habitat for Humanity once a year? What do we do for ourselves? Swill some wine with Peg and Nate twice a year? We don't even make a real difference for our own kids. They see TV at their friends' houses, even if we feel pure not having one at ours. Maybe if you'd just slow down a little, Jules, we'd be more on the same page. You're so busy with all those lonely hearts, who are just going to do the same damned thing they were doing before the minute they finish reading the newspaper, and . . . your ballet . . . and guided running. What the hell is guided running? You sound like you need a seeing-eye dog . . . you don't see the world around you and what you're giving it and what you're taking from it. Clothes and amusement parks and cell phones, Jules, the world has more to it than that. Or less. Or it should."

Perhaps I should have tried to draw him out. Right then. I might have prevented something. Perhaps he was trying, unawares, to telegraph more than a message on improving our *mutual* lives. I thought he was just being the New Leo, idealist cynic. He'd always had a potential for this. I thought also of *Homo muchas erectus,* of trekking along with Vaseline on my face, getting wrinkles and heel blisters under the New Mexico sun, of living like Laura Ingalls Wilder's parents in the potato barrens and piney woods of central Wisconsin, and mentally began poking holes in my diaphragm.

Within three months, there was the beginning of what Leo thought of as the real fly in the ointment. It would turn out, nine months later, to be a seven-pound, nine-ounce fly.

Gabe was just two years short of high school and Caroline was starting to notice boys, and we were starting over.

Leo was . . . stupefied.

He stopped dead in his tracks.

This had not been part of the second five-year plan.

While I hadn't necessarily expected wild delight, the utter absence of any emotion at all when I told him was creepy.

"You always wanted another child," I finally pleaded. I'd just given him a bubble-gum cigar. "I was the one who wanted to stop with two."

"But we didn't . . ."

"I thought you were fed up with all the doing and wanted to start being."

"I meant we'd be free . . . not raising another life for eighteen years."

"No one who has children is ever totally free, Leo. You know that. You don't want this then."

"I do. No, I do, Jules," he said seriously, taking me tenderly in his arms. "Maybe this is a sign I'm meant to start over with this child and not make the same mistakes—"

"Mistakes? I think Gabe and Caroline are pretty fine examples of good—"

"No, I mean guide him or her more on the path. . . ."

A few months later, he gave me a Mother's Day photo of myself, float-ing supine on a raft in Lake Michigan, my belly like a risen dough above and below my red bikini, with an engraving that read "H.M.S. Darling."

How could a person do that, and then do what he did later?

Right after my announcement, Gabe came into our bedroom. Doors never were anything to Gabe except a permeable membrane. "Gabe," Leo called, freeing an arm to enfold his son, "you're going to be a father! I mean, I'm going to be a father! Again. I mean, by the time I'm a father again, you'll be almost old enough to be a father!"

He was right the first time.

FOUR

Gabe's Journal

――――― ――― ―― ―――――

I planned this as an exercise in creative writing. For about five minutes.

Then it hit me that if my mother knew that I wanted—even for a nanosecond—to dime Leo/Dad out for an easy A, she'd shit. Mom.

She can lay on the guilt. She denies it. She'd say, if you hate Leo, you'll end up like him. You'll bitch your own karma, she'd say. (Not that she isn't brave and strong and there for us and witty and practical and all the junk everyone says about her; but she also is still seventies enough that, like Leo, she can say "karma" as if it were something totally real but invisible, like nitrogen.)

She wants me to still "love" Leo, "despite his weaknesses." Like she would love me even if I were in prison. Which is an entirely different thing. Any mother would. If I were in prison, it would be for a decent reason. Like breaking Leo's legs. Or a dumb one. Like possession of a joint. Whereas, with my so-called father, there ought to be a banner they fly behind a little Cessna during NFL games that says, LEO STEINER SHIT ON HIS WIFE AND KIDS BECAUSE HE COULDN'T KEEP IT IN HIS PANTS.

I always used to read my mother's letters and journals.

She didn't know for, well, most of my life; but it turned out that she didn't really mind (I think the rant about invasion of privacy and boundaries was mostly for form's sake). From my mother's letters and journals, I know Leo is a stereotype. He tried to make it sound like he had some big epiphany, but he was really only an everyday guy who turned forty-nine and figured out he was going to die. He called what he was searching for "spiritual authenticity."

Spiritual authenticity.

You're supposed to respect your father, even if he does something stupid, because of stuff he did for you in the past: He ripped your moronic civ teacher a new one, in elegant lawyer language, when you built a model of the CN tower, with a rotating viewing platform, but got a D because you wrote your bibliography with the semicolons in the wrong place. Leo did that. Because he taught you to hold the bat level, to shave before you needed to shave, made sure you knew the words to "Officer Krupke" and "Goodbye Yellow Brick Road." You're supposed to forgive him even if he goes off the tracks a little, unless he's a criminal or hits your mother or humiliates you or gives you stripes on your back with a belt because you don't want to be a bird colonel like him, or something.

But how can you respect what Leo would call callous disregard? Disregard is the worst fucking sin in the book. How can you want to keep the last name of somebody who did worse than hit your mother? Who turned out to be a totally selfish asshole to *everyone*?

Your father is supposed to be like . . . your address.

If that's true, I want to be in the witness-protection program.

I wouldn't have minded the A in creative writing, by the way.

I was going to begin by tracing the deterioration of our family through the names our parents gave us. I digressed. I tend to.

My sister Caroline and I were named, normally enough, for our grandparents. She was named Hannah Caroline, but called Caro because my grandma Hannah was still alive and well and around every day. I was named—brace yourself—Ambrose Gabriel, but always known as Gabe. My grandfather Gillis was named Ambrose; but no people in their right minds would actually call a kid that—it might as well have been Percival. When our poor kid sister came along, it wasn't that there weren't any grandparents left to name her after, it was that—it seemed to me—my parents had snapped their caps. They had replaced our little table and these sitting chairs they had on our, like, six-by-ten terrace with giant pots in which they grew tomatoes and peppers and one lousy stalk of corn. We were driving out to Farmer Griswold's and driving back with dead chickens in a bloody garbage bag in the back of the Volvo. And I thought it was their joint decision to name her Aurora Borealis.

Aurora Borealis Steiner. I pointed out that this sounded like an ethnic joke. Dad blustered, then quickly put on his Zen-understanding-the-ignorant face and said, "The wind blows all the way from the sun and passes the earth, and pushes around the nitrogen, the oxygen . . . that's what you see, the northern lights, the colors. . . ." I nodded. I had taken science. "And that's why, since she's a new light on earth . . ."

Good Christ. I was embarrassed for the guy. If I ever go this whacked over the intersection of some chick's legs, please shoot me with a .45.

I knew my father had fallen out of his tree. I knew before my mother did.

Anyhow, her name would not have been such an issue for the poor little crap if her initials had not been the same as those on this giant sign down the road from the big old Georgian two-flat where we lived.

It was a company called Atlas Breeders Services, and it dealt in prize bulls, or rather their . . . reproductive products. Until a couple of years ago, the company was called America Bull Semen. You see the problem.

In high school, I knew this girl who was crowned the Wisconsin Dairy Queen—and yes, there is an ongoing dispute with the soft-serve company of the same name—I'm not making that up. One of the privileges of her reign was to carry around in her purse a syringe of the ABS product, in case she should come upon a cow that needed a boost. She was completely shy when in her nonpageant personality, though she did have a body that wouldn't quit, especially the udder area; but I digress. Anyway, she would have to stand there, smiling brightly, while goddamned *dairy farmers* made nice comments when she whipped out her inseminator. Not to mention what her very witty and suave peers at Sheboygan LaFollette High said to her about it. (What she told me actually bothered her most was having to eat ice cream every day of the summer. She started throwing it up on purpose, though she was not bulimic. After her year was over, even the smell of vanilla gave her a migraine. But she also has these dreams of her purse opening and, like, forty giant syringe inseminators spilling out.) She told me she wished ABS had never been invented.

Everybody had a great time with that sign. The people who worked there were always putting these little slogans on it. Like at Christmas, *We Deck Our Bulls So Cows Are Jolly!* And at Fourth of July, *Red-Blooded American Studs, No Bull-oney!* And my favorite, at Easter, *Our Studs Have Something Eggs-tra!* Kids in cars would go out and rearrange the letters for maximum vulgarity, under cover of darkness. The actual farm was about a million yards back from the road, and we never quite figured out why it or the *sign* was stuck right in the middle of Sheboygan, Wisconsin, which was a pretty fair-sized town, with a halfway-decent university, though every kid in town feared the shame of having to end up going there. I don't know why. I went there a year myself, and it was a good enough place. It was only deciding I needed to put more room between myself and the Midwest that made me end up at Columbia. That and wanting to see why my mother turned out like she did, the combination of the bravest and most superficial woman on earth.

It was also sort of a tribute to my grandfather, because he left a lot of money for us that we can't have until we're twenty-one, and I'm not yet. He did this before he and Grandmother blew up in a little plane on the way to the British Open. I've never read my grandfather's books, exactly, but the Civil-War-guy-turned-sort-of-Robin-Hood he made up obviously had something "eggs-tra," because in every book in the series, he "bedded" (that's how Grandfather would put it) more wenches than James Bond could boast of in all his movies, and without aid of a cigarette lighter that turned into a ladder or a cannon or some goddamned thing. And because the books made so much money that he was once chairman of the National Book Awards. I suppose you theoretically need your grandfather more when you're a little kid, but in my case, it was the reverse. Grandfather died when I was ten, and when I was fifteen, I could sure have used being able to pick up the phone and hear him say, "A. Bartlett Gillis here," and be able to say, "A. Gabriel Steiner here." This was during the period when my parents seemed to have lost their grip on real basic stuff like three meals a day while most other people their age at least had parenthood sort of down pat.

My Grandpa Steiner still talks to me like I'm ten, but Grandfather (we had to call him that) always talked to me like I was twenty—even when I was five. "How goes it, colleague?" he would say. He listened to whatever I said, though he rarely listened to a full sentence, without interrupting, from anyone else. When he died, he and Grandmother never meant to leave us in the can financially. He could never have imagined that we would have needed our trust funds for regular life instead of a nest egg. He totally worshipped the ground my mother walked on. He just wanted to prevent Caro and me from blowing our (his) money on 'Vettes when we were young and dumb. My sister Caro would have blown it all (she now calls herself "Cat" and a person who calls herself Cat cannot be counted on; anyone can see that).

On the other hand, Grandpa Steiner, far too old to be worrying about us, was a total mensch when we needed him. He even sold their condo they were so proud of. All I'm saying is Grandfather Gillis would have done the same thing. But I digress. Again.

Back to my sister Aury and her name. At first, I thought her name, and the fresh-kill chicken, and the magazines and newsletters my dad got from people who lived in teepees and shared one truck, were just outgrowths of my father's health obsession. I thought the health obsession came about because he couldn't sleep. He told me he couldn't sleep because of his work. He had migraines. He was *chief legal counsel* to the chancellor at Wisconsin State in Sheboygan (which is sort of like being the manager of the McDonald's but *in Milwaukee* instead of Evansville), and it drove him nuts. He had to deal with lawsuits by parents over idiots who fell out of fucking second-story windows after getting trashed at frats, and with female professors of Pac-Island Studies who thought they were being denied tenure because the school wanted to give more money to the business-school guys.

He said to me, "The big clue was when everyone at work started to look like some kind of animal to me. I would say to myself, here comes the chair of the law school, Pig. There's the secretary, Ferret. There's my office mate, Clark. He looked like a Boston bull terrier. I was losing my mind, and I was scared to death I would slip up at some point, and say, 'Excuse me, Pig, would you take a look at this discovery motion?' It's interesting, law."

He also said it made him mental to have to deal with how many ways people could fuck up perfectly good lives. (As if he wasn't about to be named Most Valuable Player in this area? And as if my mother didn't get almost famous doing just that: she came to think that fucking up your life was in your DNA, part of being an air-breathing, bipedal hominid.)

Anyway, he became a basket case. He went to UW in Madison for a sleep study, and we got to see the videotape of him with electrodes stuck all over his head and body, which was at least more interesting than his slides of Stone Age man, apparently even more fixated on his genitals than my father. My dad *borrowed a TV for this*, which was like borrowing a live ram for a Passover pageant or some goddamned thing. (We had never had TV, as a daily staple of life, like other kids. We had to get it on the street, me usually at my friend Luke's house. This was weird—kids would ask you, like, how do you live? But it was far less weird than what was to come.) Anyway, we sat in the living room and watched Leo sleeping under the effects of sleeping pills in this little white motel-type room, and it about put us under. He was twitching his arms and legs about every other second. No wonder he never got REMS. He hadn't slept, in the usual sense of the word, for years, though he as sure as hell *looked* the part to us. We spent, like, months of our childhood with board games and badminton sets in our hands, waiting for Leo to wake up, and watching him sleep.

I don't know if the whole sleep business was a head fake to prove to us he needed his "sabbaticals" from his very stressful life, or real. I was just a kid, and I didn't realize then that it was sort of an American tradition to up and leave your wife for a bimbo before you hit fifty. It *would* be pretty difficult to *fake* twitching seventy times a minute.

My mother was giving *him* stress advice: take long walks at night, Lee, go swim at the Y, go scuba diving. Instead, he would stay up late on the computer. I would pass their room, and see the tiny blue fire of his laptop glowing, the way other kids would see the TV screen in their parents' rooms, though we didn't have one. I said that, didn't I?

We saw how she was.

Leo had to have seen it, too.

He didn't let it get in the way.

Anyhow, my kid sister, Aurora Borealis, was a cute little kid with black hair and blue eyes and freckles, who, like the Dairy Queen in my class, got lousy comments from other kids through no fault of her own. Just like my mother, through no fault of her own, got a wiring whack in her head. And we, through no-fault birth, got Leo.

I thought I was protecting my little sisters by keeping one off the street and one off my mother's hands. My mother thought she was protecting us by saying she was fine, even when she was trying to make both her eyes work together. My mom's best friend, Cathy, thought she was protecting my mother by muttering threats about her wish to maim Leo. My Steiner grandparents thought they were protecting my mother by making noodle casseroles and keeping the lawn mowed and selling their Florida condo. My father thought he was protecting us, as if he gave a crap, by pretending it was work driving him bonkers, not just his wanting to get away from his life—which included us. Everybody was running around trying to get everything to behave like normal, so Caro and I could pretty much do what we wanted. And that was how we hacked into the computer and set off on a trip with a fake excuse that would never have got past anyone who had been paying attention.

In the end, of course, nobody protected us at all.

FIVE

Exodus

EXCESS BAGGAGE
By J. A. Gillis
The Sheboygan News-Clarion

Dear J.,

I am a Catholic. Fifteen years ago, when I was an altar boy, my friend and I desecrated the host before mass by peeing on it and then drying it out over the radiator, as a joke. I never thought about this except as a boyish prank, until I realized things in my adult life so far have gone very badly— relationships, jobs, failure in school, and so on. I have confessed this and received absolution many times. Do you think I am under a curse from God?

Worried in Warrenton

Dear Worried,

No, I don't think you are under any curse. You may be carrying a certain amount of guilt. I think that if you spoke with a counselor, you might be able to uncover other causes for your perception of failure in pursuits that have nothing to do with your religion, and you may be seeing this prank as the cause. After all, if you were given absolution, you have removed any stain from your conscience. Often, people suffer for years over a particular event no one else knows about that has far less significance to anyone but them than they ever believed, once they look at the big picture through therapy. Good luck.

J.

———————～～～———————

"It's a girl!" the obstetrician cried, and though we already knew that—forty-two-year-olds had to have amnio—we couldn't believe the tiny splendor of our daughter. Nothing had ever been so . . . perfect in miniature. I had forgotten. The idea that I had created this little life to stall my husband gripped me with remorse. I kissed a blessing on her head, whispering, "I wanted you, personally. You're my honeycake."

Leo and I clasped arms to hold her on the bed in the birthing room. Gabe and Caroline came in, horrified with embarrassment at the evidence of their parents' physiology, and held her awkwardly, their natural graceful stances transformed into grasshopper elbows by unaccustomed awe.

"Way, Mom," Gabe said.

"She's pretty," said Caro. "She has hair."

Kodak moment.

Then Leo announced her name, and we all looked at him as if he'd dropped his transmission.

If the impending arrival of Aurora was the domestic equivalent of my leg tingling, her actual arrival opened the door for Leo's departure. Leo had been sliding and, perhaps by force of will or lifelong restraint, holding himself back. Overnight, he was a downhill racer. I'd been okay with the free-range chicken and even philosophical about the garden o' tubs. We'd always both been good, green liberals. Never cared much what anyone thought of our choices, really. But Aurora Borealis Steiner?

It was Caroline who said it. "What's with her name?"

"It's a mythic, and scientific, term for the northern lights, what we see in Door County," Leo said.

"Oh," Caroline said.

"It's Latin," Gabe said, "Like *Ursus arctos horribilis.*"

"What's that mean?"

"Grizzly bear," Gabe said.

"What'll we call her?" Caro asked.

I said, "Probably Rory."

Gabe said, "Probably Shorty."

Leo spent the entire night of her birth slumped over his laptop in the recliner at the hospital sending out bulletins to who knows whom. I tossed and nursed and worried.

But why was I worried? Leo was still wry, smart, cute as a hoodlum, just a little more habitual a complainer than he always had been. He would cope with this new child, as he did with everything, by coming around slowly. And as he did, the nuttiness would evaporate, like sweat after a steam. He'd turned forty-nine and realized he was going to die, I decided, and had wanted to try to litigate with the universe. People often went through stretches of grazing the loco weeds before settling into the back forty. That was the simple version. The one I gave Gabe at first. And I had no real reason to think otherwise. Leo was my husband and college sweetheart. My best friend of the other gender. We had a history as old as Moses. I don't think husbands and wives remain the soul mates they were at twenty for all their lives. Especially if they have families. That doesn't mean they don't have good marriages. I figured I'd ride it out and we'd have a cute kid, who, when she turned sixteen, would change her middle name to Jane.

Seventeen months after Aurora's birth, Leo announced he was taking a "mini-sabbatical."

"You're taking a semester off?" I asked, astounded. "Now? What for? It's not a great time for this, Lee."

I gestured at the room around us. Despite the intervention of a cleaning team (Leo hadn't objected) our living room looked like an abandoned base camp on Everest. Unfolded clothes, identifiable as clean or dirty only by smell. Empty juice boxes, collapsed at the waist. Game pieces that crunched like ice cubes under my feet when I went to the bathroom, which wasn't often, since I hadn't bounced back from Aurora's birth the way I had from the other kids'. That concerned me, and it wasn't only my age. I was having trouble reading my mail, even with my new prescription reading glasses. I heard funny things, like little flute solos, that no one else could hear. It was getting harder to ignore everything.

Just the week before, I'd thrown a little shower for Cathy and turned it into a disaster.

A year after Cathy lost Saren, Cathy had decided to take a real partner for life. She'd adopted Abby Sun, four months old and an edibly adorable papoosenik, from China. I'd made rum punch with floating sherbet ovals molded with some old Play-Doh forms and stuck with little umbrellas (my Sheboygan interpretation of floating junks), almond cookies, and trail mix of seasoned nuts and crackling noodles. There was plenty of baby passing, and friends of Cathy's from the rep and the newspaper who'd never met Aurora when she was born brought unexpected gifts for her as well as for Abby. Aury, who was pushing two, kept kissing the sleeping infant and saying, "Baby Abby." It was fun. Stella Lorenzo announced she'd become engaged, to Tim Downer from the Sunday magazine. I hugged her and said, "Broken hearts . . ."

"And limp dicks . . ." Cathy put in.

"All over Sheboygan!" I finished, and she blushed. We all laughed.

"You'll be a good wife, Stella," I said.

"I've had enough practice!" she said.

"I mean, you'll be a good wife not because you have big brown eyes and big boobs, which doesn't hurt, but because you have a big heart and, I know from working in the newsroom, an amazing tolerance to suffer fools with grace and see the good side of anything."

"That just about describes the perfect person," Cathy said. "So Stella, I know this isn't the usual question, but do you have a sister who's gay?"

We cracked up, and I went to get the cake.

It was when I, returning from the kitchen with the big sheet I'd had made in the shape of a sun, tripped over nothing anyone could see, dropped the plate, and stepped on it that things went jelly-side down.

I knelt in the mess and cried, and try as I might, I couldn't stop. If I began to laugh, it only released fresh spasms of crying. As if at a signal, women began consoling me with stories of emotional troughs and peaks in their forties and how theirs had been much worse and how nobody needed to eat cake anyhow since we'd had all that trail mix. Stella got down on her knees with the club soda to get the yellow frosting out of the carpet. Only Cathy pulled me aside before she left and suggested I see a doctor. She told me not to worry, that it probably wasn't anything serious, but that anemia or even a bad inner-ear infection could cause these kinds of wobblies.

It wasn't until long after that she admitted she'd been covertly watching me walking and dancing for a long while and knew that this was no ear infection.

Whatever the reason, I was in no shape to become a single parent while Leo took a semester off. I was even more dumbstruck when he announced he'd spend part of that time away from home.

"What? Are you kidding?" I asked. "Doing what? Where? For how long? Not a whole week at a time!"

"No, just a month at first, maybe two weeks later on," Leo said, and I thought, *Huh? What did this man just say? It was like the old joke, do you walk or take your lunch to school?* "I have the accrued time. I thought one thing I'd do is take a look at land in upstate New York. Perhaps consider buying a plot. Far from, and yet convenient to, the City," he told me with seductive delight. Privacy, seclusion . . . and Broadway! Closer to my sister Janey and Pete. Perhaps as a vacation home, maybe more later on in our lives. He'd already planned to meet, along the way, with some of the people he had corresponded with. I could come if I wanted, but, he hurriedly added, he knew I needed to get back to work, and he'd already asked his mother to come down from the cottage, where the elder Steiners now lived permanently, to stay part of the time with us.

"How could you have missed it?" Cathy would later ask. "It was just like Perplexed in Prairieville, or whoever it was, whose husband took bike trips with her sister because they *both loved bikes*. Julie!"

"It wasn't like that," I'd insist, knowing I was indeed Senseless in She-boygan. "I *know* he was having menopause for guys at first. People go through this all the time and nothing happens."

And sure enough, nothing did. Leo wrote to us and sent beautiful pictures of "intentional communities" where twenty people shared one snow-blower and jointly purchased twenty hardcover books each year. There were group suppers and yoga classes. "You should see my downward dog!" he wrote.

And yet, the moment his plane touched down at Mitchell Field, twenty-four days later, it was I who felt I'd come home. He *was* better for his adventures. Tanned and ebullient, Leo seemed literally to have fewer lines in his forehead. Pitifully grateful to see the kids, he kept calling them into our room just to look at them. He told me that the sight of me holding Aury reminded him of a Cassatt painting. We made love ferociously—the kind of sex married people don't have, the kind that leaves rug burns on your knees. That night, watching Aurora sleep, Leo literally cried. He said her black hair shined in the dark and how nothing he'd done could give him back the month of her changing and growing he'd missed, but that he wouldn't have known that if he hadn't missed the month.

"I was just worn out, Jules," he told me, as we stood in our underwear late that night in the kitchen, toasted bread, and smeared it with peanut butter. "That's all. Tired of being a good boy. But, hell, I *am* a good boy. A lifer. Must be genetic."

"There's a lot worse things a person could be, Lee," I said. "Not everyone has to be Jack Kerouac."

"I thought I would once, though," he said wistfully.

"We all thought we would once, honey," I told him, encircling his shoulders with my arms. "If you wanted to so badly, why didn't you?"

"I was expected to do what . . . I was expected to do," he said. "My only rebellion was"—he smiled crookedly—"falling for a WASP in a leotard."

Would I have ever thought to ask him, Leo, were you anything more than a little tired? Like, a little tired of me? Would it have occurred to me to sneak a peek at his e-mail, since I knew the password was "Innisfree."

Two weeks later, Leo decided the Unitarians were too conservative and suggested we visit a Tibetan retreat center south of Madison on Sunday afternoons.

I dug in my heels. Sundays were . . . well, sacred. I liked to spend Sunday afternoons proofing my column and reading the *Times*. I suggested he take Aurora Borealis.

"The name'll knock 'em dead," I told Leo. "She can meet some nice Swedish kids called Tenzig and Sorgay." He didn't seem to see the humor.

He brought me books about the way quantum physics and human creative thought were both wave-based. I bought him the Stephen Jay Gould book about why people believe nutty things. He bought Aury Math-O-Mozart blocks. I bought a *wide-screen* television, which was, in our family, akin to buying an Uzi. (Gabe and Caroline literally knelt in gratitude and placed their foreheads against my hand.)

When Aury was ready for preschool (it was really a sneaky form of day care, where they charged you more because they used chalk instead of crayons and had a creative-movement teacher come in twice a week; the kid was *only* one and a half), Leo suggested I homeschool her instead, giving up my column and perhaps taking on a couple of other students. I suggested *he homeschool* Aurora.

"If anyone ever needed homeschooling, it was *Gabe*," I said. "Do you know the crap he put up with from kids . . . *and* teachers? Eight years of torture because he's smarter than almost anybody in school and has every learning disability short of a Martian implant? Why didn't you care then? Why was it so important that the kids go to *public* school because you work for a public institution?"

"That's the whole point, Julieanne," Leo said. "I don't want to make the same mistakes with Aurora as I did with the older kids." Leo looked up mildly. "I knew you'd object to this." He held out a sheet of paper. "I've prorated our economic contributions to the family. Since Aurora was

born, and you went part time, you work at home, and I provide the benefits; it's only . . . well, fair, that you perform a greater share of the household management."

"Fuck you!" I told him. "I already do. Do you use fabric softener on the
towels when you dry them, Leo?"

"Of course," Leo sniffed. "Who wants old, brittle towels?"

"Beep!" I said. "Wrong! If you use fabric softener, the towels will lose
their absorbency and that's what towels are for, Leo!"

"When Gabe and Carol went to school . . . Jules, schools are no longer
benign places. They're containment facilities. They're . . . holding tanks
for the social misfits we've created with our poisoned fast food and our
McMansions and our . . ."

I left him nattering, took my bike, and rode to Cathy's, where we
spent the afternoon drinking margaritas. It was just plain old foolishness,
I thought.

It was foolishness all right. But it quickly became clear that it was
neither plain nor old.

Ecclesiastes

EXCESS BAGGAGE
By J. A. Gillis
The Sheboygan News-Clarion

Dear J.,

I finally confronted my husband with his repeated infidelities. He suggested that our marriage might prosper if both of us had other sexual relationships, a sort of open marriage that would keep us a couple but give us both diversity. I'm not sure I want to do anything like this. Yet, we have two young children, and I want my marriage to stay intact. Could this be a stage?

Leery in Lancaster

Dear Leery,

It could indeed be a stage. Or it could be a loud warning bell that your husband is seriously seeking a way out of your marriage. The only way to find out is definitely not to try experimenting with other relationships. It is to find a good counselor, who specializes in such issues, and there are even some husband-and-wife teams in the area. (Please phone the front desk at the newspaper for a list of names.) It's imperative that you work together to see what the real issues are at the

*bottom of this pattern, and they could surprise you. Your
husband could feel sexually neglected or insecure for reasons
that have nothing to do with you. Most open marriages, as they
call them, end in divorce rather than harmony. Make any
choices or agreements contingent on previously attending a
weekly counseling session, together and separately. And keep me
posted.*

J.

Just before the university opened for fall semester, Leo took me out for
dinner.

We hadn't even started our salads when he told me, "I'm taking early
retirement."

"We've been over this," I told him, rearranging my shrimp into a
wreath around my broccoli.

"I mean I'm taking early retirement now," Leo told me, shoveling in his
primavera pasta.

"Now. You mean *now*, now."

"I mean, this year."

"You mean, you're thinking about . . . Leo, you're not even fifty."

"But I told you there'd be cutbacks, sooner than later, and that I'd get
an offer. And I did. At my level, I can take early retirement, get a few
years of full salary and then my full pension earnings. I can get benefits as
if I'd been in the army. Dental, psychiatric . . ."

"We'll need the psychiatric. Do you know what I make, Leo?" I'd just
gotten a raise. "About twenty-two thousand a year."

"And you have insurance. . . ."

"All I have is catastrophic insurance!"

"Well, you and the kids will be covered. You'll do just fine. We have
our investments. I'm not going to sit around. I'm going to do some com-
modities trading with Dad. And some environmental work . . ."

"That should be lucrative."

"But first, and I know you're going to get uptight over this, I'm taking a real sabbatical. Not like the little trip before. A total break. I don't mean a *total* break. I'll be in touch with you every day by phone. But I'm going to take a real sabbatical. From all of it. I'm going to live in upstate New York, right by the Hudson River, with this great community of people I've been writing to for years. Before I go there, I'm going to visit some other people I've been corresponding with, in Pennsylvania and Massachusetts. Maybe I'll stay with one of them on their places for a while. I've arranged for everything. The mortgage will be paid by automatic withdrawal. . . ."

"Have you arranged for our divorce? Because basically, you're deserting me, Leo."

The air seemed to shimmer between us. My eyes did that separate move thing, waggling each one in an opposite direction, that they'd come to do in moments of deep stress or confusion. I shook my head to rearrange them. I shook it again. The wall between Leo and me was all but visible, shuddering. I could see it move. Even the waiter wouldn't approach.

My husband looked at me with deep seriousness in his great brown eyes. "That's what I'm trying to avoid, Jules. I don't want to get burned out on our family, on family life, and skip. I mean that. But I have to . . . get away. For a while. I have to get away from homework and Gabe's Individualized Educational Plans and the music blasting and Aury whining . . . for a while . . . so that I can stay in our marriage and renew our marriage. I can't take any more daily pressure."

Laughter, you know, is an irresistible human response. A survival mechanism. It's like hunger or thirst or sexual longing. I laughed. Leo's description of our family sounded as though he lived with seven severely handicapped children and a wife in a methadone program.

"You have to get away," I said. "For how long?"

"No more than six months."

"Six *months*?"

"I said *no more than* six months. You know how it was last time. I couldn't stay away from you as long as I'd planned to. I missed my family.

I love my kids, Julie." I didn't doubt that at all. "I love you." I did doubt this. "I don't even mind living . . . here." He made it sound as though this, his hometown, was a grimy subway station.

"You're frickin' crazy," I said, putting down my fork, whispering as the volume of noise in the room spiked. "I don't mean, you're crazy, like . . . Lee, honey, you big goofo, you're crazy, cut it out! I mean *you need help.* You really need help. You have to get help, talk to somebody, before you even consider this . . . bullshit trip."

"We're not one person, Julie. We don't have to want the same things at the same time all our lives."

"I never said we were, though that was the gist of the vows we took. Remember that? I'm not saying we have to be joined at the hip, but this is extreme stuff, Leo. Say you see that. Don't scare me. I feel like I'm in a room with a drunk."

Leo took a long breath, held it, and let it escape slowly. He did this all the time now, and it made me feel as though he were blowing me out, like a candle. Leo's long breaths were as annoying to me as a fork scraped along a plate. I wanted to reach out and backhand him. "*This* is help, Julie. This will be all the help I need. To help me plan a life that will be better for us and the kids."

"And what is the alternative, Lee?"

"I don't see one."

"You don't see one?"

Leo cradled his forehead in his interlaced hands. "The only alternative is . . . I can't be here anymore, Julieanne. I have to get this out of my system. I have to get this *out.*"

He meant this literally.

Having no alternative myself but to get out of that room then, because I could not breathe and my thigh felt as though I'd stuck the fork in it—symptoms I'd come to realize were the way my body expressed stress in the way other people got headaches, or so I thought—I got up from the table and walked along the exact center of the carpet runner. The room of diners seemed lined up on either side of me like rows of animals in cages, noisily honking and growling. The door of the restaurant was just ahead. I opened it. When we'd come in, there had been four steps that led up to the foyer. But when I stepped out of the door, the steps dissolved and I saw a sheer cliff, with the sidewalk, its silvery particulate surface glittering in the lamplight, at the foot. It was no more than five feet from the top of the cliff to the sidewalk. I jumped and landed hard on both knees.

"Julie!" Leo cried, standing behind me. I looked up. He was standing at the top of the flight of stairs, which I could now see very clearly. I looked down at my knees through my stockings. My skin was bleeding as if grazed by a chainsaw. I held up my hands to Leo, who lifted me in both arms, though he was not much larger than I am, and carried me to our car. In the car, he asked me if he should drive me to the hospital. Sobbing, I shook my head. At home, Leo bathed my knees and plucked out stray specks of cement. He massaged Polysporin into the scrapes and taped on gauze pads.

It wasn't until X rays ascertained that neither of my knees was fractured that he began to pack.

Gabe's Journal

I sometimes wish I had been expelled from high school.

But there you have it. Not even a rebel.

I never did anything wrong.

Or right.

Our father's excellent double life made school even more fun. There were a few people who used the pretext of "I-know-what-you're-going-through-my-parents-got-divorced" but the Steiners were not unknown in Sheboygan, and this was a chewy little mess.

Not that I didn't hate the fucking place. Sheboygan LaFollette didn't have huge gangs of kids with assault rifles or anything. It was just tediously crappy. Like, I did the lights for their stupid drama club shows for two years—you haven't lived until you've seen some girl play Maria who's about six inches taller than the guy playing Tony, and who's obviously Swedish and has a jaw like a backhoe to boot, singing "Somewhere," and you know that this has got to be sick and wrong, and then she falls on the bed without bending at the waist, like someone cut her down with an ax. It was a sin against nature, not to mention drama.

But the truth is, school . . . school and I never hit it off. There were the requisite roaming squads of junior psychos, who would probably grow up to be pig farmers or investment bankers, who tormented Caroline because she was sort of a tomboy-ditz instead of a full-blown ditz, wearing sporty clothes like the kind girls wear in New York (black short pants, white shirts; it's a uniform) instead of the sleazy knockoff 1970s My Little Hooker clothes her friends like the very excellent Justine had. They also tortured me, mainly verbally, though I could so not have cared less, for general peculiarity, calling me "Ed" (shorthand for special education) or worse, "Forrest Gump," which is not really that heartwarming a movie, if you ask me.

I just spent two fucking hours on physics.

Why they make you take physics and history at what's supposed to be a Barney college for "high creatives" (read that, learning disabled kids, more or less literate but unable to prove it), where I'm trying to learn creative writing and light and sound technology, is a mystery to me. I know the motherboard better than I know my mother. Do I have to know the chemical reason that makes quartz an electrical conductor?

Regarding my mother. That, what I said, is not fair. She's not my confidante, the way she thinks, but I trust her. I . . . love her, although she's psychotically overprotective and nearly clinical . . . some of the time. But she's been through a lot. You can't blame her. For being one parent with half the wattage physically, she's a goddamned good one.

I also "know" Leo. I'm acquainted with my father. That's special, isn't it? I *know* my father. Even though I've seen him precisely twice in what? About four goddamn years? These days, he visits his folks like once a year, which is very nice for his parents, isn't it? I visit him with Grandpa and Grandma Steiner, never alone. We go out for pasta. He can't spend too much, because, though he practices law where he lives now, he doesn't make a lot because he basically lives in Bumblefuck, Eygpt, and Joy, his soul mate, wants every fucking thing under the sun, and it all has to be made in Italy or France or whatever. This is fine with Leo, of course, though he once wanted my mother to use, like, dishwashing liquid on her face.

My sister Caroline (now "Cat"), of course, writes. She writes of the joys of the Happy Valley, where she has been homeschooled, probably to the point of now having the ability to put on her own hair mascara. She can't even spell. I can't spell, but she *could* spell, if she wanted to. She thinks she's a genius because she's read all the Danielle Steel books the Devlin girls had. That was their library. Danielle Steel and all these books this one lady wrote about the pastor and the butcher and the baker in this one town.

Given the caliber of her friends—including her best friend Mallory Mullis, who I gather from hints may actually have a brain but has apparently taken great care to keep it under wraps, to the point of appearing to be the dimmest bulb since Edison's prototype—you can hardly be surprised. She writes that Mallory knows all the names of a horse's parts—like "shoulders" are called "withers," and why?—but can't add and subtract as well as Aury can. "Math is so non-esentel," my sister writes.

I think personally that "Cat" is non-esental.

I shouldn't have been shocked by all the stuff she did after my dad left us.

But I fucking was.

I don't answer her letters. I read them, though. Sometimes I send her e-mails. ("Paradise" does have cable, though Cat says it's a rule that no one eats anything that requires washing a plate. If you have to wash the plate, the food is not good for human consumption.) I answer with e-mails that say, "Noted." My mother is glad we stay in touch, though I would hardly call it that. My mother would forgive Jeffrey Dahmer if he just apologized nicely. She says Caroline will "come around." I should "love" Caro, according to my mother, because one day she'll come to her senses. As if she had any senses to come to? She's just being a self-centered kid, my mother says. Why didn't I get to? Why didn't little Aurora?

My sister tells me all about Dominico, her true love. (That's a good name for a guy, isn't it? It's as rich as "Aurora Borealis.") And about how unfair I am basically to Leo and Joy (Joy is short for Joyous; she changed her name from "Joyce"). How if I would just come and visit . . .

I'm sure. I'll get right on it.

I never would have believed it was possible for her.

Not that I care. Big loss. So bad. So sad. Caro was like a vacuum when she was here; she just used oxygen and occupied space. (Would that be a vacuum?)

And it's not that I don't see her point. It was total, rotten, humiliating dregs right here in River City after my dad split, and especially after Caroline and I found out for ourselves that he'd split for good.

It's that I didn't think my sister was like, whatever, Cyndi Lauper or somebody, all kinds of brains and heart behind a goofy exterior; but I didn't know she was no deeper than a sunburn. I didn't know she'd turn fifteen and go static. Full quota of Leo genes, I guess, that didn't express themselves until the last chip was down. I shouldn't speak of her in past tense. But she is so past tense. The house we found on our Incredible Journey (more about this later) at the end of the street with no name, just off Rural Route 161, is just about the right place on earth for my sister. She belongs there, the reigning Crown Princess of the Shitheels, lady-in-waiting to Queen Joyous, in the Shitheel Capital of the World.

Do I come off as a bitter jerk?

Well, I'm not a jerk.

But I'm still pissed off, even though my own life has turned out better than I had a right to expect. It's like, I knew my sister as well as my mother knew Leo. And we were . . . related. Like, almost twins. Fraternal twins. Not even eleven months between us. Her six and me seven, me dragging her back to the house, blood all over her head, yelling for Leo at the top of my lungs, after she coldcocked herself on the neighbor's mailbox when she tried to do a wheelie on her little goddamned Barbie BMX. Me, like, ten and her nine, me holding her dress back for her so she wouldn't puke all over herself, right in the goddamned women's john at the funeral home when Grandpa and Grandma Gillis died. Me thirteen and her twelve, me walking in on her, with only her underpants and shirt on and the bolster between her legs, unable to look at her for two weeks, not that I wasn't capable of jerking off to the point of passing out, and her paying me back for this by hitting me across the back of the shoulder with a canoe paddle. Me fourteen and her thirteen, me having to pull one of the eighth-grade sociopaths off her when they rated me with the "Ed" crap. She kicked a guy in the nuts who had six inches and fifty pounds on her, and she didn't even know I was watching (neither did he; and I had a foot and twenty pounds on him).

She was tough, I'll give her that.

She did crazy shit that was not totally unadmirable. She tried out for cheerleading and was so agile given all the dance my mother made her take that she made all the squads only so she could publicly explain, at the pep assembly, how she would rather have her premolars pulled out without lidocaine than stand in front of a bunch of Neanderthals and shake her ass in a tennis skirt. She used the word *ass*. This was in eighth grade. I thought Mrs. Erikson was going to slap her across the chops. I saw the hand of the tiny blonde bitch in the white athletic shorts, a PE teacher who was the cheerleader adviser, actually go up, into the backhand position, then drop and grab Caro by the elbow. I saw Erikson look out of her little weasely blue eyes and notice the principal standing nearby them.

I wish she had hit my sister. We could have won a lawsuit. The dough would have come in handy later. Though it turned out I have gotten scholarships for the young, gifted, and maze-brained. Turned out I didn't need Gramp's stash. I'm going to take it, and probably invest it some way. I thought I'd give it to Mom, but Mom doesn't really need it anymore. It's so strange, that part, when we were so totally shit up the creek financially not that long ago. It's hard to forget the peanut-butter period. Kids aren't supposed to notice that. But I did. I knew Cathy was paying for most of the food when she moved in with us, after my father took off for good. I knew she was living there not just to help my mother through her rough periods. She was also living there because my mother couldn't have survived the Early Desertion era without Cath's financial help, unless we moved to a trailer.

But I digress again.

And again.

Caroline.

She lives in the land of ceremonial moon dinners and consensus decisions and desks made of doors scavenged on garbage day or "liberated"
from construction sites (of people who actually plan for and *buy* their
doors). She lives among the strawberry fields (literally). Her boyfriend
Dominico's brother is named McGuane. Their sister is Reno. It's a theme
family but I don't know what the theme is. (I told you this crew down by
the riverside is a real brains trust.) Leo—our *dad*—lets Dominico sleep
with her at their house. And he did when Caro was only fifteen, too.

Not that this is something I didn't envy at one time.

But self-denial has its pleasures, too. Hormones over mind is apparently our family's crowning trait. That and not seeing your ass because
you're looking at your elbow. I'm kind of determined to prove nurture over
nature. I like knowing I'm not an idiot.

Still. The whole road trip we took to find our father, when he stopped
calling us, was Caro's idea. She figured out how to transfer Dad's e-mails
to Mom's computer before he left, and she figured out how to use them in
reverse date order. To make our map. I give her that.

And there were nights out there I never felt closer to anyone in my life
(don't get the wrong impression, here; I mean close, platonically), like she
knew what I was going to say before I knew it. Times she was so quick on
her feet mentally (Caro is a spectacularly gifted liar, a truly Olympian
liar). She *so* kept us from being sent home on a bus with a nice juvie officer and a couple of granola bars.

I will never forget that. And in a sense, I guess that part of my life will
always be . . . part hers.

But fuck. I don't miss her. She might have blown off Mrs. Erikson. But
she clearly had this destiny as a cheerleader-of-the-mind anyhow. Bawling, snot running down her face in a bubbling cascade with the tears, *I
have to, Gabe; I can't deal, watching her like this; I'm afraid, Gabe. . . .* I was
supposed to feel all sorry for her. Fuck! I wasn't fucking scared to death?
Didn't she maybe notice that jumping through the woods, going to no
school, and getting a nice piece of one of the Bounteous Devlin sisters

(there were five—did I already say this?—Joy was the middle one) might have held some appeal for me? Chucking it all and forgetting about good old Mom, Semi-Suicidal in Sheboygan? Giving up being what I actually was, too young to be a nursemaid and wage earner and replacement best boy for my Steiner grandparents, and soul mate and half-assed father to a very cute but screwy and scared little kid? Didn't she think I maybe wanted, on some totally selfish level, to be Leo Two, The Movie?

But I digress. Shit. It's one of my problems. If I hadn't spell-checked this, it would have said, *"Its on o f my problem."* I think Leo might have wanted an actual, right-and-left-brained son instead of a topiary son.

To be totally honest, I would like to see Caroline again.

There was a time when I thought all the school shit I put up with before the real shit was my quota for one life. But apparently not, because everything else happened on top of it, which is so totally boring it happens over and over and over and over and nobody ever learns a damned thing about it because if they did, they couldn't possibly bring themselves to breed. I'm certain of this. Maybe it's a study. I could do research. It's possible there's a missing gene for fucking loyalty on the Y chromosome. Not to mention a missing gene for distinguishing between the smell of roses from bullshit on the X chromosome. My sister being the perfect example. My mother, well . . .

Maybe I should write a memoir. My grandfather was famous. My mother is minorly famous.

I could write about growing up young, gifted, learning disabled and dys-fucking-functional.

No.

My mother hates memoirs of any variety. She calls them "me-moirs." If you talk to her about one, she'll say there are a lot more interesting things in life to write about than yourself. You can point out that, in a sense, she wrote about herself in *Myriad Disconnections*. She would say, "I was *not* writing about *myself*. I was writing about *events*."

This has nothing at all to do with what's the matter with her. She was always like that. You can't tell people what to do with their lives for as long as she has without probably believing you know what you're talking about. Never mind the irony.

And yet, an interesting thing my mother used to say about shit that really hurts you is that writing it down drives a stake through its heart.

Maybe I'll make this thing I'm writing a long letter. A Letter to My Father, by A. Gabriel Steiner. I've written mostly about my sister. But there's a lot more to tell.

So, Pop, this one's for you.

EIGHT

Lamentations

EXCESS BAGGAGE
By J. A. Gillis
The Sheboygan News-Clarion

Dear J.,

My best friend and neighbor recently asked me if I would coach her in the labor room. Naturally, I was honored. Her children are like cousins to our two children, and I was both elated and a teeny bit jealous that my friend, whom I'll call "Lauren," was having a third—when my husband has insisted we had "two enough." After ten hours of labor, her baby son emerged, a whopping nine-pound boy, and I said, without thinking, "Why, if I didn't know better, I'd say that was Ben McAllister!" Ben is my two-year-old son. The whole room went quiet. Lauren then confessed right there that the baby was my husband's child, the result of two sexual incidents when Ben was a baby. I confronted my husband, who begged forgiveness. He and Lauren's husband—who will accept the child if we pay child support—want the friendship to continue. He has totally forgiven her. I guess he's a bigger person than I am. All three say they would have told me sooner, if they hadn't feared it would have hurt me and the friendship. I still love Lauren and I love my husband, but I don't know if I can live the rest of my life two doors down from the reminder of his infidelity. He says even good people can make mistakes. I would move, but my husband's job is here, and Lauren says that if we move, we'll never know the child. I have a dilemma. I don't want to disrupt everyone's life.

What should I do?

Heartbroken in Hartford

Dear Heartbroken,

I have a dilemma, too. It's knowing where to start. You have not said a single word about your own feelings of anger, which should be uppermost in your mind. You have been deceived and had your face rubbed in the evidence of your husband's betrayal. Just what is it you "love" about "Lauren," a woman who had no compunctions about having unprotected sex with your husband, exposing you to humiliation and possibly even disease, who now wants you to share in the life of the child who resulted from that callous act of disloyalty? And pay for the privilege?

You say you want to stay in your marriage. Okay, you're a free adult with a working conscience. Good people do make foolish mistakes, and have to pay for them; but I would have a very hard time parting with 17 percent of my family's income for eighteen years because of a mistake preventable by a little self-control or a three-dollar package of condoms. Your call. But if you do stick with him, job or no job, you're going to have to take the show on the road, far from "Lauren." If you can't see that, science has yet to create the lenses you need.

J.

"But Julieanne," Leo's dad said, "this doesn't make any sense. I understand the words you're saying, but I'm not grasping it. The Leo I know, the Leo I *raised*, couldn't do this. He never even told his mother. You say he's coming back?"

"*He* says he's coming back, Papa," I told him.

"Julieanne, your legs, did he hurt you?"

"I . . . fell, Papa. I fell when we left the restaurant . . . a couple of nights before he left."

"Because if he hurt you, ever, in any way—"

"Papa, he didn't hurt me that way."

"Julieanne, now I know Leo has a cellular phone. I need the number for that. I need to talk to my son. I need to talk some sense into him before he goes too far down this road because he might not be able to find his way . . ."

"Home, I know," I said, wincing as *my* son got up and left the room, dropping his seventy-five-pound backpack (Gabe considered school lockers a riddle and a nuisance, and so carried his entire life with him like a turtle with a shell) and making a thud that caused the windows to shudder. Caroline, on the other hand, holding Aury, pulled her chair closer to get a better seat for the show. I knew I should have sent them out of the room, but I didn't have the strength.

There was a knock at the door. Cathy, with Abby Sun in her beautifully embroidered and very PC front pack (Cathy's mother had somehow learned to spell out "I love Mama" in Chinese characters).

"Julie," she said, embracing me and removing the baby's utterly unnecessary knit hat. Abby's hair was a seal pelt that would have kept her warm in a Sheboygan blizzard, and it was Indian summer. "Julie, I can't tell you what to do until I understand. . . ."

"I don't know that I need you to tell me what do or that there's anything that I can—"

"We were just trying to get to the bottom of this," said Gabe Senior.

"I don't know if there is a bottom of this," I said.

"My father took a powder," Caroline blurted. "That's what Grandma Hannah called it. She said, 'He took a powder, the little putz. . . .'"

"Caroline!" all of us said together.

"Well, she did!" Caroline's upturned brown eyes glittered with mischief. She liked seeing the ox gored. I don't think any of us, three days after Leo's departure and the day the Steiners had rushed to help out when my knees ballooned into festive purple pillows, entirely knew what had happened, or was to come.

Hannah put Aury down for her nap. She told Caro to go into her room and get started on her homework. "I don't have any," Caroline said.

"Think of some, Hannah Caroline," Grandma Hannah commanded in a tone that brooked no sass. "Get a head start." She slouched away, but, we were to learn momentarily, never went beyond the wall outside the living room door.

I felt that those of us who remained, the adults, were some kind of NATO committee, trying to come up with an extradition order.

"These people," Hannah began, when she returned, "these hippies he's been writing to. Julieanne, you know that I love you as my own child, so you won't be offended when I ask you, is there a woman among them that he's . . . well, skirt chasing?" Hannah is the last person on earth who would have known that phrase. "What did he take with him?"

"Clothes, his camera, nothing, really," I told her. "He had everything in a duffel bag."

Caro stuck her head back in then: "He got a lot in that bag, though! Because he's been buying those clothes from Travelwise that you can scrunch up to the size of your hand. They have coats you can put in your pocket, and wash and they'll dry in an hour and come out wrinkle free."

"Tencel," Cathy said, "the big lie."

I rubbed my head. My eyes, like a sea creature's on stems, were acting independently of each other again. "I don't think anything like that's going on," I told my mother-in-law. "I think what he really wants is to figure out what he's going to do with his life after the university. And this is just his way of doing it. He's having his adolescence."

"But there's more to it," Hannah said.

"I think he wants to feel young again. Free to do what he wants—"

"He's got a wife and children," said Hannah. "That's what he needs to *want* to do. It doesn't matter that he needs to feel free."

"That's his whole point," I told Hannah. "He thinks he never got the chance to feel that way. He thinks I saddled him with babies and houses and—"

"Julie, you sound like you're taking his side!" Cathy interrupted. "It takes two to tango. Your understanding passes all understanding. Now, did you try to talk him out of this, or did you encourage him, like you did when he took his . . . other little trip?"

"I never encouraged him to do that. I allowed it, and grudgingly. And with this one, I put my foot down. I told him in no uncertain terms that I did not want him to retire and I did not want him to leave. . . ."

"And . . ." Cathy prompted me.

"Do you see him here?" I asked her, putting my arms out to cradle my goddaughter, Abby, who popped her thumb in her mouth and, wise little math genius she would certainly be, went to sleep.

"You two discussed everything," Cathy went on.

"Not recently," I admitted. "He's spent more time on the computer and at the yoga center than with me."

"That's what you wrote to that guy about his wife's e-relationship with that friend of hers in Austin. You wrote that the proportions of time should be exactly reversed, that intellectual infidelity was just as dangerous as the other kind, that confidences in the secrecy of cyberspace were just as potent and perhaps even more so, than confidences between the desks. . . ."

"That's what you told me to write. Intellectual infidelity," I reminded her.

"It *is* a nice phrase," Cathy said with a sigh. "Well, we're not sure that's what happened here. All we know is we have a guy—"

"Who turned forty-nine and figured out he was going to die someday," Gabe called from the family room. "If I hear that one more time, I'm gonna puke. Why didn't Luke's dad do this? Or Justine's?"

"Justine's dad is kind of a scum," Caroline said.

"*But Dad* is a clean-living, miso-eating saint, Caroline!" Gabe yelled back. "So what's your point, roundhead? His *not* being a scum should have kept him from doing this, not the opposite."

"I think Dad thought about life more," Caro whispered.

"Thinking about life too much is not necessarily a good thing," Hannah told her. "Some things you do; some things you think about. Some things you think about you're better off if you never do."

"Amen," said Gabe Senior. "I have to lie down for an hour or so, Julieanne. Do you mind? Will you keep your feet up and keep those ice packs on?" I nodded dutifully. Like all Jewish men of a certain age, even those who'd spent their lives selling marbles and kite string, Gabe Senior had, for me, the authoritative quality of a physician.

"I'll be here, Mister Steiner," Cathy said. "I'll look after her."

"I'm going to try to make some dinner," Hannah told both of us, "with what scraps of food I can find in this refrigerator."

"There are a whole bunch of mushrooms and some boxes of tofu in the pantry, Hannah," I told her.

"Tofu," she said dourly. "Gabe! I need some chicken, skinless, four breasts, some rosemary, French bread, some rice, normal, and a dozen eggs. . . ."

"I'm going to nap, Hannah," Gabe Senior explained.

"Nap later. I need to cook now," his wife told him. "And Caroline, you don't need to sit there looking pretty, although you do look very pretty. I want you to straighten this place up. I want you to get all your dirty laundry out of your room and your brother's—"

Outraged, Caroline cried, "My brother's . . . ! I'm not going to do his laundry!"

"So he can take Aurora to the park in the bike holder, which I know you wouldn't be caught dead doing, and play with her while we straighten this place up."

"Abby's asleep," Cathy said. "I'll do the laundry if Caroline dusts and picks up, because then I can talk to Julie."

Cathy didn't know about the night I'd spent on Friday. I was yearning to tell her, but I wanted it to be face-to-face, and everything had happened so fast. I'd spent the evening pleading with Leo as he tried to sleep, begging him to at least talk things over with Cathy—I wouldn't need to be present—before he decided to leave. Though he'd held me gently, and kept nodding as if to say he understood my panic, though he'd even tried to make love to me, nothing I could do or say would budge him. "What if I sell the house while you're gone, Leo? What if I decide to move to New York . . . *City*? Not some burg on the Hudson River?"

"You can't do that, Jules; it's a community-property state," he'd reminded me.

"I could forge your signature," I threatened him.

"If you need to do that, go ahead," Leo said. "I don't think it will accomplish what you want."

"Who the hell are you, the Dalai Lama?" I asked, jumping out of bed, the pain from my battered knees immediately shoving me back down like a rough hand. "What is this, do-what-you-think-you-need-to-do-to-satisfy-your-needs shit? Zen? Leo! Don't you give a shit what happens to us? To this house? To the holy tomato plants?"

"It's all immaterial," Leo said, lying back against his astronaut-foam pillow. "The material is immaterial." He grinned. "I just said that to getcha, Jules. You know I care about all that stuff. But you can handle it. You're a very capable woman. We have a lawn-care service. You have a strong support system of good friends. You have my parents. And a creative outlet. Sufficient money for all the face cream you'll need. The children will help. I'm not worried. And I'll be in constant touch."

He had not been in constant touch. He had not been in touch at all. He had not left an itinerary, explaining that his travels might take him to people in one location where they lived, or in another, though he'd insisted that the big, brown envelope he'd given me contained a detailed list of addresses and telephone numbers where he could be reached or where messages could be left. There was none. All it had really contained were copies of our wills and insurance papers, the number of the pager he had purchased to augment his cell phone, and a funny card, a line drawing of a guy in a little car driving in circles, signed with love to me. "I have friends in Wyoming who live in the mountains in the summer, because the cabins they have aren't plumbed, but rent in town during the winter, where they do whatever kind of skilled work can take them over the tourist season, when they don't *want* to go *near* the town, unless they sell art. . . ."

"What makes you think I give a shit about any of this, Leo?"

He'd seemed genuinely puzzled.

"As if I give a good goddamn what a bunch of selfish, aging drifters do for seasonal work. You want to know something? Personally, that kind of life sounds worse to me than . . . than camping." Leo knew I considered camping a sin not *for* but *against* nature, a form of primitive subjugation disguised as recreation, a way for men to beat their chests at the dawning and women to wash the same dishes fifteen times a day, and with sand. "What would you do with your things, while you were slipping back and forth between worlds? Between the town and the mountains? Your clothes and books?"

"Libraries have books, Jules. And most people don't have our clothing needs. You realize that most people who work at home don't need twenty pairs of shoes, nine of which—"

"Are black, right, Leo. You've only told me that fifty times. But I also give speeches, and I'm on the board of the theater, and I have a life with friends, for which I need clothing. I'm not going to debate this with you, Leo, as if I were Imelda Marcos and you were Gandhi. Neither of those things is true. Do you realize that if you hadn't got your golden parachute, or whatever—"

"Hardly," Leo said dryly.

"Well, your silver parachute from the university, from *taxpayers*, Leo, you wouldn't be free to play out this little game, this little midlife Ulysses crap. You aren't like those people with the bandanas, Leo. You might want to be, but you're a guy with a degree in business, a corporate lawyer, who sucked off the public tit. . . ."

"That would distress me, if I were listening, Jules," he said, and yawned. I knew he was faking the yawn. "How I feel is, I did my time. I tried to do some good for others. I know I did some good for a few. But I didn't do myself any good, slugging down handfuls of Tagamet, living without passion—"

"Living without passion?"

"I didn't mean it that way."

"I didn't either," I said. "I'm not talking about whether our sex lives conform to the numerical national average, Lee. I'm talking about passion for these three people named Gabriel, Caroline, and Aurora Borealis."

"That's just why I'm doing this. I want to bring as much richness into their lives as I can in the time I have with them."

"By leaving them?"

"By rediscovering my own playfulness . . ."

"You mistake shallow for playful, Leo. You think selfish people are wise. You're a fucking idiot."

"Now, *that* is a sweeping statement. And remember, Julie, always use 'I' statements. That's what Cathy, the guru of relationships who lives with her mother, says."

"What kind of sexist, homophobe bullshit is that?"

"She lives with her *mother*, Julie. She's thirty-five."

"I thought you were all for honoring the generations and interdependent communities and all that babble-on."

"You mistake codependency for respect, Julie. You mistake aberrant behavior for intimacy."

"I used to be proud of you," I said suddenly.

"Hmmm," Leo said. "What changed?"

"I used to be proud of you until *you* changed."

"Why didn't you ever take my last name then?"

This came to me as a direct shot from another galaxy. When we married, Leo couldn't have cared less whether I *became* a Steiner or a Steinway baby grand. He liked being married to Ambrose Gillis's daughter. I could think of nothing to say except, "Huh?" And, then, "But I let the children have your name."

"So you weren't all that proud of me. Personally. You were like the uptown girl. Even here. Couldn't get your nose out of the air. Did you ever think that got to me?"

"Leo, that's . . ." True, I thought. "Ridiculous," I said.

"And then after you became a media star . . . of *Sheboygan* and parts of Milwaukee County—"

"Don't make fun of my job," I quavered.

"Then don't make fun of what I care about."

"What I'm worried about is what you *don't* care about. I used to be proud that I wasn't married to Mark Sorenson or Jack Ellis. . . ."

"Julie, it boils down to this. It wouldn't occur to you to color outside the lines, so you can't comprehend it or stand it that someone else does."

"I could if it didn't mean that your children are never going to understand, and that I'm going to have to be mother and father to a toddler and two—"

"You practically make all the decisions for them now anyway. . . ."

"Now, I'm married to Leo Steiner, Ex-Former Jerk."

"I'm not a unicorn anymore, just one of all the other horses, Julieanne, dear," Leo said, batting his long, tangled eyelashes at me before turning over and dropping into sleep as easily as a man might disappear into a trapdoor.

"Do you love Leo?" Cathy asked, as she replaced the dressings on my by-now green-and-yellow knees.

"Of course," I said. "I don't know. That's not the point. Did you love Saren?"

"Of course. I don't know. That wasn't the point," Cathy said. "I didn't know anymore whether I loved her, because I got lost in the rage I felt and I couldn't see anything else. And anyway, it wouldn't have mattered. What mattered is that the rage turned out to be useful, because one thing you can't negotiate in therapy is a failure of commitment if one wants it and one doesn't. And Saren didn't."

"Was Saren really gay?"

"I don't know," Cathy said. "Maybe not purely. I don't know that anyone human really is. The most rampant sexual exhibitionist, the guy on the reality TV show with twenty women begging to marry him, is usually either a woman hater or doesn't know which way he swings."

"That so?"

"I don't know that, either. As a fact. I know what I see in practice. What I conjecture."

"So, did Saren ever try to come back?"

"She wants to be 'friends.'"

"Oh, Cath."

"She wants to meet Abby and compare her ultrasound pictures of her fetus with my daughter."

"Cath."

"We weren't talking about Saren. I asked if you love Leo and how much you're going to be able to stuff down—in terms of residual anger—if he does come back."

"You said 'if,' Cathy."

"I meant 'if,' Julie, and you know that there really is an 'if' here. You can see it as well as I can."

What I could see as well as she could was Gabe standing in the arch beyond the dining room. Not standing. Gabe wouldn't have stood. He was using his six-inch-long fingers to chin and chin and chin himself by holding on to the door molding.

"Gabe!" I said, "you're sandblasting!"

He ignored me. "Aury was hot. She fell asleep in the Burley on the way home."

"Where's she now?"

"Still in the Burley?"

"On the front walk, Gabe?"

"Yeah."

"Didn't you ever think she might be a little vulnerable out there, a not-even-two-year-old kid displayed out there like a deli sandwich for some perv?"

"Mom, do you think the pervs are out in Sheboygan today?"

"Go get your sister and lay her down," I told him, and turned back to Cathy. "I'm sorry I popped off at you."

Cathy had used the few minutes I spent on Gabe. She'd been busy. She'd written, in cursive, on the back of one of Aury's coloring pads: *Cook the main entering first. Then, fleece.*

"Why are you writing gibberish?" I asked my friend.

"What does that say, Jules?" she quizzed me. "Read what I wrote." I did. "Julie," Cathy said, "what this says is, 'Cook the main entrée and then freeze.' What did you tell Gabe a minute ago?" she asked then.

"I told him to get Aury."

"And?"

"I told him to stop eavesdropping."

Cathy sat back, her graceful narrow shoulders sagging. "Julieanne, other than the cake and this restaurant thing, have you had any other falls? Have you had any trouble seeing? With your balance? Any sensations of pain anywhere?" Mute, I tried to stare her down, Anglo blue to Gaelic green. I had to look away first.

"There's something even more important than figuring out this deal with Leo. Like, what's going on with you."

"With me, how?" I asked.

"It's time to go to the doctor, Jules," said Cathy.

Gabe's Journal

They never fought in front of us.

They would sooner have voted for Rush Limbaugh, that mean, fat, radio guy, for president.

It was a rule of Good Parenting. And they didn't break it. A few times, they had a discussion that strained the definition. In fact, Mom once dumped a whole can of powdered lemonade all over the floor. But they apologized to us later. Adults, they said, almost in unison, could be as ridiculous as children. I remember it because it was near the beginning of Caro's what-the-hell period.

"Is that supposed to make me feel good or resentful?" my sister asked, after the apology. "From most adults I know of, that's an insult to adolescents."

As a result of this observation, Caroline was not allowed to spend that evening with her friends (not watching our school's football game, but screaming "Shut *up!*" and braiding and rebraiding her hair under the bleachers at the high school).

However (*ad hoc* but not necessarily *proper hoc*, and I'm not showing off, because any kid whose father is a lawyer learns at least gravestone Latin), the next day, my father's e-mail program crashed. As the family computerian, I was the primary suspect. But I told Leo quite reasonably that I would not get up from a sound sleep to exact vengeance on Caroline's behalf, that it was she, not I, who had been grounded and she who was furious.

My father confronted Caro.

In fact, he grilled her (for forty-five minutes, during which she never glanced left, the sure sign of a lie). She mounted a good defense, pointing out that she wasn't allowed to use Mom's laptop, and that screwing up Dad's e-mail would have been as hard on her as on him, since she, too, had chat buddies from Milwaukee to Maui. With no physical evidence, he could not convict, even when Caro gave herself away by pointing out that the pulsing vein in my father's forehead made him look like an irrational adolescent. He did say, "Caroline, you are perverse. Why would you want to lip off and get in trouble because we tried to do something *nice*, like apologize to you for upsetting you?"

"You're probably right," she told him with a shrug. "I don't think it's entirely normal that you never fight. So you really didn't have to apologize."

But that was back in the good old days.

Before the *Über*fight.

My best friend, Luke, and I had to strain that night to hear the hisses and snarls on the Friday night, after they got home from the restaurant, a couple of days before Leo left. My parents were in their bedroom, and my room was right next to it. And though they were screaming, nobody was taking care to be quiet and not wake the baby or any other damned thing. I tried turning my music up as a kind of gentle signal to them that they weren't alone. I wasn't playing Evanescence or even U2 or anything normal, it was *West Side Story*; but I had it on for a reason. Louder music had no effect. I looked at Luke and sort of shrugged. He sort of shrugged, too. One or two times at his house, I heard his parents, Peg and Nate, get into it, and he'd said something to the effect of, it's their shit, don't let it bother you, it's a semi-sport for them. So, in the same circumstance at my house, we just went on with what we were doing. Which was writing a parody called *Upper West Side Story* because it was about Hasidic Jews, who were very prevalent, and very well off, in my grandfather Gillis's old neighborhood, which I used to wander around with him. He would point to the men with the side curls and cashmere coats and say, "Diamonds." Just "diamonds." There wasn't anything anti-Semitic about it. A lot of those guys really are diamond merchants.

We were writing the parody to get out of writing a comparison of the real *Romeo and Juliet* (which I'm not sure, but I believe I have been forced to read every year since seventh grade) and the movie with the pretty red-haired girl and Leonardo DiCaprio. You could do a project to replace the paper, in groups of two or four.

We talked on the phone after school Friday, and I said it was an especially good idea because we could make it a kind of double-reverse pimp because *we* lived on the upper west side of Sheboygan.

"Is school on the east side, then?" Luke asked.

"Uh, yeah, Einstein. Other than us, there's only a south and a north side. The east side would be in Lake Michigan," I replied.

"Get all pissed off, okay?" he'd said on the phone. But he showed up an hour later. "Jesus. I naturally assumed there was an east side of Chicago. There's an east side of New *York*, and it has an *ocean*."

Luke was more or less my best friend. He more or less still is.

Back then, he was the kind of kid who was a little marginal himself; but he made up for it by being this football hero, with a ton of speed but no size. And no fear. So, in other words, a pretty decent running back, by Sheboygan standards.

I should point out, he was my friend strictly at home. And from four P.M. Friday until Sunday dinner. He lived down the block, but, in school, he only nodded at me like we knew each other from church or something. He was afraid people might judge him wrong if he acknowledged hanging with an Ed.

I didn't hate Luke for this then, and I don't now, it being a fact of life of predator/prey balance that they call school, which teachers know all about, even though they keep saying, "Our school has a zero tolerance policy for bullying," and such shit. School is a game park for the lions and a sort of living hell for the antelopes—at least for the first ten years, until the antelopes either stop giving a damn, get wise enough to fight back, or go nuts.

I admit, I did feel it was a little fucking ironic that Luke could be brave enough to outrun some teeth-gnashing, slavering moron whose father had been feeding him raw liver and steroids since he was seven, and who wanted to break Luke's fucking legs backward, and not have the nerve to be seen with someone he had no problem with when he went to the cabin or even to Florida with us. We horsed around and had a decent time as long as no one else he knew was there.

The minute someone higher on the food chain appeared, he was like, right, do I know you?

My mother, who noticed more about *my* social life than she should have, went crazed when Luke had his last kid-type birthday party, a sleepover and a big cookout and junk, and invited only the football team guys who would condescend to hang with *him*—basically right in front of me, three yards over. These were not first stringers, but special teams or bench sitters, as well as one tight end who was more or less a nice guy to everyone, although a known jock. There were no quarterbacks, even second string.

And no me.

Which was the first time that ever happened.

He explained—well, I heard his mother explain, or rather I heard *my* mother's response to what I assume was his mother's explanation—that "the team" was kind of like a cult. The coach encouraged them to socialize only with one another during the season to build a dependent unit that would work like a single organism. This was semi-true and semi-bullshit, but probably exactly something a coach like Sobiano would say, but utter bullshitfulness nonetheless.

"And how do you think this makes him feel, Peg?" I heard my mother ask. I was lying on the couch, behind a barricade of my mother's omnipresent bolsters (different colors in every room), feeling divided between wanting to rip the phone out of the wall or simply grab it and say, like an electronic answering machine: "The Steiner-Gillis family is not able to take your call now. . . ."

I was writhing in shame.

Because she didn't let up.

She said, "Embarrassed? You're honestly trying to tell me you think Gabe would be embarrassed at a birthday party for a kid he's known since he was ten years old, who has been with us to our family's summer house, who's spent a hundred nights sleeping over here, because he doesn't *play* football? He *watches* football, Peg." Silence. "He plays pool. Chess. Well, that's hardly the point, Peg . . . the point is that if our positions were reversed, and Gabe told me it would embarrass Luke to have Luke meet his other friends . . . I know how kids are, Peg. I know how kids *are*. But not all kids are the same." In a minute, she was going to start comparing me to Boo Radley, and say I was like a mockingbird, and I was going to get up and stick my ball cap in her mouth. "Whatever you say, Peg. But giving Luke the message that it's . . . I know I can't manage his social life, Peg, nor can I manage Gabe's. . . ."

In any case, after one of these kinds of incidents, thankfully very few (because even my mother did not like to be as interfering as she knew she was capable of being), she would come to me, usually sitting on the end of my bed at night. She'd pat the back of my calf. Both of us knew I wasn't asleep. The routine was unvarying and yet always unique in its ability to simultaneously make me want to hug and strangle her. *I know it hurts; don't deny it hurts. You're the better man. I admire you for forgiving him.* What kills me is, she actually does. Admire me. She says she looks up to me because she says I protect the sparrows, the gist of which I haven't the fuckingest.

But she was right. It *is* humiliating to be sort of publicly iced by the friend who liked you even when you finally got the khaki baggies you wanted but then forgot to wear a belt. Still, you learn quick that fifty percent of something is better than a hundred percent of nothing. I didn't want to go to beer parties with a bunch of fucking dorks with IQs in the double digits, but I would have liked to be asked to go, which is an entirely different thing. By the way, the thing about the hundred percent of nothing. I didn't make that up. Satchel Paige, the black legend in baseball, did. He might have been, like, as good as Sandy Koufax or whoever, but he never got a chance to pitch in the *real* majors instead of the *Negro League* until he was so far over the hill, he was like forty, and I think he was a fastball pitcher, not like Nolan Ryan with his bag of tricks. Anyhow. I tried not to have this problem of Luke avoiding me, which was his because he had no balls to speak of in that regard and mine because I did embarrass people, cause maximum awkwardness between us. I will say he tried, too, not making up too many excuses when I would call him and he was waiting for a better offer. He would just say, "I gotta do something, Gabe." The way of the world, colleague, my grandfather Gillis would have said. Almost any person who catches a five-pound bass will put it on the stringer and try to catch a seven-pound bass. Take my father. Please.

And after all, I was no saint. See, a Special Ed is prejudiced against another Ed, too. There are degrees. And the thing is, I don't look the part. My mother thinks I'm incredibly handsome, and I'm not; but I'm not bad-looking. I look like any other guy, a little taller and cleaner cut than most. I look like Leo. The other guy I sometimes hung out with then, you could . . . well, tell. His eyes were too far down and too far apart, although he was a nice guy and could fix anyfuckingthing immediately. You would just set this disassembled washing machine in front of him, and he would start to hum a tune no one knew the name of, and he would have it back together in like, ten minutes, which came in very handy, for my mother and me, at our low point. There *are* . . . categories of Eds, you know. The most defective have emotional shit and terrible parents and were adopted when they were abused first or too old for it. And I didn't have that whole wagon train of baggage. Then. I didn't have *behavioral issues*. I wasn't *mentally challenged*. And stuff. And I didn't want to hang with the lowest rung of LD kids, the ones whose parents, like, drank so much when their kids were fetuses that they had brains that were like oatmeal with raisins, with just a thought here and there, but mostly mush, but who also could play Rachmaninoff. I wasn't that kind.

I just did all the homework for the semester the first week and then forgot to turn any of it in, is all. I marked the first three circles on the test in the right order and then missed one and ended up with all of the rest wrong, like you button a shirt with the holes and buttons not matching.

Anyhow, one of the ways Luke could justify his own geeky side, without having to insult me or give an excuse to his more studly friends about why he hung with Steiner, was working together on class shit. So we were doing this English project, for which we also got credit for a special, like music, and what we were doing was writing a musical. A parody. I said this already.

Like me, Luke is mixed race. A hybrid. I'm kidding.

His name is Luke Witter, which was Horowitz at Ellis Island. His mother is a Polish Catholic, Margarete, called Peg. His dad's Jewish. They argue over it, though, unlike my own parents. His mother is a *real* Catholic, and his father just recently got *big* into returning to his roots. Luke has three younger brothers. It's like a striped shirt: Old Testament, New Testament. There's Luke, then Joshua, then Johnny, then Daniel. So we're writing this musical, and both of us being fans of Weird Al Yankovic and Monty Python, it was going pretty well. We've got one song, to the tune of "Maria," that goes: *Yeshiva! My parents took me to Yeshiva! And everybody there, had beanies on their hair, like me! Yeshiva! You won't see a girl at Yeshiva! No matter what they do, girls can't be real Jews, it's true!* And then we were working on one to the tune of "When You're a Jet."

"Okay, how about, when you're a Jew you're a Jew all the way, from your bar mitzvah day 'til they cart you away . . ." Luke said, and I started typing it down.

I suggested, "Wait a minute, how about, I feel shitty, oh so shitty . . . ?"

"You can't swear in it," Luke said. "But I like it, if we do a CD."

And then we heard it.

Leo and Julie. "Fucking idiocy." Mumble. "Passion for people? What about your passion for the four people here?"

"I'm not seeing how these things fit together," I said, by way of breaking up the moment.

"They don't have to. My parents can go from why we shouldn't eat pepperoni to the Holocaust in less than three minutes," Luke said. "But your parents never fight. They're always like, 'Will you pass me the butter, Julie? How'd it go today, Lee?' I don't mean phony. Just really nice."

"My dad is a little off his rocker currently."

"Drugs?"

"Drugs?" I was knocked off my chair. "Drugs? Fuck, that would be Ripley's. Leo? On drugs? No, I mean all this health-food shit and his photography vacation, and my mom is getting fed up with it and shit. I told you about that."

"Personally," Luke said, "I'm never getting married. I think they spend about a month of every twelve just fighting. All of them. Whether they do it loud or soft. Mark Hunt's parents don't talk at all. I guess fighting is superior to that. Now, it's that my mother thinks we're going to be barred from the afterlife or some shit. . . ."

"I don't see how you can have kids, though, and have it be fair, otherwise," I said, "if you don't get married."

"You want to have kids?"

I shrugged. "I like Aury."

"Me," Luke said, "I'm never having kids. Just a nice parade of ladies. Your kids is another thing you fight about. Maybe the main thing. Your ma is spoiling you. Your dad is giving in too much. Or he's too mean. Or she has a big mouth and the kids are going to be like her. You know."

"But like, I almost wish they could fight about shit like that," I said. "My dad just sort of slips around her and goes back to e-mailing the loony toons he's friends with. It's not totally fair. It's like she can't do anything right."

"Is Justine here tonight?" Luke asked. Luke, like every other straight male at Sheboygan LaFollette, had the hots for Justine, one of my sister's best friends along with Mallory. Every male, that is, except for me, because I knew her—like working at a restaurant where everyone loves the food except you because you saw it made. I didn't know whether she was at our house. Although she and Caro were unable to spend a weekend night apart, it was always a toss-up (usually dependent on whose parents were less likely to be home) where they would sleep over. We knocked on my sister's door. No answer. "Let's walk up there and TP the house," Luke suggested.

"That's a goddamned mile, Luke," I said.

"Come on," he urged me, punching me in the ribs. We went down to the laundry room to get rolls of toilet paper. You might have thought, and I did, that throwing rolls of toilet paper into people's trees was a waste of parental rage—in other words, you might as well have gotten grounded for something worth it, like taking the car without having a license, which I had done, because despite not having a talent for concentration, I do have a talent for driving. But if you're a guy in ninth grade, refusing to TP a hot girl's house is like not wanting to go rearrange the letters on the ABS sign: in other words, it's the same as admitting you're a fag. We took out four rolls, and then my mom came flying out of the bedroom with her hair all sticking up and these big gauze pads on her knees and said, "Caroline? I have to talk to you. Now. Hi, Luke. Maybe this isn't such a hot night for you to be here."

I said, "I'm sorry, I mean, uh, Gabe."

She looked at me as though I had suddenly developed Elephant Man's Disease.

"What?"

"You called me 'Caroline.'"

"What the hell, Gabe! What are you doing with all that toilet paper?"

"What are you doing with those big pads on your legs?"

"I fell."

"You fell?"

"I fell off the steps at the restaurant."

My mom was a dancer, and she could put on panty hose standing up with her other clothes already on, which I had seen her do when I was a younger kid. It was hard for me to picture her falling. On the other hand, there had been the shaky hand and twitchy eye lately, which I attributed to my father making her nuts, but also was partly her fault because she paid attention to him when he went into one of his the-earth-is-dead rants, which none of the rest of us did.

"Did Dad push you?" I asked suddenly.

Luke said, "I better go."

"Wait," I said. "Can we talk later, Mom?" But it was like she'd totally forgotten she ever spoke to me because she went stumbling away into the living room, like someone who's trying to dodge bullets. "Are you all right?" I asked her. "Did you get a concussion?"

"I only hit my knees," she said. I couldn't see her in the dark. "Go ahead. Forget it. I'll talk to you later."

I looked into my parents' room, and Leo was rolled like a corn dog in his blanket (my mom had her own, a big poofy white duvet, because Leo was a cover hog) and sound asleep.

"Let's take the car," I said to Luke.

"Tell me what words you want on your tombstone, man," he observed.

"Leo's asleep."

"What if he wakes up when he hears the car start?"

"He wouldn't wake up if he heard the space shuttle start in our garage."

"What about Julie?"

"Out of it."

"My man," Luke said. "Our chariot awaits."

This turned out to be one of the best nights of my life.

We drove over casually and TP'd Justine's house, for which her mother came out and cussed us. But, since she sort of secretly identified with Justine's popularity, being a divorced person and the age forty equivalent of a hottie, resembling that country singer whose mother was her partner. She also asked us to come in. And Caroline was there, along with several of Luke's JV friends with the shaved heads of savages and strategically torn-up shirts; but since I'd driven my parents' car AWOL, everyone was eager to make my acquaintance over Diet Dr Pepper, which I think tastes like cough medicine but it was all they had. We all got into the car, Justine's mother being rather tanked, and drove to the place they were building the golf-course community, which had roads and even greens but no houses and should have had a sign on it that said, MAKE OUT HERE. There were so many cars already parked there with their lights out, it looked like Wal-Mart. But we drove farther back, to where it almost ended with what used to be a field, and for the first time in my life, I actually did make out, with this really cute little Thai exchange student who went to our school for about two months on a Rotary program, whom Caroline really liked. Her name was Tian, but Caro and everyone called her "Tee." We lay on the green grass, which felt better than our carpet, and it was this perfect no-bug night, a shitload of stars, like someone broke open a snow globe and threw it across the horizon. We talked about what she wanted to be, which was a pediatrician. She asked me what I wanted to be, and I said I wanted to write songs. She sat up and, in this little voice like Snow White's, sang "Younger Than Springtime," and then she asked me if I knew that song, which I did because my mother has the CD of every musical ever written, and what it was about.

"It's from that show about being a racist," she said. "About World War One or Two. On an island, there was this girl who's supposed to be a bad girl in Tonkin but she isn't, and she's in love with this American soldier. She is a Pacific Ocean girl. This actually happens all the time in Thailand. I mean with American soldiers and girls if their parents don't have any money. I have friends who are prostitutes."

"Not your age."

"My age. Younger. No bullshit."

"Kids?"

"Twelve. It's big thing. You go to Bangkok and get a girl for a week be your girlfriend. And then she get pregnant. Sometimes they get married, if she's old enough. You can't marry a thirteen-year-old kid. Even in Thailand."

"Do other girls . . . ?"

"Other girls, like me, my parents keep me locked in closet. Practically.

Like, I would never be here. With a boy. My father would kill you if you kissed me."

Which I of course did, and she kissed me, and she said it was okay, because we were in America; and I thought, I could die right now, happy. Here I am, Gabe Steiner, with this beautiful girl in my arms wearing a halter top and no bra, who's also really smart, and she's all over me—not, you know, mixing body parts; but pretty good. And me just fifteen. And Caroline was in the backseat with one of Luke's idiot friends in his torn T-shirt, and Luke finally got, well, he got a lot farther with Justine than I'm sure any of the rest of us got with anybody else that night, Justine being casual about this sort of thing.

We all laid around out there until it got to be close to midnight, when I had to break it up, because they ticket for curfew where I lived, much less driving without a license, or even a permit, with eight kids in a Volvo, and if my mother had come back to anything like her senses since my exit, I was in deep shit, not that it wasn't totally worth it. We drove out and rearranged the ABS sign: FALL BRINGS OUT THE BE(A)ST IN OUR BULLS so that it read HI GRAB SLUT BOOBS LET ALL NUTS IN FUR. Not too creative, but it was too late to mess around, and the girls were semi-offended anyhow, even when we told them the purpose was to jerk the farmers around, not to insult their gender. I then dropped everyone off but Caro and Luke, and we went home.

It was the best night of my life for a long time.

TEN

Gabe's Journal

Dear J.,

My son is a gun nut. So is his father. They go hunting, and Cody has had the safety course, and it's one of the best times they have together. They hunt pheasant or mourning doves, which are kind of hard to cook, being so tiny that they come out more or less like bird dumplings. The problem is, Cody has his walls covered with posters of different models of guns: Italian guns, Army guns, antique guns. He lied and said he was eighteen and joined the NRA. He watches gun shows and gets a marksman magazine. I'm worried that he might . . . do something. He's not the best student, and he has friends who smoke and drink beer. He is a happy kid and never disobeys us. But he's going hunting alone now on our farm, for squirrel and goose, and even though he says he's doing it to bring the game home for me, this gun stuff is getting to me. His father thinks that it's perfectly normal, that the only bad thing I can do is draw attention to it. Cody is only eleven.

Concerned in Callister

Dear Concerned,

I'm very relieved you don't seem "Calm in Columbine." It is true that all kids your son's age are fascinated with any kind of firearm, firework, firecracker—even fire, period. It's a sexual maturity thing. But Cody is beyond the ordinary pyro, either on

his way to becoming a mercenary or the next Dylan Klebold. If
your husband doesn't think it's odd to have a kid in fifth grade
whose sole interest *is guns, both of you need to consult a*
professional, your minister, a school counselor, or Charlton
Heston, because even he would think this was over the top. Do
not think you're overreacting. Not *making a big deal out of this*
would actually be a criminal offense, since it's illegal for an
eleven-year-old to hunt alone in Wisconsin. Get your kid a
skateboard and a helmet. Get him hip-hop lessons. Get your
husband a clue. Remind him that nobody ever got killed by
taking something weird and violent too seriously.

J.

This is it, the above.

I cut out the first column that Cathy and I wrote for Mom.

The first week my dad left, my mom lay in bed.

She stayed in bed like it was a second job.

I only remember her getting up once, long enough to make homemade macaroni and cheese that she was then too weak to take out of the oven. There was cheese and spilled milk all over the counter. My mother wore the same tracksuit, day and night, from Monday to Thursday. She didn't run or stretch or even wash her hair.

I figured she was letting herself go because of depression, but, not wanting to scare the shit out of my grandparents—who would have wanted her to get blood tests or something—I called Cathy. Cathy was always good in a fix. She had taught me some good stuff to say to teachers and junk. She came over with Abby, asked me why my mother didn't call me herself, and shook her head when I said I didn't know. She fixed dinner for the little girls and made me help Caro with algebra, which both of us were hopeless at.

When my mom woke up, I heard them talking.

"When do you have to turn it in?" Cathy asked. "How do you send it? How long does it have to be? Two short ones or one long one or does it matter?"

She then called me into the kitchen. She had my mother's iBook and a stack of folders.

"Look, Gabe, you're no dummy," she told me.

"You're no dummy, either, Cath," I said, wondering what this had to do with the price of cheese.

"Thanks, you big asshole," Cathy said. From the television, I could hear Jasmine-the-princess singing to Abby and Aury about a whole new world. I had the feeling that I was about to enter one and that, given the option, I'd rather not have the key.

"You know your mom is not okay."

"I know she acts funny. Is she bipolar?" I asked.

"Bipolar?" Cathy was aghast. "No, she's not bipolar. I mean, I don't think from my experience of working with people who have bipolar illness that this is what we're talking about. I think she's physically sick, and when I took her to her regular doctor, all her blood tests and her everything tests came back ordinary. She doesn't have a virus, and she doesn't have an infection or an allergy. Obviously, she's very depressed, but that doesn't account for how symptomatic . . . for how weird she's acting. And so we made an appointment with a neurologist, but it's going to take three weeks for her to get in to see him. . . ."

"A neurologist?"

"I think there's something off with your mom's balance. At first, I thought that could be from a virus that was affecting her ear, or even her brain. But she'll have to have an MRI—"

"Do you think she has like a brain tumor?" I asked.

"No," Cathy said. I could tell this was not a definite no, but a hopeful no. "What did you do?" I asked, then, "wait until we walked out the door to school and then start running to emergency rooms and doctors' offices all over the city? And not bothering to tell Caroline or me?"

"We went to Milwaukee. Obviously, Gabe, we didn't want to worry you. You might be as big as a man, but you're a kid."

"How do you do this, Cathy? If you don't mind me asking? Don't you have to work? I know my mother can do her job from our house, and I know she has Dad's . . . whatever, pension, to fall back on . . . but how do you just go tromping around—"

"I do a lot of phone counseling—"

"Like phone sex."

"Exactly like that." This was the reason Cathy was such a cool friend for an adult. You could say anything to her. Gay people are less uptight as a rule, is my observation. It's like they've already heard it all. "People don't give themselves time to go and sit in a therapist's office anymore, though I do have a regular base of traditional clients. And most of us aren't comfortable on the phone. But my partners have sort of turned the phone side over to me because I am. I guess because of theater stuff, I can hear a lot in voices, like when someone's trying to fake she's okay, whatever. Some people just aren't as comfortable face-to-face, even though I can learn a lot from them that way. . . ."

"By body language," I said.

"Even from just how they sit and where. But these days I have a couple of meetings with a couple or a kid or a woman and make a general assessment of how people feel about themselves based on their appearance. . . ."

"Are ugly people nuttier?"

"No, but fat people are eating because they're mad at someone, sometimes themselves, but not always. After that, I have a lot of appointments at eight o'clock at night and stuff. When the kids are in bed or the husband is out playing softball or the delinquent is over at his girlfriend's."

"Sounds like a nice gig."

"It has its moments. But, Gabe, it takes a lot out of you, too, y'know? To talk for two years to a woman who's getting the crap beat out of her every two weeks but who still thinks her husband has a lot of good in him because he never hits the kids? And because her father was so lousy and her first husband did hit the kids, like with farm implements, so she thinks she's better off?"

"You're always so sort of upbeat, though."

"I have to do a lot of running and dancing and horsing around to stay that way. If I kept it all in . . . I'd be like the sin eater. That's what my mother calls it. The person at the . . . well, this is gross."

"Go on."

"When my mother was little in Ireland, poor people would find an even poorer person to come to the wake when someone died—"

"Is that generally when they hold a wake?"

"Shut up," Cathy said, grinning and opening the computer's lid. "They'd set out this big meal right on the poor dead person's coffin. What's her password?"

"'Atticus.' So, about the sin eater . . ."

"The sin eater would devour this big meal, which was supposed to cause him to take all the sins of the dead into himself, so the loved soul could go right to heaven."

"What happened to the sin eater?"

"Well, he lived longer, as a result of not starving."

"Did he go nuts?"

"Well, if he was, like, a superstitious Catholic, yeah, sometimes. Some were just shrewd businesspeople, who asked for a few shillings along with the meal. But all of them arranged for a sin eater to be on hand when they kicked the bucket, for certain."

"Liability insurance."

"Yeah."

"So all these doctors—"

"First things first. All these doctors haven't come to any consensus about Julie yet. But her column is due tomorrow, and she hasn't been in any shape to do them ahead of time, and she's in no shape to write one now. I can think of the answer, if you give me a problem, but I can't write it. I'm not a writer."

"Well, call the editor. I'm not a writer."

"You're a good writer."

"But you can't read what I write, Cathy."

"Ever hear of a spell-checker?"

"Yeah, and I can use it until the end of time, but stuff is still going to come out backward and sideways in the sense of organization."

"I can fix all that."

"Isn't this, like, illegal?"

"Probably."

"Because they could probably get someone else to do it for a while."

"Gabe," Cathy told me, pressing her lips together before she continued, "if your mom loses her job now, she loses more than money."

"I would think the last thing you would want to do if you felt lousy is listen to other people's lousy problems which they caused themselves."

"On the other hand, they don't always cause them themselves. Sometimes, they're just caught in the wrong place at the wrong time. And helping someone when you feel useless and down can make you feel . . . powerful. Can restore your—"

"Don't say it. Self-esteem. If I hear that word once more, and then never again for the rest of my life, I'll be happy."

"But really. If you get dumped on, you need to know you're still a really important, worthwhile human being."

"Is that how you felt?" I asked.

"About Saren?"

"Yeah."

"I felt like I wanted to eat butter-brickle ice cream and watch *X-Files* reruns until I died from diabetes. But your mother, your mother bullied me into being in that show with her, ummmm . . ."

"*Carousel.*"

"Yeah . . ."

"I remember because they let me run the follow spot in rehearsal. What a crap show. I mean, I'm not exactly a musical-theater fan, but that was stone crap. Not as bad as *Oklahoma!*, though. That's the top."

"And what a message! I mean, *Carousel*," Cathy agreed. "A slap can feel just like a kiss! But working on it with her, being with her, and growing to love your mom, as a friend—she'd always been my friend, but she became my best friend—it made me want to go on. It made me have the courage to adopt Abby. I can never repay her."

"So you want to do this for her. The column. Until she's better."

"Well, that should be only this week. She'll be up and around pretty quick, if I know Julie. If we can get away with it. I think we can. I think people ghostwrite stuff all the time."

"I don't know," I said.

"Why don't you call your dad and ask?"

"Why don't you?"

"Because I've called him fifty times since he left, and I've left fifty messages, and he's never returned my calls."

"Has he sent letters . . . ?"

"And Caroline has kept them, and she's given me the addresses and I've written to him, and I've never heard back from him."

I took a long breath. "He probably thinks she's faking it."

"I've called him, too, Gabe. And you know what I think? He's probably just a total bastard."

"Whoa! You're talking about my father, Cathy."

"Yeah, Gabe, I'm talking about your father. And if you have an honest bone in your body, and I know that you do, you realize that sending a few letters from Illinois and New Hampshire and Massachusetts over the course of five months isn't being a father. . . ."

"He's still my father." I didn't know whether to shit or go blind. I felt the same way she did but also this blistering need to defend Leo, almost like if I didn't, what she said would be true because of me. Like, I wouldn't be the sin eater.

"Yeah, he's still your father. But he should be calling back. He should be calling you. He should be calling little Aury, every night, not sending her a box with a fucking acorn in it! How many times has he called?" I didn't say anything. I couldn't remember whether it had been three times or two times; but one of the times, I'd been out with Tian, who had only a few weeks left before she left for good. Frankly, if I wanted to talk to anyone, it was her, not Leo. Leo would be back soon enough, smelling of miso and burning anisette incense in the bathroom. Maybe trying to talk us all into moving to a happy land, far, far away. But I didn't want to move away. I didn't want to be away from Grandma and Grandpa Steiner for one thing, who now felt like the only fixed point in the galaxy. But more importantly, for the first time in my life, I felt like a normal teenager, like if my mother had noticed, she'd have said the things about me parents say about normal teenagers: *I never see him. He's hardly ever home.* You don't know what it's like to feel average if you've never felt up to average. Tian understood that I had special study halls and all, but it didn't affect her at all; she just thought they were like her English-as-a-Second-Language program after school. When I couldn't get the words to go along with my thoughts the first time, she laughed like a little bell because the same thing was happening to her. Like me, English wasn't her first language, either. To her, my head-wiring problem didn't make me an edge-feeder if not a downright geek. She didn't notice it.

I knew I was going to lose her; I knew that my life after she left would go back to being its customary empty plate with a hole in it. But right then, I had Tian. I, Gabe Steiner, Special Ed goon, had the girl everybody in the school wanted, the girl who looked like a goddamned movie star, and was also smart and really sweet and so small I could pick her up and hold her. I was in love. You can be, even at that age. And I knew that having loved Tian would change my life, that I would have lasting respect of some variety, that I would think about her forever—how perfect her skin was, how she let me slide my hands almost up to her breasts, how humble it made me feel that some creature so exquisite let my hands make contact with her.

I had actually stopped wishing I could become comatose until I turned twenty-five.

It was not a good time in my life for me to grow big shoulders and take on my mother's problems. This is a shitty thing to say, but true.

However, Cathy's face convinced me I had no choice. She looked like some kind of warrior goddess, with that look that says they'd be glad to kill you with a knife if you don't listen. I knew I was beat.

"She edits stuff out of them, too," I told Cathy wearily. "The letters. She has to. Some of the people write seven pages, both sides. Or e-mails that have three parts. She has to boil them way down, but she never changes their real words unless they have really crummy grammar. And she has to protect their identity. Like, if they say they teach at the middle school, she'll say they teach at a church preschool or whatever if that has to be in there. Usually, she leaves all that identifying junk out completely unless the woman's husband is a cop who sells drugs or whatever. She makes him a judge then, or she makes him from way somewhere like Illinois." Cathy was writing this down. "She tries to pick different topics every week. Like, she doesn't want a string of columns about, when should you have sex in a new relationship, or how can I tell if he's cheating on me? She mixes them up. Aging parents. Fights with your sister where she won't speak to you for a year. You know."

"We'll have to tell her we're going to do it," Cathy said, tapping her teeth with Aury's Scooby-Doo pencil. When we did, my mother turned her face to the wall and rolled herself up in Leo's yellow blanket.

"If you don't want us to, we'll stop right now, honey," Cathy soothed her.

"I can't," my mom said, and I could hear that she was crying. "I can't do it, and I can't not do it. I don't want to lose my job. What if I lose my job and Caro gets a ruptured appendix? When Justine had a ruptured appendix, her parents had thirty thousand bucks in unpaid coveralls to pay for. I'm too stupid. I can't think. I start to think of one thing and something else comes barreling along like a train and whams it right out of my mind. . . ."

"I feel like that all the time," I said. "I feel like I'm listening to fifty different conversations all at the same time and I can't understand any of them, particularly if I get bored. . . ."

"I do, too," my mother said. "But this is worse. It's like my head is talking to me. I hear funny little noises. Like pipers piping or little kids talking . . . that aren't there. Aurora asks me for a glass of milk, and I have to think about what 'milk' means. It takes me a minute. More. And when I try to talk, it comes out up in the wind. I mean, upside down. And if I concentrate on it, it gets more bad."

Cathy and I exchanged glances. Whatever else she did, my mother never made a mistake in grammar. Even Aury knew the difference between "lie" and "lay."

"And what else?" Cathy asked.

"I don't want to . . . talk it," my mother said. "Just pick out a sweater that has nothing to do with love." And we knew that she meant "letter" and not "sweater." I felt a cold line of sweat under my chest.

She was asleep before we left the room.

Naturally, I picked the one that interested me most, since at LaFollette, a gun rack is about as common an accessory on a car as a CD player. At this time, the governor had suggested it might not be a bad idea if there were not just armed guards in high schools but armed faculty. Which would have meant that Mrs. Erikson might have been able to shoot my sister during their little pep-rally grapple.

"Do you think this kid has a problem?" I asked Cathy.

"I think this kid's family will be a headline in about five years if something doesn't change fast."

"So it's a good one."

"The American Association of Pediatrics says that having a loaded gun in a house where there are children is so dangerous it's like . . . well, a loaded gun."

What I didn't tell Cathy was that I owned a gun, though I hadn't known that I did.

I'd been going through my father's drawers, looking for one of those strap T-shirts they call wife beaters, though my mom always made him call them "muscle tees," so I could wear it under a sort of see-through shirt that also was Leo's, when I found a handgun. It was in its box. It was a .38 special. There were no bullets. I could have shit a brick.

Now, my father had been a conscientious objector. He'd been willing to go to prison rather than to Vietnam, although being married and in law school got him out of that anyhow. He told me all the time that if a little kid with a bomb strapped to his clothes walked up to him, he'd rather be blown up than shoot the kid. This was before he got into yoga and stuff. He was always like that. He said that guys who hunted were afraid their dicks were too small, and in those words.

I picked it up, like you would pick up a snake. It was heavier than its graceful shape would have indicated, with a long barrel. And clean. I could tell he'd never used it. I then went through all his drawers and didn't find anything more interesting than an old package of rubbers and a hemostat, which at the time I had no idea what he would have done with, but which I now know meant he and my mother occasionally smoked a joint. Or they had when we were babies or something.

Why would he have a gun?

Was he secretly afraid he might run into some trouble out there, roaming among the real marginals? Did he have some psycho idea that he was going to protect us from foreign invaders? Was he suicidal? If he had it, why had he left it behind? Why had he taken his laptop but not his sidearm, partner?

That was when I knew that Leo really had lost his marbles. . . . I took the thing and threw it as far up onto his top shelf as I could, back behind the tuxedo shoes Leo had to wear every year to the Chancellor's Ball. It made me sick to my stomach to think that Aury could have found it, although Aury could not have reached the top drawer of my dad's chest.

Then I sat down on the floor of the closet and tried to think back hard, really concentrate, on the way he behaved the day he left. What he did. What he talked about. All of it had been sort of standard fare. All of it had been sort of Leo and sort of nuts.

We all got to go in late to school that day, because his plane didn't leave until noon.

Leo sat us down on the couch. He held Aury on his lap. My mother was in the bedroom. She refused to come out. He explained his "sabbatical." He explained to us about the people he'd been writing to, who were regular, educated people who just saw life as not having to be this big rat race, about the plot of clean land he wanted to buy, with a stream and maybe a prairie meadow. He explained that it was going to be like tearing out his heart to be away from us until the end of winter, but that this was something he felt he had to do and, when we were older, we would remember that he had done this, and that when people tried to discourage us from doing things that might seem unusual but that we felt we had to do, we'd have him as an example of why trusting your own instincts is always the right thing to do. No punctuation.

Then he started to cry. Not like you cry at a movie if you're a guy. Like you cry if you're a baby and you fall. "I love you so much, son," he'd said, kissing my head.

"I love you, too," I told him simply.

"Caroline, I remember the first moment I saw you," he said.

"I don't," Caro replied, her face as still as unbroken water, not a flicker, not a ripple.

"Aurora," Leo said then, and held Aury against his chest. He rocked her and kissed her. Caroline looked at him as though he stank.

"What if your instincts tell you to quit school?" she asked suddenly.

"Caroline, I know what you're—"

"No, Dad, tell me," Caro persisted, as Aury climbed down and wandered off into the room she shared with Caro. (She had slept in my parents' room until she was eighteen months. And my dad insisted that the 'guest' bedroom should be a library or office, where he could read in peace. Natually, Caro went nuts about having to share her room with a closet full of Care Bears.)

"If your instincts tell you to quit school in the traditional sense, but find a way to get the credentials to make a living, then you should do that," my father said.

"I have no idea what you mean," Caroline said.

"I have no idea what he means, either," said my mother, appearing in the doorway. Looking as though she'd drunk a quart of champagne and forgot to change out of her ball gown. She was wearing a satin nightgown and had on some kind of boots. "I know he means you can get a degree by being homeschooled instead of going to the public institution; but I have no idea what he means when he says it's okay if his instincts tell him that he can justify leaving his kids for six months under any circumstances short of having a brother who's dying and living in Saskatoon who needs his help to save the family wheat farm, and we already know he doesn't have that."

"Julie, this isn't helpful," Leo said.

"I'm not trying to be helpful. I'm trying to be rational."

"Julie, what if I died?"

"Are you asking if I would object?"

"That was a shitty thing to say, Mom," I put in.

"Don't swear, Gabe," she warned me.

"Julie," my dad pleaded, "what if I died? You'd have everything you have now, and in exactly the same way. The plane tickets I've gotten are the cheapest possible fares; I have people to stay with who'll help contribute to my room and board and so on in exchange for my helping them work out some legal issues they have. I have health insurance and so do you. This whole thing should cost me in the neighborhood of a thousand bucks. You spend that much in six months on clothes."

"I do not," my mother snapped.

"You do, too," Leo said.

"I do not," said my mother.

"I see the bills, *Julie*. You do, too," my father said patiently, in his lawyer's voice. "My point is, I'm not leaving you stranded. Aury is in day care part of every day, which is enough time for you to do your job, if you actually do it instead of spending half the time gossiping on the phone with Cathy." Cathy, sitting at the kitchen table, sighed audibly. "Cathy, I'd appreciate some time alone with my family, and I don't mean that unkindly," Leo said.

"Julie asked me to be here with her, and so I'm staying, and I honestly don't mean that unkindly, either, Leo," Cathy said.

At that moment, Aury came back with my father's old pajama pants, which she'd taken from his bottom drawer, and her *Big Book of Childhood Poems.* "Nighty?" she asked. "Dada reada story?" She thought that if she could get Leo to put her to bed, he would have to stay. That was when I started to bawl, and punched a hole in the drywall behind the window seat. I quickly covered it with one of the bolsters. The hole is probably still there, because my mom left the bolsters and made new ones when we moved.

Leo got up and walked over to my mom. He put his hands up through her long hair as she stood there, with her arms locked at her sides. "The softest hair I ever felt," he said. "Julieanne. My girl." She grabbed his wrists.

"Please, Leo," she begged him, "please don't. I ask this of you. I've never asked anything serious of you. Look at Aury. Please." He picked up his huge panier with the big frame and hefted it onto his back.

"Don't you know how this feels to me, Julie?" he asked, in genuine wonder. "I'm scared to death."

"Awwww, shit, Leo, it must really suck," my mom said, dropping her hands, suddenly no longer pleading.

"Well, it does, Julie."

"You ought to be going to a nice, big hospital with cheerful wallpaper, Leo," my mom said. "Either that, or you are the most coldhearted—"

"Take care of your mother, guys," he said to us.

"That would be, uh, your job description," Caro said.

"Caroline, let me give you a hug, please," Leo answered.

"Go . . . hug a tree," she said. I knew what she wanted to say, but our little sister was there.

"Dada!" Aury screamed, as Leo walked toward the door, where we could see the cab outside the window. My mother had refused to drive him to the airport. So had my grandparents, who would not even answer the telephone to say good-bye. "Dada! I want to come! Take me, Dada! Good girl! I'll be good!" She fell down and began to kick her fat little legs, and her face got red, then purple. Leo, crying hard, opened the door and closed it behind him.

We all ran over and picked Aury up, as if we were playing blanket toss at a picnic. As she kicked and sobbed, my mother began to sing that old song Elvis turned into "Love Me Tender," the one she sang all the time to my little sister, "Aura Lee, Aura Lee, maid with golden hair . . ." She turned Aury away from her, so that Aury couldn't kick her or hurt herself, and hugged Aury's arms firmly down at her sides. Aury screamed so piercingly that Caro shut the windows. Finally, she seemed to deflate.

"She's okay," my mom said. "She held her breath too long. She's fine. She'll be a little dizzy." My mom got up and laid both her palms against the front window. We went to stand beside her. We heard a car door slam. It was Liesel and Klaus. He waved. At them.

I'm sure that I'll hate people more in my life than I hated Leo at that moment. I've even hated Leo more since that moment. But the truth is, probably because of hormones, I thought about that fucking gun.

ELEVEN

Job

EXCESS BAGGAGE
By J. A. Gillis
The Sheboygan News-Clarion

Dear J.,

    I have a problem I'm sure that many men of my age share. I'm in love, truly, solidly, deeply, with a woman I intend to marry. She shares this commitment. Now that we recognize that our future will be together, I feel that in order to be a husband who will never stray, I need to pursue other encounters before I place that ring on her finger and seal my fate. It's not that I want any other woman particularly. My intended is beautiful, talented, and bright. But I do not want to have any regrets, and because we are both rather young, 25, I know that the experiences I do not have now are experiences I might want later. My loved one simply does not understand. She says that I had ample time, in college and afterward, to explore other relationships. She believes that finding her should be a signal that I am ready to give up my bachelor pursuits. J., I truly want a happy marriage. But I also know that too many marriages fail because one or the other partner feels cheated of things that are only possible when you're single. How can we resolve this standoff and move forward toward the future we both deserve?

                           Suffocated in Sullivan

Dear Suffocated,

First, I want to offer congratulations. To your girlfriend. She is indeed bright. She's avoided marrying you thus far and has doubts about marrying you at all. Secondly, I want to pose a question: Just how do you define falling "truly, solidly, deeply" in love? If it means that you hear the bell ring for the medal round in the race to prove your masculinity, I congratulate you, too, for self-knowledge that, I fervently hope, will prevent you from ever adding your contribution to the gene pool. What you want is not experience. You want a wedding cake frozen while you sample a tray of fresh strudel. And don't worry. I predict that you're virtually guaranteed the future you deserve.

J.

Dear J.,

Admit it. Just like the great cats and the mighty gorilla, the male of the species is not intended to be monogamous. That's an invention of women who want to have babies and take it easy living off men. If men were meant to be with one woman, why would so many of us have fathered so many children? Come on, J. There's a bet riding on this. You always tell it straight.

Manly in Menomonee Falls

Dear Manly,

You're absolutely right about lions and gorillas. Not only do they sleep around, their only activity besides sleeping and eating the food provided by the females is making more babies. Some humans have an equally sweet deal—we call them deadbeat dads. Lion cubs don't wear out their Reeboks, eat macaroni and cheese, or go to college. They don't need to be

taught to read, drive, shave . . . or learn sexual responsibility!
They don't get AIDS, smoke, or use drugs. A one-year-old lion
can hunt and survive on his own. A one-year-old human can't
survive a night outside. You're absolutely right. Women
invented monogamy! Out of desperation. Men wanted to ease it
in and then ease it on down the road. Along with that space
between their legs, they evolved one between their ears, but it's
empty. And if you think women have it easy, ask your mother.

J.

This is how it felt, the first time I was laid low.

Days of dark-edged linen light revolved around nights and mornings of thick bunting, in which occasionally I was touched by shadows that moved. I was either freezing and burning in a clammy bed. Simply getting up to go to the bathroom was not like moving, but like making a long list, a Thanksgiving list for the grocery store—swing feet to floor, measure distance to door, hold the bladder with one hand like an expectant belly until the destination; don't forget to lift nightie, to use tissues. Moving my legs was like dragging unevenly filled bags of sharp-edged rocks. I would make my path, clinging onto the bureau, the bedstead, the sink, and finally the wall. I never looked into the mirror.

After a long, dirty braid of those days, I woke up. And I was myself. Suddenly and completely.

It was a Sunday morning, because the children were asleep. The house was quiet and clean.

I could see a brown cardinal on the branch outside my window, picking at a suet cake Aury and I had long ago mounted on the half-gourd feeder she'd made at school. I watched the bird's guarded, eerily serpentine movements, observed the separation of feathers on her modest little beige cowl, and realized suddenly that *I could see the bird!* My vision was not blurred. I did not have to focus by closing one eye. I lofted my legs easily over the side of the bed. My thigh tingled, a sparkling of miniature daggers, but I could stand, first swaying like a boat in the wake of a larger vessel, then settling, calmed, still. I walked into the bathroom. I got into the shower and washed every cleft and hillock of my body, rinsing my hair over and over with animal delight. I put on my own socks, my own jeans, a white shirt that smelled of starch. I buttoned it myself.

I walked out into the kitchen and broke brown eggs into a blue bowl. I poured milk onto the eggs and shook rosemary, pepper, and salt on top of the floating orange islands, then whisked in shredded cheese. The butter was melting on thick slices of wheat bread when Cathy came scuffling out of the bedroom with Aury in one arm and holding Abby Sun by the hand. "Oh, holy Christ!" she cried, ruffling her auburn spikes and literally taking a step back, as if she'd seen her great-grandmother Gleason, who Cathy told us died on the *Titanic*, scrambling eggs at my stove. "You scared the hell out of me! I thought the house was on fire. I was getting ready to evacuate the troops."

Gabe and Caroline appeared, Gabe somehow . . . changed, grown, unfamiliar to me in his low-slung pajama bottoms, his chest broader, strapped with new bands of muscle, a wisp of hair below his navel. Perhaps I simply hadn't seen him undressed in a long time.

"Mom," he all but whimpered, bewildered, finger-combing his hair. "What are you doing up?"

"I got better," I said. "That's all I can tell you. I woke up, and I was better. Do you want some eggs? I'm starving." We all sat down and ate the eggs and toast spread with Cathy's mom's homemade raspberry jam. "How long have you been here, Cath? How long was I . . . out of it?"

"Two *weeks*," Caroline said. "Either Cath or I've been sharing a bedroom with two babies for two weeks, Mom. I don't mean that in a bad way."

"Oh, I'm so sorry. Sorry I couldn't sleep on the hall floor, Princess Caroline," Cathy said. Caro pursed her lips and tossed her extravagantly blonde hair (perhaps blonder than before?). An eerie sense stole over the table.

They were talking to each other like . . . like mother and daughter.

"Are you going to stay up now, Mom? Are you over having catatonic depression?" Caro asked.

"Is that what I had? I don't think it was. And anyway, I'm sure Cathy already has an appointment to find out what it really was." I reached around Abby to squeeze Cath's arm tenderly.

"Caroline!" Cathy reproved my daughter, and Caro rolled her eyes. "Well, Julie, you're right. You've got your appointment on Thursday. Let's *hope* that's what it was, because depression, and she's certainly earned it, responds really well to medication. . . ." Cathy was cutting Aury's toast up into one-inch squares, and Gabe was twirling the lid onto the top of her Princess Jasmine sipper cup, which she refused to give up. They were not just a family. They were also, all of them, talking about me as if I weren't there, as if I hadn't made the food they were eating, as if I were a houseplant they hoped didn't have scales. What would they do if I did, douse me with coffee and leave me outside? And yet, the smell of the coffee was as overpoweringly sensual as anything I'd ever experienced with a baby, or a man, at my breast. I wanted to pour the creamy liquid into my hands and hold it close to my face, touch the beans, feel their shape and smell them individually. Orange sections with trembling drops of juice suspended on their lips transparent as tears. The sounds of a child chewing with an open mouth, swish, gnash, gnash, smack. No flutes. No far-off voices. No sound of wet wind's constant baritone humming through a dark cave. Sunday morning ordinary.

Without saying anything that would have hinted at my asking for permission, I got up, opened the front door, and brought in the newspaper. I didn't imagine the gaze Cathy and Gabe exchanged. After years of practice, with my fingernail, I was able to flip to the front of Your Life, my section, immediately. I sat down with a second cup of coffee—coffee I could taste!—and read my column, yes, with the paper at arm's length, but without reading glasses. I read it once. I read it again. "What in the hell is this?" I asked.

"We . . . sort of . . . thought . . ." Cathy began.

"I'm going to get fired!" I spluttered, the coffee sloshing over the rim of the table. "You can't . . . insult people! You can't . . . use vulgar . . . Gabe! You know better than this!"

"Relax, Ma," Gabe told me, with an exaggerated feline stretch. "He likes it! Cathcart says you're pushing the outside of the envelope. He's sent you, like, four e-mails, saying the readers are calling in, and they're crazy about the new Gillis. . . ."

"They're like . . . give 'em hell, Julie!" Caroline said.

"That's not *me*."

"Did you ever . . . want it to be, not so you?" Cathy asked.

"What?"

"Did you just ever want to . . . tell it like it is? The way we do when we talk about the letters?"

"I don't know," I said, appealing to Cathy with my eyes. I set the newspaper down. "You know, I don't know anything anymore. You guys are probably right. I should be thanking you instead of blowing up at you."

"Well, we didn't know any other way to write it, so we wrote it honestly," Gabe said.

"I thought I was being discreet, and objective and polite. Wasn't I? I was . . ."

"Dull," said Gabe.

"Thanks, son," I said with a sigh. "Oooh, I hate your being right." I allowed myself a sharp little laugh, one I couldn't stifle. "I just *hate* it!"

"Mom, don't take it wrong," Gabe said in his soothing like-Leo voice. "You were barely there for two weeks and totally out of it for . . . We had to do something," Gabe said, sternly now. "Cathy has been totally great. She knows everything about human relationships. . . ."

"You did the right thing. I'm only snarky because I'm embarrassed."

"You don't have to be," Cathy said. "Really. Julie, we're your family."

"I know you feel lousy, Mom, and not just about being sick," Gabe said. "Because nobody's heard from Dad . . ."

"Really?" I asked, looking into every pair of guilty eyes, until each of them looked away. "He hasn't called?"

"He send a card!" Aury said cheerfully.

I burst into tears. "I feel so . . . forgotten! I wake up, and my kids have a new mother. Cathy, don't take that the wrong way. You're better at it than I was."

"Julie!" Cathy cried, horrified. "Julie. *Stop* it. I've stayed here and helped these kids handle grief, fear, and American history, and yeah, I'm proud of it. But it's not like you wouldn't have done the same thing. You would have, and you would have painted a room or two on top of it. You don't owe me anything."

"I do, and I can't ever pay you back." I gripped my coffee mug, now cold.

"Julie, listen. If you're ashamed, it's normal. But it's not fair. Look, the husband you and everyone else believed was perfect took a long walk off an emotionally very short pier over the past several seasons, and because you've been handing out tea towels and sympathy . . . no, wait, Julie, you think you should have seen it coming and maybe you could have, but you didn't. You're a person, and we're programmed to believe people we trust will treat us right. And Leo is behaving like about the most coldhearted piece of shit in the lower forty-eight if he isn't in Hawaii by now—the way he walked out on his screaming baby makes it impossible for you to ignore that there's more going on than he said, Jules. And that scares the shit out of you. It would anyone—"

"Wait!" I almost shouted, more violently than I meant to. I was crying harder now. The little girls jumped. My head drummed. I didn't want to have this deconstruction played out in front of my children, because per- haps, just perhaps, it wasn't true. Perhaps I really still had a husband who was even now recovering from his midlife crisis and heading home to me. I tried to cling to this, just as I kept clinging to the paltry hope that I'd only succumbed to a bout of . . . the flu or something for the past fortnight. "Wait!" I tried to make my voice familiar, jokey. "Caroline Jane! Gabe. Don't you have somewhere to go? Like, the moon?"

"I'm actually fine here, Mom," Caro said. "It's very dramatic. And it's nice to hear you call me something other than 'Hannah' or 'Connie' or 'Janey.'" Connie was Cathy's mom.

"You can be a little shit, Caroline," I said. "That wasn't my fault."

"Oh, I know that," said my daughter. "And I know I can be a little shit."

"I'm not going to stop right now," Cathy insisted, pouring more coffee for me. "Even if you want me to. When you got sick, it seemed to correspond exactly with when Leo left. So on top of everything else, you're not just an ordinary bat from the bat farm, you're really wacko! Institutional quality! What does all that mean? Except, what if you're not? What if you're really sick, if you have a malignant brain tumor—which you don't— the blood tests show you don't have any cancer cells in your body. But what if you have something else? What's going to become of the kids? What's going to become of you? And then, you wake up and feel good for the first time in weeks, and you think you're over all of it, and you find out your pal and your kid have taken over your job! What's left? Where's Julieanne Gillis, the swan of the Seventh Street Ballet Studio, the woman Saren used to call on to stand in front and show everyone the combinations for every show—and people said, she's forty? She's got teenagers?" I could feel tears on my face, and that sense, even at this moment, was a noteworthy pleasure. "Where is that Julie now? Where is she?"

"I want to tell you to go jump, Cathy, and not psychoanalyze me," I told Cathy wearily.

"No, go ahead," Caroline urged, leaning forward. "It *is* like a movie on Lifetime."

"Where is she, Julie?" Cath went on, ignoring her.

"At the bottom of a well, and . . ." I said.

"And what . . . ?"

"It's dark and the sides are slippery and filthy and it's a place for dirty things, and I don't know if I can climb out. I'm too small. . . ."

"What else?"

"Well, I don't know if I want to get out, either."

"Why, Julie?"

"Because there are no mirrors in here."

"Who's the fairest one of all?" Caroline asked.

"Shut *up!*" Cathy and I said simultaneously.

I looked up, then, and said to Gabe, "I apologize. Cathy's so right, it's like having the sun hurt my eyes. We've got some facing up to do, guys." I turned to Cathy. "If you can forgive my being jealous of your being able to handle everything without me, and recognize how scary it is to be me . . ."

"You don't have to, Julie," Cathy said. "I would feel the same."

"I never learned to be wrong gracefully."

"You never had to," Cathy said. "Welcome to how it is for the rest of us."

"Well, apparently I'm getting the crash course," I said. "I should be pretty fluent in Being Wrong in just six weeks!" I called Caroline, and she reluctantly slumped to my side. Aury climbed onto my lap. "I let you down. That's the worst thing a mom can do. You get that, don't you?" Caroline slowly, terribly slowly, nodded. Aurora simply held me. "Well, if you ever let anyone down, and it wasn't your fault, don't be ashamed."

I wiped my eyes with my cuffs. Gabe handed me a pot holder. "Oh, thanks, honey," I said. "This will work better." At first quivering, a bit damp and shaky, all of us began to laugh truly.

"What fresh hell is this?" I asked.

"I know you didn't make that up," Gabe said.

"No, I didn't even make that up," I said. "But I never got it before."

TWELVE

Gabe's Journal

Tian's dress was the color and had, what would you call it, the sort of sheen of something like cooked vanilla custard. That doesn't sound so good. But trust me. It looked as though it would feel like warm custard in a bowl if I ran my hand along it. As if she knew what I was thinking, Connie Gleason, Cathy's mother, said, "It's filth the oil from your fingerprints would be putting on that fabric, Gabriel. You be keeping your hands off it. And she'll be needin' a shawl, a coat if you will . . . Gabriel, this isn't the adventures in paradise she's used to, you know." I'm trying to write it to sound like she said it, but I don't know how the hell you write a sort of cross between an Irish brogue and Sheboygan vowels. When I was at Columbia, in the special program, that whole semester when I learned one thing—that I shouldn't be at Columbia—people kept telling me I had an accent. I never thought about it. I thought I sounded like people who read the news. When I went to Florida for school, nobody noticed. Nobody there is from there. When I finally went to Connecticut, nobody noticed because they never noticed anything but themselves.

But back in Mrs. Gleason's kitchen, that chilly evening before the winter formal.

"How can we dance," I asked, "if I can't touch her?"

"A gentleman doesn't need to maul a woman to have a dance," Connie said. "You touch her lightly, like this." Connie took Tian in her arms, and Tian beamed up at her, looking as tiny and slender as Aury (Tian had given my two-year-old sister one of her silver bracelets and it *fit* her). This was even next to Connie, who was, like, five inches shorter than my mother. She looked light enough to pick up and hold, which I did some-times, although Tian honestly hated it and kicked like a mad cat. They swayed together, Tian's long black hair reflecting the kitchen lights. I watched that long mirror of hair and was nauseated. Whether it was sicko lust—well, not sicko, but more lust than I can tell you I've ever felt again in my life—or from knowing I couldn't dance without breaking Tian's arches, I didn't know.

"See Gabe? No touches." Tian grinned at me, wiggling her bare shoulders.

Connie'd made the dress for the winter formal with fabric my mother bought for Tian. As freshmen, we were not strictly supposed to go. But because Tian was an exchange student, she got to do everything the school had going during her semester. We didn't find out it would be okay until there was only about ten days before the dance. There was no time for Tian's parents to get money to her for a dress, and the Rotary would have let her go to Goodwill. Plus, she was about a size minus one. So my mom pitched in, and Connie could sew anything—as a matter of fact, I still wear shirts she made for me. She made me a wool sport coat. Imag-ine this. Making a *coat*. The idea is like making a refrigerator or some goddamned thing.

Tian's dress looked like someone in *People* magazine or something made it. We got this nutty-looking card later from Tian's parents, with little silver trumpets and temples all over it, thanking my mother for "making our child have an American experience with a wonderful gift." When Tian saw the plan Connie had drawn for the dress, she literally jumped up and down. "It is like a Cinderella dress. Can I take it home?" she asked Connie. "Will it be forever mine?"

It was as if she didn't give a damn that, in just two weeks, she would be leaving me, that the time that had changed my entire life was over. It was fine with her as long as she could keep the princess dress.

"Everyone will think I am rich from America, Gabe," she told me seriously.

"Where will you wear it?" I asked her.

"Out to restaurant hotels. Out to parties that would be for my parents. At our home. They give many parties. We are Christians," Tian explained, as if this were some sort of prerequisite for party giving.

"She's going to forget she ever met me," I had told Luke on the phone.

"That's for sure," Luke said helpfully. "I mean, what are the odds? You'll never see her again. And they are Christians, Gabe. And you are being a Jew, a Jew all the way, from your bar mitzvah day 'til they cart you away . . . they don't know you don't know Rosh Hashanah from Rush Limbaugh. Plus, what are the odds you'll ever see her again?"

"You suck," I told him.

"Bet you wish she did," he answered.

I didn't know whether I did wish that or not. My, like, molecules, wanted to screw Tian. But I was . . . fifteen. Just turned. There were scuz kids who had sex when they were freshmen, but that's what they were, scuz. And so I had the equal feeling that the last thing on earth I wanted to do was put my grimy hands on the two perfect plums that held up her custard-colored dress, with no straps or anything, just a band around the top. Her unmarked golden skin, and that dress, and her hair. She looked like a ritzy dessert I could destroy.

"Are you knowing how to waltz, Gabriel?" Connie asked.

"Christ, Connie. I don't know how to walk. And, I always wanted to ask you, how come you have an accent?"

"I don't."

"You have an Irish accent, and Cathy says—"

"It's true enough that I haven't been in Ireland in thirty years and more," she told us. "But I have my relatives. And what of it?" Her mouth was filled with pins, that afternoon in her kitchen. There were those little dishes and saltshakers with shamrocks on them all over Cathy's house, except in Abby's room. "I suppose I imitated my aunties, my grandmother's sisters. It was crossing to America—"

"We know the story," I said.

We'd heard it, like, forty-two times.

"I did not hear it," Tian said. I groaned, although not out loud. She was making the dress and this thing to go around my waist to go with it. I had to put up with the *Titanic* story.

"It was the White Star Liner *Titanic*," Connie began, removing the pins from her mouth one by one, while I made motions with my index finger like I was conducting an orchestra, "from England . . ."

"I know this!" Tian cried, "Aaaah!" She jumped, having stabbed herself with a pin in a seam that wasn't yet sewn down.

"Have a care, little one," Connie told her.

"But I have heard of this in my school! The ocean ship sank in the Atlantic in the North. The water was less than zero degrees . . ."

"Centigrade," I explained to Connie.

"And hundreds of people froze to death, and now no one is left alive. There was a woman who was alive until last year . . ." Tian went on.

"My great-grandfather and great-grandmother were on that ship, in steerage, down below the decks where they kept the poor," Connie said in her voice that was like she was saying a poem. "He was Henry Gidlow and she Constance Lyte Gidlow . . ."

"Like a light?" Tian asked.

"Yes, but with a 'y' not an 'i.' They were with their sons, Patrick and Michael, and their daughters Bridget—"

"There's always a Bridget," I said to Tian.

"Be shut," she scolded me.

"And their daughter Maeve," Connie continued.

"But how were you . . . ?" Tian began.

"Maeve became friendly with a young man on the boat, also called Gidlow, from the same county, but not from the same branch of the family, a fifth cousin or somewhat, and it was during the crossing they married. . . ."

"How did they get married?"

"By a priest who was along."

"And did he live?"

"The priest? There were a number of ministers on the ship."

"No, the father of the . . . whoever. They didn't really get married, did they, Connie?" I don't know why I said that. I sensed it from something missing in her voice.

"They got married enough for practical purposes."

"And did Maeve's husband . . ."

"He died, like any man of honor on that terrible night."

"And she live?" Tian urged Connie. Whenever she became fascinated with anything, Tian began dropping little bits of her English like flakes of paint.

"She did live. She was my grandmother," Connie said, "Maeve Gidlow Gidlow. She used to say that she was like Eleanor Roosevelt. When she got married, she didn't have to change the monograms on her sheets! Not that she had monograms on her sheets. Or sheets to monogram."

Tian and I said simultaneously, "Huh?"

"Sheets?"

"No, Eleanor Roosevelt," I said.

"Her name was Roosevelt, too! Eleanor's! Do you not know the name of the wife of the great reformer? She was more president than he. She said, 'I am my husband's legs.' What are they teaching you in school? She was a distant cousin of Franklin Delano—"

"It isn't add up!" Tian objected suddenly.

"What?"

"This is not thirty years ago! This is seventy years ago. It is ninety years ago!"

"I didn't say that *I* was on the Titanic. And I didn't say *that* was the last time I was in Ireland, did I now?"

"Oh, you went back."

"Yes."

"Holiday," Tian said.

"No, to bring my grandmother's sisters here, where they lived when they were very old women . . . I did this with my husband."

"His name was Gleason?"

"Yes, and that was the only good thing about him. That and his hair comb. He was a rogue. In love with the bottle. I should have taken back my own family's name. . . ."

"That would have been pretty . . . out there for your generation," I suggested.

"My maiden name? I just liked it better. That's all," Connie said. "It reminded me of better things. Better times. Better people. And it didn't remind me of Gleason, who knows where he is now, but may he rest in peace if he's dead."

"He wouldn't be dead, Connie. You're like, pretty young for a mother. And way young for a grandmother."

"We did those things younger then."

It was a nice conversation, which I had no reason to screw up. But I still said, "Back to the ship sinking. The way Cathy tells it, it sounds like *you* were right there on the bow of the *Titanic*, the last one alive, with your father holding you above the freezing water. . . ." I guess I was sort of rude. I think you have to be rude if you're a fifteen-year-old boy. I've never met a polite one who wasn't up to something. Maybe I was just being a putz. I was. After all, they were the only people I ever knew who had any contact with the *Titanic*. That deserves some respect.

"It's spoiling a tale you like to do, Gabriel," she scolded me.

"It is a tale, Connie!" I said. "It's like a legend! It sounds so much more dramatic than it was."

"Don't be rude," Connie said. "It's by our stories we remember ourselves. And what could be more dramatic? Do your own grandparents not talk about the death camps? And your grandfather about his battles at sea?"

I was still totally pissed off for no reason. And not at Connie. In three days, I would take this girl and hold her in my arms (lightly), trying not to stumble—my mother was giving me the fastest crash course in dancing in history—all crazy with the world of what I felt for Tian. Then, after ten more days, she would leave. Boom. 'Bye, Gabe. Back home to go to restaurant hotels and become a doctor and marry some yutz who went from Bangkok to Yale, where she would probably ask me, if I turned up there—at New Haven, I mean, "Do I have met you?" I kicked a chair out from under the table and flopped down in it. And then, I looked up, and there they were, standing in the doorway of the house, where it opened in from the garage, my mother and Cathy.

They stood there side by side. No one said anything.

My mother's face was the color of Tian's dress. Tian, who was always doing stuff like this, ran and put her arms around my mother's waist. But my mother, who would ordinarily have hugged her and then held her back and said something like *Aren't you the picture of an American debutante* or some stuff, just stood there, staring past Tian at me.

"Gabe," said Cathy.

"I will do it," my mother said.

"You're the oldest," Cathy said.

I cannot tell you how fucking sick I would become of hearing this.

"I will, Cathy," my mother said. "Can you give Tian a ride home?" Tian looked confused.

"Run and dress, sweetie," Connie told her, slipping the formal over Tian's head with anxious speed. Tian grabbed her jeans and ran for the bathroom, emerging fully dressed and slipping on her loafers moments later.

My mother said, "Come on, Gabe. We have to go home. Tian, Connie, Cathy, we're sorry. You were having so much fun. . . ."

"It's you we're thinking about, Julie darling," Connie said. "Whatever you need. No matter how much . . ."

"I know," my mother replied, smiling a faded version of her toothpaste smile.

We got into the car and drove past the ice-cream place that used to be my grandparents' store, past the Italian restaurant, past the strip mall where I used to buy my model airplanes.

"Mama?" I finally said, knowing it was the word I still used only when I was in trouble at school or wanted money.

"I have multiple sclerosis, Gabe," she told me, putting a piece of her hair behind her ear the way Caro did when she was trying to think.

"What the hell is that?" I asked. I thought of Jerry Lewis on TV all night.

"It's not fatal," my mother said quickly. "It's a disease of the brain and the spinal cord. I don't know everything about it yet. It's, uh, a deteriorative disease. I don't know how I got it. It's from a virus. If your immune system is predisposed to get it, you . . . get it."

My gut killed me. "How do you get over it? Will we get it? What do you take for it? Deteriorative? What the hell does that mean? Like Alzheimer's?"

"No," Mom said, "no, not like that! Well, in the worst possible scenario, like that."

"Then what?"

"I could be . . . ill . . . like I was . . . before," Mom said softly. "But maybe not. Maybe I won't ever get that bad again. That was from multiple sclerosis. And stuff that came before. The stumbling, and the numbness, that time in my legs at ballet? And my hands. Sleeping all the time. It affects different people in different ways, and it affects the same person in different ways at different times. Back in the spring, when I felt funny, that was all this."

"Not all the time? You won't be that way all the time?" I asked again.

"No," she said, tightening her hands at ten and two. She'd been teaching me to drive. She went on, "It can get pretty bad, maybe not right now, Gabe. I have decisions to make. Like if you were diabetic. You could eat more protein and lose some weight. Or you could start taking insulin shots right away. I have choices like that. Try homeopathic—no, naturopathic things. Extra vitamins. Or what they call the smaller series of pills. Valium for the shakes and the nerves. Antidepressants . . ."

"Because you're depressed."

"Well, it hasn't really sunk in yet . . . but when it does, I guess I will be. Or the big guns. I can start right now before it gets any worse and take . . . cancer drugs."

"*Cancer* drugs?"

"Some people think that they keep MS attacks, or whatever you want to call them, from getting worse. It's pretty accepted now. You know? I thought I was nuts. Didn't you, Gabe?" She tried to laugh. She couldn't quite make it. "Gabe, I'm so sorry. The doctor said it could be very mild. So I could be normal. Just like I am now, Gabe. Not like I was a couple of weeks ago. I'll be able to work and to dance—"

"Will you be able to take care of Aury? Until Dad . . ."

"Of course. And you and Caroline."

"Will you ever get, you know what I mean, forgetful?"

"I don't know. I'd say no. Or not very often. I might have to take shots."

"Shots? You hate shots."

"Well, that's how you take the cancer drugs. The drugs slow it down. Shots, then pills. I'd just have to . . . uh, deal." Her attempt to talk like I would made me want to cry.

"What do you have to do eventually, to kill the virus or what have you."

"It's not curable, Gabe. You can't kill a virus. It goes away if it's a cold. But not this. I'll have it as long as I live."

"You have to be kidding me."

"I'm not. But we have to tell Caroline, and the baby, together."

"Are you, like, going to get sick right away? And have to go to bed again?" I thought, What about the formal? Would I have to stay at home and babysit my mother? "We . . . when? Mom, you have to stop and get some coffee or water or something."

"I don't need anything," my mother said. "We'll go home now, Gabe, and get on with it . . . and dinner—"

"Wait a minute," I interrupted. "So you might never get sick or you might get so sick you can't get up but there's no warning. . . ."

"Hundreds of thousands of people have multiple sclerosis," my mother said. "And a lot of them don't even know it for years. And a lot of them, you can't tell they do from looking at them. But some totally lose their vision, or their ability to speak. . . ."

"If hundreds of thousands of people have it, why doesn't anyone know anything about it?"

My mom sighed. It was just the most beaten-up sigh. I felt like a whiny moron. "I'm sorry, Mama," I said. I could see her eyes fill up.

"I'm the one who's sorry. This junk. And your father." Then she breathed in and set her shoulders, Gillis-style. "Look, honey, we'll figure it out. And then, we'll call Dad. . . ."

If rage can be an accelerant, that was when mine for Leo went from zero to sixty in five. I thought, You lousy scumbag. She was putting up this "We'll call Dad" front for me. My mom had to know that, in all the months since Leo had left, we hadn't been able to reach him, with all the letters we'd sent—even to the post-office box in New York State he'd promised would always be "a permanent address" during his sabbatical. Not me, not Caroline, not Cathy. She had to know he had called precisely three times in three months, but that was it—once the week after he left, once on Christmas, once on Aury's birthday. Well, at least that I knew of. Maybe he called my mother at night, when we were asleep, but no, she would have said something. Even before this medical thing, you could tell, she was worried all the time. She did things like you do when you're my age, pick up the phone to make sure it's working if you expect someone to call.

We drove up Pine Street, down the highway past the ABS sign and the high school, left into the subdivision kind of thing where we lived that they called the Gray Harbor neighborhood, even though nothing there was gray except one house and there was no harbor. My father had told me Gray was a person, the farmer who used to own the land. I didn't figure she would say anything, though normally you can't shut my mother up. And she didn't say anything, until we were practically in the driveway. She stopped the car then, and said, "Baby, I don't want you to worry. When we get hold of Dad, he'll come right home. And I'm strong and healthy, and I'll . . . I'll do what they tell me, even if it means drugs. Not right now, but . . ." She reached out and took my hand, and I let her. "I'm not going to be a vegetable, Gabe."

"It's okay, Mom," I said. I knew it wasn't.

Caro was at Mallory's. I called her and told her not to ask questions, to get her butt home. Mom drove over and got Aury from the sitter, this friend of hers from work called Stella. She made some noodles with olive oil and a salad with cucumbers and arugula.

We all ate in total silence.

Then my mother said, "Aurora, remember when Mommy had to lie down all the time?"

"And didn't wash the hair?" Aury asked.

"Yes."

"Mama was smelly," Aury said.

"That's because I was sick," Mom said. "But Aunt Cathy took me to the doctor, and the doctor is going to make me better."

"Good job, Mommy," Aury said. I kept feeling like I wanted to bawl, because that was what we said to Aury, when she learned one of her colors. "You can eat like a big girl, my mommy."

"But if I get sick again, Auntie Cathy and Nana and Grandpa will help us, and Daddy will come home soon." To tell the truth, after three months, Aury seemed to have about forgotten Leo. But she grinned and ran over and hugged my mother.

"Good mommy," she said. "Good job."

"Gay," Aury said then. She couldn't say "Gabe." To Luke's delight, she called me "Gay" back then. "Daddy coming home."

"Yep, shortie. Daddy will come home and it will be all better."

"Will, Gabe, please, will you put her to bed?" I had English homework, but the deadness in her voice scared me, so I decided to put it off. Mrs. Kimball, my so-called LD "support" teacher would expect no less of me, anyhow.

In her bedroom, I pulled Aury's little soccer shirt up over her head and zipped her into her foot pajamas with the one toe poking out. We had to cut her footie pajamas so one toe stuck out on each foot. She had fits if we didn't. I made her brush her teeth with her Princess Jasmine toothbrush. We read one of those horrifying Richard Scarry books with fifty-two pigs and foxes and snakes all working dump trucks and directing traffic and talking in little talk bubbles. Just reading one of those books was enough to exhaust a person, but Aury wanted me to "jump her" on the bed. Caro and I both did this: We'd say, "Bouncie, bouncie, bouncie, boom!" and then lay her down. Aury would have gone on doing this for about six weeks straight if we let her. I stopped with the fifth bouncie. Then, with this huge fucking lump in my throat, I kissed her sweaty little head.

I went banging back downstairs. I didn't want to surprise my mother.

My mother and Caroline were sitting at the kitchen table. I knew she'd just had the same talking-to from my mother about what multiple sclerosis was, how it affected different people different ways. Caroline looked bored. She finally asked, "Can I call Justine now?" And my mother nodded wearily.

"Use the cell phone," she said. "I need the house phone."

I got the wall phone and untaped the strip of paper with my father's cell number on it from the corkboard beside it. "Do you want me to leave?" I asked her.

"No," she told me. "Sit down."

She dialed the number.

She listened.

Then, she handed the phone to me.

I dialed the number. "This is message MC thirty-two. You have reached a number that is no longer in service or has been disconnected," said a recorded voice.

"Maybe he didn't pay the bill," I said to her.

"I paid the bill, Gabe," she told me.

"Then, maybe he's out of the area where he can get calls, like down in one of his canyons," I suggested.

"You know he isn't," my mother said.

I sat there.

I so didn't want to be hearing this.

"You know he doesn't want us to reach him," my mother said. "Okay. Okay. Maybe Cathy's right, and he never wanted us to reach him at all. If that's true, I can do this. But I'm going to wait, Gabe. I'm going to wait to hear because whatever else I know, I know Leo Steiner. I've known Leo all my adult life, and he would never, ever, ever break trust with me. No matter how confused or selfish or weak he is right now. He's a good man. He's a good man. Your father is . . . a . . . good . . . man." Tears were pouring down her face, but she didn't appear to be crying. Her breath was regular and slow. She sat completely motionless, her hands up and open.

I got up. "Will you be okay if I go to the Witts' and see Luke?"

"It's dark, Gabe," she said. "I don't want you riding your bike without a light."

"I'll walk."

My mother sighed. "Gabe, take the car," she said. "I know you do anyway. It's only a few blocks."

That slammed me a good one. I didn't even have my temps yet. I had no idea how she knew. I looked at her to see if her hands were shaking. But they were not. She was simply looking at the wall, as if the wall were a mirror.

Edward Hopper is my favorite artist. That's not true. He's actually the only artist whose paintings I ever really looked at. My grandparents had one in their apartment in New York. I like them because they look real, like photographs, but actually, they look more than real. They look like Hopper could paint the way people felt, as if he saw them from inside instead of outside. Even when he painted houses, he made them look as though he could tell what the houses were thinking.

When I glanced back at my mother, her face so pale and still under the glare of the kitchen light, her arms laid side by side on the wooden table, her hair tucked behind one ear, she looked like one of those Edward Hopper paintings. She looked like she was not in our kitchen in Sheboygan but at some lonely diner where all she could afford was coffee, and she had a long time to sit before the next bus came. She would have made a good Edward Hopper painting, except you don't want your life like one.

THIRTEEN

Psalm 55

EXCESS BAGGAGE
By J. A. Gillis
The Sheboygan News-Clarion

Dear J.,

I've had it. I'm sick of being told, "Sherry, you're the strong one." My father just had a heart attack, and thank goodness, he's going to be fine. But he's going to need someone to drive him to rehab for months, which my mother can't do because, although she's fine, too, she's about to have cataract surgery. Meanwhile, my husband and I are helping our son look for colleges, and I have a demanding job. My brother and sister, one older and one younger, only live across the border. In Indiana. Not an hour away. But do you think they can do anything? No, all my brother can do is whine about his divorce and all my sister can do is whine about her arthritis, which isn't even that bad. Why do people take advantage of you because you've managed to keep your health and make a normal life for yourself? If my husband wasn't being so great about this, I'd be hitting the bottle!

Overburdened in Oleander

Dear Overburdened,

*Okay, poof! You're not the strong one anymore. You're weak.
You're depressed. You have arthritis and your marriage is
failing. Your parents don't have physical problems they need
help with. They're already dead. Your son isn't searching for the
right college. He's in rehab. He killed another kid in a drunk-
driving incident. He drinks because you do.*

*Do you feel better now? The reason people depend on you,
while it might be a drag, may be because you HAVE managed to
stay healthy and have a normal life. That's rare. Sure, you have
more on your plate than you want. Join the club. For starters,
try being grateful for it.*

J.

Telling the kids about my diagnosis might have been the hardest thing I
ever had to do.

But getting it was a close second.

This is how it went.

Cathy and I sat across from each other in the doctor's office. We took
turns spinning in the physician's chair. We looked into the cabinets. I got
up and went out to the washroom. Cathy got up and looked at my chart
in its plastic holder bin outside the door. "I'm so jealous," she said. "How
much weight have you lost?"

Neither of us spoke of what was so obvious it was like another person
in the room. This was taking too long. Reading an MRI may take days
for a doctor to get around to doing, but once finished, it does not take . . .
now, forty-seven minutes to report to the patient summoned to hear the
results. "What the hell did he do, go golf a few holes?" Cathy asked irritably, glancing at her watch for what I estimated to be the fifteenth time.
And as if at that cue, Dr. Billington breezed into the room, whipped off

his glasses, and sat down at his desk, slapping the films of my neck and head down between us.

"Well, basically, Missus Gillis, I'm here to confirm what you probably already know. I rarely have a patient come through the door these days who hasn't already been on the Internet to find out what's going on when she's symptomatic, and by the time she gets to me, she has a list of questions as long as her arm. All of which I'm ready to answer as best I can. The most important question, the one people usually ask first, is, what is going to be the course of my disease? And that's the one question I'm not able—"

"Wait," Cathy said, "it's not that we don't know how to use the Internet. But we don't know what disease process you're talking about. We don't know if Julie has had a stroke, or if there's a benign tumor—"

"I'm sorry. I assumed you were referred here because the suspicion of multiple sclerosis was strong, and given the eruption of symptoms you've described over the past weeks, combined with the lesions that are so plain in these photos—"

"I have multiple sclerosis?" I asked him. "I have *multiple sclerosis?* I'm going to be a cripple? I'll be in a wheelchair? I have a two-year-old. Don't only . . . isn't this a disease that older people get? I . . . wait a moment. The first doctor, my own physician, said that there was a good likelihood that this was attacks . . ."

"Ataxia, due to a virus or bacteriological infection in the inner ear, or some other site. Well, while it's rare, it is possible for a viral infection, depending on the location, to cause problems with balance and coordination, even auditory hallucinations . . . and, no, Missus Gillis, you're actually on the high end of the age for receiving a diagnosis."

"Depression! Or chronic fatigue syndrome. My doctor said it was possible, that it was visually . . . virtually undetectable! Or food poisoning. Mercury poisoning. Lead poisoning . . ."

"Missus Gillis, all those things could potentially be worse for you! There was a time when MS was an exclusionary diagnosis, but now there are ways to be certain, and I am virtually certain you've probably had the disease for years. Wait! Yes. You've had some restoration. What's great about the brain is its powers of rerouting, calling on other areas to perform functions when a given area is attacked. It's like a detour, like police rerouting the cars after an accident. Usually a person is between twenty and forty at the onset. But you do not have an infection. You have a condition that gradually destroys the myelin coating of the nerves that branch—"

"I know what MS is!" I said angrily. "And that's another reason why . . . I think I need a second opinion. Given that I'm . . . fine now. I'm simply fine. I went to dance class last week, and I was a little stiff, but . . . if I had this, I'd still be hobbling and weaving around like a drunk."

"Not necessarily. What we hope we have here is a remission that can last a long time. People sometimes come all the way back after a first manifestation, and sometimes, not always, but sometimes, they stay that way. For years. But I've seen it happen. Now, what you said right there. That's a very good thing," Dr. Billington said. "You're not having problems with your gait anymore. That means we can hope that this is a milder form of MS—"

"If that's what I have!"

"It's probably what we call RR, or relapsing-remitting," the doctor went on. "That means, it's possible after the kind of month you've had, to go for weeks or even months or . . . or more without another bout of symptoms. And then, those could be mild, or the same as you've already experienced, or they could be more troubling. However, we can't be sure of any of that. You've said there are some lingering effects?"

Numbness, I thought. "A very little numbness," I said. "My hand and leg are still numb, on the outer edge, I mean. And I have a little trouble with my balance . . . and somehow with making my thoughts, this is silly, but, making my thoughts do the things I want them to do. Commanding my words or my body."

"And how long has this cognitive impairment been present?" He seemed interested, unsurprised.

"The numbness?" I thought of my leg, in ballet class, creeping across the floor, slowly unfurling. "The control problem? It, well, I've had trouble with controlling . . . my movements. . . ."

"I mean thinking. Talking. For some time? For weeks?"

Cathy said, "For almost two years. That I've seen. At least. The physical and mental stuff. "

Dr. Billington said, "I . . . see."

"I don't have cognitive impairment!" I shouted, beginning to cry and furious that I was. "I have a little trouble remembering. Premenopause stuff. I have a little learning disability. I always have had, and so does—"

"It's possible. But what you described to me sounds like an artifact of the disease. . . ."

"It isn't! I am *fine*!"

"Well. You might say that, if this condition has been present for some time with so little real manifestation, that's all to the good," Dr. Billington conceded with a sigh. "What we're going to need to do is watch this very closely. Clearly, you had a serious episode very recently. Had there been a . . . death in the family? A shock? I ask you not to be specific or to pry, but because stress tends to exacerbate—"

"Yes," Cathy said.

"But I think I need another physician, another test, not that I question . . ." I began.

"I encourage that, Missus Gillis. However, these pictures don't tell lies," said Dr. Billington. "These are images of the spinal cord of a patient with classic lesions that are present in MS."

Cathy would later explain to me the rest of what Dr. Billington told us. She took detailed notes on the course of treatment he would recommend "for his own wife." He suggested a schedule of appointments. I would need to learn to give myself injections. The injections represented hope. Some drugs you gave yourself in shot form—the only one I recognized was Interferon, which I knew to be a chemo drug for cancer—were shown to slow the progress of the disease, despite some side effects that Dr. Billington said were "not negligible." These were pills, too. It was Cathy who discussed the possibility of antidepressant medication, asked about support groups in the area, told the doctor that she heard that muscle relaxants sometimes helped both with sleep and spastic muscle behavior. It was Cathy who'd asked all those questions about dance and yoga, about the ability to use a keyboard, about the effects on me of Sheboygan's brutally hot and humid summers.

I asked about nothing.

My mind was shouting, but no sound came from my lips.

Dr. Billington handed me a sheaf of pamphlets and a two-pocket folder stuffed with green, gold, and pink sheets of phone numbers and frequently asked questions, all of which I dropped. "I just dropped those because I'm flustered," I said, "not because I'm spastic. I dropped them because it's hard to take news like this in a matter-of-fact way."

The doctor, genuinely kindly, said, "It's hard to give it. It takes a long time to grieve what really feels like a betrayal, particularly when you're as healthy—"

"I am healthy!" I shouted.

"Missus Gillis," Dr. Billington told me softly.

"What's the worst-case scenario?" I asked.

"Let's not get on that horse, Missus Gillis," he said.

"No, what? I have a right."

"The most malign form of MS is fast and steadily progressive and leads to total incapacitation and respiratory failure and death over a period of many years. We usually see that aggressive a disease with men, though women get MS more than two to one, probably because they have a different hormone structure. In other words, the best thing about women, their ability to create life and so on . . ."

"Ah, brood mares," I said.

"You know what I mean," said the doctor.

"Yeah, I do," I admitted.

"Well, for some reason research hasn't quite grasped, because gender research into this disease is only a few years along, what makes women get

MS in greater numbers than men. But the forms they get usually are milder. The *best*-case scenario is that you never get any worse than this, that if you do have symptoms they're few and far between."

"Will I be wheelchair bound?"

"Not necessarily."

"Will I die young? I mean, young for dying? I know I'm not *young,* now."

"No. That would be unexpected. We just don't know, see, Missus Gillis. You just can't tell how this is going to go until it goes, so anything I said to you would be a . . . well, it could be a lie. It's a very unpredictable thing. Many people who have multiple sclerosis walk normally; some have a little trouble; some walk with a cane. Only very rarely do you see someone who has to have help toileting—"

"*Help* toileting? You mean diapers? You mean bladder . . . problems? I would rather die. I would rather die."

"No, you wouldn't, Jules," Cathy said seriously.

"Cathy, I'm the most modest, I'm the most sort of prissy—"

"I know all that. But you wouldn't rather die. Don't get over the top. What about the kids? What about me? Even Leo?"

"I've just learned I have a disease that is going to wreck my life."

"Aren't you listening, Julie? He just said that wasn't necessarily true. You might never have another episode like you did. You might have ten little ones. No one said you aren't going to be able to walk and work and dance . . ."

"I want to ask another thing," I told the doctor urgently. "I have readers whose relatives have had MS, who use herbal remedies, even one who used bee stings. I remember now. I'm inclined to try diet and exercise and some of those things first, and move on to these heavy drugs if I have to. . . ."

"You can, Missus Gillis," Dr. Billington, who suddenly looked as old as Gabe, said, removing his glasses and rubbing his eyes. "But then, you're not . . . at least my colleagues think you're just going to *feel* better while the disease goes on getting worse inside you. In fact, there are those who think the serious kind of MS—not the fatal kind, but what we call secondary progressive, the kind that starts with relapses but gets worse dramatically each time—is really just the result of putting off the inevitable, the drugs that work. Some people think the way to go is hit the thing hard with the best drugs we have before it gets bad, because we can't really see what's going on inside your nervous system. Given that you're . . . what, almost forty-five now, I'm hopeful that you can live out an ordinary life span . . . perhaps with some impairment of function as time goes by, but perhaps not that anyone except you would know about. But I do think that using the drugs that we know can work, not for everyone, but that do work, despite the discomfort, is the way to go. Right out of the gate. Fight back. See? There may be no need for mechanical support . . . on balance, given how shocking this must be on first hearing, we can hope you'll someday be able to think of yourself as one of the lucky ones."

My mind's mouth was wide open, shouting, *Lucky! Luckyluckylucky* and *LeoLeoLeoLeoLeo*. I tried to smile. I tried to be polite. Cathy helped me to my feet.

FOURTEEN

Ruth

EXCESS BAGGAGE
By J. A. Gillis
The Sheboygan News-Clarion

Dear J.,

I know that Dr. Kevorkian is in prison, but there are those who need him. I have myasthenia gravis. Right now, I get around pretty well. But I know that, eventually, I'll be so weak that one of my sons will have to take care of me, or I'll be placed in a nursing home, using up all the savings I have in the world. I want to end my life while I'm still healthy and enjoying life. My sons have young families and live in the Northwest. They don't even know I'm ill, thank goodness. They're wonderful young men, with wives and dear little children. I'm the last thing they need. Don't get me wrong. I'm not indulging in self-pity. I just want to find a civilized way to end this before I become a rock around the neck of my children. I also don't want to spend all I've saved on nursing-home care. I've heard that there are books about how terminally ill people can end their lives with dignity.

Lost in Lancaster

Dear Lost,

While I completely sympathize with your fear of becoming disabled, don't expect me to agree with your suicide plans. People in hospice care end their lives with dignity, when the time comes. If you can still read, laugh, have a good meal, and walk, your time hasn't come. If your sons are so wonderful, how is it that you haven't chosen to share with them that you have a serious illness? Would you want them to take their own lives rather than ask you for help? And what about your grandchildren? You're a better asset to them than a laptop or a Vespa. Get down off the cross, lady. Your sons will step up to the plate, and either they'll help; or they'll find good people who will. Fess up to your family. That's what Robert Frost meant about home. When you have to go there, they have to take you in.

J.

Dear J.,

I'm in love with a man who is 10 years younger than I am. While we both agree we can have children through adoption or surrogacy if necessary, he confessed the other night that he was worried about my looks, afraid that, in the future, as I age, the comments of others who see us together would distress me. He suggested I have plastic surgery now, while I am still in my 40s. While I can afford it, I don't know whether I want to have surgery. I'm a pretty woman, in good shape. I wonder why he is more worried about this than I am. I am a widow, and he has never married.

Baffled in Beaver Dam

Dear Baffled,

Here's a three-word prescription for you: Lose the loser.
When your honey says he's worried about others' feelings about
the disparity in your ages, he's really talking about himself.
While I'm certain he looks just like Mel Gibson, try asking him
if he'll have liposuction when he gets love handles a few years
hence. There are plenty of nonsurgical alternatives for skin
improvement. If you want one, do it. But for your comfort, not
his. Or ditch Mr. Sensitivity and move to Italy, where mature
women are considered a sensual prize. Tell him what he really
wants is serving lunch now at Hooters.

> *Best luck,*
> *J.*

Though I wasn't entirely confident of the new, edgy Julie—the one who emerged from melding Gabe's and Cathy's style with my own sensibilities—a few weeks later, I got a call.

It was the one I was dreading.

My editor, Steve Cathcart, sounded urgent. I was sure it meant that I was finished.

I avoided calling him back, for in relative terms, at least, things had been going so damned well! Some minor burning sensations in my thigh, a few wobbles, and some ominous twinges in the knees, but mostly, I was right as rain. Moreover, Caro and I were in the middle of a period of bizarre closeness, fragile as a sugar egg. We took ballet together, then went "out for coffee," trying on shoes with matching leather purses we could never afford. She confided in me that she'd never gone to second base, though Justine had. I confided in *her* that I was grateful for that, and would pay her five hundred bucks if she held off "doing it" until she was out of high school.

"Five hundred," she murmured. "That's not bad."

"That's almost a round-trip ticket to Paris, in the off season," I said.

"For not doing *everything*, Mom?" she'd asked me. "Or anything?"

I thought back to my insatiable longing for my now quite-possibly long-lost husband. "Not doing it doesn't mean not doing anything, Caro. French-kiss. Feel free to . . . feel. But nothing that could lead to a big disease or a baby."

"I'll think it over," she said seriously. "But wouldn't you feel kind of queer if you got out of high school and you were still a virgin?"

What a world, I thought. "It still happens all the time, Little," I told her.

While lost in his love for Tian, Gabe, relieved no longer to be the paterfamilias, reveled in his restoration to kid-dom. I spent hours peeping over the bright little shelf of my computer screen, watching Gabe watch Tian watching television. Everything fascinated her, from the most bizarre and disturbing reality shows to reruns of *Grease*. Every so often, he would reach out and stroke her river of black hair, as if it were a relic; and she would absently pat his hand, too riveted to the takedown in progress on *Cops* to respond in kind. Tian had bought Gabe temporary chops within the school hierarchy, since she was an undeniable babe. Only rarely could Gabe tear himself away from her. But he did. When Grandpa Steiner came up from Florida, thankfully while I was still feeling well enough that he suspected nothing of the illness I couldn't bear to confide in him, he took Gabe and Luke on a nutty winter golf outing, buying each of the boys a brandy. Luke had begun hanging around at our house even on weeknights. Braving what I suspected would be their pity and gossip about Leo, I went to play bunko with Luke's mother, Peg. When she murmured something about Leo's being gone so long, I told her that he was retracing the steps of Lewis and Clark.

The silence from Leo was a dirge that had played so long we no longer heard it, except in the silence of the night. I heard it in the solitary silence of my bed. But refunded health was such a gift I couldn't afford to spend too much of it on grief. Leo would come back or he wouldn't. I would see him and love him. Or I wouldn't. My goal was to leave Leo out of my recovery, if you will, as much as possible. I had to do what men did routinely, stuff his rejection into an old coat pocket of the mind. If I did that, I thought I could handle the children and me. MS plus me plus one foot in the economic grave and the other balancing on a Ping-Pong ball minus Leo equaled me. It was better if I concentrated only on the children, the finances, and myself.

Later in the week, Steve left a second message.

I couldn't avoid calling him back.

"Gillis!" he said heartily, and cut to the chase, "Gillis, I need a meeting with you. Does three work?"

I had a women's club speech at one, so at least I'd be dressed in something other than what I was then wearing—an old pair of Leo's boxers and a long-sleeved crew shirt leftover from college. As I held the phone, I noticed right away that my left hand was jerking like a fish on a line. I knew stress could not "bring on" a bad spell, only (maybe, because with MS, it's all maybe) exacerbate one. Still, I carefully formed my answer, in my mind, like little word magnets on a fridge—I'd say *fine* and make sure it didn't come out as *fire*—and bounced back, "Fine with me. Are you about to replace me with a comic strip, Steve?"

"Yep," my boss answered, "can't fool you. No, all joking aside, I have to see you in here. If not today, then . . . ?"

"Today'll work," I told him.

But privately, I thought that Steve Cathcart's desire to see me—in person—could mean many things, but they were all bad. I tried to collate them in my mind, which was an undertaking now, not something I could do at the same time as I assembled the ingredients for, say, soup. Okay, I told myself. They've decided once and for all to cut costs and run a syndicated columnist. They've got an up-and-comer who can reel in the twenty-somethings. They were thinking of a His and Hers kind of thing—the ways in which a guy and a woman might answer the same question. However, I could come out of this still with my 22K a year if I could craft a niche, maybe, with all my recent speeches, a society sort of thing, perhaps reviews, or theater benefits and flower shows. . . . "But I can't always count on being able to walk around the orchid shows," I said, not quite realizing I was still having a phone conversation.

"What?" Steve bleated.

"Oh, one of the kids just came in." It's nine in the morning, dear God, he thinks I'm insane, I reminded myself. Even Aury was in school. "I'm sorry. Sure. I'll come by right after I do a speech thing I have. . . ."

"That works."

We hung up.

I lowered myself slowly to the cool tile of the bathroom floor and coached myself in the isometrics of denial.

The therapist Cathy had taken me to see—twice so far—had spoken about the merits of enforced denial "in situations such as this." (I hadn't known there were situations such as my own, so I thought I had a good jump on denial.) Still, one of the first things Jennet said was, "Never assume things can't get worse." A novel opener, I thought. At least, I wouldn't have to put up with happy horseshit about new awakenings and the universe closing the door on your foot while opening the window. Jennet was actually urging me to accept my lot, and then try to live as though I didn't, betting that the window wouldn't fall on my head. "Denial is really essential, Julie. People with MS, well nobody really, can live in a protracted state of crisis," said Jennet, a large, comfortable woman, the only person over the age of thirty I could think of who still wore Earth shoes. She was given to scarves she evidently wore over her coat to work and then forgot to drape around her collar on the way home, so that her office had come to resemble a sort of desert tent, a salon of many colors. She also had textural objects, such as a phallic brass tulip, a flat-sided carved granite head, palm-sized, that represented a man and a woman eye to eye, a glass egg fitted together along its deceptively shattered center, the edges of the crack smooth though they looked sharp enough to cut. Beguiling things that begged the hand. I recognized them from those in

Cathy's office. Even adults needed toys to fondle when faced with mortal memories, terrible revelations, an anguishing dilemma. There was a moment of relief that Gabe or Caro was not hunched in an opposite corner of the sofa, dismissing my plea to give up the ecstasy of Ecstasy.

For someone in a jam who doesn't know whether her ultimate destination will be, in metaphor, a tropical island or federal prison—Jennet's words—the alternatives to denial were a steady drip of self-pity or the constant unease of a guard dog on a short chain. Either would lead to emotional paralysis, for the victim. And her family. Neither was acceptable, particularly now that I was in what I supposed was "remission." (I've since learned that a "remission" may be many things, not only a time of feeling normal but a time when nothing overtly horrid is happening.) At that time, before Christmas, I had near-combustible energy and an almost supernatural appreciation of the world's elements. It was as if everything was sharply outlined in thin permanent marker. I dawdled over the darling perfection of tasks I'd once tried to rush through—to get back to my books and my music. They had become a sensual pleasure. I was being here now, as Leo would have said. Folding towels in threes. Matching all sixty of Aury's socks. Enraptured, seeing my steady hands, competent and safe, as they cut and cubed potatoes, and tossed in parsley and milk. Opening yeast. Yeast smelling like home. Dropping it into my twenty-year-old (and still wonderful) bread machine and smelling the bread beginning to brown. Each of these things was like finding a favorite earring you'd thought had been lost. I remembered recovering from measles as a child—that tremulous sense of tentative renewal. I had always appreciated my life; I had never seen it as miraculous. Now I did. Pay no attention to those brain plaque patterns behind the curtain! Nor to all those navy blue and gray blazers reproaching me from the other closet.

We'd even had a good Christmas. Dinner with Connie and Cath, blowout presents for the kids—a motorized Harley for Aury, a real stereo for Gabe, and a used but still terrific laptop for Caro. Connie had knit a sweater for every member of my family, including Leo.

I know now that those periods were a waking dream. I know now that inevitably, one day, I would open my eyes and find someone had sneaked kryptonite under my pillow. The draining away of the precious days of strength drained away hope and relief at first. But as function returned, so did hope. I didn't know this then, and even if I had, I would still have been determined to relish those good days that followed my big relapse, if only to spite Leo *and* MS. Jennet was right. Cath said she was, and so she was.

The only thing wrong with Jennet was her stubborn insistence on facing facts. I liked the truth but, as the poet said, liked it slant, a spoonful at a time.

"You don't have a terminal diagnosis," she said, during our first visit, "so you may never have another bad day, or you may have ten bad days during one summer and then no more for ten years, and then a big incident. . . ."

"My concern is that I need to keep functioning evenly, now more than ever," I told her, rolling the cool, smooth marble egg between my palms.

"Now, more than ever? Would there have been a better time?" Jennet asked. She leaned forward.

"Well, yes, when my marriage . . . when my husband . . . before he left . . ."

"You're separated?"

Separated, separated, separated. The heavy word rolled the length of the room, all its syllables growling and echoing. It had a thunderous quality, a distant fearsome sound, like *adultery.* I felt as though I ought to try to pick up my feet before this description rolled near and crushed them. "No," I said, "we're not separated. But . . . ah, my husband is on an extended trip. . . ."

"A business trip?"

"No, a sort of sabbatical . . ."

"A retreat? For how long?"

"Not in any organized sense . . . and, well, he'll be gone for several more months."

"And what does he think?" Jennet asked. "What does he think about your being aggressive about treatment?"

"I don't know."

"Well, it's common, particularly for men, not to want to deal with something like this head-on. They can't fix it or cure it, and they feel helpless."

"He doesn't know because I haven't told him," I said, putting down the egg and picking up the carven head, which looked to me like the baby of one of the Easter Island monoliths.

"Julie," Jennet said. "You need to tell him."

I sat the stone face down harder than I meant to on the marble table-top. "I haven't told him because I can't reach him to tell him." I held up my hand. "No, it's not what it sounds like. He's not hurt. . . ." Then I thought, Maybe he is hurt. I thought, Maybe he's . . . stuck in a crevasse or something, right now, dying of thirst. I thought that might be kind of nice. Then, I thought, My God, I haven't even considered that Leo might be needing me. . . . We didn't have the same last name, and my in-laws were in Florida. Had they arranged for call forwarding?

"Julie?" Jennet prompted me.

"He told me that there would be times when the plan would be for him to be totally incommunicado, and I guess that this is one of them. It's un-fortunate that this happened now." I had been mesmerized by the serenity of the Easter Island face, its expressionless gaze, looking at all, caring for nothing. I glanced at the unmarked perfection of the egg and thought, All the king's horses and all the king's men . . .

"But what was your system for emergencies?"

"We don't *have* emergencies like this," I told her helplessly.

"What was your system for *any* emergency, with one of the children, his parents?" Jennet persisted. "I know what you'd say in your column. I admire it, by the way." I felt as though Jennet had torn off my shirt. I had expected we would do our "work," behind respective masks, and agree to pretend not to recognize each other in the produce section. But this was a small city.

"It seems like we would have done something so, basic, so sensible," I admitted. "I was to contact him at one of the list of emergency numbers he left. Leo said he had left me a list of emergency contacts."

"But he didn't."

"He didn't."

"Why do you think that was?"

"I guess, because, well, that wasn't on Leo's agenda. He figured I could handle anything. I always had."

"What was on Leo's agenda?"

I bit my lip. "Let me think that over." But she wasn't going to let me slip off the hook.

"So the marriage was cracking before he left," Jennet summed up. "And this sabbatical is an attempt for him to gather himself enough to make it work, instead of coming in here or somewhere else with you to tackle whatever's stuck up his butt." Her words were bullets fired into a stuffed dummy. I felt the impact but not the pain. The mortgage was still being withdrawn monthly, but I'd just had a check bounce. When the banker reminded me that "we" had closed that account and sold some stock in the recycled-wood-products company, I laughed and said I must be getting senile. Mike the banker made a few lame jokes about a dream vacation. I transferred money from savings to our checking account, alarmed at the undeniable dearth of what was left in savings, if I thought of it in terms of years. There was stock . . . Leo couldn't call *me,* or his kids, but he could call the bank to cheat me out of what belonged to both of us. There was no escaping it.

With honest empathy in her eyes, Jennet said softly, "Leo's *agenda* was getting out of Dodge, wasn't it?"

I looked back into her eyes and said, "That about covers it."

"Damn. You're everywhere, Gillis," Steve said, when I showed up in his office, crisp in my high-necked gray silk dress, two-inch heels, and stockings with seams, my knees aching as if I'd run a half-marathon instead of taking the elevator up three flights. Standing at a podium to give an hour-long talk hadn't helped. Cathcart leaned back in his chair. I stood. I was actually worried that once I sat down facing him, I'd be frozen to the chair for the afternoon.

It turned out that the effect on Steve was psychological; he thought I was assuming a power stance.

"Well, you probably know what I'm going to say," Cathcart began, ruffling his well-tended beard. His big, even teeth glistened, ringed by an uncommonly ruddy mouth. I had never contemplated how much Steve resembled the wolf in *Little Red Riding Hood*.

"I guess," I said. "But Steve, you have to understand—"

"I do, Gillis. Don't feel guilty. As much as I hate to admit it, you need to be syndicated. That's what I told my guy, Marty, from Panorama Media. He agreed. But hey, I know it's not a sign that you're some kind of diva," he said. I grabbed the back of the chair and tried to nod sympathetically, my left leg twanging under my skirt like Elvis singing "Jailhouse Rock." Steve went on, "I have to hope you'll still do the occasional special number, a big feature or a Q and A, just for us and for extra compensation, of course. And we'll keep our special arrangement. You'll be paid for your weekly column separately from whatever Panorama gives you, and we'll run it full-length, even if your other markets cut it. You're our girl, first, Julie. Marty says he can probably get you in a hundred small dailies to start and maybe in a few bigs, now that the Lederer girls are gone. There's the *Post* girl. She's hot, but she's strictly dating. And you do it all, families, sisters, the whole rag. I hate to share you, but you should move on it. Syndication will never make you rich, but then you've got Mister Bizlaw for the important stuff. But it'll help you grow, and, don't get a big head, but you're too good for a small paper."

Cathcart handed me a slip of paper with Marty Brent's number and address at Panorama, and did this goofy thing that involved sitting on the top of his shiny desk and spinning himself around on his rear end until he was facing me without having to get up. He took my hand, a parody something between a stern shake and a gentleman dropping a kiss on a lady's hand. "You're looking sharp, Gillis," he said. "Hitting the gym?"

"Hard," I said. "Thanks for noticing. The hard drive goes first." He laughed and waved me good-bye.

Outside, from the car, I called Cathy. "You'll never guess!" I told her.

"You've been named editor of the paper!"

"No."

"You got fired?"

"I got syndicated! My column! In probably a hundred newspapers! Or more!"

"You'll be rich!" she screamed. "You won't need Leo!"

"I . . . won't be anything like rich, Cath," I said, and the melting snow on the road shimmered before my eyes. "And why . . . what do you . . . what does that mean, about Leo? I need Leo."

"Julie, you have to know—"

"I, Cath, I have to call somebody. For an interview. I'm sorry, girlfriend. I'll get back to you." But once I was off the phone, I didn't start the car.

I simply sat.

A couple of guys . . . maybe in their late twenties, drove past in a convertible. It was a nice day, though probably not warmer than forty. Too cold for adults to have the top down, but nothing could drive a Wisconsinite to excess faster than a false spring.

"Hey," one kid yelled, "hey, pretty lady!" My eyes stung. I snatched my handicapped tag from the visor. If I got out of the car now, and wavered across the street like a drunk, how pretty would they think I was?

How pretty would Leo think I was now? How proud would he be?

What if I finally needed a wheelchair?

What if I did?

I would have to find a way to get one. On my own.

I was on my own. Now.

And so I needed to do something real to stay well as long as I could as often as I could. I'd been avoiding the big, expensive, scary drugs, both for what they would cost and for what they signified. But vitamins and green tea and antidepressants weren't going to cut it. The going was going to get tough. Maybe. And so I had to get tough, too. I needed my own insurance policy; it would be pricey, especially with a preexisting condition I couldn't deny, but it would be a tax write-off. Leo's coverage of the kids would last, but there was a chance he might not be covering me in any sense for long. I had—I gulped at this—to find a support group, so people could answer my questions. There were things I could sell—my mother's real jewelry, my relatively new car. I'd start comparison shopping later that day. But one matter couldn't wait. I picked up my phone and made an appointment with the neurologist.

The thing about the shots was that they basically made the time between shots "good time." Or at least, they might have been doing that; I had no idea how I'd be without them.

But there was a trade-off. The time right after I took them was a mud slide.

And the mud slide, at first, as my body grew accustomed to the onslaught of what was de facto a poison, could last up to a week.

I began taking shots once a month, and after the first month, I knew I could count on being down for one week of four the next.

And when I was down, the kids went out. You'd be surprised how fast a house can go to hell in a couple of days if the master and commander can do no more than get out of bed long enough to go to the bathroom, or, occasionally, fry a couple of burgers before falling asleep while trying to eat one.

Gabe didn't do anything bad. He only let his natural inertia take over. He never missed getting Aury to school, although sometimes she showed up an hour late. But Caroline, my erstwhile new best friend, began working on what I suspected might be the forfeiture of her five-hundred-dollar virginity. Moreover, Caroline's last report card seemed to have gone as permanently astray as Leo's letters. I grew accustomed to the soft click that coincided with the clock striking four A.M. It meant Caro was back from I-was-glad-I-had-no-idea-where. I was *glad* I didn't formally know that my fourteen-year-old was staying out all night.

Then, Cathy had the nerve to *chastise* me about it. Well, at least to raise the subject.

"She's not accountable to anyone," Cathy said helplessly, after Caroline met Cathy in the driveway at *seven* A.M. one Sunday morning. Cath was bringing popovers; Caroline was just getting home. "She's *telling* you she wants you to make her behave."

"Well, what would you suggest, Cath?" I shot back, fuzzy but determined, sitting up in bed to nibble at one of Connie's popovers. I knew that, objectively, it was a flaky confection, utterly delicious. But to me, it tasted like soaked pizza cardboard. Every nerve ending I had was on vacation. "She minds when I can *make* her, but when I can't, she takes advantage of it. I forbid her. But she does it behind my back. I can't afford to hire a keeper." Ground her, Cath suggested. Set limits while she was still young enough for limits to matter. But Cath didn't know how tough a nut my daughter had become. I would watch Caroline, her headphones ever attached, her head ever moving in a silent seizure, complete in her oblivion, her self-absorption. I suppose it was as good a defense mechanism as any. But then, Caroline had always had a poker face, perhaps a poker heart. Even as a tot, she'd been able to keep things to herself for far longer than most children—than most people can, period, even as adults. I could monitor her groundings no more successfully than I could monitor her weight.

"At least Patty Gilmore tells me she's in school every day," I said. "That's something."

If Caro was out with an older boy on the weekends I was sick, or was using drugs, the only therapy I could avail myself of was Cath, and Cath was so familiar to Caro she was almost like another parent—destined for disrespect. The only rehab I could afford would be the kind that came with a court order. In fact, in the long run, it would be better for me to remain ignorant of any serious problems Caro had. What if she ended up in a foster home?

And there was Gabe. Gabe was a brick, and he was vigilant about Aury, but he was only a young boy, with a young boy's standards for the acceptable condition of a home. Clothes might need to be clean, but neither folded nor in drawers. When all the dishes, including the holiday china, got dirty, it was time to wash three plates. The rest were stored in the logical place, the dishwasher. When I was well enough, we'd go on a forced march through the house, dusting, sweeping, scrubbing. We'd just get it sorted out, and then it'd be time for another shot.

After my shot, as I weakened, Gabe would take up my slack, through a routine we'd developed without ever talking it over. He'd set the alarm for six, drag himself out of bed, rouse Caroline—even to the point of putting ice cubes on the soles of her feet—put Aury on the toilet and back into bed if she didn't have preschool. He'd leave bowls and raisin bran for us on the table. If Aury did have preschool, he'd call Cathy before he caught the bus, and Cath would drive Aury. Then one day, he presented me with the (perfectly forged) application I'd filled out for a hardship driver's license and a work permit. With a plummeting heart, I wondered how many other absences and detentions for late schoolwork I'd acknowledged. I'd begun throwing away notes addressed "To the Parents of A. Gabriel Steiner." What was the point? I couldn't afford a really good LD tutor. I couldn't call his "case manager," though her e-mails piled up like angry little sentinels in my in-box.

During those postinjection nights, I would wake, shivery with sweat. I'd yearn to make sure Aury was still alive and covered, so I'd creep down the hall, but often, because of the darkness and my unsteady gait, on my hands and knees. Gabe would hear me, and without a word, slip out, wearing his flannel pajama bottoms, which I finally recognized as Leo's, lift me to my feet and, hands under my arms, escort me to my bed—exactly as I had when he was little and sleepwalked. He never spoke of it the following morning. What must that have been like for him? The shame of it. What should I have said? "Thanks for dragging me back to bed last night, hon!" It would only have compounded his humiliation. And as if that weren't enough, Tian, through golden tears and kisses, finally came to the end of her time at Sheboygan LaFollette and left for home—sorry to part with Gabe but clearly eager to be with her own family, and clearly ready to fry bigger fish than Sheboygan offered. So, Gabe was hardly tooling around with a car full of Luke and Luke's friends—though having the car, even a few days a month, even only to drive to school—would have earned him back some of the status he lost when Tian left.

Gabe didn't have the heart.

I knew how he felt.

I also didn't have the heart to reply to the urgent stack of notes and reels of recorded messages from Hannah and Gabe Senior.

"Julie," the answering machine urged me frantically. "Julie. Julie! Please call us!"

Finally—and wouldn't it be just two days after my last shot?—my in-laws showed up unbidden, all the way from Florida, telling me they'd planned to come back early because they'd become bored with "all that sunshine and those old people." Bored. With twenty inches of snow on the ground in Sheboygan, mostly on my front sidewalk, because Liesel and Klaus were on an extended trip and shoveling was even lower on Gabe's radar than laundry.

Gabe sounded like a kid on Christmas morning when he yelled down the hall, "Mom! Grandma and Grandpa are here!" It was as if the Marines had landed.

"We'd rather be here, with real life around us," I heard Leo's dad say as they rolled their matching suitcases into the hall.

I tried to swing my legs over the side of the bed. My legs refused even to twitch. The last time I'd gone to the bathroom, I'd ended up pouring a full glass of cold water down my thigh, and it hadn't been accidental. I saw plainly that my skin was neither on fire nor infected, but my brain was shouting at me that I'd fallen asleep for six hours under tropical sun. The bed looked as though I'd peed in it.

I heard Hannah "tsking" her way down the hall, calling, as I imagined her skimming the soft mantle of dust on the bookshelves that lined the walls and crowned the doors on that side. "Julie, Julie, with your head in the books . . . Julie, sweetheart, when was the last time that little girl came and cleaned? What was her name? Sayonara?" Her name had been Leonora, and she had been a Filipino grad student who'd done "the heavy cleaning" weekly, and who I hadn't been able to afford since I'd begun the shots, which, because they weren't a proven therapy for MS, weren't covered by my state-sponsored disability insurance or by my paltry private policy.

I could imagine how it must have looked. And smelled.

"Julie?" Hannah peered into the murk from my doorway. I'd kept the shades drawn for the past few days because the light hurt my eyes. They were, even now, during my downtime, still pretty good, especially my right eye. Out of my left eye, I saw things haloed, as if by a smudge of oil. I was still thinking about medicine bottles when Hannah cried again, *"Julie?"*

I'd . . . forgotten she was standing there.

"Julie, what in heaven!" she cried, throwing back the curtains and raising the blinds, revealing the army of used tumblers; the empty, side-over sunken paper cups of Ramen noodles; the tangle of T-shirts and pajamas in the corner next to the TV where I'd lobbed them; and me—in an old pair of Leo's sweatpants under a long ballet T-shirt with a mustard blot on one boob. I saw the stack of newspapers that had, to Aury's delight, reached nearly to the top of my chest of drawers before she'd accidentally knocked them over. "What happened in here?"

It looked like a dorm room.

No.

It looked like an inmate's room.

"Gabe!" she called. "Come here!" and I started to bawl.

By the following afternoon, Hannah had washed surfaces I believe hadn't been touched by human hands since we'd owned the duplex. Hannah got on ladders and washed the crown molding. She made rice with beans, rice with chicken and broccoli, rice and lentil soup, rice pudding. She made matzoh balls. She starched and ironed my blouses, which had hung in my closet lately like a group of tacky Quasimodos. She dumped Gabe's backpack out on the living room floor and went through it scrap by scrap.

It being Sunday, Gabe spent six hours doing assignments, even ones he insisted were "study guides" that didn't need to be turned in for grades.

"So you study them by doing them and then you can burn them," Hannah said. Gabe gave me a look both withering and panicked. He had no idea how to do algebra.

"Call Luke," I suggested.

"He's worse than me," Gabe muttered.

"Call someone else," I whispered.

"No one else in the class talks to me," he said. "I don't know if their name is Dick or Dave."

"Call Klaus," said Gabe Senior, who'd been more or less preoccupied with the phone since he'd arrived. I knew what he was doing, trying to find Leo, calling Leo's friends, his colleagues.

"They've gone on a trip," Caro said hopefully, trying unsuccessfully to slide her own backpack into the hall closet with her foot. "They won't be back for ages."

"Unless there's a guy who looks like Klaus shoveling the walk, they're not gone anymore," my father-in-law replied without looking up. "I guess ages has arrived. He's a scientist. He should know math. Go ask him, Caroline. Or I will."

Miserably, my children went to find Klaus, who quit shoveling long enough to help the kids. My tenants were not exactly friends of ours, and they were never intrusive. But I knew they had realized something of what had transpired; and they began doing kindly, if not particularly useful things, such as bringing Aury fossilized dinosaur dung, which they left in our mailbox with a funny card. Klaus had also—in writing, on letterhead—offered to drive the children anywhere if I should need the help "for any reason." Gabe later told me that Liesel made tea for them; and that they seemed happy to work on math with my children, even though their own unpacked suitcases were sitting in the hall. They'd arrived home from Saint Lucia or Santo Domingo or somewhere, it turned out, on the same plane that had brought Leo's parents from Florida. The kids were gone for at least an hour. During that time, Hannah, with consummate delicacy, scrubbed the tub and filled it with steaming, scented water for me. She slid naked Aury, slippery and curved as a dolphin, in beside me, with the silent message that my sturdy two-year-old's physical support would be more important to me than my ability to wash her dark curls. Hannah waited outside the curtains until Aury was, at least, cleaner. Then, when Aury had run off for her Scooby shirt, Hannah found one of my expensive sponges and, without asking, began to wash my back and hair, her eyes averted. I sobbed and finally, against every previous instinct I'd ever expressed, took Hannah's spatulate hand with its imbedded gold band. "Is this from depression, Julieanne?" she asked softly. "Has my son done this to his wife?"

"No," I told her. "It's actually . . . I so very much didn't want to have to tell you."

"What?"

"I have multiple sclerosis, Hannah." Her breath quickened. "I'm not dying. And I'm not this way all the time. This is just a reaction to the shots I have to take so the symptoms don't get worse."

"What symptoms?"

"Oh, some problems with my legs. My vision. Balance. They come and go." Hannah dropped her eyes. I went on. "I . . . don't blame Leo. But I need Leo. I need Leo to come home."

We sat up late that night. Gabe Senior was talking about a petition for habeas corpus based on mental incompetence or some notion—he'd become quick with the Internet since my husband had given him a laptop, corresponding often from Sarasota with my Gabe and his golf pals in Door County. My son had never betrayed a word of this. When he once again suggested legal action, I finally sighed and said, "I can't do that, Papa. We took out a power of attorney before he left. Leo and I have power of attorney for each other. He can sell things without my signature. He can take money from our accounts. He could do that even if we hadn't got power of attorney. He can take out money whenever he pleases. We're still legally married."

The elder man pinched his brow. "In all my life, in all the years I've known my son, I imagined that he might do things I wouldn't agree with, but never that would shame me. When did this start? This hippie business was one thing . . . Julie."

"That went on for a year. You knew about that. But the trip was a big shock. It's my getting ill that's fouled everything up," I said. "I don't mean what Leo has done isn't inexcusable. But I could have made it, somehow, if I hadn't gotten sick."

"Julie, why didn't you tell us how wrong he's been acting?" Hannah pleaded.

"I thought he was having a little midlife thing . . . what do you call it . . . ?"

"A crisis," suggested my father-in-law, his surprised frown eloquent at my inability to grab the word.

"And when it was over, it would be over," I went on. "I never expected that he wouldn't be back by now. Or that I would be too ashamed to tell anyone for how long he'd been gone. And how disgusting I've been. . . . He sent the kids candles and jam at Christmas. From a zip code in New Hampshire. No address."

"Disgusting," Hannah spat. "As if you chose to be sick. You told Cathy the extent of it . . . why not us?"

"Only because she was here. You understand. I thought it would all be . . . okay." I was almost too weary to form my mouth around the words. I could feel my eyelids fluttering. "At first, I thought I was just . . . sick from grief. Then flu. And when I found out, I was . . . it was just too much to tell you. I have some pride left."

"Pride isn't for that, Julieanne. You made a graceful home for our son.

You gave him beautiful children . . ." Hannah protested. "And you didn't plan to be ill in order to get Leo's sympathy."

"Look at you! All this! And you kept up your work," Gabe Senior, prompted. "Julie, the first thing you have to do is close down all those bank accounts. Clean them out. Change banks."

"I will, Papa," I said. "About the work. I wasn't that heroic. Not at first. I can do it now," I told them. "But at first, Cathy and Gabe wrote my volume . . . I mean, my column! And imagine, they were . . . bigger, I mean they're better than I am. I got a syndication contract since . . . I got ill. Because of Cathy and Gabe. They're hip, Cathy and Gabe." I said then, "I'm sorry . . . Gabe, Papa . . . I know we weren't supposed to name him after you because you're living and Jews don't do that."

He waved his hand, perplexed both at my fumbling and the lack of sequence. "My father died when I was seven. I always thought you named him for *my* grandfather, also Gabriel. Every second person in this house is named Gabe. And why would you bring this up now of all times? We have to find a way to have Leo declared incompetent, Julie. Hannah, you see this. We have to find a conservatorship, before he cleans this whole family out—"

"Because," I said, cradling my head in my arms on the table, "you're being so nice to me. That's why I brought up the name. And he wouldn't have left maybe, if I had been, I don't know, more understanding."

"Don't be ridiculous," Hannah said. "Julie, listen. We've always felt you were a very modern girl. Very much a self-sufficient person. But things have to be done here. Caroline just tried to leave—and it's nine-thirty at night! She says her mother lets her go out at this time."

"No, I just . . . can't stop her. Not until I'm on my feet. Probably by tomorrow." I cringed inwardly at this admission of my parental impotence.

"And so I said, Missy, you have been taking advantage of your mother's illness, and that is going to change . . ." Hannah went on.

"She just lays there like a zombie," Caroline put in, suddenly standing with her hands on her hips in the kitchen door. "She doesn't even try to get up. It's like, guh, guh, I'm asleep. Like, every other week!"

"That's not true, Caro!" I said. "Shame on you!"

"It is! If Cathy doesn't come over, we're eating cornflakes. If I go to Mallory's, at least I get a hamburger. . . ."

"And have you ever known your mother to do this in your entire life before these past few months, Caroline? Ever? Didn't she always look like a fashion model?" Caro snorted, but Hannah went on, "Or a socialite, before this? Do you think she wants to feel this way?"

"I think she could try a little," Caroline said, stepping into the doorway. She looked like the Broadway cruisers my girlfriends and I used to titter at from the back of my father's car. Glittering gold eye shadow. Miles of legs under a skirt so short Aury could have worn it. And rage. Rage that seemed to seize her every muscle from her shoulders down. "I think she could take the medicine Cathy says the doctors want her to take. I think she could give a shit—"

"Shut your mouth, Caroline," Leo's father said, wearily. "Go wash that crap off your face and go to bed." Shocked, because this man, her most gentle of relatives, had never spoken to her without a leprechaun's charm, Caro slumped away to obey. "And Caroline! Spread quilts on the guest room floor, for you and Aury . . ." he called after her. "Grandma and I need firm mattresses."

From the hall came an outraged bellow, "*Me?* Me, sleep on the floor?"

"Solly, Cholly," her grandfather answered, with a kind of shrug and grin. "We'll be needing the beds. We need to stay here until your mama is on her feet."

I wakened with a jerk, realizing I'd fallen asleep at the table.

"And you get to bed now," Hannah told me, lifting me firmly by one elbow. "We'll talk treatments and condos and money and . . . these, Gabe, what did you call them?"

"Skip tracers," said Gabe Senior.

"They find people," Hannah explained.

"I don't have money for that," I told her softly, as I brushed my teeth.

"You don't have to have all the money in the world," Hannah said. "Other people also have money."

"I can't . . . take anything," I said, as I lay down on blessedly clean sheets.

Hannah sat perched on the edge of the bed, straight-backed, perhaps a hundred pounds soaking wet, pert in her khakis and UW sweatshirt, her still-black hair cut short and brushed back like a boy's. "You know in the Bible, Julie, about Ruth?" I nodded. "Well, Ruth refused to leave Naomi. She was in danger, and she wouldn't leave. And she said the thing that is probably the only thing anyone knows from that story, which was, you know it, of course, 'Whither thou goest, I will go. Whither thou lodgest, I will lodge'. . . . Sometimes people think that Naomi was Ruth's mother."

"Yes," I said.

"But she was her mother-in-law."

"Naomi wanted her to go," I said.

"But Ruth was too loyal for that. And it all worked out," Hannah told me, brushing back my hair with a hand that smelled of fabric softener.

FIFTEEN

Gabe's Journal

While passing the second semester of freshman year with Ds in every class—and these were pity Ds, purchased by ratting out my sick mother, absentee father, and the constant travail on behalf of my poor younger siblings—I also had become a syndicated columnist before I was sixteen. I, Gabe Steiner, known geek and future high school dropout, was being read by millions of fans across America.

Okay, maybe thousands.

Cathy and I were a pretty good team. She came around a lot, but she also tried to stay away as much as she could—so my mother wouldn't feel like Cathy considered her a helpless amoeba. Every day, though, she called, and when my mom would let her, she stayed over with Abby Sun.

Having to do my mother's job periodically was a good distraction, because otherwise, after Tian left, I was zoned. If I got a free minute, I played some mind-out game like Roller Coaster Magnate or listened to music on my actually-kind-of-nice stereo or didn't do a few dishes or entertained thoughts of nearly drowning myself to get sympathy. I knew my moping around bothered my mother. But she was using her good hours to go to a shrink and do all those speeches, which I gathered were helping to support us. And she was also trying, without any success, to get fucking Caroline to do anything after she'd been out all night, smoking (cigarettes) with Wonderbrain Mallory and Justine, and Caro's excellent new love, Ryan, the dumbest air-breathing bipedal hominid since Mallory. He looked to be, like, thirty, and had more hair than an Irish setter (not only on his head). Prying Caro's ear off the phone was about as possible as my being named a Rhodes scholar.

Grandma Steiner one day asked if she could "speak" to Caroline. Privately. They had stopped living with us—they stayed only for a few days—but they were over almost every day. I could imagine the topic of conversation Grandma wanted with Caro—my having heard, earlier in the week, a short but pointed lecture about the two plates with mozzarella stuck to them under my bed.

Caro showed up in my room ten minutes later, looking literally thinner from fury. Caro wasn't used to big emotions. She was a "whatever" sort of person.

"I now have a *list* of chores," she shouted. "What the hell is this? *Little House on the Prairie*?"

"No," I said. "This would be *Little Asylum on the Prairie*."

"Well, I don't give a shit, Gabe," she said. "I'm not doing laundry and . . . reorganizing 'the baby's' clothes. I have my own life."

"You would be the only one who does," I told her.

"Look, life didn't end for the rest of us when Miss Saigon left."

At that point, I hadn't hit my sister since I was about seven. But I punched her then as hard as I could reasonably hit a girl, right in the bicep. She slapped me across the face.

"You are the most fucking selfish witch I ever met," I said. "Why are you the one who gets to play Miss Popularity while the rest of us take care of Mom? I'm doing her fucking job half the time."

"Well, oh well," Caroline said, wiggling her fingers. "You're such a good little boy, Gabe."

"I mean, you could read to Aury one night," I sneered at her. "You could get up by yourself and not have to have me wake you up like I was your daddy."

"You're nowhere near being like our dad."

"Thank God for small favors," I told her.

"Gabe. Are you really being fair to Dad? I mean, you have to admit Mom was fairly . . . out there before this happened. She was all about her ballet classes and being Miss Too Good for Everybody."

I never saw our mother like that, but I could see how a person could. She hadn't been like Luke's mom, either hanging on his father or yelling at him, talking to all the neighbors and bringing them pies. Mom had her own orbit, true. . . . But I wasn't about to admit it to Caro. Partly because a lot of what my mother had been taken up with, before she got sick, had been me.

Though I had mostly hated her for it, Mom had taken on the role of engineering the push, pull, and drag method of getting me through school. I owed her at least a defense.

So I gave her one.

"Even if she was, she's your mother, Caro. Ever think that even *Mallory* might help her mother out if she had MS and her dad took a powder? I mean, she really totally abandoned you all your life, right, didn't she? When you wanted to be in shows and she'd sew the dresses or teach all the kids the dances? Every time you puked or pissed the bed or needed a Halloween costume made overnight because you found out some other girl was going to be Cinderella. . . ."

She started to cry then—mad, hot tears. "I'm not a stone or a piece of shit, Gabe! I just sort of don't want to get sucked down, all right? I'm, like, only almost fifteen! Y'know? Not thirty! I can't handle the whole Dad desertion, Mom crackup thing."

"Shoot, Caro. I understand. Because it's all about you."

"Go to hell, Gabe," she said. "Don't ever expect me to stick up for you again. Kids say you just wander around school looking like someone who needs his own shopping cart with a Chihuahua."

"You're a bitch."

"I'd rather be a bitch than a retard."

It was all very all-American and functional.

She had a point about school. I did wander around it. High school dwarfed me. Half the time, I wondered why I even showed up. I had a whole other set of responsibilities and real-life shit, and there I was every seventh hour, sitting in the dunce chair and being hocked by Mrs. Kimball for completing only half my biology lab. My *mother* was a biology lab. If Kimball had showed a teaspoonful of compassion, it might have been different. But Mrs. Kimball, LD specialist and professional sadist, thought everything I did wrong was on purpose. I was used to this, but taking care of a whole damned family in secret more or less made their bullshit about ninety percent more annoying. My mother was coherent three-quarters of the time, and what I had to explain was *how I forgot* how to do an algebra problem between the end of the ninth-hour class and the half-hour ride home. Klaus helped, but you can ask a neighbor only so much. Mrs. Kimball helpfully wrote my mom a letter, though my mother never saw it, about her belief that this was passive-aggressive behavior and I might need to be "looked at" by the emotionally disturbed specialist, too. You could try to explain it to her, but all Kimball would do was give you this constipated little smile.

The bad part was, I didn't understand it myself, and no one ever thought to question why. I didn't learn until years later that I had a language-processing disorder along with my other crap. I could understand perfectly what a teacher was saying while he was saying it, but when I tried to play it back, it was like the tape recorder had picked up gibberish. It was like he was saying, "If the missing number is X, then Y must be the factor to the right of the moon, just below one of the rings of Saturn. . . ."

Anyway, I wasn't passive aggressive toward Mrs. Kimball.

I was actually aggressive.

I didn't swear or anything like the kids with tattoos.

I just sat there, trying to do shit that would drive her nuts, like sticking a pen cap on the end of my tongue by suction. I hated her so bad that seeing her squirm was more important to me than doing what I actually could have done to get a decent amount of work finished.

Kimball looked like a cartoon of a teacher, right to the end of her little sixties flip. Maybe she had some kind of hideous scarring on her arms and throat, and that was why she covered herself from neck to knees with clothes she must have ordered specially from old Sally Field movies. No matter how hot it got in the LD room, she had on some kind of turtleneck with little initials on it and, like, a kilt or plaid pants. As soon as I came home each day, the first thing I'd do was boot up my mom's laptop and delete Mrs. Kimball's daily bulletin, which usually read along the lines of: "Mr. Molinari couldn't tell whether Gabe was awake or asleep in class today, but since he completed the paragraph about five seconds before the bell . . ." Or my favorite: "Some of the freshmen will be taking the PSAT in spring, but these tests are for the college-bound student. He'd need a note from an MD psychiatrist to get extra time to do the tests anyway, and a written copy of all test results and Individualized Education Plans going back to middle school. . . ."

Mrs. Kimball apparently thought my mother didn't know what the SAT was, or was more likely just being a bitch. "Gabe seems to have squeaked by with a B in Phys Ed. . . ." She could make even something good sound like shit, if I was involved in it.

I have observed that those who hate kids most teach Special Ed. Either they know they don't have some kind of passion for history or writing, or they figure they can't do any more harm with their fucking sadism, since their students were the heel of society's loaf anyhow. There were kids who were crazy about Mrs. Kimball and Miss Nick, her equally thick but vaguely kinder younger colleague. I swear to God, like this one brain-damaged girl who graduated at, like, twenty-two, came back to visit the LD room, with her handler. She fed dogs at the Humane Society. That was the gift Mrs. Kimball had given her with her fucking diploma. It took me fucking five years to recover from Mrs. Kimball. Just the smell of that old-lady-drawer perfume she used to wear would make me want to throw up. The principal loved Mrs. Kimball, which he would have even if she'd been Saddam Hussein. The Mrs. Kimballs of the world took the Eds out of regular classes, where they had committed heinous felonies like doodling on the margin of a paper, which, of course, would disrupt the known universe. The LD guards would then stand over the six or eight of us in our pen, and hock us with statements such as, "How can you expect to pass if you can't even remember to turn in the papers, Gabe?" They never figured out why you couldn't remember crap, though I once told the skinny, batso psychologist, who floated from school to school on her Vespa, that I felt like most of my life was one of those films where a person has a camera attached to the front of a roller coaster. She said, "That's . . . interesting, Gabe," and the next time my mother came into a meeting, there was a note clipped to my folder: *Evaluate, possible psychosis?*

Like, I'm no Einstein, but I grew up in a house where people communicated with more than clicks and grunts. I knew how to describe things. I knew what "ad hoc ergo proper hoc" meant. I couldn't spell it. I could spell it *now*. That's why God invented spell-checkers. I can write. But they didn't care about what you thought, just how you spelled it. One time, this genius English teacher decided she'd give me a list of spelling words designed just for me. Cat. Book. Milk.

This was a real fucking ego boost.

But I shouldn't have told my mother about it.

It sent her over the edge. Without telling me, she stormed into the principal's office, waving a copy of *The Odyssey*, saying, "Don't you dare, ever, ever, give my kid a spelling list with 'cow' and 'that' on it. Never. My kid has read Homer. Have you read Homer? You probably think Homer's your cousin's first name. . . ." I could have killed her for it at the time, but actually, now I think about it, she was, like, this little warrior. She didn't always make sense, but she had the right beef.

What's really neat in an extremely sad way is that even her knack for humiliating me out of overprotectiveness is one of the best memories I have of the time before The Illness.

There was this one night I got up, hungry, about one in the morning. And she was sitting at the table with her leg stretched out on two chairs doing a project for me that was due the next day. I never thought about why she had her leg up. But I bet it hurt her. She probably already had it then. All over her hair was this dust from sugar she'd been using to make igloos, and she was at that moment trying to see if she could fashion the lining of one of Aury's old mittens into a polar-bear hide she could then hang over whatever it is Inuit people hang things over to dry. When she saw me, she looked up at me and just smiled. "Go to bed, honey," she said.

"Mom, give it up already. You've got an igloo there and a couple of people—"

"Once you're in college, you'll do fine, Gabe," she said, like she was talking to herself instead of me. "This won't matter. They'll have note takers for kids like you, Gabe. You have rights. Legal rights. *Legal* rights! You're a very intelligent person, Gabe. It's just that those burnout losers they call school counselors don't get it. . . ." She looked small and white and . . . melted, like the end of a candle on a saucer. I was in about seventh grade. I wanted, big-time, to cry or something. I had honest to God just found this three-week-old paper describing the project in my jacket, along with some linty chocolate-covered cherries. I remembered that it was due and that there also would be a test the next day, so my mother grabbed a cookie sheet and starting building a model of an isolated American culture so I could at least read the chapters and sleep. I got a piece of bread out of the drawer. And then she asked, "But, Gabe, what am I going to use for seals?"

I thought she meant something to seal, to stick down the skin, so I said, "Well, how about just Elmer's glue?"

"I mean seals, animals, what they eat, and whales. . . ."

"I don't think you need, ah, seals," I told her. "I think they hunt them for pelts. Mom, you don't have to do this."

"Do you think I could use sardines?" she asked me, her eyes red-rimmed. She did use sardines. She baked them and coated them with colorless nail polish so they wouldn't smell and people still stared at me funny when they passed my project. She was so OCD. But she gave a shit. She always gave a shit.

The point is, Aury will never know how she was Before. I'm the only one who remembers that for her. Aury can't, and "Cat" wouldn't. Aury has her own . . . version of Mom. A good one. But I don't think of it as the real one.

When things got really hard, of course, I stopped bickering with Mom about anything, from homework to piano practice (no one had seen the piano teacher since Christmas). I have a theory: when you can get away with anything, you don't.

Except if you're my asshole sister Caroline.

She kept trying to sneak out the door to see Ryan the Hairy, in his car made almost entirely of body putty, and going wacko when Grandpa, who could hear like a bat, met her at the door while she was trying to slip out in her stockings, carrying her four-inch platform shoes. I think it was that, Grandpa trying to control the life of Princess Caroline, that turned the key, made her think the search-and-seizure adventure she'd only toyed with was an actual plan.

I was going through Mom's folders one week, looking up adolescent sexuality and stuff, and I saw this red folder. I picked it up because it was marked BULLSHIT.

Inside it were poems. I only read one, but I copied it down. Since I read her poems later, I guess this was sort of a baby step, an early Julieanne Gillis, poet, effort.

But it made me see how bad she was hurting, not only physically. And how much she knew. You always like to think a person doesn't know how sick she is, so you can tell her the same thing.

Mirror, Mirror

Giving up the girl
Is like giving birth
Giving up the girl hurts like hell
When the girl was to understudy the prima, woman-to-be
And was instead *la femme très jolie.*
Giving up the girl is like stretching skin after burns,

Because she was meant to be the ascension
And turned out the summit, the diamond head of the pin.
Giving up the girl is like hearing bone cut, your own,
Leaving scars only I see.
Because the woman didn't turn out to be
All she promised to be when she was grown.
Was instead an apple that fell too far from the tree.
It hurts to be the woman
Who was the girl
Who was me.

There used to be a series of three pictures of Mom in the Houston Ballet the summer of her sophomore year at the U. of Colorado. They're professional, probably done by a guy who wanted to sleep with her because
she was only in the corps de ballet; but my father had them framed and
lit, hung up as a sort of triptych in the hall.

When Grandma Steiner came, she took them down and put one of
them in each of our rooms.

You would not call my grandmother subtle.

In Aury's room, today, the picture of my mother looks like this little
arched doll, even her fingers are extended like they were little ballerinas,
she's on pointe, in what I think you call an attitude. In the one I have,
she's a blur, on purpose; she'd been in a series of pirouettes. I don't remember what Caro's was. When she took off, she took it with her. She's
sentimental.

SIXTEEN

Gabe's Journal

What I thought when Caro woke me up about two in the morning was that Mom was sick or that Grandma, who was always clutching her heart over some new outrage (like that Caro had stolen ten bucks from her purse), had actually *had* a heart attack. But instead she said, "Gabe, major truce. I'm sorry I yelled at you. No kidding. Do you have money?"

I had birthday checks and such, in the credit union at the U., totaling about two hundred bucks. "I'm not lending you any. Ask Ryan," I told her. "Have him sell a couple of his lake pipes."

"No, it's for . . . I have this idea. We're going to fix this." She brushed a middle piece of her blonde hair behind her ears, like she did when she got serious. I thought about the pictures of Mom in our hall. When Caro danced, she looked almost like Mom.

"Do you still take ballet?" I asked.

"No," Caro answered.

"Why?" I asked.

"Semester off," she told me.

"Grades," I said.

"No," Caro said honestly, "I didn't think she could pay for it. That's why we have to fix this. We have to find Dad."

"Find Dad? As in, Doctor Livingston, I presume?" I asked, punching my pillow and preparing to dive back into it. "Get out of my room. Go howl with Justine or Mallory at the Taco Bell."

"This, all this," she went on, shaking me until I sat up. "Listen. We can get Dad to come home. I can. If we can find him. See?" she went on. "He probably found out about Mom from somebody, like one of his old friends. And he's freaking out. When you have a midlife crisis, what you want is to be a kid again. You want less responsibilities. I heard this in family dynamics. So you would never want a wife with a chronic illness and one kid with learning disabilities . . . and a brat teenager, which I know would be me," she said. "But once he *gets* here, because he's probably totally homesick, he'll see she's not so bad—and, you know Dad—he'll want to fix everything. And we'll be back to normal."

I shook my head. "We've tried and tried to call him."

She stared at me. "So have I."

"So if he got any of the messages, he knows what's wrong here."

"If he got any of my e-mails," she said.

Caro looked like a scared little kid. She bit one side of her lip. "Kid, I'm sorry." I sort of awkwardly put my arm around her.

"That's why we have to go get him, Gabe!" she whispered, sitting up and jerking away, wrapping her arms around her knees. "He doesn't get how serious this is. Gram and Gramp are going to file a hubus petition against him, or whatever it is. For desertion. Freeze his assets . . ."

"I'd like to freeze his assets," I said, quoting Grandpa Steiner.

"They're going to sell the house," my sister said then.

I sat up higher, reached over, and grabbed my sweatshirt and rubbed my face. "What do you mean?"

"To Klaus and Liesel. They're going to sell the house and . . . I heard the whole thing. They're going to let us rent our place from them, but Klaus is going to put up a big greenhouse or bug house lab in our backyard. In *our* backyard . . ."

"When'd you hear this?"

"I heard Mom tell Cathy and Grandma. Like, a couple of days ago, they came up while we were at school, and she told them the whole thing. That's why we have to act fast."

"We can't stop her from selling the house," I said. "I heard Grandpa say that if he can take out both their money and junk, she can sell the house without him."

"Yeah, but if we find him fast enough, and he gets the message, and Gabe, you know I can talk him into anything. . . ."

So I listened.

Turned out it was no spur-of-the-moment idea. She had it all down, in a folder with our spring-break schedule taped on the outside. A folder! My sister! While there was nothing wrong with Caro's wiring, at least when it came to logic, I didn't think my sister cared to do much planning at all, beyond deciding on Thursday to go shopping on Saturday. Actually, she's very smart. And she has Leo's gene for knowing exactly what she needs.

The folder she showed me was filled with e-mails. They were all Dad's e-mails, and they were some fascinating reading.

Before Dad left, Caro had downloaded all Dad's saved e-mails onto Mom's computer, slugging it "Caroline's Diary," thus ensuring that Mom, who was pathological about not invading our privacy, would never look at it. Then, when Caro got her own laptop, she downloaded the whole schmear from Mom's onto hers.

They started a couple of years before, with a man named Aimen and his wife, Mary Carol, who had started what they called an "intentional community" in New Hampshire. The first place it had been housed had been a gutted Kmart, where the people just partitioned off their individual "living spaces," but since then, the people involved had all moved to the same neighborhood—too much closeness being too much of a good thing. As far as I could tell, they all believed in the same ethical stuff—like universal health insurance, keeping kids out of public schools, buying all their organic food in big bunches from farmers and sharing it out among the families. The families, I gathered, now all lived on the same couple of blocks in a town in New Hampshire, but in their own houses. They saved a lot of money because the whole group of them—Caroline said she had figured, from reading all the e-mails, that there were eight or nine families—co-owned only two vans and a truck as their only vehicles and, like, one snowblower and one TV, which they used only for movies and seeing stuff of outrageous significance, like the Olympics or 9/11. They had a meeting each week, "and it can get a little uproarious," said Aimen, who had been a Marine and whose wife, Mary Carol, was the New Hampshire State Champion Skeet Shooter. Caroline asked me what a skeet was. I had no idea, but I thought of the gun in Dad's drawer.

Aimen wrote, "We make joint decisions, such as curriculum, and when there are people who want their kids to read only novels that have modern social themes, and people who want their kids to commit Shakespeare to memory, and everyone over the age of fifteen has a vote, we have to do some real diplomatic negotiation. But we have a nice mix." Rituals, he wrote another time, "are one way we stay a community. The coming-of-age ritual at thirteen is a big one. Nothing religious about it. No. We don't 'do' religion; those who have their own faiths practice those faiths in their own way. But we think attaining maturity is a big deal, as have most indigenous cultures, and we have a feast, with gifts, an engraved Book of Life for the young person to fill with his or her own memories. . . ."

It sounded right up Leo's alley, especially given the sprinkling of names throughout, some of which were normal, but others of which were obviously chosen by parents who really wanted to crawl down into the earth and be it. There were kids named Willow and Muir and Diego. I *hoped* they were kids, anyhow.

There were various others, some from some fucking hostile survivalist nuts Dad didn't correspond with for long. But the next big batch were from two locations. The one we could tell was sort of in upstate New York, because the Hudson River was mentioned; and one was in Vermont.

The one in Vermont had a return address of crystalgrove@popper.net, and it was another community like the one before, only more so. Everybody who lived there had, like, three full outfits of their own, period. They lived in what they called "little houses" (an attachment had a picture of one of these) that were like something Aury would play in, but they had real rooms, only tiny-sized and with everything built into the walls. Your bed folded down. Your desk folded down. Your goddamn kitchen table folded down. This was supposed to encourage you to be outside more and at the Gathering (this sounded to me like some creep horror movie, about people who went to paradise and got turned into clones), which was this big lodge with a table longer than the one in the Last Supper and a lot of little ones—I assume for the children—where everybody ate every single meal together, and every single meal was made from stuff that was grown at the place, even the meat. The kids went to regular school, but they had to work on the place every Saturday as their "tithe." (I looked it up and it meant their tenth or percentage or something.) Adults had regular jobs, but—this blew me away—they put all their money together! I mean, one worked at a garage, and one was an orthodontist, and they put all their paychecks in one big pot and paid everything out of that. They were totally in it for life! Some people only worked for the place, farming and sewing and canning and junk. There were pictures, though, and the place was beautiful-looking. Like a magic place, with a waterfall the kids were playing in. The waterfall was supposedly connected to a pool with a hot spring. I hadn't ever heard of a hot spring in Vermont, but why not? They have them in Alaska. There was a class of graduates and what colleges they were going to, and some of the high school kids who went to a mountaineering camp—they had a big banner in front of them that said STRONG PROUD BODIES—including one really cute girl named Jessica Godin. The old lady—she said she was an old lady—who wrote to our dad seemed totally nice. Her name was India. She said it was her real name because her parents were teachers and she grew up in Delhi.

"Our life is not for everyone, Leo," she wrote in one of the early ones. "So I would advise you to counsel long and hard with your wife and per-haps come for a visit, for as long as a month or even two before you make a choice. We have had very few members leave, but the few families who have left (mostly due to marriages ending or the needs of elder relatives) have had a very hard time adjusting to the other world. . . ." Dad had written that the other world was just what he and his wife were so anxious to leave. He'd also written a lot of stuff about himself that wasn't necessarily . . . true, like that he'd done half marathons and such. I don't know why he said that, maybe because he wanted to look like the macho guys in the pictures, who were all buffed from chopping wood and making little houses and butchering oxen and shit. The correspondence with India went on until she was the one to stop it, gently suggesting that Leo needed to come to see Crystal Grove because they had talked about it as much as was feasible for her with her own "research" and her duties in the community.

In the one from the last place, the one in upstate New York, he seemed to be talking to this one person, "J." J's address was Jdevlin@devlingood-jams.com.

"J." was a very sympathetic person. She sympathized about how selfish Julie and "the three children" were, how they wanted to work him into an early grave so they could have more junk food and electronic gadgets. "It's the way of the world, Leon," she wrote—who the hell was Leon?—"and most people don't have the courage to recognize it. As my mother says, most people live lives of quiet desperation."

Her mother and Henry David Thoreau.

I couldn't believe it. Electronic gadgets? We didn't get a TV or DVD player until I was in middle school. The parents had their laptops. They wouldn't even give *us* a used one, until Caro's guilt gift. That was it. I didn't even have a Gameboy thing, though I used Luke's. Not only did Luke have one, so did every one of his brothers. Even Caroline had to save for a year to buy her disc player and headphones. We had to buy CDs out of our allowance and birthday checks. Wrote J., "When my mother first brought us here, Leon [Leon?], my father was corrupting all our lives with the same stuff. Plus, he was cheating on her with a cocktail waitress. Imagine, her taking five girls and moving to a remote little town in the Hudson Valley. She was like a pioneer woman. Like Sojourner Truth. ["J." did not sound like the sharpest pencil in the box. It was funny that this was how my mom signed her columns.] But our whole community at

Sunrise began around her, around my mother. She loved my father, but she had to leave him behind because he couldn't let go of the world. . . ." That was Julie all over, my father wrote back. No inner life. Just a shell.

The coldhearted bastard, I thought. A shell? A shell was what I figured Leo had in place of a heart.

At some point, Caro left the room and went back to bed, but I kept unfurling this long, long, long string of e-mails to "J." and they got . . . sort of sick. My father was picturing himself with his body pressed against "J.'s" back, feeling safe and clean for the first time in his life. One equally sick part of me wanted to go on reading it, but this is *so* stuff you don't want to know about your father. I was also nauseated. Safe and clean? What were we, a methadone clinic? How could he be such an asshole as to call Julie a "social climber" with "trivial" friends and his children "self-absorbed" and "materialistic"? I'd had the same backpack since the fifth grade.

In the car the next morning, Caro asked, "Like the part about all our electronic gadgetry?"

"I don't get it!"

"He was just trying to impress her, you know, the way you do a girl." Caro was completely calm about this. "He was trying to make himself sound like this poor victim."

"He's married, Caro!"

"I told you, we heard this in health, a lot of guys do this! They e-cheat. Anyhow, that's not where he is. He's at the Crystal Place. I have a sense. That India lady was the one who was talking like he did before he left. So that's where we have to look first."

"And when Mom notices the car is missing . . . ?"

"We aren't going to take the *car*, idiot," Caroline said. "We're going to take buses. The whole way. And when—"

"Mom notices we're gone—"

"I have this worked out. I told Grandpa and Gram we were totally stressed out and Aunt Jane asked us to come to the summerhouse at spring break; and Grandpa and Gram wouldn't know how to reach Jane if she was on fire, plus they're leaving tomorrow for Florida. Then, I wrote to Jane and told her we were totally stressed out, and she sent us, like, six hundred bucks to buy plane tickets to go see Gram and Gramp in Florida, and said not to worry Mom by telling her, just to say Gram and Gramp invited us. So, I figure we have about a thousand bucks between us, and—"

"We're going to be able to find him, on buses, staying at hotels—"

"No, Gabe, they have these youth places in every town in the world, hostels, where kids can stay if they're runaways and they give you money to call home and a bus ticket home. . . ."

"But they call the cops if you're underage."

"But we aren't underage." She reached into her backpack and produced two beautiful professional driver's licenses, describing her as Elaine Drogan, eighteen, and me as Kevin Drogan, nineteen.

"No way could I pass for nineteen!" I told her.

"You could. You're really tall. Look at Cathy. She looks about twenty-five and she's practically thirty-five!"

"Where'd you get these?"

"Ryan."

"Who's Elaine Drogan?" I asked.

"She's dead," Caro said, again with that complete nonchalance. She was staring seriously in the driver's-side mirror at her eyeliner. "She's a dead baby. So is Kevin. That's what you do. You get a birth certificate for somebody who died and apply for all their stuff under their name. They died in a fire."

"Is it against the law?"

"Yeah, probably. But we aren't going to rob banks with a couple of fake driver's licenses. We just want to find our lost father for our sick mother." She pressed her hands together under her chin like a choir singer and closed her eyes.

I saw how God created Leo.

Gabe's Journal

Probably because it was two days before we left, I got sick two days before we left. I lay in bed on the day before spring break started, shivering and burning, and my mother made chicken noodle soup with her own noodles, and I wanted to puke and tell her the whole thing.

Caroline kept coming in and warning me, "Don't say anything. You'll blow it all. . . ."

But I knew we had to tell one adult.

We *had* to.

If we got goddamned arrested or hurt out there, what would we do? We'd be unconscious, or dead, and we'd be the dead Drogans, who were already dead, so who'd care? We'd end up in some unmarked grave in fucking New Hampshire, and my mother would eventually find out when the animals uncovered our molars and would commit suicide.

So when I packed, while loading up on jerky and peanuts and raisins and junk, I called Cathy and asked if I could see her at her house. She was immediately leery. I got about two sentences into explaining when she began shaking her head. Honor bound by being an adult, she immediately vetoed the whole thing as irresponsible and nuts.

"You do it, then, Cathy," I said honestly. "You're her best friend. Somebody has to go find him. Gramp hired a private detective, and he paid him a thousand bucks, and he's spent two weeks going through Leo's bank records because he has strict orders not to ask Mom any questions or upset her. . . ."

"I can't leave her now, Gabe. You know how sick those shots make her. On the other hand, your grandparents could come over, and I could fly out—"

"Out where, though, Cathy? You'd have to look all over the eastern seaboard. . . ."

"I can't take off that much work, Gabe! I've taken off so much already because of—" She stopped.

"Because of my mom," I said. "That's what I *mean*. And we can't send my grandparents."

"Why? You probably could. Well, theoretically."

We exchanged a look of unmixed comprehension. We both knew why. What we found might not really kill them, but close enough. So I said something more neutral. "Well, there's the practical reason. They're going to Florida to get their stuff. They already sold their share in the condominium. And there's . . . He wouldn't listen to them. We have at least a chance. I stockpiled some columns," I further offered. I was getting to be a real reporter. Stockpiled. Words my mother used.

"What were they?" she asked.

"Some woman asking if their having a baby would help their marriage have more common ground between them . . ."

"And you said . . . ?"

"It would *definitely* put more ground between them, like a continent, so that unless she wanted a child for reasons completely unrelated to her marriage . . ."

"You're going to be a therapist, Gabe."

"Not me," I said. "I already feel like the sin eater whenever I read those letters."

"The . . . ?"

"The story you told me. They had to hire a starving person. . . ."

"Maybe that *is* what I do, and what your mom does."

"I think you do it more. I mean, they walk out feeling better. . . ."

"That's what I want," Cathy insisted.

"But don't you feel like all the air's been let out of you?"

"You develop a tough hide, but maybe. . . ."

"Anyhow, that's what I feel about the column. I don't want to know their problems. And they're always the same problems. People never make the same mistake once."

"Your mom used to say that."

"I heard it from her," I confessed.

"Why did you stockpile more than one column?"

"In case this time she got sicker, or we had a hard time convincing him."

"Maybe," Cathy said thoughtfully, touching my cheek, "maybe you feel that way because . . . you're her son. I mean, you're more her son. Maybe I wouldn't think another kid could do this. And I don't think you *should* do this. But I think you can." She brushed Abby Sun's long hair with her long fingers. "Well, you have to take a cell phone. I'll get one today, in my name"—she held up one palm—"no, I'll give you mine and get another one. You already know the number of mine. And I do. My mom should have a cell phone, I guess. Be wise and don't object. You have to call me every day. At the same time. Eastern time. You have to take enough extra money from me to get plane tickets home if anything, and I mean *anything*, goes wrong. You can give it back. And didn't you even think your mother was going to want to talk to you, while you were with Jane . . . ?"

"We thought we'd tell her we were lousy about calling and that stuff."

"That's so limp, Gabe," Cathy said. "Here's what I'll do. I'll let you talk to her a couple of times. You say, Fine, Mom. Fun, Mom. Yeah, I met a girl, Mom. She'll be half out of it, especially at first, so I don't think she'll remember all that much. . . ."

"Do you think he'll come home when we find him, Cath?"

"I think he'll come home, Gabe," she said, taking my one huge hand in her two little ones, a gesture I would loathe as phony from anyone but her, "but I don't think he'll stay."

"That was another letter. The guy had an affair, and the woman wondered what they should do to try to repair the marriage for the children. . . ."

Cathy leaned back and tried to pull Abby onto her lap, but Abby had other plans and ran off to get her goldfish tambourine. "You said try counseling. Try hard. But—"

"But it won't work. It usually doesn't."

"Which is true. But it buys the kids some time." Cathy sighed. "Well, I shouldn't let you do this. But Leo needs to come back here. He has to face the music. At least make sure that you're safe. That she's safe. He owes her at least that much."

"Well, no matter what, she'll feel she's come down in the world. Being a tenant. Having nothing."

We let that sit between us for a moment.

"Well, *she* might have a tenant," Cathy said.

"She's going to take in boarders? That's a bit . . . out there."

"I was thinking of me, Gabe. Your mom told me once that now that I'm a mother, I'm too old to still live with my mother. And Connie's thinking the house is getting too big for her. She'd like a little condo. Julie and I talked about it. We could help each other out."

"I could see that you'd help her out, but how would she help you?"

"It's not all about money. It's about company, too. She helps me by just being there to listen." Cathy punched me on the arm. "Come on. It would be like our own little community. You've got Leo's sacred room and no one's using it."

"That's what my dad wanted!" I said. "You should hear about these places. Caro cracked into his e-mail. She can read whatever he writes."

"She figured out his password?"

"Yeah."

"One of your names?"

"Yeah. It is now. 'Aurora.'"

"Huh. Well, as for those places. They're not all loonies, Gabe. They're getting more common. They're not like . . . the Manson family. They're just people who want time more than money. It's not that big a deal these days for married couples to share one job, or get a smaller house on purpose. . . ."

"I'd *hate* that. A house with no privacy; they have these little houses where all you have is a bed and a chair for everyone to read, and the parents' room is the only one with a wall. . . ."

"I've heard about them. I even once, Saren and I considered—"

"Jesus, Cathy, I thought you *weren't* nuts."

"It was in Big Sur, Gabe. Not Nebraska. Come on. That nuts I'm not. But there are some big pluses to . . . having less stuff to worry about and maintain, and sharing a common vision with the people you hang around with."

"You should definitely go," I said, disgusted. "You could bond with Leo."

"But, Gabe, isn't one of the things that drives you nuts the most about your school the percentage of assholes per square foot? What if you went to a school where everybody wasn't just like you, but they were okay with however you were . . . we just thought that would be good for Abby. I don't mean *Abby*. I mean if there ever was an Abby; she was theoretical at that point. But I thought we'd stay together and eventually have a child or adopt a child. And we wouldn't have been deserting anyone to do it."

"I'm glad you didn't do it, though."

"Yeah, so am I. For a lot of reasons."

She rummaged in her purse and pulled out her cell and the charger. "Here. It has national roaming, for conferences I go to. About every thousand years. I'll get another one in a couple of days. But call me at your house." She stopped. "You look like shit, Gabe."

"I think I have the flu or something."

"Then you should wait a few days."

"I would, but we have to go while it makes sense that it would be a time when we would go. I have to beg her and tell her I feel better . . . or she won't buy it, and Gram and Gramp are only going to be gone a couple of weeks. If that. They're leaving tomorrow. They're talking about selling the cottage, too, in Door County."

"That's so sad," Cathy said. "But the Steiners are two of the thirty-seven great people. . . ."

"What's that?"

"You're the one who's Jewish. It's a Jewish saying. They say that in any given time, there are thirty-seven great people on the earth. Hannah and Gabe are two of them, for sure."

I went home and desultorily packed my three allotted outfits—jeans, khakis, rain pants, a rain poncho, T-shirts, one silk shirt with a dragon on it that tended to make me sweat, about six pairs of thick wool socks, running shorts, a swimsuit in case I had to shower in some den of lunatics in front of other people. A disposable razor (pink, the only extra Caro had) and bar soap you could use for your hair, too. Two toothbrushes (I'm a little OCD about my teeth). I picked the Beatles' *White Album* and the soundtrack from *Hell Hath No Fury,* and then I ran out of room and figured Caro and I would fight over her disc player.

I called Luke. "Mon," I said.

"Dude," he said.

"I'm headed for points east. See Jane."

"See Jane run," he said.

"See Jane golf," I replied.

"Why would you fucking do this to me when you know you have a driver's license?" Luke asked. "It's spring break. We could go to . . . Lake Geneva!"

"Why would you fucking act like everyone but your fucking jock tribe of hairy beasts didn't exist for four months and then expect me to be your chauffeur? You let me finish the musical alone. I had to pay Kelly Patricia to sing the songs, like, fifteen bucks. . . ."

"You finished it? You—"

"I made a cover. I turned it *in.*"

"You are my hero, mon. I totally owe you my life."

"I'll bring you a key chain from goddamned Nantucket or wherever. I haven't been to my aunt's since I was, like, twelve."

"You sick?" he asked idly. I didn't think you could tell.

"No."

"Something's fucked up with you."

I was holding the gun in my hand. The cell phone and the charger I put outside Caro's bedroom door. The gun went in the bottom of the backpack, all of it in one of the fancy dust bags my mother used to get purses in. I'd researched the gun on the Net and found it was old, a 1937 Colt police revolver, .38 caliber. I had no goddamned bullets for it, and I wouldn't have known how to put them in if I had had them. I had no idea whether they screened your backpacks to get on buses. I knew I would have to throw it in the trash if we had to take a plane. I had no idea why my dad had it. There was the skeet-shooting lady. Maybe he was trying to learn shooting as an art form. Maybe he had it for protection. Maybe he'd planned to kill us all in our sleep. Maybe we'd started to look like sheep to him.

I also had no idea why I was taking it with me. The worst I could do to anybody was throw it at them. The weight of it in my hand felt sneaky and dead. "I'm fine," I told Luke. "Hasta la bye-bye."

"Dude," Luke said.

"Yeah."

"My mom says Julieanne is really sick. Sucks."

"Thanks," I said.

"Julieanne is a decent unit."

"Yeah."

"Even my dad says fucking Leo should come back."

"He doesn't know. He's, like, in the wilderness. . . ."

"Fuck. That's not fucking okay."

"Yeah. Well. Cathy's here."

"I'll . . . uh . . . mow the lawn or something while you're gone. I owe you for the English project."

"It's April. The snow just melted. There's nothing to mow."

"Okay, I'll pick some shit up off the ground and put it in garbage bags. I'll take Aury to the arcade with one of my many fraternal units. I'll have my mom drive us. Since you're fucking leaving and you're the only freshman in the whole school who can use a car."

"Good," I said, my voice box hurting, whether because I was sick or lying I couldn't tell. I put the phone down and wrote him a note. *Luke, if I don't come back from here, write Tian and give her the earrings I got her for her birthday. It's in July. They're in my nightstand in a gold box. You can have my Hawaiian shirts and my boombox. It's only minimally busted. Dude.* It sounded lame, but I didn't want Luke to think I liked him overly much, even if I happened to be dead. Still, I wrote, *You were a good friend unit. Out, Gabe.* I left the note taped under the May page, figuring they'd see it when they turned over to April. It took me a couple of days to realize that, if we really did die or shit, no one would ever bother to turn over my room calendar again.

As it happened, I didn't myself turn over the calendar page until June.

EIGHTEEN

Proverbs 24

———————

EXCESS BAGGAGE
By J. A. Gillis
The Sheboygan News-Clarion

Dear J.,

In the past few months, the spark has gone out of our marriage. I'm starting to think my husband is tired of me. He's making critical comments about me, comparing my cooking to his mother's cooking, going out with his friends on Friday nights. I'm starting to think we need a baby to be more of a family. I think having a baby would give us some common ground, and it would help me feel more like an adult. We are both nineteen.

Lonely in LaBurton

Dear Lonely,

Having a baby right now would definitely put ground between you—like a continent. A guy who's having trouble staying home at night is telling you in big neon letters: HELLO! I DO NOT WANT TO BE RESPONSIBLE! And you're thinking of presenting him with another human being. Unless you have always had the secret desire to be a single mother on welfare, try getting a hobby instead of getting pregnant. Become a marathoner. Paint in the nude. A sad but true fact of human nature is that people pay more attention to people who aren't paying so much attention to their not paying attention. The real question is, are you sure you really want his attention?

J.

Dear J.,

I am just 14, and the total love of my life is 19. You would think the age difference would matter, but it's as if we were exactly the same age. When we're together, we're like two little kids playing in the sun. We love all the same things, from sunsets to anchovy olives! The thing is, he wants to have sex, and so do I, but I'm terrified of one thing. If my parents find out, I'll be grounded for life, and I'll never see him again. Help me, J. This is totally the perfect relationship, and my darling says only one thing could make it more perfect.

Dreaming in Delavan

Dear Dreaming,

If your major concern about whether you're old enough to have sex is that you'll be grounded if you do, you aren't even old enough to ask whether you're old enough. I don't care who you are, unless your boyfriend is very slow—and bless you if he is—there's no way a guy who's out of high school can "love all the same things" as someone in eighth grade. The only thing that can turn this delusion into a disaster is sex. And the total love of your life should be the first one to tell you that. Ten years from now, this age difference won't be a big deal. But trust me, neither will this relationship.

J.

"When's the closing on the house?" Cathy asked me some few weeks later. I'd just had my shot of Interferon, but the period of shakes and nausea that followed was lessening with each round. I'd learned to administer my own shots, practicing on an orange, and was feeling a backhanded competence. If I had to do this, at least I was going to *do this*. The shots would lay me down, but I'd be like one of those Bobo dolls we had as children; I'd take the blow and come up standing. I wanted to talk about the progress I'd been making, but Cathy was unusually upbeat and busy, skipping from topic to topic while making iced tea—but not eye contact. Cath was a big eye-contact person; I was feeling too woozy to get suspicious.

"What do you think the kids will find to do with Janey for eight days?" I asked Cathy. "My sister wouldn't know what to do with a kid for eight hours."

"Well, she's probably got tickets to every Broadway show that's playing, and she'll probably buy them their whole summer wardrobe, which will be, ah, good. . . ." Cathy said vaguely. It was not an incisive analysis.

"I hope they won't be too bored," I said.

"Oh, I think a break will be good for them, and you," Cathy told me. She was now straightening my closet, rearranging shirts *by color*. "You can spend some real time with Aury. We'll take them to, ah, the zoo and stuff. You know, Jules, speaking of which, I have to run. You're sure you're okay for now? I'll give you a call later."

"Sure," I said, puzzled. Cathy usually tried to hang around on my first, worst days.

Cathy was a lousy liar.

That night, as the inevitable sleep-and-crackers fog drew on, the kids were great. Extraordinarily great. They brought me ginger ale. They stayed in my room while I corpsed on the bed, too weak to hold up a book, covered in my thickness of blankets. Gabe gave Aury a bath and read to her.

"What d'you want to do, Mom?" Caro asked. "Want to watch TV? Want us to go get you a movie?"

"I couldn't pay attention to a movie," I said. "Just . . . whatever. You guys have already done as much as I could expect. You can go see your friends if you want."

"No, we don't want to leave you when you feel so crummy," said Caro, and at that moment, I actually believed her. "Let's . . . uh, play a game," she said.

I almost sat up, so great was my astonishment.

Given permission to leave, and not even a halfhearted attempt at a cur-few, Caro was electing . . . to play a game?

"You know, like a car game," Caro continued. "Like we used to do on the way to the cottage in Door County."

"Okaaayyy," I said softly, wondering what wires were attached to the detonating device. Gabe returned, reporting that Aury was already snoring.

"C'mon, Gabe, you start. It'll tire you out, Mom, and you'll be able to sleep," Caroline said, and she lay down on the big bed next to me.

Looking back, I really think she was sad that night. I really think she understood the enormity of what they'd planned, and wanted her mommy's protection. She wanted to be a regular kid again, just for that few hours. Maybe I'm wrong. But she nestled against me, rubbing glitter from her eye paste onto my arm.

"Okay. Greatest name of a football player," Gabe said.

"N'fair," I said, trying as hard as I could to enunciate. "I don't follow the game."

"Living, playing, or all time?" asked Caroline, and Gabe teased her, telling her she couldn't say "Brett Favre," because it was the only name of a football player she knew; and right then, it hit me.

"Johnny Unitas," I said. I'd always thought that name sounded like a comic-book superhero. I couldn't believe it belonged to an ordinary person.

"I can't beat that," Gabe said. "You pick."

"Presidents who served more than one term," I murmured, figuring they'd be unable to think of one.

"Jefferson, Clinton, Johnson, Reagan," began Caroline. We were stunned silent.

I finally recovered. "What about Roosevelt?"

"I thought you meant two, not four," said my sister.

"Three," I said.

"No, four," Caro said placidly. "He died during the fourth term."

"You pick," I told her.

"Greatest name of a Triple Crown winner," said Caro. "That's a horse that won the Kentucky Derby, the Preakness—"

"I know what a Triple Crown winner is," Gabe said irritably. Through the slits of my eyes, I could measure him wondering how he could sidle back to the kitchen table, where my computer was, and do a quick search.

"Secretariat," Caro said quickly.

"He was the fastest," I said. "I know that. Still is, I think. But I wouldn't say that was a great name."

Gabe said, "War Admiral."

Caro said, "Man O' War."

I said, "Okay. You pick."

"Greatest name of a play."

"Now or all time?" I asked.

"All time," she answered.

I thought so long I believed I'd fallen asleep and dreamed the names that paraded through my head: *Suddenly, Last Summer, A Midsummer Night's Dream, A Raisin in the Sun*, but apparently what I actually said was, *To Kill a Mockingbird.*

Gabe said, *To Have and Have Not.*

I said, "'S a movie."

Caro trumped us all with *A Streetcar Named Desire.*

"Best song that won an Oscar," said Caro, and voted for "Under the Sea." That was still her constellation: *The Little Mermaid*! She still thought *Sleeping Beauty* was a big romance. Panicked, I thought, *I can't do this. She's still too young. I can't put this poison in my body and leave her alone for days at a time. I'd almost come to believe in her ever-so-grown-up act. But it was an act. Leo, I thought. Leo, your dearest little girl needs her dad*. But we were playing a game. All I could think of was my mother, taking every chance she got to say that, when she was a girl, "The Man That Got Away" should have won instead of "Three Coins in the Fountain."

Gabe said, "Maria."

I lifted one hand and made my index finger nod in assent.

I saw them look at me. At last, they must have thought, Mom was blessedly asleep. I wondered what they would do. Caro covered my shoulder and kissed my cheek. A tear slid from under my lid, but she didn't see it, absorbed in pulling the tasseled cord on the bed lamp. My aching back and neck nagged for a painkiller, but I listened as they left the room. Gabe asked, "How come you knew all that shit?"

"Because I know all that shit, Gabe, that's how," Caro said.

"I didn't figure you for the two-term-presidents type," Gabe said.

"No, you think I'm a valley girl with shit for brains," Caro said, unperturbed. "But I'm not. That makes me all the more dangerous."

I hadn't told them to remember their acne cream or their thank-you cards for their birthday gifts. Not even kissed them good night—and I wouldn't have ever thought I was kissing them good-bye, really good-bye. I hadn't even asked them what they planned to do with Janey. Or reminded them to pack something other than jeans. But anything they did had to be better than this, no matter how gray and billowy the ocean at the summerhouse, no matter how greasy the air in Manhattan. They *did* need a break. I felt I saw a wave just then, rise up then, a great, gray glacier, and I dove into it and slept. When I woke, they were gone, and I didn't see them again until Leo walked them in through that same door.

NINETEEN

Gabe's Journal

I slept practically the whole first two days on the bus. When I woke up, we were entering the town of Pitt, Vermont. I'd stumbled onto the bus carrying a plastic bag in case I hurled, still sick as a dog.

Caro had fobbed Cathy off when she picked us up at six A.M., telling her I was "always like this in the morning." But after sitting in the next seat for thirty hours, feeling as though she was sitting next to a toaster, even Caroline started to think we should stop in some big town, like Manchester, so I could go to a hospital.

But when I woke up from feeling sick, I woke up completely well. Purged, like. I was desperate for food, and immediately ate everything in both our backpacks. The driver stopped, I washed as well as I was able in the lobby of some Holiday Inn with paper towels and liquid soap. Then, I bought six bottles of orange juice and three plain bagels in plastic wrap from a machine, ignoring the internal voice of my grandma Steiner about the slimy way the bagels looked ("Oy, gevalt!"). I found out that I'd been asleep for so long I'd forced my sister to finish reading *Andersonville* ("And," she said scornfully, "I *hate* literature!"). She grabbed two of the bagels and one of the juices. "We're practically there! You ate everything but our socks!" she said. "Have you figured out what you're going to tell them? The people there? About us?"

"I figure," I told her calmly, "that if our father is there, he's going to walk up to us and take us back to his little hut and we'll figure it out from there, so there won't be any problem."

"Have you figured out how we're going to get to the Crystal Grove or Cave or whatever from"—she consulted the gazetteer, the other thing besides her cell phone that Cathy had forced us to bring along—"there? From Marshfield?"

"Yes," I said, "we are going to hitchhike."

"That's suicide," said Caro. "We're going to end up raped in a ditch."

"Only in California," I told her. "You can't kill your hitchhiker in Vermont. It's a state law." I thought of the gun, wrapped in my sweatshirts. I could at least brandish it. No one was going to be tying us up and leaving us in a ditch.

No one was apparently going to be picking us up, either, we soon learned.

We sat for the next couple of hours in silence, watching minivans go past, the drivers doing the thing you do when you notice somebody who's, like, handicapped, but you're determined for them to think you didn't see them. I grew considerably more conscious of how I'd sweated and dried in the throes of my virus or what have you. I longed for a hot shower and clean clothes, and pulled the parachute silk of my jacket hood more tightly around my face. I must have looked retarded or dangerous or both. I tried to read a Michael Crichton book, one of a couple of paperbacks I'd grabbed out of my mother's donation box before we left, but I couldn't concentrate. I didn't really know what Dad would think of us being there, or what we'd say to him. Not that you should have to think over what you'll say to your own father, but these were bizarre circumstances for a surprise visit. I kept trying to plan my sentences for maximum impact, the way I'd heard him do when he did one of his arguments. How *do* you beg your own father to come home and take care of you? It's his job. *He* should have been the one trying to hitch a ride to get to us. The whole thing made me want to vomit, this time from nerves instead of flu. I didn't know how I'd feel about talking to Leo again, after so long, but I knew it wouldn't be good. I could see my mother lying there, her lips barely moving, as she said, *To Kill . . . a . . . Mockingbird.* I hoped to Christ the goddamned shots of cancer medicine worked for what she went through after taking them.

After a while, we walked a little way.

There was a store in Marshfield that looked like stores in old TV shows. It had a shelf of cereal, like, two kinds, Raisin Bran and not Raisin Bran. Oatmeal in a barrel. Six boxes of detergent.

Caroline asked for pita bread. I wanted to clock her.

I asked, "Pardon me. Can you tell us how to get to Crystal Grove?"

The old man who ran the place asked, "Whose grove?"

"It's a . . . I don't know, a place where everybody lives in the same place and they have little playhouses they live in."

"Oh, you mean the hippie joint. Nice folks, generally. Ayuh. Except they're taking in ex-cons now. Try to teach them better ways. I don't know that everyone doesn't deserve a second chance, but seems funny, with all them children there, to take that kind of a risk. Those are men who grew up in New York, Chicago. Not from here. Seems impossible they could adjust . . ." Caro began tapping her foot.

"But, we have to go there. . . ." she said. "Pretty much right away."

"Well, it's about seven miles to the crossroads, County C. Then you go left at the fork, another seven, eight mile. They have a sign about as big as my two hands, but you'll notice the apple trees, not just Granny Smith or Golden Delicious, but Garland, too. . . ."

"Can we hail a cab?" Caro asked.

"A cab?"

"Can we find a . . . ride? We, I don't think we can walk there. My brother is sick, and we just rode the bus from Wisconsin."

"No cabs around here."

"Oh," Caro said. There was a five-minute silence.

"Ned Godin. He'll be in shortly. He lives out there, does carpentry. Built the porch here for me. Nice porch. Good workman."

"And, so?" I asked. I wanted to say, Your point is?

"He might give you a ride back, once he gets his nails and such," said the old man. "One thing they can't grow's nails. Nobody can." *Ayuh, I thought*. They were slower here than in Sheboygan.

"And he'll be in . . . ?" I asked.

"Lemme see. It's ten now. Twelve, latest. He called. They have the one phone there. That's the sum of it. Don't see why they want to do it that way. Seems a person can do with a little privacy during a conversation . . ."

"Daniel!" came a voice from the back of the store, where, we saw, there was a little curtain, "Don't you go chewing off those children's ears." A tall old woman appeared; she had the best posture I've ever seen other than my mother's. "You can wait right here. There are two chairs by the window; that's right, where the checkerboard is. . . ."

We felt we had to buy something, just to sit there that long, and so we bought a bunch of doughnuts, and I don't think I've ever played more consecutive games of checkers in my life. Finally, the doorbell tinkled, and a big, heavy man with a beard strode in—he literally strode, like Paul Bunyan—with a big square wooden box on each shoulder.

"Snow again, you think, Daniel?" he asked.

"Could be. Sugar snow. Won't stick."

"I need fifteen pounds of sixteen-penny sinkers, Daniel."

The old man said that thing again, that sounded phony, like he was in a movie about a guy who owned a general store. "Ayuh."

"And a thirty-pound bag of wheat flour, two peck of potatoes," the man went on. The whole thing was like a movie about how you'd act in a small town—in a previous century. The guy was going to need a hand truck. I felt like I was going to crawl out of my own skin, waiting for them to talk about syrup and leaves and shit. The big guy had brought about seventy pounds of stuff out to the car and old Daniel was scribbling on a pad of paper and no one had mentioned us. Caroline kept kicking me in the shin.

Finally, I stood up and said, "Let me help you carry that stuff out."

"Eh, Ned. These here two young people need a ride out to your spread. Do you think you have room for them?"

"What business have you got at Crystal Grove?" the big man asked me, as if I were the CIA or something.

"We think our father is there, or at least we know he was there," Caroline said. "His name is Leo Steiner."

"I don't know any Leo Steiner."

"Well, he wrote lots of letters to India Holloway. We know that. They were friends."

"You say. Did you try to get a hold of him, by writing letters or trying to call him?"

"Of course we did; that's why we are here. He hasn't answered."

"Okay," said Ned Godin, "get in the truck. You look like you could use a sleep and a good meal anyhow."

People ordinarily converse in a car, but Ned Godin didn't say a single word for the entire twenty minutes it took to get from the town to the sign (really, about as big as your hand) over a huge wooden mailbox that read CRYSTAL GROVE. There was also a NO HUNTING and ABSOLUTELY NO TRESPASSING sign, which I guess is more severe than merely NO TRESPASSING.

"I expect," he finally said, "I'll let you wait in the car while I find India. Then she can talk with you."

We sat there and watched the windshield fill up with snow, for about ten hours.

At last, the passenger door opened, and there was this bright-eyed little old woman all in purple, even wearing high, purple, suedelike Sherpa boots, who said, "Hurry on into the big house. You look a sight."

Long story short, she wouldn't listen to anything we wanted to say until we got showered and changed and fed. They gave us coats and boots and sweaters and jeans from this other lady with gray hair but a young, rosy face, whose hair was twisted into a bunch of ropes and twists and clipped down. She asked us for our wash, and I said, "You don't have to bother, ma'am."

But she said, "I'm washing anyway. Doesn't matter how many socks I do." She said to call her Janet. It was also this same woman, Janet, who gave us big plates of soup with lentils in it—the kind of thing that Caroline would have moaned at if my mother served it, but was glad enough to have it after two days of nothing but two bagels. We ate all that and some homemade applesauce, and then Janet said, "You can meet India in her study. It's at the top of the stairs."

The *stairs* were the size of the whole front of our house and they led up to this balcony or gallery about ten feet across, all with big timbers of wood, whole trees it looked like, holding up a peaked roof where some birds were flying around. Off the gallery, there were some real little kids in a schoolroom, and a bunch of closed doors, and finally this massive couple of double doors standing open, with an iron owl holding each door, and we could see India at her desk, which also was big, bigger than our porch. I'd seen strange offices at the university, but India's office was undoubtedly the strangest office I've ever seen anywhere. For starters, where regular people would have a vase or a statue, she had bird nests. Like thirty of them. She had a stuffed snow owl so big it scared the hell out of me even though I knew it was dead. She quickly told us she had not killed it; it had died of natural causes and one of her sons, Pryor, had found it in the woods when he was a boy. There were rocks holding down stacks of paper, and little jars of colored water on the windowsill, a regular birch tree in a pot and, most peculiar of all, a human skeleton I had the feeling was not a model hanging on a stand, with India's woven purple hat on its spotty head.

"My husband," she said, gesturing with her pen at the skeleton, "Doctor Hamilton Holloway. This was his wish, you see, that he remain here, and I thought, why scatter ashes, when what better way to teach people, the children and the adults, the names of the bones than with a genuine human skeleton?" I didn't ask and hoped to Christ she wouldn't explain how Hamilton Holloway had been transformed from a dead body to a skeleton. "He died six years ago, at the age of eighty-five, and I think his bone structure speaks well of an active lifestyle, don't you?" We nodded. I didn't know what to say. I don't think anyone's skeleton looks particularly terrific. Caroline poked me in the back. "Moreover, it comforts me to have him here."

Mr. Holloway wasn't the only skeleton in the room. There were a few other heads, a deer, I guess, and something little, a squirrel, and the whole room smelled like the inside of a nutshell.

"But you're here about your father," India said, motioning us to sit down on some fairly normal chairs. She was herself sitting on a big blue exercise ball while she worked at her computer. "Your father was here, for a month, several months ago. He loved the place, and he was a genuinely nice man. But we had to ask him to leave."

"You did?" Caro squeaked.

"Yes, but not because of anything he did wrong. Although we have our own system for wrongdoing here, and it's not unheard of, the reason Leo had to leave was because our Gathering didn't believe his reasons for being here were consistent with our philosophy. You see, my husband started this intentional community with simply ourselves, our daughter and sons, and one other family, the Godins. They're still here, but so are about twenty other family groups, a few single people, and a few guests of my son Pryor. I'm sure if you spent any time with Daniel Bart at the store, he told you about the dangerous convicts. Well, they're not. They're young people who made a couple of serious mistakes in their lives, with drugs or thievery"—I had never heard anyone actually speak the word *thievery*, but she went on "—and it's Pryor's contention that working and living here can undo what their previous lives and their incarceration has done to them. I don't say it isn't a challenge."

"About our dad," Caroline said.

"Yes, of course," India apologized. "I'm continuing my husband's work, a study of the evolution of this kind of closed community, the ideals, the adjustment of new members, the inevitable conflicts of trying to live outside the so-called normal world, the personal stresses and rewards; and Leo was very interested, and I must say helpful, in helping me see how it was possible to set up a judicial—"

"I'm so sorry to interrupt," said Caroline, "but this is so urgent. Our mother is so sick, and we have to find our father. Why did he have to leave?"

"Well, that was just it," India said, as the lady named Janet entered quietly with a pot of tea and some cookies for all of us. "We don't accept members who are running from something, only people who are trying to find a way *toward* something. Leo was leaving behind a family, and it wasn't difficult to gather from our conversations that this was not an amicable or mutual parting. It's not that we don't accept divorced people. But we didn't think that Leo's reasons for leaving his family were valid, that he'd explored all the ways of healing before making a permanent break."

"A permanent break," I said.

"Yes, he intended to stay," India told us. "He said he'd brought everything that he needed and he intended to enroll, I believe along with a close friend of his from New York, whom we never met, after the mandatory three-month period of probation. He made a substantial donation. But though I can't say there was honestly anyone here who—excepting my son Pryor, who's rather the alpha male and I think was a little threatened by Leo's advanced degrees—didn't like him, we didn't want to put him through the waiting period knowing we weren't going to be able to accept him. So he left after, perhaps, a month, and I believe when he wrote last week, he said that—"

"He wrote you *last week*?" Caroline gasped. "We've been trying to find our father for months. We've been in hell. I mean that. I'm not making this up. Our mother is sick, and we had to sell our house. . . ."

"That was the problem," said India. "We thought Leo lacked responsibility for dealing with his past."

His past, I thought. Here we were, fifty percent of Leo's past, zero percent of his future.

I said, "Thank you. I guess we'll . . . walk back. . . ."

"It's snowing." India smiled. "You may have noticed. No, it would be irresponsible of me to send the two of you off in this weather and after you've had a shock. . . ."

"What did he say?" Caro asked.

"He said, I believe, that he was doing well, that he'd found the place for him, that he remembered us fondly. . . . I have two grandsons, Muir and Paul, who are about your age, and Jessica Godin, Willow Sweeny, Maggie and Evan Menzies, the Calder boys, and the Ramirez girl—Liliana— they're all within a year or so of you. You stay with us for a couple of days; get your strength back. Then we'll take you back to the bus. Do you need money? We can give you passage to the Hudson Valley."

"We're okay. We have money," Caro said softly.

"Then I'll ask Janet to show you to the little house we keep for guests, unless you want to stay here in the Gathering house. I hope you don't mind sharing a house; there's a private bedroom space. . . ."

"No, it's fine," I said. "We don't want to impose."

We sat facing each other across the pull-down table in the little house, neither of us knowing how to begin or whether it was worth saying anything. Caro finally tossed her head and said, "What does she know? Maybe he meant he'd found the place for him for the rest of his time away, not forever. At least now we know where he is. . . ."

"I'm for we just go home."

"Well, no, Gabe. We came this far."

"I got to sleep on it then."

I pulled down a bed, and heard Caro, as if I were dreaming her, talking on the telephone to Cathy. I heard her leave and return, after trying to shake me awake for dinner. Then, when it was dark in the room, I felt another hand on my shoulder and knew it wasn't my sister. Jumping up, I almost pulled the bed out of the wall. "Don't be scared!" the girl laughed. You could barely see her in the dark, but she was the pretty girl from the picture in the computer, Jessica with the long auburn hair. "I only came down here because your sister is watching a movie with the others, and I thought you might like to see the waterfall in the snow. It's something else."

If she hadn't been so cute, I probably would have pulled the blankets up and gone back to sleep. But, while she waited outside in her coat, I got dressed, then followed her along this twisty narrow path she said was a deer track until we could hear the water rushing. "Slow," Jessica said, holding me back, her small hand on my chest. There was a buck and a couple of does at the waterfall, drinking out of the tumbling water as if it were a bubbler. This was all pretty surreal. I'm standing in the snow, watching deer about six miles from the four corners of Nowhere. "See, they won't drink from the pool. But the waterfall, they like." She stepped out into the clearing. "Hi, deer people," she said, and the deer regarded her gravely with their dark golden eyes. "You better take off, because we're going swimming." The deer, in no hurry, ambled up the slope behind the waterfall.

Great, I thought. They've adapted to the point that they no longer feel cold.

"Come on," Jessica said, pulling off her coat and hat and then her sweater. She had on this stretchy sports thing under it. I had such a hard-on I thought I'd stab myself in the intestines.

"Uh, I don't think I can. . . . I don't want you to think I'm stupid . . . but I don't do ice-cold water."

"Neither do I," Jessica said, jumping in, basically only in her underwear, a jet of steam applauding her entrance. "Come on. You'll be surprised." I smelled the sulfur then, and I realized it had to be a hot spring, that the waterfall was runoff from a spring somewhere farther up in the hills. And so I pulled off everything but my running shorts and slid in. It was hotter than a bath. I felt my muscles melt. "There," Jessica said, "you were so scared. I thought guys from Wisconsin were tough."

There was nothing else to do. I kissed her. I felt sort of like hell about it, but you don't jump half naked in a pool with a guy at night if you don't want him to kiss you; and though I thought of Tian, and my private vow to never kiss another girl, Jessica was so beautiful, and I was clearly not the first person she'd ever done this with. When I ran my hand up her ribs, she kind of sucked in her stomach so I could get my hand under the sports bra. Then, she let her stomach back out and gently moved my hand away. "I like you.

But I'm not ready for anything else," she said. "My parents and I agree."

"Your parents know you're here, with me?"

"Sure."

I thought of her father's size, relative to my size, and felt like a popsicle stick. Suddenly, the idea of loyalty to Tian and the pull-down bed seemed very appealing. "I got to get back," I told her.

"Okay," Jessica said pleasantly. "Isn't this a cool place?"

"Yeah, but how can you stand the same people all the time?"

"Well, are you with different people every day?"

"No," I said. "But . . . well, yeah, I guess that makes sense. You're with the same people anyhow."

"See?" She began to climb out of the pool. "Turn your back," she said, "I can't put my clothes on over wet underwear." The thought of her stripping off her underwear behind my back was excruciating. When I turned around, she had her cap and boots and coat on, and I asked her to do the same. She was really a nice kid. I wished she lived in Sheboygan. Her "little house" was back farther in the woods, so she pointed me the way back to the guest place, and I started walking, seeing already I'd left the light on.

But as I got nearer to the guesthouse, I heard voices, muffled but you could tell they were angry, where the path cut to the left away from the waterfall. I veered off, curious. There was a little clearing, but the snow had stopped, and I could see a wide circle of tamped-down grass around a big old oak. There were two people either . . . well, fooling around or fighting. The one on the bottom was much smaller. Then I heard.

"Let me up, you bastard! I mean it, I'll scream!"

"Go ahead! No one will hear you," said the deeper voice.

But the first voice had been Caroline's. And she did scream. But the scream was cut off, as if someone stuffed something in her mouth. I heard fabric rip. My first impulse was to wade right in there and pull him off her. But the guy was about six twelve, and I had nothing in my hand but my pair of wet gym shorts. Running on my toes, I got back to the little house, rifled in my backpack, and got out the gun. I had to pray to God there wasn't some obvious way a normal person could tell, in the dark and at a distance, that it wasn't loaded. My chest literally thudding, I stopped at the lip of the clearing and called softly, "Get off her." The big bastard rolled to one side, and Caro began to kick and fight, but it took only one arm for the guy to hold her down, easily.

"Who the hell are you? Go away," he said.

I took a step forward, tried to remember various Mel Gibson movies, and took what I hoped looked like a military firing stance. "Let her go, or I'll shoot your balls off."

"Not at that distance," he said easily.

"Can you bet on that?" I was panting. "After all, you can barely see me, but I can see you perfectly, in the light. That is my sister there, you son of a bitch. And she's fourteen years old."

"You said you were eighteen," the guy scoffed, but he didn't let go.

"Gabe, he tore my shirt; my lip is cut!"

"Big man!" I said. What in the fucking hell were we doing here? Dipping in the pond and fighting off big, crazed rapists in the peaceful paradise of Vermont? "Big man to cut a little girl's lip! Get up," I said, waving the gun enough so the moonlight hit it and it sparkled.

"Okay, man, settle down," the guy told me, getting up first to his knees, then his feet. Stumbling, with one shoe off, Caro ran to me. "Put down the gun," he said.

"You gotta be really stupid. I'm from the real world, asshole. I've watched a lot more reruns of *Law and Order* than you have. This is a .38. You come any closer to us, and it'll make a hole in you big enough to throw a softball through. What I want you to do is walk in front of us until you get to the . . . shed or garage where the trucks are." He made a fast move toward me, but Caroline tripped him, and he fell, hard, his thigh against a shard of stump.

"Fuck," he cried. "You know my father owns all this? I'm Muir Holloway!"

"I don't care if you're Muhammad Ali! I'm the one who has the gun!" I said.

Grumbling, he began to walk, or limp, along in front of us until we reached this long tin shed. "The key's in the red one," he said, turning.

"Stand still!" My knees were rubber. "Caro, go check and see if he's lying." Caroline ran, hopping and prancing on one foot.

"They're in there!" she called.

"Get in!"

"Gabe, all our stuff is in that little shed. My shoe is in that clearing. . . ."

"You have your tennis shoes. . . ."

"And our money, and Cathy's cell phone."

"Run and get it then, our bags. That's all, fast. . . . So this is what the peaceful life of the commune leads to, you loser," I said to the back of this guy. I could see his muscles tense and roll under his shirt. The guy probably didn't need a coat because he had a full pelt of hair. "You know, you're named for one of the greatest naturalists in history, and you—"

Of course, he wheeled around then and knocked me on my ass. And as I was getting up, still holding the empty gun, he grabbed for a hoe and started to draw back.

Never since that night and never before it have I ever intentionally hurt another person. But I flipped the barrel of the gun in my hand and hit him first across the jaw with it, then when he reached for that wound, across the back of the head. He went down in the straw. I knelt and felt for his pulse, and it was strong and regular.

"My God, Gabe! Did you shoot him?" Caroline cried, throwing our stuff in double handfuls into the back of the truck. "And where did you get a gun?"

"Get in the truck, nimble wit," I told her, because Muir was already beginning to moan and stir. We gunned it out of there in fourth gear, down through the woods, and drove south for half an hour before either of us said anything.

"What were you doing with him?"

"He said he'd show me the hot pool," she told me. Must have been the night for it.

"Couldn't you tell he was an asshole?" I asked, thinking all the while, this is the girl who thinks Ryan, the Were-man of Sheboygan, who says 'Nam, as in Vietnam, so it rhymes with lamb, is a total hero.

"Where'd you find a gun?"

"Did he get to you? Did he rape you?"

"No," Caroline said. "No, I fought the whole time. Where'd you get the gun?"

"At home," I said. "In a drawer in Dad's dresser."

"*Dad* had a gun?" she whispered.

"Caroline, we don't even know Dad," I said, and she started to cry so hard she finally fell asleep.

You get to know far more, faster when you break the centrifugal pattern that holds you in the same routine of things you do and think and believe. In our case, it was more, faster than we ever wanted to know, and we didn't know anything yet. I called Cathy and told her I was on the bus to New York State. She let Mom hear me say "Hi," but said my mom had basically been asleep for two days. I was glad of that. She'd never know this.

I drove, so keyed up I could never have slept, feeling like my blood was full of little wires, hearing over and over again the crunch of the butt of the gun against that kid's jaw. How awful and how satisfying it was. I wanted to be home, and yet I knew that home was changed, forever, if home is something you keep in you, like a memory or an idea.

I drove until morning, until the light hurt my eyes. Then I pulled over in a rest stop outside a town called West Springfield, Massachusetts, and, after locking all the doors, fell down a hole into sleep.

We woke to the sound of a state police officer tapping on the windshield.

TWENTY

Gabe's Journal

The only reason that we are not in foster care in Massachusetts *to this day* is that, if there were ever an Olympics for liars, Caro would medal in every goddamned event.

I'm sort of exaggerating.

But it was tense there for a while.

The first thing the cop asked for, obviously, was the truck's registration. In fact, the truck had no registration, in the glove compartment or anywhere else. It did, however, have a revolver, in plain sight on the backseat. The guy asked for my driver's license, which I gave him, but then he asked me to get out of the truck and open the back half door.

"You can't do that," I said softly, standing quietly with my hands at my sides next to the truck, adding, "sir."

"And why would that be?" It was early in the morning, probably not even seven o'clock, and this guy looked like shit, either having just ended a lousy shift or just begun one. His eyes were red and his breath was evil and he wanted prey.

"It's, uh, and I mean no disrespect, it's illegal. You have no probable cause to search our car, and there's nothing in it but our clothes, and it's a violation of my civil rights. And on top of that, I'm not a minor. This is my sister, and we're going to my father's, and he lives right up the road about two towns. But we can't take a bus until one comes. . . ."

"Why do you need a bus if you got a truck? What if I book you for resisting arrest?"

"You'd have to arrest me first, and . . . look, I don't want to say any of this, my father's a lawyer . . ." I told him sadly.

Caro leapt out of the truck with cell phone in hand. "The reason the car has no registration is that we're *supposed* to leave it here to be picked up by Missus India Holloway of Pitt, Vermont. She gave it to us to get this far and we arranged in advance for her grandson, Muir, to pick it up here. Call her. She'll tell you." I wondered how she'd come up with this whopper. Caro, as she had probably done more than most people ever do, was just leaning on the arm of lucky charms. It had worked in the past. She smiled winningly and rubbed her eyes. Even I would have thought she was a little doll.

"I have my own phone, young lady," the officer said, but he didn't try to open the doors of the truck. This *was* Massachusetts, where they started all this rights-of-people junk. He walked back to his car and I could see him on the radio, then on the car phone. He then tipped his hat over his eyes and seemed to fall asleep while I stood there, unable to move or barely breathe but utterly wretched with the psychotic need to piss. I think police are trained to do this—to foster maximum frustration so that people become crazed and confess to shit even if they didn't do it. I had to wait his pleasure, and he knew it. My father once said state cops don't really have to wear black leather gloves. They buy them, themselves, because they like to. I knew if I moved, he'd, like, kill me. *His* gun had bullets.

Finally, he seemed to wake up, to notice us, and he walked back to our car. "I spoke to Missus Holloway's grandson, and this is your lucky day, because your story checks out. But you can't leave an abandoned vehicle in a rest area, because it's going to take them a day to come and get it, so if you'll just follow me into town, we can leave it in the parking lot at the station."

"Excuse me," I said. "Is it okay for me to use the bathroom here first?"

"No," answered the officer.

So we drove into town, about ten minutes of feeling my bladder fight to pop out of my body, and the cop watched us as we cleared our stuff out of the backseat and shoved it into our backpacks. As it happened, the gun had fallen off and was under the way-backseat, but I could see the tip of the handle from the corner of my eye as I shoved my socks and books and now-dry shorts into my backpack. I wondered if I should lunge for it. My gut said leave it there. It could only get Muir in more trouble, which would be a good thing. The cop then drove us to a diner, where he waited while we bought ham sandwiches, and then he drove us to the bus terminal, where we got our one-way tickets to Peekskill, New York, the only name of a town in New York, outside Manhattan, we could think of.

The first thing I asked Caroline was, "They lent us the truck?"

"Look, I didn't think he'd *buy* it! I figured," she said, with her mouth full, "that Muir would go to them with this bullshit story of how you beat him up and we stole the truck. But I took a chance because his grandmother didn't seem like an idiot. When we left that night, she told him to be careful and take a flashlight. She'd nag him until he told her what really happened, or most of what really happened. . . ."

"That was so likely, Caroline!"

"I didn't say it was likely! I said it was an off chance. I didn't think it through that far! I had to do something. You were talking about an illegal search. That's more balls than I've ever seen you show. . . ." She held her hand up as I began to object. "Except out there in the woods. Which I appreciate, of course. God, I don't have to tell you that. And the gun. Well, it's basically a collector's item if it doesn't have bullets . . . it doesn't have bullets, does it?" she asked me.

"No. But I'm completely sure they wouldn't have seen it that way."

"Well, like you said, Dad's a lawyer. Don't get all dramatic. We got lucky. That's all."

I had a headache the size of the Goodyear blimp. "Whatever you say, Caro," I told her. "Shut up long enough to let me sleep."

We got to Peekskill and found a bed-and-breakfast place and we splurged on a buck and a quarter for two rooms. I slept twelve hours, during which time Caroline ate two breakfasts, but the lady was nice and saved a bunch of food for me.

The problem was, we were there, in the Hudson Valley, but there's a lot of the Hudson Valley, and we didn't know which part of it contained Leo. That night, when we called her, Cathy commented on how tired we sounded. And my mother, now rallying and sitting up and eating miso soup and in her right mind, said, "You don't sound like you're having much fun. Let me speak to Jane."

I said, "She's out shopping. She's having this big dinner thing tonight with people who have kids our age." Couple more days, I'd be as gifted as Caroline. I went on, "Most of what we've done is sleep."

"That's good," Mom said. "You're kids. You've had too much going . . . I'm glad. Kiss Janey for me."

"We'll be home . . . soon," my voice began to crack as if I were fucking twelve. "We, uh, love you."

The next morning we had to ask the lady where the bus station was. She told us. It was like, twelve blocks, and she offered to drive us. "I hope you don't think me out of line," she said, "but I know you aren't nineteen. I also know you must be in terrible trouble to come this far alone, young as you are."

"We are," Caroline said stiffly, her lip quivering. "I'm just small for my age. I'm . . . anorexic."

"I know you're not," said the woman. "I didn't say I was going to do anything about it."

Caroline began to cry. "You don't know how far we came."

The woman didn't move, didn't try to hug her or anything, which probably made Caro respect her more. "I can imagine," she said. "Where are you going?" Caroline kept on crying. Her hair fell across her face, frizzed and helpless-looking.

"We have to find someone. We don't know where he is," I said. "Actually, I have no clue. I know he's somewhere next to the river, because he wrote about it in his e-mails, and we have all of them. We're really desperate right now, because we're trying to find him. We have to. He talked about a place called Sunrise . . . Hill? Road? Crossing?"

"The weavers. Yuh," she said, "the ones who sell jam."

"He didn't say that name. Weaver."

"No, they weave. They sell weaving, cobweb scarves and afghans and things at the art fair. And jam. They're famous for their jam. Let me think. Sunrise . . . Valley. Is that it?"

"Thank you, ma'am," I said. "That's it."

"How do we find it?" asked Caro.

"If you took the bus, you'd take the bus to Irvington, then . . . but you can't do that. Let me get my wallet and such . . ." she said.

"How far is it?"

"Good two hours."

"We can pay you," Caro said. "We'll pay you . . . what does it cost? The gas? I . . . really don't drive. I'm fourteen."

"Thirteen, fourteen and about a minute, I'd guess," said the woman. "And no bigger than one. My name is Virginia. I won't hurt you. Though I reckon if I were you, I wouldn't trust anyone about now."

"Look, it almost doesn't matter," I said.

"Well," she said, "I don't need the money that much. We'll just call it a benefit of the breakfast package." She wrapped up thick slices of bread for us, with peanut butter and jam, and called upstairs to her husband, "Warren, I'm going to run over past Irvington. You want anything?"

"We have people coming in at two, and in the Rose Room. I think those need to be seen to," a gravelly voice called back.

"See to them then, darling," called Virginia. We went out the back door and got into her Dodge Durango.

The country we drove through was some of the most beautiful I have ever seen in my life. The river birches had their little tongued leaves out, and there were clusters of little purple flowers in the sunny spots, even if there was snow on the other side. We drove up these lanes of sugar maples, and a couple of people waved at Virginia from these little houses that looked like houses never look in real life, white and covered with little lattices and scallops of painted wood, not dirty but shiny white with scallop-shell drives. You could imagine lives in those houses, how even the sweaters would smell clean. You could imagine wanting to hide there. I thought of our house, which to me smelled sort of perpetually like urine.

At Irvington, Virginia stopped at the Central Perk for coffee, and she bought Caro and me each a cup, mine chocolate-toffee with whipped cream. "You look like a toffee man," she said.

"Yes, ma'am," I said. "Thank you, ma'am." When she saw me eyeing the slices of lemon cake, she bought a couple of those, too.

We drove up some hills with these fields of horses and their little-legged babies and down into a long valley between two hills that followed a creek.

Finally we rounded a turn with a big square yellow sign that read BREAKDOWN LANE.

"What's that?" I asked Virginia.

"Well, that's . . . I don't rightly know what you call it where you come from—where you pull off when your car's in trouble. . . ."

"The shoulder of the road," I said.

"The shoulder of the road," she said. "I've never been out west. Sounds romantic."

Caroline leaned forward from the backseat. "Do you think he'll want to see us, Gabe?"

"Sure," I said.

"Do you think we should call Cathy, right now?"

"Nope."

"Gabe!" Caro cried, and I don't know what she expected me to do. I gave her my ball cap, which she stuffed on her head, pulling all her pale curls in a brush out the back of the rim. Then, she sat back and bit her cuticles.

Right below the sign that read BREAKDOWN LANE was one of those little clusters of signs on a pole, all pointed in different directions, like a stripped Christmas tree. One of them, which pointed down a gravel road to the left, said SUNRISE VALLEY, BEWITCHING WOOLENS AND SACRED WORKOUTS.

"She teaches classes. Dance or some such. And she makes jam I get by the case for my breakfasts. It's that good. The one, maybe Jane? Jean? I'm not sure what her name is. But she's the one that makes the jam. I know the mother a little, a Miz Devlin, Claire Devlin. I've bought several of her scarves and quilts. Gifts for my daughters in Boston. She has five daughters, and they all have kids and husbands, and then there are other families who all live on the same acreage. Share expenses and such. They built an exercise building down in there they call a 'kiva,' as the Indians would. It's basically a shed with a wooden floor and curved walls. People come from all over . . . nothing sacred about it if you ask me."

The shadow was deepening under the maples, some still heavy with wet snow. Virginia stopped at a mailbox and got out of the car, and before she could even get to the walk, a woman about her age but a lot thinner and prettier came out and hugged her. "Virginia Lawrence! What brings you all the way over here?"

"I have two friends with me," she said slowly, "who need to find a man they think . . . they think might be living here."

"Well," the other woman said, peering at us, me in the front seat and Caro in the back. "Children?"

I got out and stretched my legs. I wasn't as tall as I would get, but I was nearly six feet. I could see the woman measure me. I looked back at her with what I hoped was a look that said nothing except, we come in peace, like we were aliens. Caroline and I had been like creatures staying out of the light the whole way, and we were at the end of the road. The getting here had been one thing. The being here was another. I looked at her and considered the years between us, the insults we tossed at each other like wads of balled-up paper, the slammed doors. It all seemed like such kid shit. And we weren't kids anymore. I walked over and got Caro out of the car and put my arm around her neck, trying to goof off a little.

"There's no Leo Steiner around here," Virginia said dryly, as she came back to the side of the car. "But up in that house where Joyous Devlin lives, is a man called Leon Stern."

Leon.

I began to walk, with Caro slipping along behind me on the wet leaves. So did Virginia. "You don't have to come," I told her. "We don't expect you to do any more for us. You've done more for us than most of our family, to be honest."

"No reason to stop something I started," said Virginia. "What if he's not the man, your father?"

"We never said it was our father," Caro murmured.

Virginia smiled tightly. "Lucky guess."

The girl who opened the door was older than Caroline, maybe twenty. She called for another girl, who was probably a little older than her, maybe . . . you can't tell how old women are. Maybe she was twenty-five. "Hi," she said. "Do . . . can I help you?"

"Well," Virginia said evenly, "they want to see Leon Stern. Is Leon Stern here?"

A voice came from the back of the house. "Is it Jim? Tell him I'm not done. Rome wasn't built in a day." And he came in off some kind of porch, wearing his stupid rubber shower slippers he always wore in the morning, and a shirt with little woolen checks over a plain white undershirt. He was thinner and had a beard. He was my father. He was carrying a little baby who looked just like Aury looked when she was practically a newborn. Caroline cried, "Daddy!" and began to step up into the house, but the older girl blocked her way.

"Wait a minute," she said, not unkindly. "Just . . . wait a minute. This is my house. My little boy is in there. What's going on here? Leon? Who are these people?"

"Hi, Leon," I said.

TWENTY-ONE

Second Samuel

―――――――

EXCESS BAGGAGE
By J. A. Gillis
Distributed by Panorama Media

Dear J.,

I could die. Really. We were at this outdoor cookout and suddenly my best friend blurts out this horrible, embarrassing thing we did when we were about twelve years old. She was laughing hysterically, but everyone else got silent, and stared at me! And now, everywhere I go, someone acts like they've heard about it, and I'm sure they have. There were fifty people there. This was the person on earth I totally trusted. Plus, she did it, too. I don't know what my kids are going to think if they hear. But I don't want to lose her friendship! Because it's been forever! My best friend and I are both 37.

                                        Outraged in Oregon

Dear Outraged,

You have what they call on cop shows a legitimate beef. You have every right to feel hostile and hurt and to behave like a ninth-grader—all of which you're doing, by the way. One thing you deserve is an answer, a chance to find out why, after so many years of closeness, she felt the need for an overt act of *hostility, and don't kid yourself, this is what that was. Maybe she's been holding on to a grudge. Maybe you two can talk it out. But if she says it was all a joke, ixnay with the friendship. Even if she apologizes, which I wouldn't expect, remember you're accepting a "pardon me" from a snake that bit you. Some people don't get another chance.*

J.

Dear J.,

My mother totally invades my privacy, reads my e-mail, makes me leave a phone number wherever I'm going, has me call *her from there, and generally is ruining my life. I'm thinking of running away.*

PO'ed in Plankinton

Dear PO'ed,

Ask your mom to respect your privacy in certain things, like written communications and phone calls. Tell her that if she has to ask questions, and all good parents who give a damn do, to try doing it without being judgmental. In exchange, you give your promise to be honest. It has to be a two-way street. But if you really want to punish her, by all means, *do run away. Of course, you'll also ruin your own life and spend the next twenty years trying to get it back, and you'll learn how it feels when nobody at all cares whether you leave a number or not. But your mom will be really miserable.*

J.

On the Saturday before Easter Sunday, I woke feeling exceedingly odd, as if someone had subleased my body during the night. I probed for what the difference was.

It was this. I wasn't dizzy.

I stood up. I wasn't dizzy.

I walked around the room. I wasn't dizzy.

I took a ballet stand and spotted on the Chinese powder jar on my shelf. I did a cabriole, expecting a concussion. But I didn't fall. I did another. I ran down the hall to wake Cathy, too selfish in my exultation to realize that she'd been the sole caretaker of a preschooler, a toddler, and an invalid for nearly a week, and deserved to sleep past seven A.M. I felt good, not just better, or getting over my reaction to the medicine, but really better. *Good.* Like myself. Cathy would fall over. But she was already awake, Aury was in her bed, playing with Cathy's hair.

"Cath!" I whispered. "Watch."

I did it again, in the hall, the cabriole.

"Julie!" she cried, with appropriate amazement and joy.

"Oh, please, Cathy, can we go to class? Please? Can we leave the girls with Connie just for an hour? This stuff is working, can you believe it? I feel like . . . like a person. Like me!"

She smiled and yawned and said, "Sure. That's so great. Jules, I'm happy."

I showered, marveling at the splendor of the grains of oatmeal in the soap, at my ability to lift one leg and soap my toes, clip my own nails into the toilet without following them in, pull on my unitard and lace my shoes. Myself! Good girl, Mommy! I ran out into the kitchen and swung Aury around. She felt as though she weighed seventy pounds—maybe she did weigh seventy pounds—but I could spin around and not hurt my little girl. We bought the girls breakfast sticks of some variety from the Culver's custard stand, then headed to Connie's. "I want to take them in," I begged Cathy. "Look, Cath. There's a snowdrop. There's a daffodil, Connie! Watch," I commanded her and did an open pirouette in the driveway.

"What's come over you, Julie?" she asked.

"I don't know, I guess, I guess this is what they were hoping would happen!"

"Don't be overdoing," Connie remonstrated, drawing the girls to her, "you know that can lead to worse."

"But I feel like overdoing! This didn't used to be overdoing, Connie. It used to be doing."

"I know," she said, "but you're ill now."

"Not right now," I told her. "Not right this minute."

Except for Leah, who said, "Hello, Julieanne," the rest of them behaved as though a ghost had walked into the room. They placed themselves along the barre, giving me extra room.

It was hellish. I hadn't done any exercise since Caroline and I had gone to ballet months before. My arms felt as though they were wrapped in sandbags, my legs ached, and I could feel the muscles object, then refuse my long-neglected turnout. After fifteen minutes, I was covered with sweat. After a half hour, I had to go and sit down on the Pilates mats and slug down a whole bottle of water.

The time for center-floor work arrived, and Leah, for reasons inscrutable to me, prescribed a combination that included a series of glissades ending with a *ballotte*. "Julieanne, please demonstrate," she said, and I looked up at her, horrified.

I could not get up off the pile of mats.

I willed my arms to push me off, and they remained rigid, my hand clenched around the water bottle. The women watched; one teenager tapped her toe. Finally, Cathy walked over and pulled me to my feet, and, as if I were a wind-up toy set in motion, I walked to the far corner of the room and did the combination. Grand jeté, now, the instructor continued, and I did . . . three, the sensation of flight now a sensation of pulling a large animal from sucking mud.

"Now, let us stretch," she said. And as we began walking back to our places, this little red-haired woman I recognized only because she lived not far from me and seemed to have a dozen or so red-haired children whom she was always pushing or carrying on her back as she jogged, began, lightly and timidly, to clap. Cathy joined heartily, and soon all of them were clapping. The instructor walked over and took my shoulder. "Brava, Julieanne," she said. And no one said another word. We stretched.

My second shower of the day was accomplished by sitting on a rubber stool in the bathtub.

I wasn't disease-weak. I was worn out. Good tired. I'd moved that morning more than I had in ages. But I was grateful to feel that way. Still capable of feeling that way. Cathy went to her mother's for lunch and then said she was going to take advantage of the weather and take the little girls to the park.

So I slept for five hours, even though I was afraid I might sleep through the kids' call. The kids would be home from my sister's tomorrow anyway, and the closing for the sale of the house would be Monday. There's a strange sensation—you recall it from childhood—about sleeping in the afternoon. You rise into a different world from the one in which you lay down. The shadows have been rearranged. There's a sensation of sad sweetness, as if something has been overlooked. I used to feel it coming out of the movies just before dinnertime, after the matinee. How, I wondered, did Broadway actors face it, this bittersweet sense of time's slipping past. When I woke, the first sight I saw was the windmilling shadows of the blades of the ceiling fan above my head as I lay in a room darkened by the approach of sunset.

I thought I was dreaming then, because I heard something. A cry. Not Abby or Aury. I heard a little baby cry.

TWENTY-TWO

Gabe's Journal

My father is probably unflappable, or he would have flapped his way out the nearest window the minute he saw us. He recovered quickly, though I could see him swallowing as though he had a bread ball stuck in his throat. How glad he was to see us, his best beloved and bedraggled children, after fucking six months, was touching.

He looked at us like we were bringing him a subpoena.

"Umm, Joy," he said, after a pause so long it was more expressive than any words could have been, "I want you to meet my children. My *other* children. This is Caroline and this is Gabe." In some miserable fashion, I wanted to laugh. Here we were, like the people Cathy talked about so much. *Othered.*

The older girl shook hands with us. She had long, freckled hands and smelled sweetly of peach. "I'm Joy, and I'm sure you've guessed that this is Amos."

We sure hadn't guessed that this was Amos, or who Amos was. But that was quickly cleared up. "Amos is Joy's and my son," said my father, not just the new Leo, but the newborn Leon.

"Dude," I said, "have a cigar." I would have fallen down in a chair had there been one.

"How did you . . . get here?" my father asked.

"Jeez, we're glad to see you, too," I told him.

Virginia was still standing in the doorway, a solid pillar of Yankee outrage. "I drove them here, sir. And I want you to know, they've come all the way from Wisconsin on a bus."

"We had to find you," Caroline apologized, slipping under Dad's free arm. He handed the baby to Joy. It was a pretty cute baby. Still is. But then, Aury had been a pretty cute baby. Still is.

I said, "I'm sure my father would also have liked you to meet his other daughter, Aurora Borealis Steiner. She's two, and not old enough to bus cross-country."

Joy, dressed in black tights and a long sweater, looked bewildered. I was to learn this was her regular look.

"Well, I'm grateful to you," my father said. "I'm grateful for your making sure they got here safely."

"I made sure they got through the last two hours safely," said Virginia. To Caro and me, she said, "Good luck. And remember, if you need a ride back, please call me." We thanked her. And she left, angrily shaking her keys out of her pocket.

" 'Bye, Missus Lawrence," Joy called. "Imagine, of all the people in all the world, you meeting Missus Lawrence. I'd call that a miracle, though my mother is pretty well known. . . ."

"Well, it saved us a two-hour bus ride and, oh, about a two-hour walk," I said.

Then everyone stood there.

"I guess I should explain," Leo finally said, with a sigh. I gazed pointedly from Joy and . . . Amos (he was probably named after Tori Amos, judging from the look of the place). You can tell if a house is normal by a quick scan of the books. On Joy's shelf, there were about eight—three of them by Danielle Steel. The rest of the shelves looked like India Holloway's office: birds' eggs and dried grasses stuck in straw holders. India had at least three yards of books, all serious. But I digress. "This is Joy's sister, Easter," my father added.

"Call me Terry," said the younger girl, or woman, what have you. She was also very cute and curvy, and if I hadn't wanted to rip out Leo's lungs, I would have spent more time staring at her. As it was, she made some blithe excuse about having to get something "at Mom's" and made herself scarce.

Finally, I leaned against the front door and said, "Come on, Pop. Calm down. We don't have to leave right away. Quit making such a big fuss."

"Would you like something to eat?" Joy asked. "I guess we weren't expecting anyone. Or some iced tea? I make great green tea with spices on ice. Don't I, honey?"

My father winced. "This looks very different from what it is, Gabe," he said. "Actually, there was a tacit understanding between your mother and me—"

"She's pretty tacit all the time now, Dad," I said. "She has multiple sclerosis."

A legion of emotions crossed his face: pity, relief, and a sort of eye-rolling "what next" expression. Finally, he slumped and slapped his forehead. "What are you telling me? What are you talking about? Are you sure?" he asked and sighed.

"I came, uh, about fifteen hundred miles to talk to you, and that was going to be one of my higher-agenda items," I told him.

"We got fake driver's licenses . . ." Caro began.

"I think *somebody here* needs to eat," Joy announced, jiggling the baby, who was whimpering. She headed for the sunroom, God granting at least one small favor in that she didn't whip out a boob right in front of us. "There's mint in a dish on the windowsill if you want it with your tea." I had to drink the tea her hands made because I was so dry my tongue was mortared to the roof of my mouth. Caroline began wandering around the room, picking up and examining things. She held up one little carved wooden statue of a barrel-chested little guy with a huge dick.

"Looks like Muir," she said to me.

"You met Muir?" my father asked. He had not yet invited us to sit down.

"I've got a better question. It's a 'why' question. Why is Amos living?"

"Come on," Leo said, "let's take a walk."

"Well, no, Leon," I told him. "These here boots are pretty much soaked through, and Caroline's tennis shoes are from last year. We've had to tighten our belts a little and cut down on all the electronic gadgets and such. Like, clothes. So if we could just sit down here in your house for a moment."

"You know, I love both of you very much," he said.

"We know, we know!" I said, parodying Grandma Steiner. "With this much love, I'd like to try hatred."

"Look, come and sit in my study, both of you. There's a great view of the woods. . . ."

I lost it there. "Listen, you dumb asshole, no disrespect intended, that's a description, not a cuss word. *Your* daughter, the one who's here, almost got raped on the way here. I almost got arrested. I'm fifteen fucking years old, Dad, and I've already stolen a car and pistol-whipped a guy. I'm doing part of Mom's job, and half the time she says 'banana' when she means 'backpack.' We found a gun in your bedroom drawer! Are we getting through to you? I don't care about your view of the fucking woods! I don't care how at peace you are! You need to answer to us, Dad! *Leon!* You need to tell us what gave you the right to ditch us and refuse to answer our phone calls, so that we finally had to track you down like you were some fugitive. . . ."

"Gabe," he said mildly. "I am a fugitive. Or I was. Until I found home. You'll understand someday. Home is not a place. It's a place inside you—"

"Listen!" I shouted, and from the other room, I heard Joy whisper, "*Shush,*" and quietly close the door. She began to say a rhyme.

Goodnight moon, I thought. I was standing here talking to some stranger who'd once thrown me up over his head, who'd taught me to read by spelling out the letters in headlines in *Rolling Stone,* who gave me half his genetic material, and who obviously was as attached to me as he would have been to a virus. On some level, buried, I realized I had hoped, even until the last step up into this house, that Leo would still want us, that he would still be our father. I think I had some vestige of belief in that most adults are good. Or at least most adults I'd known. But he sat there like a mope. Like it was tiresome how we'd shown up and stomped his day. I finally said, "You're totally happy. Zippy for you. But your happiness means that our mother, your *legal* wife, is completely miserable, not to mention in really bad pain. And there's the matter of us, and you have another little kid, you remember her, you must have guessed, that would be Aurora Borealis Steiner. And she's using your power whatever to sell the house. . . ."

That got his attention. We were in his study in ten seconds. It did have a really great view of a ridge topped by trees. "Gabe," Leo began, "you're not really old enough to understand this. But I'm going to talk to you man to man."

"Talk to Caro man to man also," I suggested. "She was the one who figured out how to find you."

"That's my girl," our father said, beaming. "You've got a good head on those shoulders, Caroline. You'll make a lawyer someday."

"Whatever," Caroline said, picking at the tapestry on her chair.

"Well, it's a matter of passion," he told us. "I felt all the passion had drained from my life. Julieanne is a terrific person. She's a wonderful mother—"

"Save it," I said, noticing for the first time how I towered over him.

"But her life was *you,* Gabe. You and Caro and Aurora. And appearances. The right thing to do. It was what Romberg calls an 'apparent' marriage, not a soul-completing relationship. We appeared happy. We *appeared* to have attained the American Dream. But I was miserable, Gabe, since before Aurora's birth. I felt like a man in prison. The challenge had gone out of my work, and my personal life, my life as a man, was completely eclipsed. I told you, it made me near psychotic. The desire to get out of the law department. There would be people who would say I should have been more honest, but wouldn't that really have just been—"

"There would be a lot of people like that. Including your own parents," I said.

"Well, I expected you to be angry. I want to honor that."

"Will you please talk like a person?" I begged him.

"When I found out that Joy was pregnant," he began, "I . . ."

"As a result of . . ." I interrupted.

"Our last visit," he said, "that month, last year. I had to make a choice. She's a very honorable person, Gabe. An alive, energetic, seeking person. Happy, congenitally happy. She wants to fix the world's problems, Gabe. She knows that's impossible, but she runs on hope. And she would not violate any bond between your mother and me until I could assure her that the bond was irrevocably broken . . . so we waited," he said.

"You waited?" I sneered, pointing in the direction Joy had gone with Amos. "Why didn't you wait until you assured Mom the bond was irrevocably broken?"

"She should have known that!" Leo burst out, getting up to do his attorney's pace. "I tried to tell her over and over, but she wouldn't accept it. I tried not to be cruel. I tried not to say, 'It's not there for me anymore, Julie.' But she just kept dancing her way through life. . . ."

"Don't worry. She's not wasting a lot of money on ballet lessons anymore," I said.

The room felt like a hothouse, probably because every flat or hanging space was filled by some sort of plant. I took off my coat. "All I want from you is this. First, you have to get us home, and second, you have to come and tell Mom this yourself. We're not going to carry your dirty laundry, Dad."

"I know that. I intended to come. It just seemed, well, kinder, not to keep up a pretense. . . ."

"Kinder how?"

"Kinder to Julie."

"Like you so care. I told you she had multiple sclerosis and you acted like I was just trying to fuck up your day."

Caroline asked then, "What about us? Are we supposed to go on taking care of Mom, if you stay here? Are you going to support us?"

"You have your college funds, and I can break those trusts easily given the fact of your mother's incapacitation. Can she still work?" he asked.

"She can still work. In fact, her column was syndicated," Caro said, lifting her chin.

"Well, there you have it, and with your trust fund money—"

"You know we aren't supposed to have that until we're twenty-five, and Mom isn't going to let you break into our trusts for her sake," I told him.

"That's a little unreasonable, Gabe. That's what breaking trusts is for."

"Yeah, but she has a mental problem, Dad."

"What do you mean?"

"She's a decent person."

"I can see I'm not going to convince you of anything," Leo said, summation over. "I didn't expect to. But I do want you to stay here as long as you like. . . ."

"We have to be back in school in three days," Caroline said.

"Well, I'll have to take you home then, though that's complicated, because Joy and I are right at the stage of approving the blueprints. . . ."

"You're building a house?" I asked. The guy was un-fucking-believable.

"Well, Joy is . . . pregnant, again," our father said. "We didn't think that was entirely possible, given that Amos is only four months old and she's breast-feeding. But as she said . . ."

I finished for him. "Miracles do happen."

"And I'd hoped you'd want to spend time with me here, you and Aury and Caro. We have to have a place with at least four bedrooms. I never wanted you out of my life. Look." He opened a folder of letters, addressed to Caroline and to me. He gestured to our photos on the shelf. "I tried to explain, but I knew I would have to come back to do that, and I was trying to find a good time; then we learned about the pregnancy. . . ."

"You've really got yourself a full plate here, Dad."

"I do, but there's a major difference. The difference is, I'm not expected to do anything. Joy is completely grateful for whatever help I give her, and completely self-sufficient. She's told me, over and over, she's entirely capable of raising our children within the community, without a formal marriage. She doesn't want to bury me. I can do as I wish, study what I wish, work when I want to."

"Well, goody for you, Dad. I don't know if I speak for Caroline," I said wearily, "but I'd rather sleep on a barbecue grill than spend a night in this house, so if you'll direct me to a quaint inn somewhere, I'll leave now."

"I want to stay tonight," Caroline said, in a meek voice. "I'm too tired to go anywhere else."

"Gabe, however you feel about me now, I am your father."

I said, standing up, "Don't blame me."

"Gabe, I'll drive you to Amory's Inn. She's got rooms. We don't get the tourists here until May. But I wish you'd stay here."

"I'm not asking you for anything," I said. "I'll take the ride. Caroline, give me the cell phone." She did. "I just have to ask you one thing. Why did you have a gun? The gun in your drawer?"

"It's not mine," Leo said. "I found it in the acoustical tile when we redid the bathroom. It looked old, like an antique, so I kept it. I don't even know if it works."

"We met your friend, India Holloway," I told him. "You know. The grandmother of the excellent would-be sister raper."

"India's a special woman," Leo said.

"Did you hear what the hell I just said?" I hissed at him.

"Leave it, Gabe," Caroline told me.

"Look, I admire your self-reliance, guys, but this wasn't a very mindful thing to do."

"You should know. Can we please leave?" I asked him.

And finally we did. Caro's face was a little white disc at the window.

Ten times, that night, I dialed home, and ten times I didn't press the SEND button. What would I say? What did I owe Mom to say? Did she need preparing for what would be a helluva shock (but, my God, she couldn't be so dim she didn't know he wasn't coming back, when we already did, at least subconsciously)? Was I the one to do this?

Was I the one to do any of this?

I didn't relish the prospect of assuming permanent guardianship of my little sister. I didn't relish the prospect of . . . like, dropping out of school and working at ABS or someplace to help Mom make ends meet. It was sort of old Jimmy Cagney–movie semi-appealing, but also appalling. It also made me want to shake my mother, actually. Since this whole thing began, I don't think I'd had an uncharitable thought toward her, probably because Caro had so many. But at that moment, I envied old Leon, with his soul flown through the open door of the cage. Paying boarder or not, Cathy was only Mom's friend. I couldn't expect her to take on the role of full-time helper if my mother had spells or switchbacks or whatever. And though I had never raised the subject with her, I knew she would never agree to take money from Grandfather Gillis's trust funds for us; she'd rather have died.

I decided to drop out then. I wasn't sure exactly when, but school was so over.

In fact, childhood was so over. It had been for a while.

It was like some stupid pop song. Drop out, get a manual labor job and a fast car. I decided to drop out when I turned sixteen, take the GED and go to school later, like when our trust funds matured. Or maybe they had special scholarships for idiots who could write advice columns. There would be no choice if Leo went through with this. The thought of never having to see any of the goateed assholes at Sheboygan LaFollette cheered my misery considerably. The thought of never having to see Mrs. Kimball again after a few more months about made me have an erection. I lay on Mrs. Amory's perfectly soft and nice mattress and searched for sleep without any luck. I saw the red numbers flip over to one, one-thirty, two. I wanted to call Tian or at least Luke and say, *Get this.*

But there was no one to call. I almost wished I'd stayed back in Sunrise Holler with Caro. At least then I'd have had someone to compare notes with. I wondered what they were talking about now, Joy and *Leon* and my sister, over a dinner of lettuce and water.

I finally got up at six o'clock and took a walk, my shoes having dried a size smaller next to the woodstove. I found a diner. The pretty girl with the auburn hair, the sister of Joy, was a waitress there. I didn't recognize her at first, because all her hair was pulled up. "Hi," she said when I sat down. "You're Leon's kid."

"His name is Leo," I told her. "His name is Leo Steiner, and he's a lowlife piece of shit who left my mother and got involved with your sister—who I'm sure is a nice person—without telling us."

"I kind of gathered that," she said. "You want coffee?" I tapped my cup. "Food?"

"Yeah, the whole left side of the menu," I told her. She brought me the eggs and toast I ordered and some waffles I hadn't, and she sat down with me for a minute.

"You know, Joy really *is* a nice person," she said. I remembered her name then: Terry, short for Easter. I was in the county of the Land of Oz. "She's a little bit trusting, though. Leon's a lot older than she is. She's twenty-eight; she's the oldest, and she's never really been involved for long with anyone before."

"How old are you?" I asked her.

"Twenty-one," she said. "I love my sisters and my mother. There are three more of us. I have a sister who's eighteen, Liat—that's from some musical. . . ."

"*South Pacific,*" I said. "The girl was Tonkinese." I thought of Tian.

"You know a lot about history!"

"I don't really consider musical theater history."

"And there are Kieron and Grace, who are both older than me and have three kids each. We all live in the yellow submarine. But not me, not for long. I'm getting out of the valley."

"How come?"

"Just, it just creeps me, everyone always on top of you, and I want to have a life of my own, live on a New York street like any other single girl, go to school, quit weaving like the miller's daughter in the fairy tale. . . ."

"What if you couldn't leave?" I asked. "What if your mother was stone sick?"

"I'd find someone to take care of her, or I'd find her someone to live with who'd take care of her in exchange for rent. But I'd take care of her, too, when I could." She gave me a straight-alley look. "I wouldn't give up my life."

"What if she'd given hers up . . . like, for you?"

"What? Did you have a terminal illness and she gave you bone marrow?"

I thought, What the hell, I'll never see this person again, so I said, "Yeah, I did."

"Then you owe her more. You owe her to *have* more life for yourself. Like, see my mother? She's a cool person, but she's completely into the idea that the sun rises in this valley because she came here. And Joy buys that. Our father named her for his mother, Joyce? She changed her name to Joyous. Joyous Devlin. And I was Easter?" She pointed to her name tag. "My mother did this to me when I was eight? Easter's over. The second day I'm out of here, I'm Terry again."

"I can see you better that way."

"Well."

"Well, I'm outta here in the morning, if not today," I said.

"Good luck, and listen up. He didn't want that second baby or the first."

"Who?"

"Leon. Leo. Your loser dad. I heard them. I used to stay over there? And I heard them. He was like, I've done this. I wasn't good at it."

"He can say that again."

"So consider yourself lucky, kid. You got one sane parent. Sick or not sick."

"Where's your dad?"

"He died. He . . . died after my mother left him." She looked up at the acoustical tile. I didn't want to ask any more details. "I don't even remember him. Just that he used to feed me bacon off his plate when he came in, in the morning. He worked the graveyard shift."

"Where?"

"At the graveyard," she said. "I'm not kidding. He was a night watchman at a graveyard."

"How do you get *that* job?"

"Well, he wasn't all bad. I don't remember. But I know this. Not wanting to live in trees doesn't make you all bad." I put money down on the table and gulped when she stuck it down her bra. "Every little bit helps. Next time you see me, I'll be gone."

With that thought, I trudged up the road to where the sign turned left at the Breakdown Lane. Caro was still looking out the window. She reminded me of somebody's dog. When she saw me coming, she threw open the front door. "He's taking us home today. He has to take Amos. He says Joy is too sick. Funny, huh? He wasn't that worried about Mom being sick."

"Well, she is sick," I said. "Joyous is."

"I thought she had to feed the young prince twenty times a day."

"He didn't tell you?"

"Tell me what?"

"Why Joy's sick?"

"No. Look, I could so not care if she had Lou Gehrig's," Caro said. "She's not a bad person."

"Oh, yeah, I can see that from her behavior."

"It wasn't all her idea. What about our very excellent father?"

"But why does he have to bring the baby? Talk about insult to injury. What about her mother and her dozen clone sisters?"

I shrugged. I didn't feel like explaining. My father came out of his office and I jumped. He looked like his normal self, in a turtleneck shirt and a sport coat. He had his old duffel over one arm and a diaper bag as big as our trash used to be under the other. The baby was strapped to his front, asleep. He looked like a bomb ready to go off.

"Let's go," he said, touching Caro under the chin. He looked at me. "Where's your stuff? Still at the inn? We can pick it up on the way."

Joy wouldn't come out of the bedroom.

"She's tired," Leo explained. "The early months of pregnancy are hard."

I tried for Caro's sake to pretend that he meant the early months of raising an infant. Or I must not have wanted to hear him say one more inexplicably despicable thing. But I heard Caro gasp. And I snapped.

"I thought that the beauty of Joyous Devlin—yeah, I know that's her name—is she doesn't make you do anything. I thought," I said, "that she was perfectly capable of raising him and his successor in this community without a formal commitment."

"Go get in the car, Gabe," he said.

TWENTY-THREE

Amos

EXCESS BAGGAGE
By J. A. Gillis
Distributed by Panorama Media

Dear J.,

Six months ago, my sister borrowed ten thousand dollars from me. Okay, it was because her husband was laid off and she didn't have enough money to buy a car that her two boys and new baby would fit into, or Christmas presents. I didn't tell my husband. I took it out of my own bonds, which I got for college graduation. Now, she tells me her husband bought her a fur coat because he felt so bad that he was laid off at Christmas and he can't pay it off. So she's asking me for another thousand just until they "get their feet back under them." I said no, and she started to cry and rant and rave and say I was a hard and vengeful person and that she felt soiled by taking my money. I told her, well, feel clean again, give it back. She threw a Tupperware container she'd borrowed at me and nearly hit me. What do I do? She's my only relative.

Broke in Boston

Dear Broke,

Some days, I don't know why they pay me to do this job. You know the answer to this question. One of the people in your letter is a user. One is a loser. One can certainly change, by closing her purse and turning off her phone. One may not be able to. You guess which is which.

J.

I sat up when I heard the baby's wail.

And then, before I could even slip into my flip-flops, there was Leo. Leo, standing in my doorway.

"Lee! It's you? For real?"

"The very same," he said, and sighed. "It hasn't been that long, Julie."

"It feels longer. Time has been sort of fungible. I got sick. . . ."

"I heard."

"How'd you hear? You disappeared."

"I have my sources."

"Did you *just* hear?"

"Yesterday."

"And you came right away," I breathed, gratitude like honey filling my throat.

I reached up and touched his face, ignoring his flinch, like a leap in the line of a lie detector's pen. "I'm memorizing your face."

"So soon forgotten!" he joked.

He leaned over and kissed me, my husband, flattening his hand on my belly, opening his lips to just such an aperture through which our inner lips could touch. It was not, no, it wasn't passion I felt, but redemption, a wafer on my tongue. He smelled of Leo, coffee beans, wintergreen, and Ivory soap. His arms sinewy, never large but strong enough, were around me, pulling me upward as if I were a child. "Were you in a place that had no phone service? Did something . . . what happened?"

"You don't know?"

"Don't know? Were you hurt? In the hospital? Because I—"

"The children came to find me, Julie. Caroline and Gabe."

"Honey, the kids were at my sister's. All of spring break. Don't tell me you were in the *Hamptons*."

"They were never at your sister's."

"Wait." I sat down on the bed.

"They, ah, told you they were going to Janey's, and they told Janey they were going with my parents, and they took a bus to New England. . . ."

"A bus? Alone?"

Leo chuckled. "They were pretty intrepid."

"Intrepid? I can't even take this in. You knew about this and you didn't stop them?"

"I didn't know about it. I gather only Cathy knew about it."

"Cathy. *Cathy!*"

And then the baby cried, again. It had been no dream. And all the swords that had been hanging over my head fell at once.

I said, "Who's that?"

"Well, Julie, that's Amos."

"Amos?"

"My son. I had a baby, Julie, with a woman in upstate New York, a woman I love very much. Maybe not the way we loved each other once upon a time, not the way you can love someone the first time, but not every love has to—"

"You had a baby! You had a baby! You brought your baby to my house!"

"Well, he needs his father, Julie. You'd be the first to say that. Joy isn't feeling well right now. . . ."

I tried to swallow the irony of this. Then, I stepped back and spit on his chest.

"Jesus!" he cried, leaping up as if I'd scalded him.

The older kids sidled in then, one after the other, Caroline holding the little dark-haired baby, her eyes the huge eyes of a child in some cheap painting. Gabe fixed his stare out of the window at the swing set where all of them had played.

"You can feed him, Caro," Leo said. "Just put some . . . do you have spring water . . . ?"

"*And* juice," Gabe said softly, "*and* fresh air. And windows that open and close."

"Just warm it a little. Joy likes him to take it room temperature."

"Give me the telephone, Gabe," I said, standing up, thankful that I didn't falter or wobble. "I have to get a witness for this. I think this may be unprecedented." I began to dial Cathy's number, believing that I otherwise might abscond my body and kill him. I might try to take the receiver to bash in his skull or the half smile on his face. Then I realized I was dialing Connie's number. Cathy had lost her cell phone. "You were at my sister's house." Gabe shook his head ruefully, hating even then to disobey. "You weren't at my sister's house. You lied to me and got away with it because of the medicine. You knew I couldn't catch you. You went to . . . him." I am putting them in the middle of him and me, I scolded myself, making them a prize or a carcass. "And you made Cathy go along with it."

"We went to *get* him," Gabe said.

"And you got him. Now what?"

He huffed, exasperated. "Wasn't that what you wanted, Mom? Just a chance to talk to Dad? Wasn't that what you kept moaning for when you were out of it?"

"I don't know. I didn't imagine this! I didn't want his . . . spawn."

"There's always catch and release."

"Don't joke," I said, my head throbbing. "I want to work some things out before Cathy gets here with Aury. I don't want a scene for Aury. As for what you did, it was foolish and stubborn. You could have been killed or hurt. . . ."

"We called Cathy every night. She knew."

"It was foolish on Cathy's part then." I went into the kitchen, and reached up into a cupboard for a bottle of aspirin. But I couldn't manage the aspirin bottle; Leo had to do it, and the water kept sluicing through my fingers as I tried to cup enough to wash down the chalky pills. Acutely aware of being clad only in a flannel shirt, I asked everyone to leave while I went back into my room and dressed, which I did with care and extraordinary slowness.

As I pulled up my slacks and wrapped my belt—my once-upon-a-time once-around belt—around twice, I thought about the fact that Leo had not come home until someone cornered him in his lair. Played music on his guilt. As I tucked in my shirt and turned up my collar, as I brushed pigment on my jaw to fool the eye away from the slack, I thought about the fact that he had another child, another marriage. Not a marriage, better than *marriage*. A love match. I didn't dare consider how this made me feel. Practical action. I would think only about what I might do for myself with Leo's transgression. I brushed out my hair and ran mousse through it.

Wisconsin was a no-fault divorce state.

Surely, they could make an exception. If this wasn't fault, I didn't know what was.

No.

Well.

I thought about how I could manipulate whatever there was left of him, against him. But I didn't think there was much left. He seemed too assured, too impatient with our dullness, our mess. He'd probably anticipated everything. And I still loved . . . *the rain-drenched . . .*

No. A guy who could kiss his wife, then draw his very next breath, and explain how very much in love he was. . . .

No.

Some people don't deserve second chances.

But he doesn't want one, a carping notion nagged. If only Leo had something he needed that I could refuse.

His parents would be home tonight.

A last glance in the mirror and then I walked, with what I hoped was a regal bearing, out into the living room. Caroline was feeding the baby in the rocking chair.

"You wouldn't happen to have a cradle I could use?" Leo asked.

"I wouldn't," I said, "happen to have a cradle that you could use." I crossed the room and selected one from a group of my father's canes, canes he'd used as an affectation. I didn't really need it that day, but I wanted, perversely, for Leo to see me using it.

"You need a cane?" he asked.

"Yes, for some things," I told him. I studied his face, the shifting kaleidoscope of my children's features that surfaced and vanished with his expressions. "I could use it now to crack your skull, but I don't want to go to prison. I would like *you* to go to prison. However, what you've done isn't against any law, except the ones that have to do with personal morality. Biblical-type laws. Your parents will want to see you, before you leave. . . ."

"I was planning on staying a few days."

"Where were you planning on staying?"

"At a hotel. A friend's."

"Leo, you have no friends," I said softly, realizing that this was, in fact, true.

"I have friends in Sunrise Valley."

"Is it possible that you—" I began to laugh, despite my shame—"live in a place called Sunrise Valley?"

"Is it possible that you live in a place called Sheboygan? On Tecumseh Street? West Side Julieanne Gillis?" Leo sniffed.

"Go upstairs, kids."

"We, uh, don't have an upstairs, Mom," said Caro. "We have a down the hall."

"You know that's what I meant, sweetie." Despite her holding the sleeping Amos over her shoulder, I kissed her. "I missed you. You were very brave. But lucky, too."

Caro smiled sadly.

"Be careful with his head, and you have to burp him more than once or he'll throw up . . ." Leo said as Caroline left.

"He changed his name," Gabe said over his shoulder.

"I call myself Leon there," Leo said as Gabe disappeared.

"I call you beyond belief," I answered. "Anywhere."

"Julieanne, I don't expect you to understand or forgive this. I might not have been able to, at one time in my life. But I've read up on this. Relationships have a shelf life. Between adults, that is. Our relationship had a life. It doesn't mean that it wasn't real."

"And so, this thing with . . . I didn't get her name."

"Joyous?"

"Joyous? Her name is Joyous?" I was being gutted, and yet I couldn't help enjoying this one on some level. "Your . . . pal's name is *Joyous*?"

"Well, Joy, yes. It's a chosen name."

"Like Leon. I'll bet she's . . . don't tell me. . . ."

"She makes jam."

"Oh, God help you, Leo." I sat down on the window seat. "You're a caricature. And do you expect this meeting of souls to last? Forever?"

"She's also a Pilates instructor."

"Oh that explains it, then. She reminded you of me."

"In answer to your question, we're taking it one day at a time. That's the only way Joy would do it. We'll take this as far as it works for both of us. . . ."

"Are you a complete idiot? You have a baby in the other room. *Is that taking it one day at a time?* You erased one family; are you going to erase another?"

"No, this feels, somehow, different."

"Lee, it feels different because *she* feels different. Like, her boobs. Get a grip. She makes you feel twenty-five, too. Do you think that'll last? And why the hell do I even care? I guess because you're still *my* children's father."

"This was never about the children."

"But you said it was, Leo. You said it was about too much of too much. You never went to Colorado to take photographs—"

"I did, but she went with me. She wanted to know that I was completely free of . . ."

"Of what? The family you snookered?"

"I didn't *decide* to have another baby," Leo whispered. "I didn't even *decide* to . . . leave you. It unfolded that way. It was a turn of events I honestly didn't expect. But when it did happen, I thought things happen for a reason. . . ."

"Just not necessarily a good one, as Gabe would say."

"I thought it over, and I realized that this might be my last chance. . . ."

"For a young girl? For a young girl to fall for your over-the-hill self?"

"For a life of passion. For a life of my own."

I pointed down the hall with my cane. "Good luck with a life of your own. You have four children now, Leo. But three of them live with me. And I assume that after we divorce, you'll be paying child support in the amount of twenty-something percent—is that right—of your salary?"

"Jules, I probably don't make half of what you make anymore. I do a lot of pro bono work and work for the community I live in."

"Well, you can still give me twenty percent or whatever it is of what you make. Not for me. For them."

"That's why we need to talk, to do this fairly for all the children involved here," Leo said. "I love my children, Julie. If you're not up to their care, I'll gladly take them back with me. All of them. I think the fairest thing we can do is to let the money your father put aside for the education of the children go to work for you now. This is the time for you to break that trust. Let me invest it. Or let someone else invest it, if you don't trust me."

"I'll think about it."

"Really?"

Why shouldn't he think so? Did he think I wouldn't take care of my own, now that I knew the chips were *irrefutably* down? I had the present on my mind, how to afford Interferon, not the Ivy League.

"Well, I'm glad you're being reasonable, given your condition and its instability. Before I left to come back here with the kids, I scanned the Net about MS. It can really throw you some curves. I know that."

"I did cabrioles earlier today, before class, and a ballotte, in ballet class."

"You can still do that?"

"Yes. Sometimes."

"Because Gabe gave me the impression that you were virtually bedridden." He glanced at the cane.

"I can do that, too."

We stood like prizefighters, listening to each other's breathing.

"Do you know what time my mother and father will be here?" Leo finally asked.

"Six. About six. They'll go to their apartment. And then probably come here. Their plane lands at four. They sold the condo in Florida. Their share."

"Why? I promised—"

"Don't even think about it. Leo! Your parents are never going to let Joy into their house."

"You'd be surprised what a baby can do."

"I thought that period of your life was over, Lee. Circa our daughter. Our *two-year-old* daughter."

"You make it sound like a crime."

"A crime? It's a sin, Leo. And boy, talk about retiring and *being here now*. Little Amos is going to punch some holes in that bubble."

Leo sighed. "And, well, you might as well know. You're going to find out anyway. Joy is pregnant again."

"Well, Lee, that about covers it," I said, surprised by my own restraint, my ease at speaking around the stone in my throat. "You aren't just a man who's had ridiculously bad luck and bad judgment. You are a world-class twit. You will now have *five* kids to support. You make me want to go take a shower. And *Aurora* was supposedly what pushed you over the edge. You blamed me and you blamed little Aurora, and I bought it."

"Who is . . . where? Some kind of day care?"

"She should be here soon."

"I hope you send her to a decent place."

"I do, Leo. I send her to Connie's. About two mornings a week. The rest of the time, I am her day care. Just like you always wanted."

"Leave it alone, Julie. Where is my daughter?"

"She's out with Cathy and Abby. Cathy and Abby live here now. They rent a room from me. I need the money and the company and sometimes the help. You must know that I sold the house to Liesel and Klaus. . . ."

"I heard that, yes. From Gabe."

"Well. No one was able to find you. None of your family."

"Not keeping in touch, that *was* wrong. I see its effect on the children. But I was desperate, Julie. I was as ill, in my own way, as you are."

"You fruitcake," I said. "I think of you as *many* things, Leo. Snake comes to mind. But I never think of you as stupid. There is no comparison between your so-called desperation and my health. There is no way that, in *any* way, you were as bad off before you left as I am now."

He smiled mildly. "I don't expect you to understand. It's all colored by rage for you. And pride."

"Well, yes," I said. "But hey. You know about market studies. If you took a hundred women and asked how many of them would feel *rage* if left alone with three kids, with diminishing health and mysteriously vanishing funds, by a husband who didn't even have the grace, not to mention the balls, to explain what he was really doing, I wonder what percentage of that target population would feel . . . *rage*."

The front door opened, and I could hear Cathy half laughing, shouting down the little girls, "Wait, wait! I want those boots off."

"Here," I said. "We're in here."

"Daddy!" cried Aury, as if she was seeing an exotic animal.

Leo's face crumpled in honest longing and misery. "Dolly! You must have grown a foot!" He held out his arms and kissed Aury's head, shaking his own head as he did, beseeching me with his eyes. He really felt it then, and my heart did not go out to him. Aury gently disengaged herself and stood back shyly.

"The prodigal asshole," Cathy said, unwinding her scarf. She stood astride the arch of the door. Her yellow coat and braided knit hat shouted health and functionality.

"Hi, Cathy," Leo said, recovering. "Didn't Connie ever teach you that if you don't have anything nice to say, don't say anything at all?"

"I don't see anything nice in this room except Julieanne." Aury ran past her and clambered up next to me on the window seat, popping her finger into her mouth and trying to diminish herself behind me. "And now your daughter."

"She hears in your tone of voice that you despise me. That's why she ran over there."

"Maybe she just has good taste."

"Stop it," I said. "This is . . . it's sickening."

The baby wailed, and Leo startled.

"*No!*" Cathy said. "What's that?"

"That is Amos," I told her. "Amos Stern. Leo here goes by another name when he's having adventures in paradise. Amos is one of those," I told her. "And wait 'til you hear. Amos isn't the only member of the new clan. Leo here's starting a dynasty with his new love."

"Tell me you're kidding," Cathy said. "Leo, even you wouldn't be such a shit."

Caroline called. "I don't have any more baby milk." Cathy's eyes saucered.

"She means formula," I quickly explained. "It's not Caroline's baby. It's not that bad. Leo's new friend, in New York State, is on the way to having *not just this baby, but another baby.*"

"You make it sound worse . . ." Leo began.

Cathy sat down hard on the hall bench. "No, Leo. It's actually worse than it sounds."

"A baby?" Aury cried. "Daddy, did you bring me a baby? A really baby?"

It stopped being funny then. Even in a lousy way.

"Aury," I said, and gathered her onto my lap. "Aury, listen . . ." Caro came stumbling into the room, the wriggling Amos having squirmed halfway down her cropped sweater.

"Daddy, help!" she cried, and Leo leapt up.

"Daddy, help!" Cathy and I repeated, but tears sprang into my eyes, and I stood, holding Aury's hand.

"Daddy?" Aury asked tentatively, "can we keep the baby?"

"My God, Leo!" I told him. "Go now, out of mercy. I'll try to explain it to her. . . ."

"I want a chance to see her, Julie," Leo whirled on me. "I want a chance to see my little girl!"

"You should have thought of that oh, about sixteen months ago!" Cathy scolded him.

"No . . . don't," I told her. "Not in front of them. Leave it alone, Cath. I know you're trying to help, but you're making it worse."

"Julie, will you let me take her to the hotel with me? After my folks get here? So she can swim in the pool and we can get reacquainted?"

"Would you like to go to the hotel with Daddy? Aury?" I turned her to face me, softly holding both her shoulders, her birdlike little shoulders. *No*, she mouthed, *no*. "She doesn't want to go, Leo. It's been a long time . . . and she's shy. . . . Don't take offense. I would let her; I would."

Caroline spoke up. "Aury-o, don't worry. Gramp and Gram will go there," Caroline said soothingly. "They really will. It'll be fine. You can play with the baby." Gabe and I stared at Caroline, looks that might have turned her to salt. "Well, she would be fine. Gramp and Gram *will* come there!"

As it turned out, Gramp and Gram would not. Not then.

They came to my house first.

Cathy discreetly decided to visit her mother. I promised to call if there was anything I couldn't handle. Caroline gave Cathy back her cell phone, and I could hear her, out in the kitchen, treating Cath to an appropriately lurid account of their near-miss. It was the first time Cathy had heard about it.

Then my in-laws arrived. And I tried to explain, softening the sharpest parts, what had happened to the children while they were gone. Hannah still clutched her chest. Gabe Senior stood on the back porch, hatless and coatless, staring into the darkness.

Then Leo arrived, offering Amos to his mother as a warrior priest would offer his child to the sun, withering as she said, "He's sweet, Leo. God forgive you. What have you done?"

"Dad?" Leo turned to his father. Gabe Senior shook his head and put his hands over his face. He sat down heavily on the couch. "Look, Dad, I'm not the first person on earth to have ever wanted to leave a marriage! I'm not the first man who ever wanted to live the latter part of his life, alive! You don't even begin to imagine the joy I feel, simply from being—"

"If you have no respect for yourself, Leo, have respect for your daughters and your sons. Don't say anything else." He stood up. "I do have an imagination, Leo. But it doesn't take imagination to see what's happened here. You've deceived your wife. You've deceived yourself. And you have no shame."

"No, I don't, Dad, Mom," said Leo. "I don't have shame for having a heart, and a need to feel! I love all these children equally! I take full responsibility for them."

"But three of them, you ignored. You didn't take responsibility. To the point that you put two of them in danger."

I glanced at Leo, to see if his mother's chastising had an effect. It hadn't. He said, "That was their choice. And they have a mother. I . . . didn't know Julie was ill. Well, as ill as she *says* she is. I never meant to ignore them for any extended length of time. First of all, the baby was born," Leo began.

"You talk as though babies fall from trees, Leo," Hannah said.

"Does that mean he shouldn't be loved? And by his own grandparents? Because he wasn't part of this neat little plan?"

"No one has said that, Leo," Hannah continued.

"That's how you're acting!"

"How you are acting," Gabe Senior said, "is like a child yourself. We're going back to our place, Julieanne."

"Okay, Papa," I said.

"It's like," Leo said, "you only see her side of it! Don't you want to spend time with me? With Amos? At least come over to the hotel."

"Leo," his father said gently, "we will. We have to . . . get settled first. We love you. You're our son. And you have made us proud in your life so many times. But there were times over the past few months we thought Julieanne might die, and you not only didn't seem to care, you didn't seem to want to be bothered."

"She doesn't look so bad now," Leo said.

"No, she looks wonderful," Hannah told him. "You do, Julie. No thanks to you." She turned to me. "You're so dressed up and shiny. Like your old self."

"Not hardly, but I had a good day. Despite . . ."

"That's good, honey," said Hannah. "We'll take Aurora over to the hotel and then maybe she can stay over with Gram and Gramp, hah? Aury can help Grandma find some surprises in her boxes!" Aury ran to get her little backpack. "And Art and Patty said, use the condo in Florida whenever they're not there! Isn't that nice? You can bring the children."

"I can't. Heat . . . makes it worse. What I have."

"Then we will."

"Thank you, Hannah," I said.

"Why don't you get your things and . . . Amos's things and we'll speak at the hotel?" Leo's father asked. "Let Julieanne have some rest."

"I'm not so sure I want to now," Leo said, and their bracing scorn felt like an injury even to me.

"I'm not so sure I want to, either," said Gabe Senior. "But if this mess is to be straightened out, someone is going to have to talk to someone. I have a mediator, a friend of a friend, a lawyer."

"I'm not crawling back here for any sessions or negotiations," Leo told him, motioning to Caro to hand him his coat and to help him drape his various traps around his shoulders.

"Crawling. No. Crawling is what you're doing now. This shame you don't feel," Leo's father said, "we do, son. We do."

TWENTY-FOUR

Gabe's Journal

There was this John Ciardi poem I read in sophomore year, just after I got to New York. It stayed with me. "Snail, glister me forward/Worm, be with me/This is my hard time." That was the part I remembered.

Perhaps you think we were already over the hump, bad-time-wise.

No.

You'd think you couldn't sink much lower than turning your dad up like something you'd find under a rock, after a six-month lapse, with his illegitimate child no less.

Very urbane for Sheboygan.

But like Mom's therapist, who I went to myself a couple of times, says, it's a mistake to think stuff can't get worse.

The phone rang all weekend. Leo wanted to see Aury. My grandparents wanted Leo to see a lawyer and set up mediation. They wanted my mother to talk him into this. Mom wanted to know if Leo would come to the house closing, and he did, but at a separate time. He agreed to go to the title company before Klaus and Liesel showed up and sign the papers. I guess he didn't want to run into Liesel and Klaus. I wouldn't have either. Klaus later helped move some of our stuff out to the garage for the sale we were going to have. My mom offered my dad all his good clothes. He mailed one box of things to *Joyous* and said for my mom to sell the rest. She asked me if I wanted to keep any of Dad's sport coats. It was like she didn't notice I was already four inches taller than he was. I said I'd pass.

Klaus and Liesel brought down noodle kugel, which I ate the entire pan of by myself in one sitting, after having given Mom and Aury the stamp-sized portions they requested and didn't finish. They sat the obligatory mournful ten minutes at the table with my mother, and then Liesel said, "We have found life is too short for small talk, Julieanne. This is our home, and we will be glad to also have more of a chance to expand, an office for Klaus over the garage, a small lab. But we also feel that, as long as you need to, this is your home, and the rent will never change from whatever you can manage to pay us." My mom started to object, but Liesel said, "This is our wish. We have saved all our lives, and this house is already paid for. We have no need to take money you need now more than ever. Think of what is fair, but modest, and we will draw up a paper." They went back to their own apartment. Caro and her squealing gerbil friends reacted with feigned horror to the Vermont Hot Springs and Rape Retreat. ("Was he cute?" Justine asked. I'm not making that up.) On Sunday night, I got a long letter from Jessica Godin, who said she hoped we'd found our father safely, and maybe we could write. She already knew about Muir, and more shit he'd pulled with his father's lost sheep convicts had emerged. I answered, it seemed like, for hours. I thought my wrists would swell. Telling her about my mother, how half of me wanted to just let my reptile father break our educational trusts so I could run, become an emancipated minor (I had looked this up) and how his selfishness made me want him to have to go back to work, to put on a suit each day over there in Nature World and go hump to support us. Later, unable to sleep, I wrote Tian, but I didn't expect to hear back from her for days, e-mail between here and Thailand is always a little sluggish. Cathy was unpacking her boxes of old stuff, and as fast as she did, Aury and Abby took out whatever looked good to them, a scarf or pancake turner, until junk was scattered all over the house, Mom's and Cath's. After they got into all the makeup in Mom's room and Aury cut Abby Sun a nice little mullet, Connie came over to watch them. No one else had the strength.

Luke Witt stopped by twice that weekend, just to view the rubble.

"Dude," he said, the first time, coming into my room, where I was pretending to read my English. "Hell's a poppin'."

"Yeah, my dad's back in town."

"I heard. It's all over Tombstone. Gunfight at the OK Corral. Heard there was . . . trouble."

"Well, if you consider that he has a girlfriend old enough to be my sister and that they have a baby, then it's trouble, yeah. It's not very confusing, though."

"Say hey."

"I mean, I don't have big divided loyalties, man."

"My mother's p.g.," Luke said. "They want a girl now."

"How does that synch with what I just said? I'm the one who's not supposed to make sense."

"Well, it was on the general theme of even the oldies howl at the full moon."

"Your parents are married. To each other."

"It's still embarrassing. My littlest brother's, like, nine."

"Point of order. Luke, my mon, you don't know what embarrassing is. As a matter of fact, you don't know what shit is, to tell you the truth. No offense."

"None taken."

"Because I don't know what the hell is going to happen to us. We could end up in a double-wide before he's through."

"Not happening. It'll work out. I bagged the wet leaves."

"Dude." I nodded.

"You took buses all the way out there?"

"Who told you?"

"The Caroline."

"She's actually proud of it, I think. She could have been porked by some ecosavage if I hadn't pistol-whipped him." Luke guffawed and threw his size-fourteen feet up and folded his arms against my headboard, as if he was doing a reverse crunch.

"You pistol-whipped him, huh?" He laughed again.

I gave Luke a once-over, not sure whether or what I wanted to say. Luke was still my best friend. More or less. On good days. He also had a big mouth. On the other hand, the pistol business might not hurt my reputation among both the normal and the un.

"There were no bullets in the gun," I said.

"I'm sure." Luke smiled.

"It was a 1937 Colt police special."

Luke sat up. "What the hell? You *really* pistol-whipped a guy?"

"Yeah."

"Where's the gun now?"

"Under a car seat in New York. Or not."

"Jesus fuck. I thought you were fucking with me. Where'd you get a fucking gun?"

"I found it. It's a long story."

"Dude!" Luke said. "This was some hairy adventure."

"Then there was our excellent encounter with the Massachusetts State Police and our fake driver's licenses. . . ."

"I never thought you had it in you, dude. No offense," Luke said.

"Why?" I asked. "Because I don't get a hard-on about running up and down the hills with the cross-country weenies? You think everyone who isn't a jock is some kind of pussy?"

"No," Luke said honestly. "Get over yourself, Gabe. I didn't think that. You just don't seem . . . c'mon, Gabe. You don't seem like the pistol-whipping type. But it's cool. I admire it."

Well, I had finally arrived. Fought my way out of geekdom.

And it didn't matter.

I watched my mother, physically better than she'd been in months, constantly in motion. Shopping. Making lists. She cooked stew with dumplings on Saturday night and took Aury to one of those places where little kids jump on trampolines into big foam pits—just the two of them. Like she had to prove she was among the living. I think it was at the foam pit that she explained that Dad, although he loved Aury very much, had to take care of little baby Amos. Mama would take care of Aury, and Aury would be able to visit Daddy when she was just a little bigger. I assume that was what she said. We didn't even hide Easter eggs for Aury. We forgot about Easter, even Cathy the Catholic. Gramp ran out Sunday morning to the Dollar Bonanza and bought the girls Easter baskets the size of Trump Towers that he hid under the shrubs in front for them to find. We kind of left clues, in picture language, around the house. They were pretty cute, searching. Cathy took her and Abby Sun to the egg-rolling contest at the Laurel Tavern, which isn't what it sounds like. It's this sort of fish-fry place, and they have a big egg deal for little kids in the back every year, where there's a little park.

I kept wondering when Dad was going to attempt the "Son, we need to talk" thing, and he did, on Monday when Mom was at the closing.

He came over with Amos, limp as a doll in his front holder. I saw him come up the walk, talking on the cell phone, gesturing at the air as if the person on the other end, I assume it was the Joyous one, could see him. When he came in, he said, "For Christ sake, Gabe, take him a minute and lay him down. I have to go to the bathroom and wash the barf off my hand." When I hesitated, he said, "Look. He's your brother." And yeah, he was, the poor little bastard. I stuck him lengthwise between the couch pillows, the way I'd learned to do with Aury when she was little, and heard the little catch in his breath as he relaxed into a baby snore.

"So," Leo said, returning, "you hate my guts."

"Something like that."

"I don't blame you for being angry. . . ."

"Big of you."

"But hate's a massive word, Gabe. I don't know if it does me or you more harm, you know?" About this, he had a point. My guts were literally twisted. I couldn't stay off the toilet. Having Leo around was like having the flu that followed you from room to room. He sat on the end of my bed. "Remember, Gabe. There were good times. Remember when we made the Pinewood Derby car? And . . ." I groaned. "How is school?"

I pretended to laugh, bitterly, though I sounded like some old guy in a tux in a black-and-white movie. "Nonexistent or shit, depending on the day," I told him.

"You have to try at that, Gabe. College is going to be easier for you. There's a program at UW-Baraboo for bright kids who are LD. . . ."

"I'm not LD. I have LD."

"You know what I mean."

"I do, actually. I hear it every day of my life."

"You could get help with the speech thing. And that would help the writing thing. Do you take meds for the ADD?"

"No."

"You could."

"Uh, okay."

"Your mother told me that there are programs."

"They run about one-forty an hour. Are you offering?"

"You know I'm in no position to do that, Gabe," he said. "But I can help your mother break the educational trusts so you can get the help you need. . . ."

"So that her kids have *her* father's money, instead of having to bother *their* father."

"There's probably some sort of aid for that."

"Christ, Dad, you think she'd accept, like, aid? She does for her medicine from drug companies who give it free, because she can't really buy much insurance from anyone, but she's not the aid type."

"That's what it's there for."

"I didn't think you could amaze me anymore, Daddy of mine. But you know, I was wrong there. You'd rather have Caro and me take state aid than have you work full time?"

He looked away then. "Remember building that tree fort? How you thought there had to be boards that fit over the tree, like the neck in a T-shirt?"

"Skip the walk down memory lane." I looked at my watch. "I have to, you know, go look for a job and junk."

"Gabe, someday you're going to understand why I did this. I don't know if you'll ever forgive me, but someday you're going to want something so badly, just for yourself, just to live, that you're willing to risk anything."

"I'm missing something. What exactly did you risk?"

"The respect of my son, for starters."

"Okay. Point taken."

"And I'll come. When the baby . . . well, the babies, are a little older . . . and you'll come to see me. If you knew Joy better—"

"Yeah, count on that. In fact, it's about as likely as me going down right now and taking a little dip in Lake Michigan. They say the water temp's up to about fifty-three near shore." I got up. "Are you nuts? Dad, I don't want to talk to you like this, but you force it. Why would I come and visit you? Why would I want to come and visit you and get to know *Joy* better? I think the two-hour visit I already had with Joy about filled me in on the whole scope of Joy, and even her own sister can't wait to get out of that happy horseshit."

"You'll change your mind."

"Don't lay money on it. Once I can find . . . a way, and I shouldn't have to be saying this, to make sure Mom has . . . help, and is okay with Cathy, I'm outta here. You know, mention my name in Sheboygan, but don't tell them where I am."

"I don't blame you for feeling like this."

"Dad, you're breaking my heart."

"How would you feel," he asked, and I had to fight myself, hold one arm like it was broken and in a sling, not to go to him, "if you were me and I were your son? If your own parents felt like you were something they wanted to wipe off their shoes?"

"I'd feel like shit, Leon," I told him. "I would honestly feel like shit. Hey, I would feel exactly like I do right now."

"Want a sub?" Cathy called from the kitchen.

"Yeah," I called back. "Roast beef and turkey and—"

"Russian dressing. I know the drill," Cathy called back.

"I have to admit," Leo said. "She hates my guts, but she's been a good friend to you guys."

"She's sort of the father I never had, Leon. Not that I haven't enjoyed this, but I really have things to do. . . ."

He left then. I took my fist and put a hole in my headboard—it was kind of a lousy headboard—then, and semi-cried like a complete ass until I fell asleep.

TWENTY-FIVE

Gabe's Journal

My mother went to physical therapy on Saturdays. If she could take it, after all the leg lifting with weights and the therapist rotating her ankles, she took ballet afterward. Sometimes Caro went with her. About half the time, she made it, and the rest of the day the rest of us all lived as if we were holding our breaths. She kept getting better, though, not worse.

My father was coming back—without Amos—for the divorce. I kept hoping to start feeling weird and sad and drained and sort of nostalgic about Leo and my childhood and junk. But all I felt was dead to the touch, like the crooked scar on my knee from when I cut it down to the bone on a broken bike handle.

The feeling never came back.

It still hasn't.

The divorce just seemed like a normal fact now. Not even like something you'd change from tennis shoes to loafers for. And this was a thing that I would have thought as unlikely as a Martian installation in Klaus's greenhouse, only a year before. The past six months had been the longest five years of my life.

Now, the only thing I wanted was for my mother to look good in court. I didn't want her to be limp and skinny, even though it would probably help her cause with the judge. We already knew that my dad was going to have to pay her some kind of money each month because she couldn't work full time—unless she got married, which it was obvious she wouldn't.

She kept acting like she more or less couldn't give a shit about Leo or Amos or anything. In front of us, at least. And I thought I knew part of the reason why. Sometimes, at night, I would hear her through the wall, singing along to some music, but more and more often, I'd hear her talking on the telephone. It was kind of comforting, even if she was crying while she was talking. It reminded me of when we were little, and we'd hear our parents, well, I suppose, screwing, my mom kind of making little whimpering noises and my dad gasping out her name, "Julie. Julie." I wondered who she was talking to. It wasn't Cathy, because Cathy now lived with us, though she was away then at a conference and afterward was going to see her brother in Denver. It wasn't Stella, because she and Stella didn't talk on the phone except to say "Later," just to arrange to meet for coffee. That left my aunt Jane. But then, no one sane would talk for more than five minutes to my aunt Jane, and Gram was always around and about and went to bed at, like, eight-thirty. All my mom's university friends, the professors' wives, had ditched my mom like she never existed after Leo moved out.

It was one night when my mother took Aury to a play for little kids that I sat down at her desk, to try to find out who the mystery talker was. It didn't occur to me that I was violating my mother's privacy by rifling her things. I didn't think of her as a person with limits and a life apart. She was our mother. She belonged to us.

Anyway, that night, I found two things of immense interest. One was a little magazine called *Pen, Inc.* Mom didn't read magazines, and she was always hocking us to read books you couldn't lift in one hand, like *Anna Karenina,* so I flipped through it. And there was her poem. Not the one I'd seen before we left for the Breakdown Lane. Another one. I don't know if it was better. I don't know anything about poetry except the Robert Frost poems she made us memorize when we were little, and the fact that you could sing all of Emily Dickinson's poems to the tune of "The Yellow Rose of Texas." But it must have been more or less decent because they put it in this magazine.

This is it:

Remission

I will have to pay for this remission,
Shell out, with drooly dawns and stuporous mornings,
Listen to winces, proffered help, tongues clucking or scorning.
Pay with rage and fear and regret and mourning
A new bruise on my hip, a fat lip, vertigo, nausea, all warnings
That there's a price tag on this holiday of health,
No such thing, for me now, as a wealth
Of it. I dance and sing, but in a closet, with stealth,
As if to escape notice, forestall the time it takes its commission
At the end of it, I shall remit,
This isn't joy. It's intermission.

I thought it sounded pretty damned bitter. It didn't mesh with that perky-Julie phone voice I heard through the wall at night. "He did? And what did you do? Well, yeah, there may not be emergencies but it's still a big responsibility. And accidents are emergency cases. Well, it doesn't have to be *mortal*." She sounded like a less stupid version of Caroline, talking to Mallory.

But the really interesting thing was this folded piece of gray paper that fell out of the magazine. It was a note from a guy.

Matthew McDougall here. I know you don't remember me, Julieanne, but I remember you. I sat behind you in art class at PS 17, and I was madly in love. You danced with me exactly three times at Rec, to "God Only Knows." You said it was your favorite song. It was Paul McCartney's favorite song, too; and he used to drive his kids nuts by playing it over and over in the car. In fact, I have a daughter, who's eighteen, and I drive her nuts playing it in the car. I read your column from time to time in the Herald, *and when I saw your poem in* Pen, Inc., *I decided to write. I don't know if you'll ever get this, but if you do, call me and we'll catch up. Fondly, Matt.*

His phone number was on the letterhead, and his name was followed by MD. A doctor. Probably the class nerd. It made me think about what it would be like if my mother were ever to have a . . . date, or what have you.

Maybe he was the one she talked to on the phone.

But if he'd read the poem, he knew she had MS.

So why was he flirting with her?

I'd read enough MS pamphlets to realize that people fled from women with MS, even if they'd loved them before. They deserted them because they could get stumbling and ranting and disgusting, though it wasn't their fault, and just meeting the base physical needs of people with the worst cases could practically kill the people who took care of them. So far, my mom's case seemed pretty mild, but you never knew. I put the gray paper back into the magazine, carefully making sure it was on the same page, and cut open the bills with the paper knife. I had always been pretty adept at my mother's signature, how she'd respond to a dunning letter, how she'd schedule a speech. The bills were part of my routine. I just printed them out and signed them, along with permission slips, answers to letters, Caro's detentions, and anything else that came along.

It was the next day, after I spied on her, that my mother started having her bad spell.

It was short, and really the last one she's had since. But it was fairly awful.

I never wished Cathy was home more than I did that week.

It began with a little more trouble with her eyes. She would press her good eye basically *against* the computer screen as she wrote, her fingers moving. It made me think of Anne Sullivan and Helen Keller. It gave me the creeps, to be honest. I had to drive her almost everywhere there for a while, and it was speech season, when hospitals and stuff were having their year-end banquets.

The week before my father came back was the week of my mother's Interferon treatment. She gave herself the shot, and it was routine. But this time, I heard her, from the bathroom, say, "Shit!" and I asked if I could help her. "No," she said. "I got a damned blood return. I hit a vein. Go away." This was . . . a little not Julieanne. Her shot finally administered, she came out and literally slung some hash at Aury and me, Caro having departed for her evening's revels.

"I hate fried eggs," Aury whined, looking at the quivering runny orb on her hash cake. I couldn't blame her. I eat them hard-boiled or scrambled, but a fried egg creeps me out. It reminds me that it's one cell.

"Fine," said my mother, dumping Aury's portion in the flip-top trash can. "Don't eat."

Aury began to cry. "Gay," she said, sniffling, "make me a PBJ."

"Don't you dare, Gabe," my mother said. "I'm sick of her picky eating crap. That was perfectly good corned beef and potatoes, Aury."

"But the egg was touching it," Aury whined, beginning that passionate snort of rage and sadness that made snot come out her nose and made smoke come out the ears of any adult in earshot.

"Get up then," my mother said, grabbing Aury's arm and hauling her to the door of her room. "And leave the table. And don't come back." She turned to me, then. "Not good enough for you, either?" she asked. "I can dump yours out, too."

"I was just kind of caught up in the floor show here," I said, raising both hands in surrender.

My mother checked her swing, but she almost slapped me in the face. I couldn't believe it.

"Fuck this!" I yelled, jumping up. "First you crap all over a little kid—"

"I did not! I took her forcibly to her room, which even Doctor Spock said was okay. And I gave her perfectly normal, even banal food, and she wouldn't touch it. She whines *constantly*. She never *stops*." I put my plate on the dish drainer. My mother picked up the plate and, with satisfaction, broke it in half across the sink. "Go ahead and make your own god-damned meals," she said.

"Would you like that?" I asked her. "Would you feel more like a martyr than you already do?"

"I'd like you to shut up and go to your room."

"My pleasure."

I lay there suffering, waiting the obligatory half hour before she came in saying, *Gabe, I'm tired. Gabe, I'm sorry. Gabe, I still miss your dad and our old life so much.*

But she didn't.

I knew she was dreading what tomorrow would bring, the nausea, the chills, the veg out. It didn't last long, only a couple of days, but she dreaded it. Still, I didn't give a damn. She was acting like a complete ass-hole. And instead of apologizing, what she did for the next hour was to bang around the house, slamming doors, picking up all of Aury's scattered toys and throwing them in a trash bin that she carried with her, shouting to Aury that if she didn't want her toys, well, her mother didn't want to trip over them so she'd give them to a child who could pick them up. I went in and got Aury, and put her to sleep in my bed. She'd cried so hard she'd thrown up, so I changed Aury's bed, too. You ungrateful bitch, I thought. And she *kept it up.*

"Look at you, her protector," Mom mocked me. "Do you think I'm a lousy parent, too? Like he does? Do you think I've lost my mind?"

"Currently," I said honestly. "Not permanently."

"Well, fuck him and fuck you," said . . . my mom! My mom who never swore in front of us, for whom a softly uttered "damn" was acceptable only for a traffic accident or a tornado warning. "By this time tomorrow you'll be free to eat and do whatever you please, because I'll be in bed, shaking and stiffening up. Have a ball!"

"Mom, you need to lie down," I said.

"I never need to lie down again!" she screamed. "I've lain down for the best part of the past six months. My husband accidentally left me for a jam maker, my son refuses even to fake doing homework, and my daughter is probably the town whore."

"You forgot Aury."

"Oh yes, the flower of your father's age. Or wait, did he get a new pistil or whatever they call it? The previous apple of your father's eye. Don't stand there and look at me. Leave! Leave, like every other stinking rat—"

"It's either stinking rat or rat leaving a sinking ship, Mom. You can't have it both ways."

"Shut up!" she shouted, advancing on me. I grabbed her wrists and held her arms down. "I hate you," she sobbed.

"I hate you right now, too," I told her.

"I hate what I have that passes for a life."

"Do you want me to call a suicide hotline?"

"So they can tell me suicide is a permanent solution to a temporary problem? Well, what about a permanent problem? One that plays with you like a cat with a mouse. One day, your leg. The next week, an eye. Left hand Tuesday. Right hand Wednesday. Neck so stiff you can't turn it. What about that? And how you feel about the person it makes out of you?" She pounded her fists together. "Gabe! I wish I could say I'd make it up to you. I don't know how you feel, but I can imagine. Like I'm the child, and you're the parent. I wish I could say, if I get better, or if I get some money, I'll buy your childhood back, but you get only one. And I used yours up. But, Gabe, you don't know how I feel, with all these little crappy things picking at me and my life . . ."

"It sucks," I said, and I meant it. She had a right to go ballistic. But she had no right to treat us like shit, because we were the only people in the world she could depend on. On the other hand, I could see how you could hate that—being dependent on the people who were supposed to be dependent on you. It would make you want to treat them like shit.

By then, she had finished breaking plates and throwing Aury's toys away—of course, I took them back out of the trash—and gone to bed. I wondered if I would end up hating both of them, her *and* Leo.

I had saved my most recent letter from Tian. And I figured this would be the time to read it, when I needed it most

Practically the whole front of the letter was stamps, and it was so pitifully short. Yeah, English wasn't her first language, but she had a way of being sweet and yet distant that was unbearable. She had "so much sorrow" over my mother and father.

I am without the words to say this. These were such good people to me. I come from a stable family, and it is difficult to imagine my father describing himself that way. Perhaps he is having a mental illness and will get better presently. And so, Gabe, you must be very brave, because it will pay off. I am now a junior in my school because of the acceleration. I went to school all through my holidays. It was so that next year I will apply to Yale. And I will go the year after. I would like to see the United States again, and have ice cream. I remember my days there like a dream that girls have in a legend. Will Yale be far from Sheboygan? [As the moon, I thought. As far as the moon.] *I will hope you will come over and see me. Your friend, Tian.*

The "your friend" didn't help.

It wasn't like I hadn't tried getting over her. I dated, for a while, in the laziest sense of the word, a girl called Rebecca, not an Ed. She was cute, along the lines of Easter, sister of Joyous, all long legs and purply red hair, nearly as tall as I was. But then I'd get one of Tian's letters. And her handwriting, even the spicy smell of the paper she'd written on, made me sick, as if I had the flu. Nauseated. Sweating at night. I'd fake having to work or take care of my mother two weekends in a row to avoid seeing Rebecca before I got over it. I thought that if I weren't a Jew, I might become a priest, because it was obvious I was never going have Tian, who would marry some Yaley doctor, just like Luke said, about five minutes into her internship. After a while, Rebecca told me gently she thought she wanted to see other people. I put up a minor struggle, for the sake of it looking right. But it was kind of a relief. I mean, I had proved my point. I'd dated a regular girl at fucking LaFollette. And I had no desire to do anything else.

That night, after my mother went bonkers, was when I called Tian. It probably cost about eighty dollars, and over there, it was, of course, about four in the morning. Her dad had a shit fit until she told him it was Gabe from Sheboygan United States, and then he was all nice.

"Why is it?" Tian asked.

"Why's what, that I called?" I replied. "I . . . miss you. Still. I miss you like you don't miss me."

"Wait," Tian said. "I miss you. I don't have a boyfriend. But I am practical. If I miss you all the time, I get depressed and I cannot do work or be a good person to my friends."

"My mother's so sick."

"I know. It is horrible to think of beautiful Julie sick and weak."

"And my father is a bastard."

"Don't say that, Gabe. It's worse for you than for him to say that."

"That's what my mother says. She says I have to think of my own karma."

"She's right. Because if he will be a bastard, hating him can make you into a bastard."

"So, what's new?" Well, there was a lot new. A lot of social parties and a lot of dancing parties and very hard schoolwork, not like Sheboygan, and a trip to Italy planned with her choir, and . . . she just had so much good going on in her life, I wanted to hang the hell up on her, too.

"Gabe, I know you are so sad," she finally told me. "I wish I could come and kiss your mouth."

"There's nothing I wish more in the whole world," I told her.

"But I will come soon. In two years. And we will have coffee," she said.

"Oh, Tee," I said to her. "You know we won't. You know . . . you don't know about me. You don't know I'm not a smart medical student kind of kid like you. In fact, I'm giving it one more semester, just for my mother's sake, and then I'm quitting."

"Quitting school? Gabe, you must not do this ever."

"It's not getting me anywhere. I can take this test that proves you learned everything you needed to learn in high school, and any idiot can pass it, and then I'll go to college later. My mother has Cathy here, and she's better a lot of the time now, and she doesn't really need me."

"I know that you have a special class for reading. This is not a lack of intelligence. Gabe, you told me that yourself."

"And you believed it." I looked at myself in the mirror. My skin had gotten bumpy, probably from stress and junk, and I realized why the comparison is often made between people with acne and pizza with sausage. "Well, you won't feel that way in two years."

"We'll see, Gabe. After the coffee, right?" She was so relentlessly practical and upbeat. I had gotten all the way to upstate New York, why not Bangkok? We could run away and pretend to be Mr. and Mrs. Dead Kevin. But even if I showed up there, Tian's father, after giving me food and tea and probably a shirt handmade by his personal tailor, would put me right back on a plane home.

I could never escape.

I grabbed my coat and sat on the porch.

Even if I quit school and somehow got into a college on the basis of test scores, I would still be a sixteen- or seventeen-year-old kid who would have to ask somebody for help, even though when Gramp came to America, boys my age got married and went to work. And did I even want that? Did I want to go to work flipping burgers alongside girls with mall hair?

I felt so sorry for myself that I didn't hear the screaming until after I came back inside and was about to flip on the TV. My mother was hoarse; I don't know how many times she'd called me. In the dark, I couldn't see her on the bed, so I went to flip on her light. "Don't, Gabe," she said. "Don't turn on the light. Go call Gram. Right now."

"What, Mom? Did you hit your head or something?"

"Just . . . go call Gram. Wait. Before you leave, let me tell you something."

"What?"

"That I'm a lousy person. Getting sick doesn't give you the excuse to be a bully. I'm a bully, Gabe. Maybe it's because I'm scared and I think that being a bully will make you behave and be safe because I can't."

"It's doesn't work that way."

"I know that. And right now, I deserve to have you hate me for the rest of my life. But please don't, Gabe. You're a mensch. Gabe, you're more of a human being now than most men I know ever get to be. Stay that way. Be a bigger person than I was tonight. God forgive me, Gabe. Because I'll never forgive myself."

Gram was over there in about fifteen minutes. But it turned out I had to pull Mom up out of bed because Gram was too little. I could smell the sharp tang, the stink of piss. Gram drove her to the hospital, and the doctor decided to put in what's called a Foley catheter for a day or so, the better for my mother to conserve her strength for the formality of losing my father. Gram slept on the blow-up bed in my mother's room. Every time I emptied that rubber bag, I didn't want to know myself, and when I'd come back into the room, she'd put her face in the pillow and pretend she was asleep until Gram got it hooked back up. I would stand in the hall.

I know she wasn't asleep.

All that time, I wanted to tell her I forgave her for almost slapping me and for scaring Aury. I wanted to tell her that there were houses I knew of right on this street where crap like that happened all the time, and nobody took people's kids away for it. I wanted to tell her that she wasn't a monster, she was just in a bad way at a really bad time.

But I couldn't. She was out past the fence of shame, in new territory. She was out there by herself, and we couldn't go.

TWENTY-SIX

Gabe's Journal

My grandpa Steiner was the one who told me that my parents' marriage was over, officially history. My mother hadn't wanted to come right home from the courthouse, so Cathy drove her around for a while, I guess.

But Gramp and Gram came right back, to make sure we were okay. Both their eyes were red, but Gramp at first seemed like he was almost celebrating something. "The judge gave it to him, Gabe! He told him that his wish to work less and live more was incompatible with his wish to procreate, that he had four minor children to support, not one, and a disabled wife, and that his earning *capacity* far exceeded Julieanne's, no matter what the current status of her health. He said that he could either give Julieanne half the proceeds of selling the house up in la-la land or he could give up his share of the proceeds of this house, and he would have to pay support for you and all the children until your eighteenth birthdays, in the amount of about thirty percent or something of what he used to make at the university unless Julieanne remarried, which we know, God help her, she never will, plus college, but Julie spoke up and said that college was taken care of, by her own father's estate. Leo was all red in the face; he was so mad. You could see why no lawyer I ever called would mediate, because he was all ipso facto Havana banana and all that, just like they said. His knowledge of the law so far outruns Julie's, it would have been a joke. But the judge just finally said, Look, Mister Steiner. I respect your abilities as an officer of the court or I would not instruct you to use them to your fullest capabilities to provide family maintenance for the children you have chosen to abandon, however you choose to describe that abandonment. You are at the peak of your earning power, Mister Steiner . . ." And then Gramp began to cry. He took his handkerchief and blew his nose so you could hear it in Milwaukee, the way old men do. And he just sat there.

"Gramp?" I said finally.

"Here I am. Kvelling over my son's loss. And his idiot behavior. Here I am cheering against my own child," he said, hanging his head.

"It's pretty hard to cheer *for* it, Gramp," I said, sitting down next to him. "But, look, Dad could change. He could wake up. I don't really . . . think he'll ever come back here, but he could still have a good relationship with, like, Caroline, even just summers and holidays, because she's basically so shallow she'll end up being best friends with Joy and Amos. Aury's just a baby. Mom says we're going to start calling her 'Rory,' because it's more normal, and she'll start liking little Amos, and when they have the new baby—"

"The new baby?" Gramp cried.

"What baby, Gabe?" Gram asked.

"She's expecting," I said. "Joy is. Dad's girlfriend." I hated myself for the misery I saw further crease their old faces.

"Gotten Himmler," he said, though I didn't see what it had to do with history. "And you, Gabe. What about you and your father. If he should wake up, as you say, will you forgive him?"

"Sure," I said.

"You're lying," Gramp said.

"Yeah, I'm lying," I admitted.

"But he is your father, Gabe. You'll never have another. And there is good in him. People make mistakes. He didn't kill anybody. He's wrong. But he's done so much in his life that's good, for me, for you. You know that."

"I know that, too. But I can't see how I could ever see his point."

"Maybe when you're grown up, and you fall in love," said Gram.

"I have been in love," I said.

"Puppy love," she said. "Milk-tooth love."

"No, Gram, real love. I don't mean, like, for the rest of my life. I'm not going to be that lucky. To keep her. But I know how he feels. But then I just look at Aury . . . or Rory, and I think I wouldn't hurt her even for that, what I felt. And she's not my kid, she's my sister."

"I'm changing my name, too," Caroline announced, walking out of her bedroom, still blurry from sleep, wearing her pajamas and socks, her earphones hanging around her neck.

"To what? Lead Ass?" I asked. "It's one-thirty in the afternoon."

"To Cat. I like it. Cat Steiner. It sounds like a visual artist. Or singer."

"When did you make this decision?" my grandmother asked her, putting her arms around Caro and nuzzling her hair. "Let me get you some toast or a bagel before Mama gets home."

"When I was out there, out where Dad is," Caroline went on, and bounced over to the window seat. "I liked the way they chose their names. They were all free, you know? They all did exactly what they wanted. . . ."

"He won't be doing that anymore, Caroline," said Gramp.

"But he'll still be happy. He'll still be tapping his own trees for syrup and stuff. And making birdhouses and shelves. He might even start making guitars. He'll still be able to drink out of his own spring, and he'll still wake up every morning and hear Joy singing. She's really a good singer. When I stayed overnight, she was singing 'Once Upon a Dream' to the baby. . . ."

"Mom used to sing that to Aury," I said murderously. "When she was a baby."

"Yeah, that's right! But Joy has a better voice. I like mezzos. I'm a mezzo."

"You're a ditz."

"He can't call me that, Gramp!" Caro said, kicking off one of her puffy monster shoes, which hit me in the chest.

"You can't call her that, Gabe."

"Sorry . . . Cat."

"It's okay," she said. "Are they back yet?"

"They were going to get some coffee and pick up Aury," I told her. "I mean, Rory."

"I meant Dad."

"Dad's not coming here."

She sat down. Grandma had gone to toast her a bagel. She selected a piece of hair and wound it around her finger, examining it for split ends. I knew this was her way of looking like an idiot while she thought something through, and, in fact, she finally said, "Well, he is, Gabe. He's coming to get me."

"I'm not going to dinner with him," I said.

"I'm not going to dinner with him, either," said Caro, now Cat. "I'm going with him. I'm going back with him. School's almost over, and I can finish with the homeschool program out there, and I already have two teachers who are going to let me take my finals early. . . . Dad's going to wait until the end of next week. . . ."

"For how long?" I asked. "Not the whole summer. I can't do this all alone the whole summer. It's not fair to Cathy."

"That's what I thought," Caroline mumbled. "So I thought, I'd stay out there. And then, there'd be one less mouth to feed, and one less person taking up space in this place, and there's plenty of room for me in the new house, Dad says, and Joy says it'll be like having two little sisters, and she'll need the help, with two babies—"

"Are you out of your fucking mind?" I asked her, ignoring Grandma's *"Hush"* as I jumped up off the couch. She stood between me and my sister, the bagel on its blue plate with its cream cheese spread delicately to the edges of each half held in her hand like an offering. "You'd leave Mom? You'd go there and live with that bitch and her babies? You'd leave Aury?"

"She's in a phase, Gabe. She's a whiny little brat. She's always taking my things. . . ."

"She's practically a baby!" I grabbed her arm. "You blame her for using your lip gloss? You won't help your own mother crawl to the bathroom after her shot. You think it's 'gross.' You're mad at your own little sister? But you'd help *Joyous* with *her* babies? Have you even *mentioned* this to Mom? Because if you do, I swear to God—"

"I don't have to tell Mom! I'm almost fifteen, and I can make my own choice! Dad says—"

"You want to know what Dad cares about, *Cat*? He cares that he won't have to pay support to Mom for you, that's what. Ask Gramp! He can feed you a couple of alfalfa sprouts a day and have free child care and not have to spend so much time working, which would suit him fine! He wouldn't feel all confined and start thinking people looked like badgers and hedgehogs! You think this is because he loves you so much? *Did you see his face when his slut opened that door and he saw us standing there?* That wasn't love, Caroline. That was 'oh shit.'"

"Gabe, stop," Grandma said.

"He *does* love us, Gabe," Caroline said. "He'd love to take Aurora, too, if Mom would let him. But she won't. She says Aurora's too little to be away from her mother! But nobody around here has any use for me any-how, and anyway, I'm sick of school. Joy's going to homeschool me, and teach me how to put up jam and weave, and introduce me to all these kids that go to their Quaker meeting."

"Quakers?" my grandfather bellowed.

"Well, Dad and Joy aren't Quakers, but they hang around with them, and they're really nice, and they don't believe in war and there are, like, fifteen kids my age right in the same valley. They go there sometimes. It sounds neat. You don't have to pray or even stay awake. You just think."

"But can you bring your headphones in? And wait! You'd leave *Mallory and Justine*? You'd leave *Ryan*?" I was starting to feel sick to my stomach, starting to think that she really meant this, that she really was about as deep as the sole of her shoe, that my mother could lose her husband and her child, that this was not my problem, but also that it would be this bog I'd be stuck in for the rest of my life.

"Ryan is so over with, Gabe," she said. "And I can come back and visit.

I won't, like, never see you again."

"But I'll, like, never speak to you again."

"Fine," Caroline said then, and I could see the puma part of her gathering to attack under her fluffy yellow pajama top. "Don't ever speak to me again. Spend your whole life changing your mother's diapers, you freak!"

"Caroline, God forgive you!" my grandmother said, with the obligatory heart grab. "Gabriel doesn't change his mother's diapers. Your mother doesn't wear *diapers*."

"Well, you do it, or fix her pee hose or whatever! I saw you last week. I couldn't bring anyone in this house. They'd think she had . . . cancer or Alzheimer's."

"And if she did?" my grandfather said. "You wouldn't want to know her?"

"Gramp, I love my mother. I love the mother I *had*! But it isn't just that she's sick, it's that she acts like . . . she's mean to Aurora, and she's always depressed or busy with one of her talks or picking on me to do something, Caroline! *Do something!* If I wanted to be a nurse, I'd be one. I don't want to live with Mom and her friend, the lesbian. I want to live in a normal household. . . ."

"Oh, then definitely go live with Joyous and Easter and whatever their sisters' names are, Tree Frog and Sunflower. They're a real normal bunch."

"It's better than here! Anything's better than here!"

None of us saw Mom standing in the arch, holding Rory by the hand. She tried for a smile that quivered and sort of dissolved into a puddle.

"Cathy went to see her mom," she said. "It really isn't fair to turn her out of her own house while I have *ma petite crise*, is it? And I have them so often. But . . . I guess this is the last one. Huh? It's . . . so funny. Isn't it? They make you go together, to be apart. They make you go to the courthouse and sit side by side—some people have lunch afterward—while you cut your marriage up into steaks and chops. You get this haunch. I get this quarter. A slice here. A slice there. You cut up your life. You sign the same papers, the way you did when you got married. I, Julieanne, give you, Leo, away forever. Before these witnesses." Her face crumpled up like Rory's did before she cried, and was suddenly a waterfall of sooty tears, which she made worse by rubbing her eyes. "I had to give Leo away, and he said, 'Why so bleak, Julieanne? You're getting what you wanted.' And I said, 'No, Lee, I'm getting what *you* wanted.' And he put his arms around me and patted my back! Papa, Hannah, how can he leave me?"

Caroline got up, quickly, and tried to duck around our mother on her way to her room. But Mom reached out and held her. "Don't be angry with him, Caro. My sweet girl. My beautiful sunflower head. He loves you so. He loves Gabe. I know he does." My mom held Caro against her, crushing Caro to her, leaning down to put her head against Caro's cheek. "It's not always going to be like this, sweetheart. I promise. I heard what you said. This is the worst it will ever be. Mama will make it better. We'll have fun again, Caro—"

"I have to go get dressed, Mom," Caroline said. "Don't cry."

"Okay," my mother said, and then she turned to look at the rest of us, crouched on the sofa like the three monkeys, with hands over various parts of our heads.

Caroline stood in the hall. "Mom, listen. We might as well—"

"Shut *up!*" I shouted at her. I think the whole neighborhood heard me. "Shut your stupid mouth!"

"What?" my mother asked. "What's wrong? Are you sick, Caroline?" There were tears all over the front of her good white satin blouse. Her nose was running.

I don't want to remember the rest of that night. My mother kept going back into Caroline's room as Caroline packed, resolutely, also crying, but placing roll after roll of her embroidered jeans and her minuscule sweaters into her big Land's End duffel, the one from camp, embroidered HCS. We could hear her, pleading, "Caroline, no. Darling, wait. Please think it over . . . just 'til summer, how about that, Caro? Just until summer? Huh?"

I personally couldn't wait to see her walk out the door.

That is a lie.

I . . . loved my sister. More or less. Then.

I still think about her. It was all part of that time, but you are supposed to have your future with your siblings. That's a guarantee. Like that your father will take care of you.

But I had also heard enough to know that what Caro was doing could throw my mother into a relapse. Stress was hard on anybody, but particularly hard on a person with multiple sclerosis. It must have been so hard for her to beg like that. But then, there was nothing she wouldn't have done for us, any of us, not because she didn't want us to be with Leo—it was never like that—but because she wanted us to be with her. She thought it had always been her job to take care of us, to be the one of them who was the most parent, the less outside support. It wasn't like Caroline finally said, the next morning—as though Mom was Grandmother Gillis and had this set of china that would be missing the gravy bowl. We were literally all she had left.

I tried to jam my pillow over my ears, stuffing it around my head like a life preserver, so that I wouldn't hear them crying, all that long night. I know Caroline finally went to sleep, but I heard the coffeemaker click on at about four in the morning, and Mom and Gram talking.

". . . be back after she has a little . . ."

". . . imagine him being able to . . ."

". . . so foolish, because of her age. It frightens her."

At one point, then, Mom sort of shouted, "It frightens me, too, Hannah! Just because I'm an adult doesn't mean that I don't know I'm going to live my life alone, when the kids grow up, or with some kindly helper I pay to feed me. I want what I have left while I have it, Hannah—"

"Hush, Julie, you'll wake the children," Gram said. I wondered why she was still there. We were sort of the Holiday Inn of the Fucked Up. You could drop in anytime. I got up and sort of curled up next to the crack in my bedroom door. "There's Cathy—"

"You know that I want Cathy to fall in love and have her own family one day. Hannah, I know how you feel about . . . how Cathy is, but she's the dearest friend. . . ."

"I won't argue with you there. I admit I had my concerns about her influence on the children."

"Be quiet. She'll hear you. I heard her come in."

"But her door is closed tight."

"She's been the most loyal friend I've ever had."

"I see that."

"But she's going to want her own life, and perhaps another child. She's only thirty-five, Hannah. And Gabe will grow up and go to school. . . ."

"Every one of us is afraid of being alone, Julie," Gram said, and I heard the clink of her spoon as she added more sugar.

"It's one thing being alone if you can travel, or go to lectures, or whatever it would be that I'd do. It's another being alone if you fall and have to lie in your own excrement until the mail carrier comes."

"We'll get an alarm, Julie, and a beeper, when the need for that arises, and it may never arise. You might never have another bad stretch again."

"But I might. I had a really severe onset of this, Hannah. I have to face the fact that in a few years, I might be using a wheelchair."

"Julie! Let's burn that bridge when we come to it."

"And, Hannah, more than that. I'm not some kind of saint, but really, right now you should be with your son. I don't want to come between you and Leo. I don't want you to think that being loyal to the children and me means ruling Leo out of your life. . . ."

"We won't, Julie. When things settle down. Right now, Gabe is having a very hard time dealing with what Leo did to his grandchildren and to you. Julie, remember. You've been married so long to our son. You were a pip-squeak, you and him, under the canopy. I've known you all of your adult life. You're not like a daughter-in-law to me, Julie, but like my own—"

"I know, but this has completely messed up the plan we had for you. Your friends, your traveling. All of it."

At some point, I must have fallen asleep. I dreamed of Tian, in Connie's kitchen that day, saying she felt like a princess of America. But she had grown taller—well, tall for a Thai person—and had short hair cut to turn under and was wearing one of my mother's jackets. *Gabe, she said, taking my hand and patting me on the arm, how good to see you. What grade are you in now?* And I was still the same age, still fifteen. In the dream, I kept trying to stand up taller, willing myself to be taller and more imposing, so she'd see me as a man, but she was walking away, telling me how great it was to have seen me again, that I should do good in school. That she'd see me again . . . but that wasn't a dream. It was really Caroline, crouched down next to me on the floor.

"Wake up, Gabe," she said. "I want to go while she's asleep and Aurora's asleep. Dad is outside."

I got up and walked past her to the bathroom, and took my time, brushing my teeth. I knew the silence would drive her nuts, but I also didn't trust what I might say.

"Gabe," she whispered, outside the door. "Come on out here. I want to give you the number of their house and the Quality Inn, so you can call me if Mom needs me. Not like I won't come back here to say good-bye to her, but she's too upset now. I don't want to upset her any more."

I threw the door open and Caroline almost fell in. I walked past her as if she were invisible. "Goddamnit!" she said. "You don't have to be so rude." I went into my bedroom, the door of which did not lock, and got into my bed. As zonked as I might have looked, my mind was banging like an engine opened up full bore. Should I try to talk sense to her? Beg her? Curse her? What would ultimately be best for us, all of us, for her to stay here and resent the hell out of Mom, get pregnant, smoke dope, whatever? Or would she settle down after he left and stopped filling her head with pictures of the glories of the Happy Valley in spring. I could imagine the Happy Valley under three feet of snow was probably a pretty grim and isolated place. There was also the matter of what kept spooling through my mind, the pictures of her and me huddled in the bus station in West Springfield, Massachusetts, wondering if we'd get out of town before they found the gun, the two of us sitting pressed up next to each other as if a storm had broken over our heads. Just her and me. My sister. Irish twins, they called us, born in the same year. Another part of me wanted to remind her of that, of the fact that she was not only leaving Mom, who would always be more loyal to her than Leo, but me. Me. Who saved her, who followed her all the way to the road across from the Breakdown Lane sign. Caroline, I wanted to say, you're a fool, but you're part of . . . I secured the pillow around my head, harder. "Gabe," I heard her say. "Gabe? Aren't you even going to say good-bye to me?" I wouldn't let myself speak. "Gabe, you're my brother," she said, and I could tell by the break in her voice that she was crying. "Not everybody is the same. Okay, maybe you're a bigger, stronger person than I am. But I'm not evil, Gabe. I'm not mean. I don't want to hurt anybody. I'm afraid I'm going to hurt her feelings. Mom's feelings. That's why I'm going, partly. It's not just for me, Gabe." Like, a sixteenth of my brain knew she was telling the truth. Finally, after what seemed a couple of hundred years, I felt her reach out and put her little hand on the back of my head. "I'll write to you, Gabe. I'll call you from the hotel. You'll always be my bro, Gabe. I'm sorry I called you a 'tard. You're the smartest person I know." Oh, shit, I thought, this cannot be happening. It was some, like, surreal fucking joke. I could imagine how kids would act. I didn't want to go there. To the Steiners, the award for best transformation from an ordinary family in the lower forty-eight. After a couple of minutes, I got my mouth to stop shaking and lifted my head. I wasn't sure what I was going to say to her.

But she was already gone.

TWENTY-SEVEN

Psalm 78

～～～～～

EXCESS BAGGAGE
By J. A. Gillis
Distributed by Panorama Media

Dear J.,

Who the heck are you to give other people advice that could change their whole lives? Tell them their marriages aren't going to work out, when it's completely possible that if they prayed and tried to give up their pride, they might turn out to be very happy? That's what happened to my husband and me, after he stepped off the path. We found the lowest place in our house—in our case, the basement powder room—and got down on our knees and asked the Lord to heal our marriage. And he did. I think you're crazy yourself, and that's why you don't want anyone else to be happy. What are you, a psychologist? A minister? Or just a busybody with a big mouth?

Curious in Clayvourne

Dear Curious,

Probably the final choice.

I have no credentials. I never went to school to try to help people live their lives. And mine hasn't been anybody's idea of a

rousing success, especially in certain areas. But I do the best I
can. And I listen. Isn't that all any of us can do?

                              J.

———————————————————

Caroline had not been much of a presence in our lives after Leo left for the first time. She'd made sure of that. But when she left for good, she was an absence. Though I was sure (almost hopeful) that I would become symptomatic (a little mental sludge can't hurt once in a while), I did not. I felt great. In fact, I've never had as bad an episode again as I had around the time of the divorce, which is probably no coincidence.

My mind remained brutally lucid. I could see my Caroline's pixie-ish upper lip as I gathered the detritus left behind by her hurricane departure: barrettes with tendrils of blonde hair; notes folded into those complicated, eight-sided paper pyramids you can only manage to construct when you're an adolescent; a half-empty bottle of Eau Leonie (mine). I could see her, hair twisted and pinned up, wearing the things she'd left in her closet—her long black formal skirt, her parka, the Mary Janes that made her feet look so dainty and trim, that she, of course, hated. I boxed them up, first pressing each to my face, as I had boxed up my mother's cardigans after her funeral. But I realized then I'd nowhere to send them. So I gave them to Hannah, not really wanting to know Leo's post-office-box number.

My sense of my own worthlessness was past measuring. I don't know if it's possible to put yourself inside the body of a woman who's been ditched by her husband, her child, and at least some big part of her health. Perhaps what had animated the marionette was the sense of being Julie-who-was-wife-and-mother-and-writer. And then all but one of the strings was snipped. One hand moved, jerkily, up and down over my keyboard. Gabe was there, and Aury-now-Rory. But I couldn't give myself to them, or only sporadically, and in bursts of affection, rather than a dependable level of maternal steadiness. I would look at them and see Caro's wrinkled nose cross my little girl's face. I would hear some note in Gabe's laugh that was hers and want to shut myself away from him. And so I behaved . . . like shit. Rory would get a stack of Golden Books one night, a rude wave from me the next to go away and let me sleep. One week, I'd be emptying the book bag each night with Gabe and going over his calendar. The next week I didn't notice whether he came home. Jennet said some of this might come from the lesions that either were or were not cratering away in my brain tissue, crumbling the tissue surrounding my nerves like burned toast.

Gabe was like a rock. Actually, he was like a stone. He showed almost no range of emotion or motion. He moved like a weighted diver traversing the ocean floor.

But he always made sure his little sister got home.

He always made sure she got fed and to bed, whether Cath was working late or not. I took him so for granted. He knew it.

With Cathy, there was almost a shame, a smell of failure. A sense that Abby Sun would never leave Cathy as Caroline had left me. She greeted me each morning with a strong shoulder hug I had to force myself to return with a pat of my hand. It was not my finest hour. These were not my finest six hundred hours. The perpetual dull pain and intermittent bursts of flame along my legs and the tremors in my hands and brain that made me have to S.T.O.P. and T.H.I.N.K. to type drove me mad with rage. The inability to recover words I knew as well as my own name—and, more than once, when someone answered the telephone, I had to pause and reflect before I could say my own name—had the same effect. I knew that it was necessary for me to lie down each afternoon, and that when I had my bursts of energy or creativity, and "overdid," I paid later with hours of falling asleep during conversations or talking like a drunk. I took Valium to stop the jits and the rampant anxiety—there were times I was certain I could see Caroline lying dead in the Vermont mud, knocked off a bike by a drunk driver, while Leo and Joyous toasted each other with fucking grapes they'd stomped themselves and congratulated Leo on his excellent sperm count. I took antidepressants to thrust me out of bed in the morning, or I'd have lain, without washing my face, for days, past caring how I looked or smelled. The children never seemed to notice, and though Cath made tentative hints about the importance of getting up and at it every day ("If you get dressed and showered, Jules, everything thereafter can legitimately be considered a nap . . ."), it seemed so much easier just to brush my teeth and haul my computer up onto the bed. Eventually, Cathy or Hannah would wash the sheets.

Did I think I had this kind of sloth coming to me because I was a poor lady who had MS and had been dumped?

Uh. Yes.

I showed Cathy my poem "Soup in Winter," on which I'd worked for two months, counting out dum-da-dum-da syllables. I was kind of proud of it.

Soup in Winter

An onion, as a symbol for love dissected
Translucent skin making visible the rejected,
And the layers—a tree's memory rings, halves bisected,
Is too easy.
And yet we do it.
An exercise, a verbal excision of a small dark place of rot,
The sharp poignancy, blended, easily forgot
Over low flames, a boost to flavors more kind, lost to mind.
We forget, until we cut again, how shrill are love's demands
And how our eyes fill and stream, the scent stubborn on our hands.
How easily an onion falls to pieces,
How fit for disconnection.
As if in its conception
Was its insurrection.

Cathy looked at me and said, "Well, it's not that it's really bad writing. But, um, the message is that love stinks, right?"

I hadn't thought of that.

But I had to agree. Damn her!

"It doesn't necessarily, Julie. It's not written that you'll never fall in love again. You're a young woman—"

"*Oh, please!*" I brayed at her, my dearest friend. "I mean, women my age can't get a date if they're millionaires. How about if they're broke, have neurotic children and a debilitating deteriorative disease? I think that describes the dream date of the millennium."

Then I pounded on the table until my hands hurt and apologized profusely.

"I think this thing is getting to my brain, literally. I never used to be so prone to, well, ups and downs of mood," I said, expecting Cathy to hurry to deny that. When she didn't, a cold black shaft opened inside me.

It was entirely possible that I was having what they call "cognitive" issues—in other words, brain damage.

With Jennet, I worked it out that I somehow believed Leo was to blame for having leached away my health by leaving me behind. I somehow seemed to think that if Leo would come back, I'd behave like a tape played in reverse—all the strings would connect again if Leo would love me. And yet, much as I loved Leo, my fantasies about Leo were not sexual but homicidal. I pictured him coming to me, frozen and bleeding, and my closing the door against him in a blizzard. I actually dreamed that, so it wasn't my fault. Jennet said that images of Leo as cold and threatening were not bizarre, but rather ordinary. But also, I would take out his letters to me, our honeymoon scrapbook, and stare into the faces of those smug, slim, utterly sensual young people and think, Where is the clue? Where is the seed that grew into the Whole Holistic Leo? His pinch of arrogance? His touch of impatience? I was a dozen times more arrogant and impatient any day of the week, even back then. But I never, not ever, would have slipped through my wedding band and fled. As closely as Jennet questioned me, trying to probe for the soft spot, the place that admitted a certain immune deficiency in my marriage, I could not honestly find one for her. Gabillions of people have midlife wackies and come home, wagging their tails behind them, I alleged. No, Jennet would argue. That was not true. Those who take off on extended flings are practicing divorce, as a suicide practices with shallow cuts. But he had been such a wonderful father, I would counter. So were many wife beaters, Jennet came back at me. Many never laid a finger on their children.

"Okay!" I shouted at her one day. "I knew I was being a wuss, letting him go on photography vacations! I knew he was juggling with torches and he was going to drop one on me! But if I'd forbidden it, he'd just have left sooner, right? He'd just have speeded up the whole thing and booked out."

"And would that have been the worst thing that ever happened?" she asked softly.

"I loved him!" I cried. "I was used to him! We were a team. Are you suggesting that a nice clean cut, sooner, between the children and their father would have been better than the good times we had—and we did still have good times—right up until the last trip?"

"Yes," Jennet said. "I am."

"Why?"

"Because the way it happened was sordid and deceitful and, for both Gabe and Caroline, has created lacerations that will remain open for years. Hate to be the one to say it."

"And you blame me?"

"Wait," Jennet held up a hand. "I didn't say that. In fact, I don't blame you for closing your eyes to what seems obvious to me, because you're not me, and I wasn't the one married to him. Behavior that starts gradually, the way you describe Leo's, becomes customary, and anything customary seems preferable to something awful and alien. Like living alone. Like losing your daughter, too. But making a pastiche of Leo and your health is going magical, Julieanne. Some coincidences are coincidences. In fact, though I don't want to offend whatever religious beliefs you have, I think most coincidences are . . . coincidental. In other words, if they hadn't happened . . . if you asked God for proof of His existence and an eagle *did not* fly overhead, well, that would have simply been a day you didn't remember."

"So this leaves me?"

"With a lot of anger work to do."

"Oh that sounds so psychie-wyckie. Anger work."

"Well, it might. But you've got to acknowledge to your kids that you're absolutely furious with their father, stop telling them to 'respect' him, that they want to 'love' him one day. That's their choice. And right now, while you can help them honor their memories, their dad has snapped his cap. And you have to stop thinking of yourself as a victim. And stop looking like a victim, in baggy pants and sweatshirts. Get a life, Julieanne."

Well, it was easy for her to say.

Talking to Matthew, there'd been that. Little Matthew MacDougall, my secret seventh-grade crush, now a big-shot surgeon in Boston. I was flattered at first that he'd read, much less liked, my poems.

But it wasn't as much fun after Leo's and my divorce. Talking about my woes with someone who was smart and funny and (tragically, but I hadn't known her) widowed felt as if I were on a par with Leo. He'd lost his wife in a car accident that his child thankfully survived. Better yet, he obviously was smitten with his quarter-century-old memories of me. It had been a kind of vengeance. Harmless vengeance. You got a Pilates instructor who makes jam? I got a *facial surgeon,* a real doctor, not a dentist! He rebuilds jaws instead of picking berries. He makes baby's faces whole instead of doing the Hundred.

But I didn't really "have" Matthew, or want him.

I remembered Matt MacDougall as an absurdly short, almost elfin boy—I'd been tall for my age, and dancing with him was like talking to the part in his hair—who worshipped me through mournful aquamarine eyes and let me copy his math papers. Over the years, when a notice came round for one of our high school reunions, I would read of him vaguely—he hadn't been a crush. His wife, Susan, who'd died when their child was just a toddler, had been the first person from our class to be lost, except in

Vietnam. On my stationery, *JSG*, which I now used for grocery lists, I'd sent him a note. Though the publication and the huge check (fifty dollars) of my poem in *Pen, Inc.*, had been a thrill, I wondered why a doctor read a "little" (really little) poetry magazine.

In fact, I wondered why he wrote and asked me to call, and why I did. I was lonely.

I wanted someone who couldn't see me to want me. I wanted someone who didn't know that I tripped or staggered, slurred, or stammered, to want me.

"What did you do tonight?"

"Oh, it was big," he'd say. "I got the car washed, and I went and bought the new Elmore Leonard novel. I got a cup of coffee on the way home, though I know I'm too old for that, and it's going to keep me up. . . ."

"That's more than I did this week."

"Oh come on," said Matt. "My friends tell me I'm the most boring man they know. Go to the gym, buy carryout, fall asleep after ranting at the news. Last month, I tried to cut a couple of my big shrubs into a topiary shape. I thought it would be fun to make them into dolphins. I got a book from the library. Well, I'm a surgeon, right? How hard could this be? Let me tell you. It looked like kids had vandalized the house afterward. No, it really looked like the KKK had vandalized the house."

What he'd said, about his shrubs, his fireplace, his pal Shawn, and his pal Louis, from New York by way of Nigeria, made me feel connected to a normal world of people doing ordinary things for fun. The three of them had decided to go pheasant hunting. Shawn's father lent them the guns. They'd driven to the game preserve the previous fall, but it happened to be the day that the gamekeepers were unloading that year's stock. The pheasants hopped out of the truck and stood looking at Matt and his friends, making no attempt to fly or allow themselves to be stalked. One by one, the men exchanged glances and, without a word, put the guns back into their cases. "That was my hunting period," Matt said. "I'm entering my fly-fishing period in a couple of weeks, when I go on vacation. I'm sure no trout will be in peril. I think my guitar period will follow that."

He made me smile.

But after Caroline was gone, and the long, languid summer began, I was too sapped to talk to Matthew or even much to Cathy or Gabe. My daughter "Cat" sent a few desultory duty notes, about her adventures in Quaker-dise, about learning to fish, Amos beginning to crawl; but even I, after a while, began to feel that she was rubbing my face in her father's new life. I still called her every week on her cell phone, leaving messages when she didn't answer. She rarely called me back. When she did, she was eerily breezy. "Mom. Hi. Great. Yeah. Love." Nothing I could do touched her. Her birthday card to Gabe, which he threw away and I rescued, was signed "Cat Steiner."

Leo's insurance, which had covered all of us for the first years after he left the university, lapsed. And though the divorce required he cover Gabe, Caroline, and Rory (so Gabe *finally* got therapy for his language-processing problem), I began to have to pay for my medicines, my little sentinels against the dark, which no one was sure were effective, but which everyone was pretty sure were too risky to stop. *No* insurance company covers medicine for MS, because all treatments for an "incurable" disease are experimental. I did get my physical therapy paid for by a state program, with a little finagling from Cathy. I sold the last of my mother's antique bisques and her little Renoir sketch. I had another critical look at my closet and decided I really needed only three good winter and three good warm-weather dress-up outfits. One lovely lady gave me eleven hundred for two armloads of suits and dresses—some my mother's and some mine. Hannah gave me a box of her voluminous matching scarves and gloves, and I ended up looking—on purpose—vintage.

With seventeen thousand dollars in the bank, after the garage sale and all that other selling, I felt rich—but with physical therapy, food . . . it was an illusion. Eventually I knew I had to find an insurance policy. Which meant I had to find a full-time job. But what nice company would want to hire a reporter who sometimes had to lie down two hours a day? And had a weird preexisting condition. Maybe one that wanted federal brownie points for hiring the handicapped.

Until then, I had to find a way to do more, to make a dollar stretch more, with less. I made small economies. Although Cathy paid for most of the groceries, I began experimenting with various ways to make rice and beans more interesting. We bought into a vegetable co-op, and I made soup, soup over pasta, pasta with soup and extra beans.

Leo would have been in heaven.

This, was, then, to be my life. Speeches, when I could catch one, were increasingly farther and farther away, as the column was picked up by far-flung newspapers. But the airfare often was flung in with my honorarium, which I boldly raised to two thousand dollars. I would look after Abby when Cath had to go out of town—unless it coincided with a shot week, when Hannah or Connie looked after all of us—so she was glad to take over with my little girl when I went away. I sometimes believed that Aurora thought Cathy was her mother, but when my mind went grazing there, I tried to think that she was lucky to have such a good other mother. If I had to go to Atlanta, or even on hot summer days up in northern Wisconsin, the heat was enervating, but not, so far, problematic. If I got a nap, and I learned to fall asleep instantly on any moving conveyance from backseat to airplane, I was okay. Increasingly, I used one of my father's canes. People thought it was a fashion accessory, especially the one with the silver peacock he'd been given by some lord or laird.

When I had a moment, and they were few, I messed with poems, trying different forms, trying to work out whether I was angry or heartbroken. I got contact lenses for my birthday from Cath, and cut and sewed a bat costume for Aurora. It took two months of evenings.

Then, two things happened simultaneously and disastrously.

One Friday night, when the shiver under the murk of August heat portended fall, Gabe came into my bedroom, where I lay watching the ceiling fan, counting beats to a minute. Rory, who'd adjusted rapidly to her new name, climbed up next to me and nestled into my neck, tucking a finger into the corner of her mouth.

"Most banned book in the history of public schools," said Gabe.

"Okay, wait," I temporized. "Um, that Judy Blume book."

"God and Margaret and having your period, but no," he said.

"Okay. Gimme another chance."

"We don't do two chances. It's *Lord of the Flies*."

"How can I prove that, lying here? And anyhow, that reminds me of your father's first commune." According to Jennet, I was not supposed to ignore Leo's existence: I was supposed to bring up his name.

"It's true."

"More than that wrestling book?"

"Yeah."

"Okay," he went on, lying down at the foot of the bed. "Top jingle of the twentieth century."

"Had to be by Barry Manilow," I said. "I wish I were an Oscar Mayer wiener. No wait. It could be 'Winston tastes good like a cigarette should.'"

"Ma, they don't have cigarette-commercial jingles."

"They used to."

"I think your, uh, mind is playing tricks on you, Mom."

"*No*, Gabe. There used to be cigarette commercials on TV, with big TV stars singing about cigarettes. There was the Marlboro Man, and he was this big macho symbol. He died of smoking. Before he died, he made a commercial saying, 'This is what happened to me. By the time you see this, I'll be dug.'"

"You mean dead."

"Right."

"I *so* believe there were commercials for smoking."

"Look on the Internet, big shot. Anyhow, I think that was the top one."

"Wrong again, Ma," said Gabe. "It's 'You deserve a break today.'"

"Well, there you have it," I said softly, noticing Rory had fallen asleep. "I don't eat garbage. So how would I know? Anyhow, I was partly right. Barry Manilow wrote it."

"You're such a good loser."

"I get a turn now. What TV actor said 'Nano, nano'?" I asked.

"Mom, no seventies crap. It had to be, like Gramp says, since the flood receded."

"Okay. God. Name the thirteen colonies." I surrendered.

"So she goes back two centuries."

"Well? That much you know by the time you become a sophomore."

"Okay. New York. New Jersey. New Hampshire. North Carolina, South Carolina," Gabe said.

"Well, that's all the News and Norths and Souths, but I only count six."

"No big wup. I'm not going to be a sophomore long."

"Yeah? Skipping a grade?"

"No. Quitting."

"Carry Rory to bed," I told him, because some form of human electrical charge from my body had already disturbed her, and she was whimpering. "Please make sure she goes to the potty first."

"Come on, squirt," Gabe said, rolling his limp little sister into his arms. "Okay if she just sleeps in this? I'll change her in the morning."

"Uh-huh," I murmured, thinking, *Cathy, Cathy will talk him out of this.* It's just an anger reaction. It's a form of disgust. He can't bear the thought of facing Mrs. Kimball again, and who could blame him? I'll get his case-worker changed. I'll find a way to pay for homeschooling once the checks start coming—what's good enough for Caro is good for Gabe, too. I had all my arguments mustered when he came back into the room. I burst into tears instead and took his big hand. "Don't hand me one more thing, please. I don't want to guilt trip you, but, Gabe, I beg you. Don't give me one more failure. Please."

"I don't want you to think of it that way," he said gently. "I want to learn. I'm going to keep reading. But I hate that place. . . ."

"We can find another school. . . ."

"Yeah. Sojourner Truth? Mama, I don't want to go to school with kids who have designs they cut into their own arms with bobby pins. I don't want to go to school with kids who may be perfectly nice people, but who wear black leather vests with nothing underneath them in the winter and have purple hair. I'm not that kind of weirdo. I'm just an ordinary weirdo." He sighed. "I know this really sucks, on top of all you've been through. But I'm sixteen and I'm not your ordinary sixteen, for bad or good. I know you aren't getting the checks from Leo yet. I can get a job—"

"*No*, Gabe," I pleaded. "No, I know you hate it. I'll think of another way. But once you drop out, you never go back."

"Some big shots have. Doctors. Steve Jobs."

"He dropped out of *college*, Gabe. He was driven by a violation."

"A violation of what?"

"An . . . idea. A . . . plant. A vision! That's what I meant. And he was, like, a genius."

"Well, I know I'm no genius, but I don't want to end up digging a ditch. I'll go to college. But I'm going to LaFollette exactly one more semester. If that. I'll finish in January because I like things neat. But that's it."

Something will change by then, I thought. Something will have to change. There is no justification for this, this, this endless persecution. Then, I thought, why am I taking this personally, thinking of it in terms of everything happening to poor me? The kid's lost his father, who'd previously been out to lunch for probably the past two years; he's lost his closest sibling, and he has virtually lost his best friend, the only thing that once made school fun at all for him. Luke was even more too cool, this year, for Gabe . . . he'd have to be a summer friend, and Gabe just couldn't accept that anymore. And he'd lost his love, too. Tian. I was still thinking of this mess as the most legendary tank in history, the sinking of the good ship *Julieanne*. The ship *was* burning, but all hands were on deck; other people had worse problems. Think of the letters I didn't answer publicly. The ones for whom I called professionals and made sure the professionals found ways to contact the writers. The ones from teenagers whose father crept into their rooms at night, whose mothers washed their mouths with soap when they tried to ask for help. The wives who "walked into kitchen cabinets" or "tripped" and went to work with their arms in slings. The priests whose superiors could not hear the sins they needed to confess. The mothers whose children had been taken away, who'd never see those children again because of what they'd done to them, or what their boyfriends had done to them. The women with breast cancer that had come back after eight years. The people with . . . multiple sclerosis, who could no longer walk; who had timers they set when they held meetings at the offices they still somehow managed to run, to remind them when to stop talking; whose husbands had to give them colonic flushes, feed them oatmeal on a spoon.

"Gabe," I said, taking his hand. "I don't blame you. I don't want this, but I don't blame you."

"Listen, please, Mom. It wasn't easy, but it was possible, to face it when I had you to help me out. I can't face it now. I know we can't afford tutors. I just can't. There's too much to do here. And we can't live our whole lives on vegetarian chili, easy on the soy burger."

"The checks will come soon. The whole thing should be sorted out, property, everything, before Christmas." He sat there patiently. I knew there was no changing his mind. I knew that well over half of dropouts never go back, and dropouts earn half of what graduates do, for the rest of their lives. But he was my son. To push him would be to seal the decree to this.

He said, "Rory needs me, too. You're not here sometimes, and when you're here, there're those few days when you're out of it."

"I'm getting better. Every month, it takes less out of me."

"Mom! I have to do three hours of homework to do the same stuff people get done *in the class*. It'd be different if I could use a laptop. But we can't afford a laptop for me, and if I try to get on one at school, there're three psychos in front of me playing Viking Samurai who'd kill me if I tried even to ask them if I could use it for a while; and then *I'd* get suspended. There has to be a place where I can go, where I can show what I know without having to write it down in this stupid, stupid writing that looks like Rory's stickman drawings. There has to be a place where you can carry a computer without some psycho throwing it up on the roof."

What do you do with the truth when it's more than you can endure? What do you do when the assessment of what has to be the wrong choice is so sound in so many ways that you can barely argue against it? And when there is nothing left to change it that you haven't tried? There had to be a place, and I would find it. I would find Gabe a college, and make sure he got tutored for his entrance exams. Maybe he could start at seventeen. His IQ wasn't through the roof, but he'd never been able to take a reliable test. It was at least as high as my own.

Dreams that you believe you own can come to seem as though they are your destiny.

Finally, I said, "I hope you change your mind, but if you don't, I believe you will go to college. And if you don't do that, you can take over my column and live cheap and support me." I was only half kidding. I thought maybe he could write, something for teenagers. He had a gift, in speech at least, for the word. We both laughed, and I hugged him a little longer than was comfortable for him. Our laughter a little weak, a little damp, and I fell asleep as he made his way down the hall.

When the telephone rang, I grabbed it in a clumsy cacophony of clattering medicine bottles and used water glasses. I was sure that it was midnight and Hannah was calling from the hospital, that Gabe Senior had finally had his stroke, and that this, too, was my fault. When I found out it wasn't, I was furious.

"Julieanne," said a male voice, soft, intimate, abundantly cheerful. "Are you in bed?"

"Shut up, freak!" I snapped. "Call your mother!"

"Is this Julieanne Gillis?" the voice was abruptly reserved, shocked into decorum.

Matthew.

"Oh my God!" I sat up. "Oh my God, Matthew. Oh my God, I thought you were some psycho who saw my column picture and decided to kill me. What time is it? What *time* is it?"

"It's . . . nine-thirty in Boston. Guess it's eight-thirty there."

"Eight. Thirty? Only eight-thirty. I thought it was the middle of the night."

"Long day?"

"Yeah. I can't believe I was asleep. Yeah, Matt, it's been a long night, and a long day's night."

"Sounds like it." His voice was puzzled, embarrassed.

"I'm sorry. We haven't talked in a while, Matt. And I told you I was separated from Leo? Well," I drew a deep breath, "we're divorced now. And he has a baby. And his girl is expecting another baby. And—"

"Jesus, Julie . . ."

"And my daughter Caro moved in with my husband and the girl, who's this alpaca-weaving workout instructor who's about twenty-five, and she's in New York State, and my fifteen-year-old son, who's brilliant and dear, but who has learning disabilities, just told me he's dropping out of school when he turns sixteen, quite a melodrama. . . ."

"Wow, I . . ."

"Pretty gruesome? Not what you'd think would become of stuck-up Ambrose Gillis's baby girl, huh?"

"It's more than that." He had no idea, I thought. He went on. "You poor kid. I can't believe you're still walking." He didn't know how close to the bull's-eye he'd hit. "What I went through with Susan, I thought that I'd never recover, that I'd never have a day in my life that was completely free from pain. And this is no time for a sermon. But you do. You wait eighteen months, Julie. And I guarantee you, you'll have a day when you catch yourself smiling at something. I won't say you won't feel guilty for that. But you will."

"It's not like that for me, Matt. Eighteen months from now, there's still going to be a big problem." And I was going to tell him then. What the hell? He had the sweetest voice. I had begun to correspond, through e-mail, with other people who had MS. Maybe he knew someone I could correspond with. I was ready to be out of the closet.

But he said, "I called, Julieanne, because I'm, ah, coming to Milwaukee for a meeting, and I thought I'd stop and see you. It's not until November—"

"Oh, gosh, I'd love that, but no, see, it's impossible," I said, remembering that fleeting, world-beating sense of being cherished. "I'd love to see you again."

"Too soon, then, and there's always the chance, of course, that you'll work it out. After all, you and Leo had a long marriage."

"It's over," I said flatly. "It's so over. That's not it."

"But you're just not ready to . . ."

"Are you talking about a date, Matt?"

"Well, is that against the law? To ask? I've been a widower for sixteen years. I've had a relationship that lasted four years but just never reached the point where I could make a commitment, though she was terrific, really terrific. A really athletic, happy person."

"If she was so terrific, try it again," I said, jealous and pissed off because his voice took on this the-way-we-were quality. Why in hell was I talking to this guy? "Anyone that terrific, I'd be with right now, if I were you." But he went on to explain: The primary problems were his sweetheart's touchy ego, her near obsession with her body, to the point of becoming anorexic. I looked down in dismay at my steroid-plumped body. I knew I wasn't fat, but I'd always believed I could pass for the younger Katharine Hepburn. Well, the young Katharine's Hepburn's body double, boyishly slender. Oh, well, that's it then, I thought. He likes them nuts and skinny.

"So," he said, "how about we don't think of it as a date, how about we think of it just as a visit? I can bring over hamburgers if you want." I thought, He's probably still five feet four, and now bald. He probably wears belts with big silver buckles with whales on them, because he's said he sailed on Cape Cod. He was probably a frumpy little guy who read frumpy little magazines. But why not have a new friend? I could think of it as the beginning of my new life as a celibate.

"Okay," I said. "But you should know, Matt, that there's every chance I could forget what you're saying while you're saying it. Or I could have to go out to get my meatball sub using a cane. I have multiple sclerosis, Matt."

"Oh, I know that," he said.

"You know that? *Nobody* knows that."

"Your father-in-law knows that. He told me how wonderful you were, how you fought it like a tiger. . . ."

"When did you talk to my father-in-law?"

"One Saturday I called, and you were at ballet class, and we got to talking. He's a nice man. He loves you very much. I can't believe you still take ballet. I'd throw my back out if I played football. I can remember seeing you dance in the variety show. You could have been professional, Julie." My head was still cranking. I wondered how long he'd known this. I wondered if he had something wrong with him, beyond the baldness and the belt (by now, in my mind, it was a big piece of turquoise surrounded by heavy silver). Something that attracted him to sick women.

Matt MacDougall, a pervert.

But he had been such a sweet, funny boy.

"That's why I can't . . . have a relationship. Now you get it."

"I don't understand," he said.

"What don't you understand?"

"The relationship between having a chronic illness and having a relationship, not necessarily with me, but with, well, say you had diabetes. Would you say, Well, I'm never going out with a man again?"

"It's not the same thing, Matt. You're a physician. You know there are issues with MS that make it impossible for all but martyrs who were married twenty years before their diagnosis."

"I know a woman who has MS. She's one of my patients because she was having some dental . . . well, it wasn't related. But she's only twenty-six, and she uses a little chair/walker thing, and she has a boyfriend she's crazy about."

"He's the one who's crazy," I said. "No one, Matt, and I am not putting down your patient, no one would buy into this, Matt."

"Why do you get to be the judge of that?" he asked me.

TWENTY-EIGHT

Gabe's Journal

That quarter, for the first time in all my hideous years at school, I made honor roll. I got an A and four Bs. The A was in English. When they e-mailed my grades to her, bullshittingly before I could delete them, it made my mom cry. Since being in remission, she'd become harder to control. She was more on top of everything. So she found out, and, naturally, she pleaded with me to reconsider.

But there was a huge price for those grades. It was a mission. It was proof to Kimball that I wasn't retarded. I simply, totally, fucking did nothing else. I forced myself to write down every fucking word every fucking teacher put on the board. I filled in every fucking sheet copying the answers to every fucking question out of every fucking book. I had dreams about the Teapot Dome scandal. I lay in bed with Rory and read to her from *To Kill a Mockingbird*, every page, so I'd remember every word, and, just like my mother, I got fucking choked up when the guy left the courtroom. At the end, Rory asked me, "What happened to the bird?"

I painted the entire apartment for my Gram and Gramp and with the money I earned paid a cute junior girl basically to do my geometry homework. The proofs reminded me of my life, which I think of as being evidence of negative numbers. The day after the report card came, I brought my mother the paper giving me permission to withdraw.

That about killed me. But I did it anyway.

She was shaking, she was crying so hard. The next day, I went around to all of my teachers, none of whom was intrinsically a bad person, just clueless, and I said good-bye. I saved Mrs. Kimball for last.

She lowered her reading glasses. Wouldn't she have reading glasses that were cut across the top like little amputees? "Well, Gabe," she said.

"Well, Missus Kimball," I said.

"What are your plans?" she asked.

"Do you care?" I asked.

"I don't think this is a wise choice."

"I don't either. But then, I'm a kid. I'm not wise. I'm not learning how to be wise here. I'm learning how to be a victim. And I'm learning how to hate what I love."

"What do you love?"

"Uh. Reading, I guess. Writing."

"If you'd written one half of what we'd asked you to do, you could have been an A student, Gabe. Do you intend to take the GED? Are you going to enter the armed forces?"

"Yes, I am, Missus Kimball. I'm going to enter the armed forces. Not really. I'm being sarcastic. Do you really think a lot of guys would like me to have their backs in combat? I'm a little easily distracted."

"Well, good luck."

"Do you mean that?"

"What?"

"Good luck."

"I mean you're going to need good luck."

"Good luck to you, too, Missus Kimball. Now that I'm no longer officially your student . . ." I saw her glance from left to right, to make sure she had a clear path to the exit. "Don't worry, Missus Kimball. I don't have a rifle under my jacket. I just want to ask you a favor."

"What?" She began clipping and releasing her ballpoint with her thumb, a gesture for which she would have interrupted Guided Study to say to me, *Mister Steiner. . . .*

"Don't ever do this to another kid. Don't pick one out and make him feel lower than a snail's belly. Don't mock him for what he can't help. Cheer him on. Try to look for some good thing about him. Honest to God, I mean this in a nice way. . . ."

"The fact that you didn't . . . prosper here doesn't have anything to do with me, Gabe. But you know that. That was your choice."

"But you could have helped me make a better choice," I said. I had thought long and hard about this. I had made notes. "It has everything to do with you. Because you can take a kid's hand, not really, but you can tell him he's okay, and find him the help he needs, if you're interested."

"Only if you have a student who's interested."

"But how would you know?"

"I have a group now. I need you to go, Gabe. Leave."

What did I really want Kimball to say?

What did I expect her to do? Tell me I wasn't garbage? Tell me she was sorry it hadn't worked? Tell me that she cared? Tell me she was going to get Lou Gehrig's and die a slow death? Say she was sorry about my family? Say she even *knew* about my family? She handed me a file of official papers about the GED. I made a point of dropping it into the trash on the way out the door. The whole thing hadn't gone as I'd rehearsed it. Had I really expected it to? Mrs. Kimball being who she was and I being who I am?

Had I expected, finally, some guidance from the guidance counselor, for the principal to be a prince and a pal?

What had I thought my leaving would accomplish that my being here never had?

I left Sheboygan LaFollette for the last time through the gym door. I saw Mallory, my sister's friend, changing classes. "Gabe!" she said, "I totally can't wait until Cat comes for the four-day weekend at Halloween. Aren't you excited?"

"Totally," I said. I had no idea she was coming at all. I had no idea where she was staying, or with whom.

"Are you okay?"

"I'm fine," I said. "Take it easy, Mallory. I dropped out today."

"That's so cool," she said. "My parents would kill me."

"Mine, too," I said.

"So?"

"So, well, say hi to my sister, and tell her we're fine. Just fine."

"Isn't she staying with you?"

"You know she isn't. Maybe you didn't think of it. Bet she's staying with my grandparents. She won't talk to my mom. She thinks my mom hates her for moving out there. But she doesn't. And, y'know, Mallory, why don't you tell her that?"

"She has the coolest boyfriend. He's, like, eighteen, and Leo and Joy let him stay with her—"

"I don't want to know this." I knew I shouldn't have stopped to talk to Mallory. It was unprecedented.

"But it's the most natural thing in the world, Gabe. They don't want her to have her first sexual experiences in a car or with some creep. They made sure she was protected, and they had this long meeting before, with his parents. . . ."

"I *so* don't want to know this. And please, neither does my mother. 'Bye, Mallory."

"Well, 'bye, Gabe. Is your mom sick or something?"

"More like, or something."

"Are you going in the army?"

"Marines," I said. "Special Forces."

"Cool," she said.

As I opened the door, Luke and a cadre of his jock brothers stumbled out of the gym. They were talking about who had been "trashed" the past weekend, who made "time," what an asshole Burke was in Algebra II. I looked at Luke. He looked straight back into my eyes. Then, he pretended to see something on the floor, nodded the briefest nod, and turned away.

I began to turn away, too, when he said, "Dude."
I said, "Dude."
Luke said, real low, "Want to hang out Sunday?"
I said, "Maybe."

TWENTY-NINE

Daniel

EXCESS BAGGAGE
By J. A. Gillis
Distributed by Panorama Media

Dear J.,

I met a man last spring who was absolutely everything I wanted. We clicked immediately. Bright, funny, so caring and interested. He couldn't do enough for me. Notes, flowers, surprise dates planned—even a dance class! After a long, long dry spell, I felt I'd died and gone to heaven! As the fall progressed, however, he got more preoccupied and distant. I knew that he was working on his PhD dissertation, so I gave him space. Occasionally, he dropped by for dinner and an overnight, but he was distracted. At last, he told me that he'd be finishing his dissertation the following week, and defending his thesis, and then he'd be all finished, getting ready to look around the country for a place to be happy. Naturally, I assumed he meant that for both of us, and I began to tidy up loose ends at work. Two days after his defense, when I knew he'd be home, I dressed in a beautiful new sundress and loaded the car with wine, cake, and flowers. I drove to his house. It was empty. There was a FOR RENT sign in the yard. There was no note. His phone had been disconnected. J., I immediately came home to write this note. We were in love! What am I to think?

Hysterical in Hoboken

Dear Hysterical,

Do you still have the cake and the wine? Sit down. Eat the whole cake. Drink as much of the wine as you can without doing permanent damage. Take a long, long nap. Then, get down on your knees and thank whatever deity you embrace that you didn't quit your job or in any other way change your life for someone who clearly is a flake at best and something much, much more treacherous at worst. Studies show that more than half of the people with whom you "click" the first time are sociopaths. They know what you want and they give it—but only for as long as they want to. And they never look back. You are obviously a decent person, so don't you look back, either.

J.

Dear J.,

My boyfriend of two years just told me last week he felt he needed to end the relationship. Naturally, I asked why. He said that the most honest answer he could give was that he just didn't feel the way he needed to feel when he wanted to get serious. He certainly felt serious a year ago—like twice a night! But then, when I'd make plans for us with friends for the weekend, he'd start getting sulky. He raved about the sweater I made him, then never wore it! His job has become more complex and is taking more of his time, so I know that's a factor. But I've just heard that he's been coming on to a mutual friend who is known as the biggest here-today-gone-tomorrow girl in town!

Nice Girl in Nantucket

Dear Nice,

I don't want to be the first to tell you. Your mother should have. Nice girls do finish last. It's an unfortunate fact of male nature that the hunter is not going to want to eat the game he didn't stalk—in a manner of speaking. Next time you fall in love—and you will—make a rule. Every time you ache to return his phone call, wait twenty-four hours. The new flirt is the girl with the most classes, most consultancies, most meetings, most girlfriends—the one who's always just on her way out the door. Yeah, it's incredibly stupid. But it's been the guaranteed recipe for bliss—or at least getting what you think you want—since mothers were writing "Do not call him" on the walls of caves.

J.

I heard the door open and knew that it was Gabe. I sat up straight at my father's desk and concentrated on my computer. In fact, I performed a parody of a woman lost in utter concentration. I didn't know if he'd come into my room, but if he did, I wanted to make sure I was so absorbed I didn't notice. He did. I could *feel* his facial expression. He dropped his book bag onto the floor and said, "I think I'll wash this. I returned all the books, Mom."

And I knew he had done it.

I breathed in deeply, but not, I hoped, audibly. I'd held out hope that something about proving to himself that he actually could succeed would spur him on for the meager twenty months it would take to finish. But to a person of Gabe's age and temperament, twenty months was an eternity. For *anyone,* it was an eternity, if you were spending it in purgatory.

On the other hand, there had to be a limit to my tolerance. He may have usurped a part of my role, but I still had the influence. I knew he cared about what I thought. "If you want something in the way of my saying okay, I'm fine about this, Gabe, what you're going to need is a different mother," I said. "I do have something for you." I handed him a stack of job applications I'd picked up on my little errands around town, to the bank, the doctor, the physical therapist. "Time to start living the life of an adult, pallie. Get a job."

On the bed, Gabe seemed to sink deeper into the contours of my mattress. He sighed noisily.

"Well, you're being a real sport about this," he said. "You're showing a lot of sympathy."

"This is the kind of thing they call Social Services on parents for being a good sport about," I said sharply. "Want a pack of smokes? Want to be able to drink beer, but just at home? It's not me, Gabe. Healthy or sick, single or double, I'm still the same mother I was. And, damn it, I spent ten good years of life trying to get you past the, okay, past the thick-headedness, the intolerance of public school. . . ."

"Yeah, and it helped me. But it didn't change anything."

"Sorry I couldn't change the world, Gabe. I'll try to get to that next week."

"I thought I'd take a little time to orient myself," Gabe said, as if by way of changing the subject. "And it's not like I haven't worked. I've done, uh, some writing, as I recall. Unpaid."

"I could count that toward room and board," I suggested, sounding tart as a lime even to myself. "The deal is you support your minor children as long as they're in school—did you realize this is going to mean that your dad no longer has to pay for your support at the same level?"

"Do we have to tell him?"

"Do you think we'll need to? Caro has her sources, Gabe." I didn't even know whether this was strictly true. But he deserved it. "Now, if you agree to some kind of homeschooling, plus work, that might be a different story."

"I never thought it would cost you money," he said, kicking off his shoe. "I'll go back, if it means that."

Unwilling to let him off the hook, I said, "Okay, fine. Un–drop out. Or go to a different school, Gabe. You can drive. It doesn't have to be So-journer Truth." I looked him over. He was almost the same thickness as the comforter. Had he lost weight? He could ill afford it. "Forget it," I finally said. "But I *don't* want you to think this is going to be the beginning of a nice, long nap, Gabe. What kind of person would that make me?"

"You're one to talk," he muttered.

"Uh, I can't help that, and you can take that back."

"I take it back, but you're pretty up on your high horse since you don't have to have people pull you out of bed."

"Would you rather see me . . . the way I was?" I held out my hand, which jigged obligingly. "I'm not exactly ready for the biathlon, Gabe."

"No, but I'm worn out, too, Mom. This hasn't been a banner season for me, either. I'm sick of having a surrogate child, for one thing."

Despite myself, I was proud of his using the word *surrogate* correctly. "Okay, what should we do? Let Aunt Jane raise her? Send her out to Happy Hollow with the other little Sterns or Steiners?"

Gabe sighed even more gustily, and said, "I love her; don't get me wrong. But I'm . . . I don't want to be Rory's daddy. And that's how she looks at me."

"What do you want to do about it? I mean really. This wasn't the plan. . . ."

"Have her spend more time with Gram and Gramp, for one thing. They don't have jobs, and they're always calling and asking if she can come over, and if Abby can come over. Let her, sometimes. So I don't have to drive her everyplace and go through her book bag and fill out her order for ivy plants and Christmas wrapping and crap."

What I felt for him was disgust. And sympathy. I thought of telling him what it felt like to have a catheter inserted. "I can raise my kid, Gabe," I said. But he didn't shut up! We both should have stopped, right then.

"You know, Mama, this isn't all about you and your being the proud-though-challenged Julieanne Gillis. At some point you're going to have to admit that we've, well, gone down in life. We're not having people over for little wieners and wine before the ball game anymore. We're not having a Christmas open house. We're renters. You, me, and this poor little kid Dad didn't even want. We're, like, renting our own lives on a month-to-month. People weren't ever calling to have me over, but you haven't gone out for dinner with anyone but Cathy or Stella since Dad left for his little trip. You know what they say about the smell of a winner? That works in reverse, too."

"You're saying we're . . . losers?" I reached down into the permanent files and pulled out one of my copies of *Pen, Inc.* "I'll have you know I'm a published poet now, Gabe. This isn't easy to do. Okay, they didn't pay me much, but I'm trying to do different things from the things I used to do."

"Yeah, but one little poem in a little magazine published by a guy in his garage isn't going to mean that anything, anything ever, is going to be like it was again."

"Thanks for the vote of confidence, Gabe."

"That's what Jennet said. We have to be optimistic but not unrealistic."

"If I'm not a little bit more than optimistic, I'll hang myself," I told him.

"Yeah, well I see your point. And plus, it's really, really boring. I think of Caroline out there frolicking through the woods, doing whatever the hell she pleases, and here's old Gabe, holding down the fort. . . ."

I tried with all my might to see this through Gabe's eyes. It wasn't so difficult. He had endured an uncommon amount of responsibility. Maybe he did need a break, time to sleep late and stay up watching stupid TV, like most teenagers. Maybe he needed a dumb part-time job as a bagger at the co-op. Maybe he needed to veg out. It was my own humiliation that was forcing my hand against the back of his neck. This, my last hope at a proud ending, at least until Rory, who seemed unnaturally bewildered and timid in the face of the world, grew up, had, as my mother would have said, seen its final inning. It was I who'd wanted Gabe to nail a thirty on his ACT tests—to smite Leo. It was I who wanted to watch him toss his mortarboard into the air—as a reward to me, for all my hard work.

"What do you want, Gabe?" I asked finally, letting my hands drop into my lap.

"A rest," he said. "A couple of weeks off to figure out what I'm going to do."

"Okay."

"And I will figure out what I'm going to do." I thought that was about as likely as him separating the jeans from the towels. But I nodded, and he slouched into his room. The book bag was still on the floor.

Rory couldn't quit preschool. I supposed I could withdraw her, saving Gabe even the possibility of needing to give her rides, but that would be a four bagger. Everyone in my life, loused up by Leo, administered the coup de grâce by MS and me.

I wouldn't let that happen.

But the next day, I took an ad out in the newspaper. Within four days, I'd sold my single-carat diamond, my mother's wedding ring, to a nice young couple from Milwaukee. With the proceeds, I bought Gabe an old Toyota Corolla, with no rust, no dents, complete with air bags (Gabe Senior made sure, and chipped in by buying new tires), and I called one of those places in Minnesota that take young men out and march them around the rim of Lake Superior or through the Everglades with a pack of matches and a spoon. Gabe would find himself, or at least bulk up.

The program I could afford had quotes on the Web site that I could more or less agree with, and was for kids who weren't overt felons. I paid the deposit for a three-week stint beginning in April. He'd go out with a group over spring break and then continue for another two weeks on a "solo" with a counselor I hoped wasn't a rapist.

I presented him with both, as accomplished facts.

When he saw the car, he got tears in his eyes. "I don't deserve this," he said. "I just said a bunch of shitty stuff and dropped out of school."

"You do deserve it. You have to get places. And you have to take Rory to Gram's. And the shitty stuff you said, well, I kind of asked for it."

He smiled. "And I have to drive to work."

"Yeah. Part time."

"Mom, you can't afford this."

"Let me worry about that, huh?"

We agreed that he'd find a job, and then we'd look for a minimalist homeschool teacher, someone who would coach him for college exams, acquaint him with the basics of what he would have learned from biology, geometry, and so on—a series of tutors from the U. at ten dollars an hour were probably all I could afford—so that he could either earn a high school diploma by virtue of my certifying he'd completed the equivalent of four years of science and four years of English (the law allowed that), or the GED.

"Hour about four hours a day?"

"How about two?"

"Gabe, what can you learn in two hours a day?"

"That's basically all you do in school," he argued. "The rest is fighting the crowd, listening to stupid announcements, going to assemblies and junk."

"Okay, but two hours and you have stuff to do afterward."

We shook on it. Then he hugged me, tight, as he had when he was small. "I love the car, Mom. It's a cool car. What did you have to do to get it?"

"Oh, I sold a novel for an advance of . . . about a hundred thousand bucks."

"That's so great," he said. "Let's buy a lake house, too."

"I sold Grandmother Gillis's ring."

Gabe looked as if the car had turned into something foul. He put the keys down on the kitchen table.

"Look," I said. "I have your father's ring to give Caroline. And I'm counting on Rory marrying to great wealth. And you, well, you're going to have to give your wife—"

"One from the machine at the grocery store, in a little plastic egg." Gabe laughed.

"You're never going to get a girl anyhow," I said.

"I know."

"Come on, mope," I said. "I meant, you have to learn to dance."

"Nuh-uh."

"No, I have my shot tomorrow, and then I'll be soup for a day at least, so tonight I'm going to teach you to dance."

"Nothing . . . no way, Mom. I can dance enough for practical purposes."

"Can you swing dance? I know people do it again now. I see it on TV."

"Please, God, don't make me do this."

"Dance!" Rory cried, cranking up the CD player to about five hundred decibels. Gabe strode across the room and grabbed her. I followed them, and rifled through my CDs until I found something I'd grabbed in a coffee store, I had to crack the thing open on the edge of the kitchen counter.

"Watch it!" Gabe cried. "You know, we don't own this place!"

We started the music and Gabe stood, helpless and embarrassed, while we octopus-armed each other until we had the approximation of a couple's stance. "Now, listen, everything else you do is based on this: one side, one side, back, front. That's it. Do it." Of course, he couldn't do it. "Come *on*, Gabe. A chimp could do this. One side, one side, back, front." Rory was already in the rhythm, bouncing up and down in her footie pajamas. I don't know what the song was, some updated forties jive, though I guess I should have remembered it, given everything. He finally got it, and we did a tentative few minutes on the basics. "Okay, next, you're going to spin me, *not too fast*, and then we just go arms out straight, then side, side, back, and front, again. Okay?"

"Okay," Gabe said, half laughing. I hit the button again, and was just coming out of the turn when I noticed that Rory had opened the door and was standing in the front hall with a tall, dark-haired man in an olive trenchcoat.

"What? Rory! Hasn't Mommy told you never, ever to open the door!"

"But he knocked! You didn't hear him," Rory said mournfully. She ran to me, tucked her thumb into her mouth, and hid behind the wide panels of my trousers. I pushed my hair up from my sweaty brow.

"Can I help you?" I asked.

"This has to be one of the most charming things I've ever seen," said the tall man, who had masses of wrinkles around his wide, greenish eyes, but beautiful thick, dark hair. I crossed the room, glad Gabe was there beside me. The guy was taller than Gabe. Gabe was six-two.

"Listen," I said, "whatever you're selling—"

"Julieanne," he said, "I'm Matthew. I'm Matt MacDougall."

"But . . . you grew!" I said like a damned fool.

"Well, I've had thirty years!" He leaned down and hugged me lightly.

"Well," I said, "you didn't . . . you didn't tell me you were coming."

"I left three messages on your machine."

"Mom?" Gabe asked.

"Oh, Gabe, this is my old friend from New York. My boyfriend from eighth grade. Seventh grade?"

"Maybe a little of both. Maybe neither."

"This is Matt. Matt, this is my son, Gabriel Steiner, and my daughter, Aurora Steiner."

"Gabe Gillis," Gabe said, taking Matt's hand to shake. My mouth opened to protest, but I shut it.

"Well, I didn't make anything for you to eat or plan anything. I didn't even wash my hair. Can't you come back tomorrow?"

"Sure," he said, "why not?"

"But you drove all the way from your conference?"

"I can drive all the way back."

"Well, you want a cup of coffee?"

"I brought a bottle of champagne." He'd brought Cristal! I wanted it desperately.

"I'm allowed, like, a half of one glass. Like a little girl at Christmas," I told him. "How about coffee?"

"Mom," Gabe said urgently, "can we turn down the music?"

"Gosh, yes, sure," I thought of how I must look, my already spiky hair peaked by sweat, my mascara running from sweat and laughter, one of Leo's old dress shirts hanging over a pair of baggy khakis, bare feet. Well, it wasn't as though he has come a-courtin'. He has come . . . from curiosity. And now I recognized him. He had a dimple in his right cheek. He'd been able to draw horses. He drew horses all the time.

"Do you have any horses?" I asked him.

"Two. Why?"

"You used to draw them in art class."

"Huh. You remember that."

"So, I was thinking, I'd take Rory to the Culver's Custard and drop by Gram's," Gabe broke in. I thought for a moment he was trying to leave me alone with Matthew. But then I remembered. He hadn't had a chance to drive his car.

"Well," I said, with a shrug, "she doesn't have school tomorrow. And you don't. So, okay. But don't be long. And put her long coat on over her—"

"I know how to do this, Mom," Gabe said, already swooshing Rory's parka over her head.

"And don't forget her booster seat!"

"Mom!"

"New car," I explained to Matthew. "Sixteenth birthday."

"Nothing like it." He smiled, and the wrinkles deepened. He looked older than I did, but not, somehow, in a ruined way. As if he'd spent far more time in the sun. As if it didn't much matter to him.

Gabe gave me a kiss. "I'll stop at all the lights. Full stop. I'll put Rory in the back."

"Go on," I told him, and turned to the stranger on my hall rug. "Can I take your coat? Is it snowing or anything? Do you care if I go and wash my face?"

"I don't care," he said easily, with a Boston accent, removing his coat carefully and folding it over his arm. "I can hang up my own coat, and I've nowhere else to go."

There was nothing to do about the state of my face that wouldn't require a half hour of repeal and repair. So I rubbed colored moisturizer onto my face and wet my hair even more, scooping out a dab of Gabe's hair pomade. I took the mascara off with cream and put on some new stuff, a few strokes. I rolled up the sleeves of my shirt. All this seemed to take hours, as I didn't want to smear the stuff all over my face. After a few minutes, he called, "I know how to make coffee. I even have the same machine. Just tell me where you keep it."

"The freezer," I called. "And the grinder is in the cabinet above the machine."

The last thing I did was put a cold washcloth between my breasts and force myself to breathe deeply. I looked in the mirror. I looked like a very flushed Cyndi Lauper with my apple steroid cheeks. What the hell, I thought. I heard Matthew humming as he flipped through the CDs. When I came back out into the living room, he had just pressed the button to close the machine, and punched up, of course, "God Only Knows."

"Look. Wanna dance?" he asked, his blush, if possible, more savage than my own.

"Well, you're taller than I am now," I pointed out.

"Yeah, and I can lead, too," he said.

Afterward, we sat at my kitchen table and talked, about old acquaintances and what had become of them. His sister had been in my sister Jane's class, as had Suzie, his wife. Nothing more than a sidelong glance betrayed him as he described what he considered the single worst moment of his life, waiting in the hospital mortuary for a curtain to be drawn up so he could identify the side of his young wife's face that had not encountered the steering column, while upstairs, surgeons worked on his little daughter's collapsed lung and broken jaw. "You go mad for a moment thinking that maybe it isn't her; maybe a friend of hers was driving Kelly somewhere; maybe it's all been a mix-up. And then they raise the curtain. I'll never forget that sound, so authoritative. And she was lying there, covered to the chest by a sheet. They had brushed back her hair and washed off her face, and the young patrolman with me held my elbow so I would not fall. I said, "Suze?" As if she would answer me. She was a fourth-year nursing student, and I was an intern. Everyone we knew was the same couple we were, a nurse and an intern. I'd been in dermatology. I wanted more kids; I wanted a predictable life. But I switched to surgery the next week and took a specialty in rebuilding faces, after I watched how long it took to rebuild Kelly's jaw and palate, feeding her through a straw, her crying and asking why Mommy would let people hurt her."

"Is she okay?" I asked then. "Does she have lasting . . . ?"

"Scars? No. She was two. She doesn't remember. She has an impression of the crash, but she's not sure if it's a memory or a dream. One of our horses is a jumper. That's her passion. She's after me to take a semester off because she thinks she could try for the American team, and from what they tell me, she could. I'm leery, though. I think school has to come first. She knows that." A semester off to try to make the Olympic team as an equestrian. I wondered what he'd think of Gabe, sixteen-year-old ex–tenth grader.

"In the smallest way, it was like that when I was waiting to hear what was wrong with . . . with me," I said.

"And Leo. That sounds like it was rough, and so bizarre that people probably get lost in the bizarre part and forget that, really, you're someone whose marriage is breaking up and you're just hurting, like anyone would. Even I suffered just the absence of the woman I was with, Suzie, and I wanted it to end. But you come across something she'd owned, or hear a song . . ."

"It's like that," I said. "I have my rage to keep me warm, though."

"Do you think you ever get over it, if you've been happy?"

"Look, Matthew, you'd know more about that than I would."

"I think I have."

"I think I will."

"Speaking of warm, let me look outside." Matt opened the door and roared, a man used to allowing himself laughter without cynicism. "I hope you have a Holiday Inn around the corner. Look." There were eighteen inches of snow on the ground. "It's November second, Julieanne. Are you people crazy to live here?"

"Come on! I've never had a normal flight out of Boston. The fog there is permanent. It's just lake-effect snow," I told him, reaching past him to pick up a handful of it. It was as insubstantial as cotton. "It will be gone by morning. Wait," I said then, and I grabbed the telephone, glancing at the clock. It was nine-thirty. "Hannah," I breathed gratefully into the phone when she picked up, "I know Gabe is there with Rory. Will you let them stay? I don't want him driving her in this."

"Of course," Hannah said briefly, something just off in her tone of voice. "They're here."

"What, Hannah?" I thought perhaps Gabe had said something about Matthew, and she was reacting to our being here alone. "Hannah, Cathy will be home from her rehearsal in a little while. Abby's sleeping over at her grandma's."

"It's not that, Julie. It's . . . they're all here. Caroline, too. She . . . wants to talk to you." I caught my breath, and realized it was attempting to stay caught. Finally, I was able to gasp, "Not now. I can't handle that right now."

"She's here with this boy."

"I see."

"Leo lets him sleep with her."

"That doesn't mean you have to," I said, my brain cartwheeling. Caroline, fifteen years old, with a live-in lover. My little daughter, little in every sense, little feet, breasts, a waist I could almost still span with my hands. "How long has she been there?" I asked.

"Two days. He's sleeping on the sofa. Decent boy. I mean, he says please and thank you. But Julieanne, I can't and Gabe can't stand this. . . ."

"Of course not. Is . . . Gabe, my Gabe, okay?"

"He's watching TV with Papa in the den. They didn't say two words."

"Well, maybe he should bring Rory home then."

"Rory's all over her. She couldn't be happier."

"Well," I said, "it's nothing I can't deal with in the morning. If I can get my car out."

"Okay," Hannah said tentatively. She was seventy-eight years old. This was even more alien land for her than for me.

"It's all right," I told her. "I'll come first thing."

I put the phone down and turned back to Matt. "There's a Quality Inn in the next few blocks, but you can stay here. I'll make up Gabe's bed with clean sheets."

"Let me try to shovel a little. So you can get your car out tomorrow. Where's your shovel?" I told him where to find it. Then I heard him laughing out there as I picked up Gabe's socks and opened the window a little to get rid of the wet-dog smell of a teenage boy. I looked out, and the snow was feathering down.

"It weighs nothing," he called over to me when I rapped on the window. "I haven't shoveled snow in years. It's fun. I feel as if I'm in a Frank Capra movie."

"You have snow in Boston," I said, handing him a towel as he came back inside.

"I have a long driveway. A guy plows. I have to get out of there early in the morning for surgery." The moisture had turned his hair to ringlets. He was so . . . conventionally handsome. Just a big, cheerful New England guy. It had been so long. I had forgotten the oxygen a man takes up in a house.

"Do you mind if I shower?"

"No," I said. "Do you mind if I do?"

I gave him a few towels and one of Gabe's clean robes. "I'm afraid I can't offer you pajamas. Leo's would have been sizes too small, and I'm afraid I don't have them anymore."

"I don't sleep in them, anyhow," Matt said, and I felt another alien thrill, a thrum in my abdomen.

We both emerged half an hour later. Vain unto the end, I'd put on more mascara after drying my hair.

"Now, there you are," Matt said, "the same girl I knew."

"Hardly," I told him. "But that's nice."

There was nothing left to do but for him to kiss me. I leaned deeply into the kiss, knowing there would be nothing but this, and perhaps only this for a very long time, perhaps always. As if it were a natural thing to do, he reached down and, with one movement, undid the belt on my robe.

"Not," I said. "No."

"Don't worry," said Matthew. He let his hand trail down my cheek to my neck and the outer edge of my breast, from my hip to the small of my back. "That's all. I'm not going to ravage a snowbound woman." He could have, then, and I would have let him.

But we both went off to our respective beds then, and cool as it was in the house, I kicked the covers off and stroked my own neck, which had already committed that touch to memory.

Proverbs

―――――~~~~~―――――

EXCESS BAGGAGE
By J. A. Gillis
Distributed by Panorama Media

Dear J.,

   *My worst nightmare has come true. My daughter is pregnant.
She's seventeen, and she insists that she and her so-called
boyfriend, who as far as I can tell has never done a day's work
in his life, are going to raise the baby themselves. She's dropped
out of school and has a job as a hostess at a restaurant. She's
taking night classes at the technical school. Nothing like this
ever has a happy ending. I've told her over and over. She can
still end this thing in time. Can't I make her see what she's
doing to her life? And mine? We had plans for this child!*

Frantic in Fitchville

Dear Frantic,

   *No. You can be a supportive mother. Or you can be an ex-
mother. If this is the worst thing that ever happens to you, count
yourself fortunate.*

J.

―――――~~~~~―――――

The telephone rang two mornings after Matthew's visit. I hadn't gone to Hannah's to see Caroline after all, since Gabe had shown up within five minutes of Matt's pulling out of the drive. Though nothing had happened, I had stripped all the beds and was washing sheets, and settling in with Cathy for a bout of good girl gossip. It was a few hours before I'd take my shot. Rory wanted to put on her bat costume, as she had every day for two weeks, and it was a good half hour before I could tell Gabe it had been fun talking to my old friend, how about that snow . . . and, by the way, how was your sister?

"She's going to call," he said, just as the phone went. "Let her tell you." I picked up.

"Mom," said a small, shy voice.

"Caroline," I answered softly, my eyes spilling.

"I want to come and see you. I want you to meet the guy I'm living with, Dominico," she said. "Is that okay?"

"Which part?" I asked. "Your coming to see me? Or your living with a boy. You're just fifteen, Caro."

"Cat," she said.

"Sex is not for people who are fifteen, Cat," I said.

"Mom, it's natural. And Dad and Joy understand that," she said.

"Come and see me by yourself. Ask Gramp to drive you. I have to take my shot and then we'll have a cup of tea. Herbal, I promise. And we'll talk, woman to woman." There was a muffled series of squeaks and rustlings on the other end.

"Dominico says that if you can't accept him, you can't accept me," Caroline said finally.

"I can accept him as your friend, and you're my child. I'll always accept you. But no, I can't accept you as a person who's making such a risky choice," I said, holding the receiver with both hands to steady it. "First of all, are you using protection? And secondly, do you know how many other girls he's . . . ?"

"You can't just come out and ask someone that, Mom," Caroline said.

"Yes, you can. And you have to. You can get a virus just from fooling around, without having intercourse. You can get a virus that could hurt your baby if you ever have a baby, or hurt your brain. Human papilloma virus can lead to cancer of the cervix. This could have consequences that can last the rest of your life," I told her.

"I know about all that."

"Your emotions are way ahead of what your mind and body are ready for, Caro. I know that the desire is real—"

"Don't talk to me like I'm one of your letter writers, Mom," she said.

"I'm talking to you like a mother," I said.

"Dad discussed all that with Dominico."

"Oh. And Dad gave him your hand, huh?"

"Duh. So can we come?"

She was reaching out for me, my precious, my girl. My daughter whose first party dress and baby book were bound with a ribbon in a cedar box in my closet. The child who'd asked for an egg every morning of her life for five years, and who had once said to me that she loved me as much as "sunny-up" egg. Yes, she'd been Leo's girl, more than mine. But she *was* mine! We'd washed angora sweaters one day, and Caroline, perhaps eight years old and trying to be Mommy's helper, had dried them in the dryer. Even the zippers had shrunk. We couldn't have fit them on her doll. If I didn't see her, she'd be angry. She was a passionate kid. On the other hand, it would imply approval. Anxiety coursed through me like an electrical charge. "I wouldn't do what you're doing. It's irresponsible," I said, thinking of Matt's long and yet carefully un-explicit caress down my naked body. "Even at my age, it would be irresponsible." I watched Cath's eyes for guidance, watched them fill with tears as she nodded. "This can't be a long-term relationship, Caroline. You've been gone for only six months. Sex is for people who are committed to each other. . . ."

"We are, Mom. He's not seeing anyone else, anymore."

"Please come and talk to me, Caroline. I love you. I want to see you."

"I'll only come with Dominico."

"Then," I said, fighting to keep the fracture of hurt from my voice, "you'd better not come this time. When are you leaving? Think about it. You could change your mind."

"I won't change my mind. This is why I left. You can't understand anything that doesn't go along with all your little rules. Neither can Gram or Gramp, and Gabe wouldn't even shake hands with Dominico. You think you know all the answers, Mom."

"No, I don't! I just know that what you're doing is wrong. It's wrong by anyone's standards. It's . . . how old is Dominico?"

"Eighteen," she said smugly.

"Then it's also illegal."

"I so care."

"Well, I wouldn't expect you to care. But he's taking advantage of you. Your father is a lawyer, Caroline. He's served as a guardian ad litem. Does he have shit for brains? You're just a kid, Caro."

"Thanks for always being so understanding, Mom," Caroline said. "You always come through for me."

"Caro . . . I mean, Cat, wait. Let me talk to both of you. You and Dominico."

"We don't need a newspaper writer who thinks she's a therapist, Mom. If you hadn't been so . . . so conceited about everything, Dad might have never left you in the first place."

"Stop that! This has nothing to do with your father and me."

"And now he has to work six days a week, Mom, because of you. Because you're so poor and sick, and Gabe is such a helpless nerd. His whole life is turning out to be just what he never wanted, Mom. He's doing *house closings,* and court-appointed defenses. All to make enough money so that you can still have your Kenneth Cole shoes . . ."

I couldn't even wear my Kenneth Cole shoes anymore. The heels were so high I felt as though I were walking on tiny and torturous skyscrapers. "That's wrong and cruel and you know it! Your dad has a responsibility to Rory, just as much as to you and . . . Amos and . . . what's the baby's name?"

"Scarlett."

"Jesus," I said.

"What, not WASPy enough for you, Mom?" Caro sneered. "What would you have named her? Gertrude or Matilda? You think everyone had to come over on the *Mayflower,* Mom."

"You know I'm not like that. Nobody in my family came over on the *Mayflower,*" I said. This was a lie. My mother's family roots were that deep in New England. "I'm not a snob. But even you said, when Rory was born, what's with the name? Don't you remember?"

"Well, I was wrong then. Rory? God. You changed her name and didn't even tell Dad."

"Uh, Dad had a baby and didn't even tell me."

"You're so small-minded."

"I can't let you talk to me this way."

"You can't stand to hear the truth."

"Maybe. Maybe I was small-minded. Maybe I didn't see how badly your father wanted a change. Don't you think I've thought about that thousands upon thousands of times? But I'm not small-minded. I'm being practical, Caroline."

"That's another thing I hate about you. It's all, like, beige for you, Mom. Beige and little stationery with edges on it and thank-you notes and stockings that match your shoes."

"Stop that. Nothing about this was my fault."

"You can't admit it was."

"I could, if it were." Could I? I thought. Should I have followed Leo to that place in the clearing he'd wanted, at first, for all of us? Given up my job and learned to put up preserves? Would that have spared the shatter-ing of my family, Gabe's bitterness, Rory's fears and confusion? My own anguishing doubts?

"You could have had everything we have if you weren't so uptight and, just, old-fashioned."

"Maybe," I said again, sadly. "But maybe I wouldn't want what you have. Maybe I would never have been good at it. There's only so much you can give up, Caroline, even for your marriage."

"You didn't even try! Dad's told me! How hard he worked to make you see how stupid the life we had was!"

"I don't think it was a stupid life. It just wasn't the life he wanted. But, look, Caroline, it was the life he wanted once. He helped create it. He chose it."

"Only because you never let him do anything the way he wanted. Everything had to be Julie's way."

"Caroline, just come and talk to me. Or, or meet me at the coffee place. We'll sit together—" I was talking to a dead phone.

And I had been, all along.

Caroline needed to know she'd at least made the effort to see her poor, benighted mother. I don't think she'd meant to come to my house at all. She just wanted to show off for her friends that she was a fully fledged sexual being. I put my face in my hands.

"Do you have an ouchie? Baby Bat will fix you," Rory said to me, prying my fingers from the grate they'd made over my eyes. I pulled her onto my lap. She felt so fragile, as if her bones were hollow, just as Caroline had felt, all sticks and knobs.

"Mommy loves her Baby Bat," I said to Rory.

"Is she coming?" Gabe asked from the door of my room.

"No."

"Bet she wanted to bring the excellent hippie. He can't string two words together without saying, 'You see where I am, man?' He's a horse's ass. I'm glad she's not coming," Gabe said.

"Gabe, that's your sister. And she's not the only person in the world ever to have made a lousy choice. Go look in the mirror." Gabe made a parody of firing a gun, with his thumb and index finger.

"Bingo! Well, Ma, all I can tell you is, get ready to be a grandma. I wouldn't have minded Caroline coming here, but him?"

"What?"

"I'd have killed him," Gabe said. "He's a slob and a user. He smells. Caroline must have inherited her taste in men—"

"Watch it," I said.

"I'm sorry."

"I still love your father," I said. "I don't regret that we had you guys, and there was a lot we had going for us, once, Gabe."

"Or so you thought."

"Or so I thought."

The phone rang again, and it was Matthew. This time, I picked up when I heard his voice on the recorder.

"Julieanne!" he said, "I have to scrub in, in about five minutes, but I had to ask you, are you avoiding me? Did I step out of line?"

"No, you were the perfect gentleman, in a sense," I said. "I just don't know if I can have feelings for anyone but Leo. At least, not yet."

"So you still have feelings for Leo?"

"Don't you still have feelings for the woman you loved just a little while back? And Suzie?"

"I have feelings about the time we spent together. Not about them, as individuals. That's what I came up with last night, after we talked. That chapter is closed. You can't make your whole life a shrine to the past, Julie."

"I'm not doing that."

"Well."

"I'm glad you called."

"But you don't want to see me again. Really see me."

"I didn't say that."

"Not now."

"Well, I don't know," I told him honestly. "That would depend on what your expectations were."

"That would depend on what you wanted me to hope for," Matt said. "Julie, I have to go. But I wanted to ask you, do you know you were the first girl I ever kissed? When you were elected class president?" I'd forgotten. But now, I thought I could remember. Sweet, Doublemint-smelling breath. Tightly closed lips. My back against the wall of the library extension at school.

"I remember, now," I said.

"Well, I waited twenty-five years to do it again, Julie. All through high school. All through college. Until I met Suzie . . ."

"Do you think you're just wishing yourself back to a time when you didn't know that all good things, all innocent things, are spoiled in the end?"

"But that isn't true, Julie!" he said, and I heard him tell someone he'd be right with her. "Not all things that stay with you all your life, and my memory of you stayed with me all my life, are just because you were a kid and foolish. Sometimes they stay with you because they mattered."

"You're a romantic. You have to pardon me if I can't be one right now."

"Julie, let me come and see you again. . . ."

"I don't know if that's such a hot idea."

"Let me come and then we'll decide. No pressure." Cathy was nodding. Yes. Shrugging. Why not?

"Even your asking to come is pressure," I said.

"Well, okay, then."

I heard myself say, "Well, okay then."

"Okay what?"

"Okay, come and see me. When? After Christmas?"

"I was thinking, ah, Saturday," he said.

THIRTY-ONE

Gabe's Journal

I got a letter from Leo right before Thanksgiving, asking me to come out there and spend the holiday weekend with him. He would send me a plane ticket. Since I had time before my tutor, who was this really nice older lady who got right down to business and made sure you had food throughout the whole two hours, I decided to answer his letter.

Dear Leon, [I wrote,] *I have to decline your invitation on personal grounds, those being that I hate your guts. I don't mean that in an unkind way. You're supposed to be able to admire your father. I tried to make a list for Mom's therapist of all the things I admired about you. I admired your vocabulary. I admired that you did nice things for your parents. I admired your knowledge of baseball statistics. That would be it, Leon. I figure if you have to make a list of ten things you admire about your own father, and you can come up with only three, and if you can think of thirty things you admire about your little sister's preschool teacher, this is an indication that either you're not an admirable person in my eyes or that I'm still too angry to see you, as in, during this lifetime.*

[I signed it *Gabe Gillis,* adding, as a P.S.,] *The new thing in our so-called family seems to be changing your name. I wanted to get in on it. I thought about it for a long time, and decided to use Steiner as my middle name, because otherwise it would hurt Gramp's feelings. Gramp is such a great guy. Funny thing, genetics, huh?*

I mailed it on the way to my tutor Donna's house because I thought I'd otherwise never do it. Either I'd lose my nerve or forget it.

The guy Matthew came to see my mother again after Halloween. They had dinner, and she looked all rosy and pretty in a dress Cathy loaned her. She was doing most all of her own work now, only occasionally asking me to look something up for her or make a phone call—for which she paid me, ten bucks an hour—I hadn't had much of a chance to look through her files. Once Rory was asleep, I did. And I found another poem, this one with the envelope in which she was to send it—actually, a couple of envelopes. One to *Urbane* magazine (fat chance, I thought) and one to the *Pen, Inc.*, people.

I used her copier to make a copy of it.

A Lamentation of Insects

Why did the ladybug fly away home
If her house was on fire
And her children were gone?
Did she need proof there was not just one left,
One beetlet uncharred,
Last jewel of her breast?
Did she need (really!) to kiss the charred shells
To bless her nest's pyre,
Enter ladybug hell?
Why not toss back a cold single malt?
Or tequila like swamp ice,
In a tub rimmed with salt?
Rubbed rumps with a moth in some fleabag bed?
Drowned her memories of fire?
After all, they were dead.
Why didn't the ladybug fly to Belize?
Where hulabugs writhe in the amethyst seas?
Why didn't she simply do as she pleased?
Why did she waste so much precious time?
Had she been a boy-bug, we'd not have the rhyme.

I thought it was funny and probably halfway decent, but it was creepy how she seemed to think about men. I wondered if she included all men, myself, in that poem, or just my father? It didn't seem to include the Matthew guy, who came the morning after he took her out to dinner and took all of us to brunch at this big hotel in Milwaukee. I thought, Aha, the old try-to-win-over-the-kid thing. But he hardly paid attention to me, beyond telling me why he reconstructed faces for his job. Really sad story. I don't mean that sarcastically. All he could do was look at my mother, as if she were some kind of really rare painting. I thought it must be nice for her, to have someone she knew once still think she was pretty. And he was a fairly nice person. He showed Rory pictures of his daughter on her horse, Diva. The horse, not the girl. The girl's name was Kelly. She was in college in New York, at the New School. She wanted to be a journalist or a professional equestrian or a vet. Or train horses for a living. The girl was amazing-looking. She had the longest blonde hair I ever saw on someone who wasn't nuts. He had a big farm between Boston and Cape Cod—well, big to apartment people—maybe twelve acres. He commuted, and traveled a lot, teaching other doctors how to do this one thing he'd sort of invented for cleft palates.

I walked with him to get his rental car, because my mom tried not to walk too far, especially in front of other people. She was still worried she'd fall and humiliate herself, though her balance was halfway decent now.

"What do you do, Gabe?" he asked.

"I go to home school," I said. "I have learning disabilities."

"Bad?"

"Yeah, I think, like they say, one more chromosome, and I'd be a cricket."

"But you're smart. To talk to."

"I didn't say I was stupid."

"Do you want to go to school?"

"Maybe. If it seems worth it."

"People all get to it at different times. Maybe your time won't be until you're in your twenties."

"Maybe," I said. It was a long walk, like, two city blocks. "So, was my mother much like she is now when she was a kid?"

"Yes," he said, "almost exactly. Smart. Pretty . . ."

"Stuck up," I said.

"Yeah."

"You'd think she would have gotten over that by now."

"For her, it's not a matter of being really stuck up, Gabe. I mean, I don't know her now. But when she was a kid, it was more like she had to keep her dignity."

"Maybe that was it," I said. "Because my grandparents were great, but they drank a little, and she didn't like that. She always wanted to be in control of herself, she used to tell me."

"Which is why this disease is probably so hard on her," he said.

"Trust me," I told him. "It would be hard on anybody. But she's way better now than she was."

"Do you mind that we're dating?"

"Is that what you're doing?"

"No," he said, as I swung up into the passenger seat. "But I want to. I don't know if she does."

"Do you know anything about multiple sclerosis?"

"Only what I've read. And I had a patient with a facial deformity who had it."

"Jeez, two strikes."

"Yes, but she was great. She didn't let anything stop her. Even using a walker. She danced with her walker."

"Christ, I hope that doesn't happen to my mom."

"It puts a lot on you."

"That's not why. It's, like, what you said about her being so into her dignity and so forth. She'd feel like she could never go out of the house."

"I'm very taken with her," he said. "I always was. But you had to get to the back of the line to have a prayer with Julieanne Gillis."

I tried to think of my mother, then, as a hottie, someone guys would kill to go out with. True, she had a semi-famous father, and she lived in a ritzy place. But I couldn't manage to see my mother that way. "I always thought she liked me. But I wasn't on her level. Like, her father."

"And you are now."

"I don't know. Maybe."

"MS. The big leveler."

He stopped the car. "No," he said. "You're a kid, but that's kind of a slam on your mother. I meant, I'm a doctor. People seem to think you have some brains to do that. Back then, I was basically a poor kid who went to public school because there was no other choice, not like your mom, who went to public school because her parents were liberals and didn't want it to seem as if they thought their daughter might get diseases from mingling with the common horde."

"I didn't mean anything," I muttered.

"And she *was* kind of stuck up," he said, laughing. "I went to her house once, for a party—"

"You were at my grandparents' house?" I asked, suddenly missing them, unable to make the picture of my grandmother's face form in my mind, able only to summon her voice, saying, "Ambrose, it's time we got on."

"Yes, it was when she was going on to Miss Whatever's School, and there were maids passing out—"

"Cucumber sandwiches," I finished for him.

"Yeah! To kids."

"That would be them," I said.

"But she was so embarrassed, for all of us. She wanted us to go fly kites in Central Park. And finally, we all did. I can still see her, climbing up the rocks with her kite, letting it unspool. She was a really athletic girl. Strong."

"The ballet."

"Yeah," Matt said, starting the car again. "I thought she'd go pro," as if the American Ballet Theater were the Dallas Cowboys.

"She was too fat and too tall," I told him. "She didn't want to do the anorexia thing. She says dancers live on vodka and chocolate and cigarettes."

"She's perfect," he said.

"You should live with her when she gets in one of her everybody-out-of-the-boat moods," I said.

"Well, Gabe, I intend to," he said.

THIRTY-TWO

Psalm 37

EXCESS BAGGAGE
By J. A. Gillis
Distributed by Panorama Media

Dear J.,

I can't tell anyone. My husband hits me. Last week, I was too bruised and swollen to go to work. I'm a nurse. You'd think I'd know better. I see people like me every day in the emergency room. But I'm afraid to leave. First, I know he'll find me and kill me. And second, he's a wonderful father. He's well known in our community. No one would believe me. And the children would hate me for it. How can I get him to stop? He's sorry every time, so terribly sorry; but he says it's the combination of the demands the kids and I make and the stress of his job that makes him lash out.

Miserable in Manhattan

Dear Miserable,

I believe you. And others would believe you. I promise you that. If you tell one person and that person doubts you, tell another one. I want you to write down a plan. And start packing, slowly, the few things you and your children will need to relocate. A good nurse can find work anywhere. Change your

name, and, if you have to, change your birth date. Most people
who leave are found because they don't change their birth dates.
Use one from someone who doesn't need it anymore (see my
confidential answer for details). Your kids may be angry at you.
All kids get angry at their parents when they have to do things
that mean big changes for the kids. But the worst thing you can
do for them is to allow them to believe that what they're seeing
is something that's acceptable. Get out while you still can. Get a
cell phone to call 911 for any reason, if you suspect he's found
out. Get a gun if you need to. Just get out. Don't try to help him.
He's beyond help. You're not. Yet.

J.

The beginning of the second beginning of my life happened unexpect-
edly, as so many things do. I hadn't exactly given up on planning, even
knowing it to be an exercise in futility. But I had decided to try to be
happy within the confines of what I could do, and stop lamenting what I
couldn't, as much as was possible for a person of my kind, who had finished buying and wrapping her Christmas presents by September.

I began dating a guy I met through a show Cathy was in. He was a nice
enough person, though I could feel myself pale when he told me he was a
lawyer; but it turned out that he was a corporate lawyer for the big sporting-
goods company, First Gear, which I didn't find nearly as threatening, for
some reason. "So," I asked him, the first time we had dinner, "what you
do is try to get people off the hook when a kid falls on one of your skate-
boards and gets brain damaged?"

"You do come right to the point," he said, "but what I do is try to get
people benefits for the child when that happens, without bankrupting the
company. You know people in our world now; I don't think that anything
bad should happen, and if it does, someone should pay."

But after a few months, during which I saw Matthew twice and Dennis almost every week, I resigned amicably from Dennis.

Nice enough wasn't good enough, even for me.

I'd believed I would be abjectly grateful to anyone who showed the slightest interest in me. It turned out that when *Urbane* did accept my poem, and paid me a thousand dollars for it, it was Matt I wanted to tell, even before I told Cathy or Gabe.

He was ecstatic on my behalf. He told me he was going to buy copies for everyone on his staff and for all his friends, and he had many friends. There was one weekend when I offered to come to Boston to see him, but he was headed off on a football weekend. For the next two weeks, when he called, I didn't pick up. I felt rebuffed, slighted. Finally, he sent me two dozen white roses in a silver-and-blue trophy cup. The card read, *Is it me you don't like or the Patriots?* And I called him. A week later, I received an engraved invitation to a gathering at the home of Matthew MacDougall for two weekends hence.

I didn't want to go. I did want to go, but I knew that something would happen, in front of his physicians' wives' friends, something that would prevent me from ever again crossing the Massachusetts border. But I thought, then, it was a party. How hard could it be to sit on a sofa and talk to regular people? I had once been a regular person.

And I thought I might go to see Cat. It had been months, with no word. She'd sent Rory a set of cloth dolls for Christmas, but they frightened Rory, since they had only eyes but no mouths or noses.

I might rent a car and drive to the place that I could no longer really recall the name of, since Gabe and I had, so often, called it the Happy Valley. It shouldn't be too difficult. I could get Cathy to keep Rory, and Gabe was fine on his own, with Cath in casual earshot. It turned out, when I mentioned it, that he and his grandparents were going to Door County that weekend, to do some preseason work on the cottage. He wanted, he said, to fish while it was still cold. "It makes me feel like a mariner," he said. "In summer, anybody can sail."

And so I readied myself carefully. I packed garment by garment over a period of weeks. A clinging black dress with a skirt that descended sharply in back and which ruffled around my legs when I moved, a movement I thought might disguise movements of my own—the unintentional kind. Wide-legged flowing trousers and a satin blouse. Funny big fake pearls on a fishing line. Jeans and two sturdy sweaters. A pair of boots and a pair of tennis shoes. Gabe asked me if I was moving.

A few days before I was to leave, the editor of *Urbane* called me. She asked whether she might give my e-mail address to a publisher who'd expressed interest in my "poems of anger." I hadn't known they were that, but I agreed in any case. What if there turned out to be a few bucks in it? I wrote the poems for a twisted kind of fun, and having had them published wasn't even the icing on the cake, it was the frosting roses. I never expected anything to coalesce around my poems. Even Gabe called them my "so-called poems."

The woman, an Amanda Senter, a name that seemed oddly familiar, wrote and asked permission to call.

"Julieanne Gillis," she said when I picked up.

"Yes?"

"The last time I saw you, you were hiding under a piano." It was that, then. The Dad thing. "I was your father's agent, Julieanne, for a very short time a very long time ago, when I was very young. Before I moved to the other side of the desk. You probably saw me twice in your life. But when I read your poem, I thought Ambrose would like knowing that I recognized his girl's work."

"Thanks," I said. "It's kind of fun."

"And what do you have in the trunk?" she asked.

"The trunk?"

"I mean, do you have enough poems amassed for a collection? I see it as a sort of woman's triumphal rejection of the old male rule . . . and they're kind of fun. You know, a poem to read when you're furious at him." I had no idea what she was talking about. The poems I had written were the poems I had written. Four. There were no odd slips of paper and jottings of consummate power tucked away in my drawer, to be found with breathtaking consequences by the children after my death.

"I'm an advice columnist," I said. "I'm not a poet."

"Why not let me be the judge of that. I have my own imprint now. I do very few things. . . ."

I ended up, conscious of the firm, approving stare of my father from on high, sending her two. One of them I wrote after we got off the telephone, in perhaps twenty-five minutes.

Some Days Are Better Than Others

There is nothing wrong with me
A new body wouldn't cure.
How about a side of spinal fluid?
Got that in the color pure?
There is nothing wrong with me;
But I need a couple legs, size eight.
Then I'd be secure
Little larynx tune-up, diaphragm tuck, pair of new eyes,
Some agile hands, a brain that works not just in reverse,
Or maybe just a promise, say, nothing worse?
Just settle for me, order filled, not my three.
Just that. I'll endure.

Promptly, the following morning, she wrote me and told me she'd cried upon reading it. I thought she must be going through some rough times mentally. She talked about positioning and presentation, about line drawings or the lack of them.

"Wait, Miss Senter," I finally said.

"Amanda," she replied.

"Amanda, just what are we talking about here?"

"Well, poetry, as a rule, isn't a major seller. But what I'm thinking is that, there are enough women out there who've been dumped, or who have gone through similar trials, for all sorts of reasons, that we could almost present it as a book of friendship, of solidarity. . . ."

"A book?"

"We can't offer you much."

"I don't have a book of poems! How many poems go in a book?"

"Twenty-four, I think. I see it small, very rich-looking, almost like a thickish greeting card. . . ."

"It would take me six months to write twenty-four poems!"

"Well, we wouldn't expect them for a year, at least. But we can give you five now and five upon acceptance." She meant thousands. I was grateful to be sitting down. A year's worth of therapy and home schooling. More if I petitioned the school district and won, so they had to pay for Gabe's schooling. I didn't know what to say, so I said nothing. "I'm sorry it's not more, Julie."

"Well, I think it would be nice to be public."

"I'm sorry?"

"Published. I think it would be nice."

"So it's okay? Who is your agent?"

"Uh. I have to get in touch with her." I had to think of something. I had to think of an old (and that would mean really old) friend of my father's I could call, to ask for the name of an agent. But I didn't know any of those people! Not as an adult! They knew me as a little girl in my high school uniform. I called Cathy at her office, and was too tense and excited to remember to ask for her by name. "I'd like to talk to the psychologist."

"She's in session."

"I'd like to have her call me back."

"Are you suicidal?"

"No!" I burst out laughing. "It's . . . Julieanne Gillis. She's my housemate. Cathy Gleason."

"Oh! I'm sorry, Missus Gillis."

Cathy and I spent the evening looking at the spines of my father's signed books. We picked out the name of a woman who had at least a hope of being alive and sentient, found her agent's name in the acknowledgments, and when I called, she not only remembered me, she greeted me with the vocal equivalent of open arms. She was glad to go over my contracts. She'd love to have me to her home for dinner, next time I was in New York (next time I was in New York?). She knew my father would be proud. She thought the advance was a little on the stingy side, and she would try to keep foreign rights out of it. "We can pick up money on foreign sales," she said. She might as well have been speaking in Aramaic. She used words I had heard my father use, but I had been trying to ignore the words at the time.

The publication of my poems was a terrifying crack in an opening door. I was afraid that the light from that opening door would hurt my eyes. I was afraid I would disgrace my father. I was afraid for the world to see what seemed, to me, like the little pages of scribbles Aurora held up at the dinner table. ("I have an excusement to make," she would say, "I wrote a column.") Abruptly, the trip to Boston was no longer a source of anxiety. It was a relief.

Matthew met me at the baggage claim, carrying a Patriots fan card with the words GILLIS PARTY written on it. "Enough with the Patriots jokes," I said, meaning it. "How far is it to your house?"

"About twenty minutes if the traffic is good."

"I don't think anyone has ever said anything else to me," I told him. It struck me funny.

"What?"

"I mean that no one has ever said anything to me except 'It's about twenty minutes from here.'"

"And all clocks in store windows are set for twenty minutes after eight."

"Isn't that because it's when Abraham Lincoln died?"

"No," he said. "I think it's because it shows the hands better. The hands of the clock."

"I think it's because of Abraham Lincoln. And don't mess with me. I'm a trivia expert. And the strangest thing happened." I had rehearsed this revelation. Girlish and flirtatious? Proud but somewhat bewildered? Surprised yet confident? "There's going to be a book. Of my poems."

"Julieanne," his reaction was different from what I'd expected. Very un–football fan. A quiet approval. A proud, proprietary nod. We passed through the center of a small town called Briley, and headed down a country road. When he turned in at the columned house, I thought he was stopping to buy eggs. "My humble abode."

"It's a fucking mansion!" I said. "I'm sorry, Matt. For cussing. I hang around a sixteen-year-old. But I never imagined . . ." A cream-colored horse watched us with amused, kindly eyes as we passed. "That's my girl's girl, Diva. My horse is Carver. Kelly gave him to me. The name? It's her idea of a surgery joke. He's a good old boy, though."

"I used to ride," I said, thinking of Central Park, my mother in her jodhpur boots.

"We can take a turn tomorrow," Matt said eagerly.

"I couldn't sit a horse now."

"Don't be so sure. With Carver, you just have to let him do the driving."

"Matt, you're one of those guys who's always thrashing off to do something, aren't you?"

"I guess," he said, taking my suitcase out of the trunk. "That a bad thing? I stand still all day, using my hands to make tiny motions. So I like to make big motions in my time off. It makes sense."

"So what do you want to do hanging around with a lady who used to be able to jump three feet into the air and now has to take her time going up three steps?"

"There's more to life than thrashing around," he said, and opened the door.

It looked like my memories of Tuscany, from a summer when I was nine or ten. Golden walls and thick green rugs. Brick-red furniture with striped pillows and a chandelier that looked like Cleopatra's barge. I flopped down on the couch, from which I could see the long table, cherry, plain and shining and the kitchen with its painted tiles and strings of garlic. "Hey, congrats to your decorator."

Matt nodded, then shrugged. "I picked up junk because I liked the colors. I bought the chandelier when Peter Mangan sold the prototype from a restaurant I like to go to in Seattle."

"You did this yourself?"

"I hate, you know, single guys with white walls and navy blue furniture. . . ."

"I do, too, but how do you do all this?"

"Listen, I have one kid in college. I didn't plan that. Even with doctor's hours, that leaves a lot of time on your hands. You decorate a house. You take piano lessons. I don't know. Suzie and I traveled. I never felt . . . I always wanted another child. I still do. Don't laugh. People do it all the time at our age."

"I'm not laughing. I have a three-year-old. People think I'm insane."

"Do you want tea?"

I nodded.

"Y'know what Brits call the tea they take at four o'clock? Solace. Isn't that kind of cool?"

"I like it. It sounds like another word I like. My parents were sort of Episcopalian. Vespers. I liked that word."

We drank the tea as the light outside sank and the lights in Matt's house, and outside, among the trees, obviously on a timer, rose in mellow increments. "When are the guests coming?" I asked. "I want to lie down, maybe take a shower. If you can show me where I'll be sleeping?"

He led me down a short hall to a room with a bed I knew I'd need a three-step ladder to climb onto. I meant only to lie there for a moment, but when I woke, the room was black. Despite myself, I called out, "Help!" And I could feel, smell, Matt beside me, his clean woody scent, within a moment. "I'm sorry. It was so dark. I thought my eyes were acting up."

"Does that happen much?"

"It used to."

"Not now."

"No."

"Can you see down the hall?" I could see candlelight, immaculate cloths on the shining table, and as my senses returned, coming alight one by one, I could smell the aroma of garlic, roasted.

"Are people here?" I whispered. "I have to dress. . . ."

"Take your time," he said. "No rush."

He turned on the lights, in the bathroom—the tub actually did have steps—and left me alone. I bathed carefully, finger-brushed the silly short hair for which I'd come to have a rough affection, and put on my soft black dress. I brushed the color across my nose and applied lipstick that barely had any color, best for older women, the girl at the drugstore said. I looked good. Now, my shoes. I opened my shoe bag. Running shoes. Boots. I sat down on the bed, ready to weep. I could see them, exactly where they were now, on my desk chair, each of them in its own little cotton bag. "Matt!" I called. There was music on. Something soft, old. Julie London. Funny guy. "Matt!" I couldn't hear him excuse himself from a conversation, but he was carrying a bottle of wine when he came to my door. "I forgot my shoes."

"You're just this . . . sweet, delicate—"

"Be quiet! I don't want anyone to hear us! I can't walk out there in my stockings!"

"Oh, but you can, unless your feet are cold."

"What will your guests think?"

"The whole party's here," he said.

"But you sent me an invitation."

"You're the party," he said. "Come on." The table was set for two. Pasta waited for a simmering peppery sauce. He'd filled my wineglass, exactly half.

I stood on the tiles. There was nothing I could think of to say.

Matt said, "Don't be mad."

"I'm not mad. And I'm not scared. Don't get me wrong. I can't think of the word for what I am."

"Shocked?"

"No."

"You think I'm an asshole?"

"No," I began to laugh. "*No,* I don't think you're an asshole. You're not the class nerd, Matt; you're a catch."

"I've waited thirty years to take Julieanne Gillis to dinner. I wanted to do it up right."

"Don't get all, you know, funny. No, I mean defensive."

"I'm not."

"Is everything ready?"

"It's a dish, okay, look, it's the only dish I can make. It can sit here all night while we talk and it'll still taste the same. We can have some cheese, first."

"I was thinking you'd show me the rest of the house."

"Okay!" he said heartily, putting down the wine. The staircase that rose like a wave out of the front foyer had, I counted, seventeen steps. I looked at Matthew. "Julie, let me help," he said.

"I'm not a teeny-weeny woman, Matt."

"But I'm not five one anymore, honey." The "honey" about did it. Something splintered, and I began to cry.

"What did I do?"

"You called me honey."

"What, I didn't mean anything—"

"No, I mean, I felt so, I don't know, cherished. I haven't felt that way in a long time." As I said it, I realized that I meant a *long* time, as in *years.* And so he carried me up all those seventeen steps, without having to stop and pant. Down the hall to his room where he lay me down gently on the bed.

"I have to tell you, this disease, it's about nerve endings, Matt. It takes forever for me . . ."

"That's what I was hoping," he said.

THIRTY-THREE

Song of Solomon

EXCESS BAGGAGE
By J. A. Gillis
Distributed by Panorama Media

Dear J.,

I'm 51 years old, and I'm a widow. I'm pretty, okay? I'm in good shape. I have two kids, good kids, never in trouble. Two years after my husband passed, I signed up with one of those Internet dating services. My best friend, she writes, and she wrote my profile. I'm a librarian. I love to dance. I love motorcycles. I got a lot of hits. A lot of dates, two or three with men I really liked. But as soon as Mike whined about something, or Cheryl, my daughter left her shoes and book bag on the floor, or argued with me about the car keys, the calls stopped. They don't want the complications. Well, they're not complications, they're my kids, and I think they're, like, value added. Good people. There are no good men left out there. All the good ones? Taken or gay. I'm not going to fool around with a married man. This is it, huh?

Fed up in Philly

Dear Fed,

I hate when people say "I know how you feel" because usually they don't, or they say it because they just don't want to hear about it anymore. I do know what you mean. My husband *ditched me for a girl half my age when I was in my forties, and though I didn't know it, I had multiple sclerosis. If I can find a good man, anyone can. And I did. They are out there. Keep dancing, sister. Chance favors those in motion.*

J.

I woke up alone in Matt MacDougall's massive bed, and began to laugh wildly. He hadn't heard me, because he nearly dropped the coffee mugs he'd carried up when he got to the door and saw me kicking my feet and howling.

"I can't believe this. I've spent the past year selling my clothes and feeling like something wet that crawls along the edge of walls, like I'd never see the sun. Now, I'm sitting here in the mansion built by my eighth-grade dance partner. I slept with you, and we made love and it worked, Matt! I never thought I'd do that again!"

"Do you always wake up this happy?" he asked, flopping down in his (blue-and-white) sweats.

"No, sometimes, I wake up terrified that I'm not going to be able to see out of my left eye that day. Or knowing I'm going to have to take my shot. And always by myself. Unless Rory's on the end of the bed. But the next time I do that, I'm going to, you know, I'm going to remember last night. Because it was mine, Matt. I want to thank you for giving me this wonderful morning."

"Julie," he said.

"I'm not crazy, Matt. I just want to thank you."

"But are you hungry?"

"Oh, we forgot to eat! Your pasta. All that work. My half glass of wine!"

"I got up and put it away. We can have it tonight. You were out like a light!"

"Uh, satisfaction will do that to you. Very careful guy, you are." I reached out for my coffee, holding my wrist with my left hand. "My hand is damn shaking. I mean, my damn hand is shaking. No! Not right now! Out damned hand!"

"Don't worry, Julie. Let's get this straight. I don't care. I mean, I care so much I don't care." He kissed me, on my overnight mouth, and together, with me lost in one of his huge terry robes, we walked carefully down that sky-suspended staircase, into a kitchen filled with sun. "Give me your coffee cup," Matt said. "I want to give you the good stuff. My mom's china." I sat down. There was a cup at my plate, and a sugar bowl with tongs.

"You do this every Sunday morning?"

"Are you kidding? I had to climb up into the attic and find this stuff behind the Christmas ornaments."

"Lump sugar?"

"And tongs, Julie. These weren't my mother's. I got them from Kelly after she told me it wasn't that cool to pull the cubes out with my fingers. But here, do it the right way."

The ring was on top of the pile of raw sugar cubes.

It looked like one of the brown lumps had been transformed, by a genie, into crystal. It was that big. Plain and simply set, but the size of Mount Rushmore.

I reached around it and put sugar into my coffee. "Do you have milk?" I asked.

"Well, will you marry me?" he asked.

"Do I get milk then?"

"Now, you think *I'm* crazy."

"I think this is a gesture of overwhelming sweetness, Matt. And I've never seen a ring like that, much less worn one."

"Try it on."

"Matt . . ."

"That sounds like a big letdown."

"I don't mean it to. I thought we were having a good time."

"And then I had to spoil it by offering to make you my wife?"

"We haven't seen each other in almost thirty years, Matt! We've had six dates. We've had sex once. Well, twice."

"And we've written back and forth and spoken on the phone for hours for nearly a year. You've seen other men. I've seen other women. You know that I love you. I hope you love me. You know people depend on me for more physical challenges than your disease could ever offer us. From now until, well, we kick the bucket."

"What would you say if I couldn't see? Or had to zip around on one of those little scooters, if we took Aurora to Disney World? Think about that, Matt. Think about Suzie, climbing mountains and, I don't know, jibbing the mainsail or whatever she did. What if I couldn't do that? Or couldn't always do that?"

He sat down and folded his huge, clean hands. I shivered, looking at those hands. "Well, don't think I haven't thought about this. I know that you could remain this way the rest of your life, or be badly disabled. And I want to sign on."

"What if I lose it all? My mind?"

"I'll have the privilege of really being the support and help for someone. Really mattering to someone. That's no small thing. Anyway, you don't say to yourself, when you fall in love, gee, what am I going to do if my wife can't talk when we're eighty? Or if she makes mistakes with words? We're in our forties. Should I do that? I could easily be the one who ends up buggy."

"Well, those are the things you should think about long and hard, if you're marrying a woman with a disability. . . ."

"So you confirm that I am marrying a woman with a disability."

I waited, as he slipped the ring on my finger, for the flashing red sign that would restore me to my senses.

It didn't ignite.

I felt only a great and consuming peace of mind. I thought of a forever of last nights, safe in this house. This *house*! Seeing things with Matt, a man who, apparently, wanted to devour the world. Someone who didn't hate his work, but who had a passion for it. A big, handsome man with friends! He loved me as I once was, and as I was now. Tears gathered in my eyes. He loved me even as I might become, or thought he could. It took my breath away. I could be . . . myself again. With someone I knew, or had known, as a good and honest person. My first kiss, and my last. A symmetrical union. The possibility of joy. A loving, comforting presence beside me on quiet nights, or festive ones. When the demons descended and, even better, when they didn't. Matthew MacDougall, a good man, a patient and, I'd discovered, sensual man.

Did the thought of health insurance occur to me? I'm not stupid, or a liar. Did the thought of a stable home for Rory, a stable father figure who actually wanted a child, did that cross my mind, too? For Gabe, perhaps an understanding friend who might repeal some of the cynicism he felt about the loyalty of men? Was I crazy?

I was not crazy.

I would be crazy to turn him down.

I was knock-over-the-moon lucky.

I was going to walk out of this house with this ring, like a little star, on my hand. The possibility of the book, the luckiest thing that had happened to me in years, now was pallid in comparison with the richer happiness I envisioned. One was a little help, a little payback. For a little while. One was sanctuary. I didn't kid myself. I wanted Matt now. I would need Matthew as time went by.

But who among us does not need other people?

People have been far bigger fools for far less.

Matt spent the rest of the day asking me, "How's engaged life?"

Much as I hated to leave him, I knew I had to face the drive to Vermont in the morning. I knew that he would insist on driving me, and that I ought to refuse, but also that it was okay for me to give in! He would go with me. I had a partner. And after the day and the next night, much as I hated to leave him, I couldn't wait to spill the bittersweet revelation to Gabe, and to Cath. This house! I wandered around, examining the towels, the sunroom, the massive game room with pinball machines and a TV the size of Montana! Gabe would love this house. I examined the old glass doorknobs, the curve-legged table with its frieze of Poseidon on the waves.

I had no idea whether Gabe would be hurt, relieved, or elated. I suspect there would be a tincture of all three.

At least, he would know that he would be free.

Then I thought of Hannah and Gabe Senior.

Every blessing has its blemish.

How could I leave them? *Whither thou goest.* Perhaps there was a way I could convince them; but no, there were all the friends they had who were in Sheboygan or in Door County. On the other hand, flights to and from there weren't outrageous.

It was a three-hour drive to Pitt, Vermont, where we stopped at the bed-and-breakfast Gabe and Cat had mentioned, just a map step shy of the New York State line. We brought the owner a flowering plant, and I explained who I was. She had no trouble remembering my children; and her face toughened with disdain, but she made no comment, when she gave us directions to Sunrise Valley. We made the ride in silence, the way obligingly variegated to reflect my mood. I was going to be a doctor's wife. I was going to be a published-ass poet! My kids were going to be safe.

I was going to see the great love of my life, and the great love of *his* life. I was going to see my little girl, who'd grown up too soon. When we finally drove down the avenue of maples and turned left, the first thing I saw was the new house, still raw, but glittering with oversized south-facing windows, riotous with plants of every span and plumage, just beneath the crest of the ridge, I grabbed for Matthew's arm. Who was this man? A complete stranger. I was going to march up to the front door of Leo's love nest with my seventh-grade crush—and by the way, it had been *his* crush, not mine! What was I doing? Why had I not thought it over?

I would not have done this, any of this, had I thought it over.

And there was no point starting to think now.

So we walked up the flagstone steps that led to . . . my ex-husband's home. Caroline opened the door. Involuntarily, she leapt toward me and threw her arms around my neck. I could have eaten her up. Her neck was wet with both our tears.

"I take it you know this young woman?" Matt asked, gruff, almost abashed, so lost were we in each other.

"*This* is my daughter! This is my beautiful daughter, Cat Steiner!" I told him. "Cat, this is Matt. That sounds ridiculous. Cat, this is, well, my sweetheart." I put out my hand.

"Mom! Is that real?" Cat burst out, ever mindful of the important things in life.

"I'm afraid it is, yes, and I'm afraid it's what you think it is," I told her. "Ain't that a kick in the head?"

"Mommy! I'm so happy for you!"

"Are you? Is everything just as . . . wonderful here as it looks?" Something passed across her face. I'd have called it a cloud.

"It's great!" she said, and I thought, she is my daughter, too. Living in Deny, Vermont. "Dad's out right now . . . but Joy is here."

"It was you I wanted to see!" I said. "I'm here only for one day. Cat, will you come to our wedding?"

"Cat!" A voice in the background bellowed. It was okay. I bellowed. "I told you to change that load of whites!"

"How are you doing in school?" I asked.

"Really, really good," she said. "But I don't have that much time for it, because of the two babies and with Dad working so much. . . ." I noticed, then, with a bit of alarm, the little blue hollows under Caroline's eyes. She changed the subject.

"Are you feeling good, Mom?"

I spun around on my boot heel. "Don't I look like I'm feeling good?"

"Yeah," Cat said wistfully, leaning against the door frame. An actual cloud pushed across the sun, and she shivered. "You look pretty good. How're Gabe and Rory?"

"He's good, Cat. He dropped out, but he's almost ready to take the GED. . . ."

"You can't blame him, Mom. You don't know what it was like for him."

"I don't blame him."

"You don't?"

"No, I did, but I don't. Not everyone goes the same way, like you said on the phone. How's Dominico?"

"So over. He was, like, sleeping with three other girls. He was so trash." I froze, and Cat whispered, "I had all the tests. Everything's okay with me. But what an asshole."

"I'm sorry."

"Why?" Her back stiffened a bit. "You were right."

"I'd much rather have been wrong than see you hurt."

"Mommy, it's cool to see you happy. You were so lousy—I don't mean lousy—"

"Yeah, I was pretty lousy. I was lousy to you. You can say it. I was pretty hurting."

"Well, I didn't help. It was better I left."

"I'll never think that."

We all turned as a car crunched down the lane behind us. A truck really, an aging Dodge. But the stroller on the porch was a Zooper Baby, with every gadget on it except a foot massager. Leo got out of the truck, slowly, and used a sheaf of papers to shield his eyes as he tried to place the stranger with the big man on his porch, talking to his daughter. Then, he recognized me, and his shoulders seemed to drop from their position of defense.

"Julie," he said.

"Hi, Lee," I said, taking his hand. "Mazel tov. I heard you have a baby girl."

"Yeah," Leo said to me. "Joy is very fertile. The baby's a doll, though. Joy, too. And this doll has been my right hand." He nodded at Caroline. Leo shifted, slipping his sheaf of documents under one arm. "Leo Steiner," he said, putting out his hand to Matt, who gave it a perfunctory shake (I took smug pleasure). "I didn't get your name."

"Matt MacDougall."

Leo grinned. "You sound like an actor. Look like one, too. One of Cathy's friends?" he asked.

"I'm a surgeon," Matt said.

"Huh," Leo appeared a bit distracted. I watched his eyes flick toward the windows of the house.

"We thought we might take Cat to lunch before I go home."

"That would be great, Jules, any other day. But she has chores and a whole lot of back homework, and she's been mouthing off like crazy."

"Make an exception, Lee," I urged him. Again, that flick of the eyes, toward the interior. "Gabe, well, he's doing . . . okay. He dropped out of school."

"My dad said. Tough. The longer he waits, the less likely it's going to be that he ever goes back, so try to steer him toward getting something started. . . ."

"Like I wouldn't," I said. "And you can, too."

"Like he'd listen," Leo mimicked me, and I had to smile.

"Aren't you going to introduce us to Joy? Is she your wife? Hannah and Papa don't . . . say much about her to me," I told him.

"Uh, no," Leo said. "We haven't quite gotten around to that." He paused in his door frame. "You look wonderful, Julie. You look like a million bucks. Like a dancer." *The rain-drenched man.* I felt a sting behind my eyes.

"I'm happy, Lee. It's been a long time. No offense meant there. Matt, well, Matt and I just got engaged. We've actually known each other since we were kids, with a gap of about twenty-five years."

"You're getting *married*, Julie?"

"Isn't that something?"

"Well, yes, yes it is."

Matt put his arm around me, and I leaned back into his great, solid chest. Leo regarded me. Christ, if he didn't look . . . no. Well, I was sure he looked a little bit wistful.

"Let me take Caroline, just for lunch."

"Can't. She made her bed this morning, and she's got to lie in it."

"Well, I'm glad you're setting limits for her. But, Leo, you're a lawyer. You know that I have a right to see my daughter. I have a custodial right to my daughter, if you want to make an issue of it—"

"Yeah, okay." He looked gray, worn. "Go ahead, Caroline."

We ate at a little restaurant with good pie.

"Are you really happy here, honey?" I asked Caroline.

"Sure," said Caroline.

"You seem worn out."

"I have a lot to do. When you're part of a community, everyone depends on everyone else. There can't be one weak link."

"I wouldn't call being a kid a weak link," I said.

"Well, a lot is expected of me. But in return I get a lot of freedom." She let her hair fall across her face.

"You can come home, Caroline."

"It's Cat, and no, I can't. I told everyone back there that I had the perfect life. And I do. It's fine. I'm just having a hard time right now."

"Is Joy hard on you?"

"I'm fine, Mom," Caroline snapped. "You should be hysterical with joy. All you ever wanted me to do was *chores*."

"You know," I said, "when Matt and I get married, I'll be moving to near Boston. That's practically right down the road! You don't have to live with Dad full time."

"We'll see. Dad does really need me," Caro said, eating the crust first, as she always had. I didn't hear the ring of conviction.

"I need you, too, and I don't mean because of my sickness."

"You have to know how much your mom loves you," Matt put in. "She talks about it like you're this princess in a tower. Maybe you could cut her a break."

"I did. I left."

"Is part of the reason you won't even think about it that it won't be just me living in the house? That you'd have to get used to someone new? But Rory'll be there. She misses you so much," I said.

Caroline put down her fork. "I miss her, too. I can't eat anymore."

"You could go to"—I looked at Matt—"a residential school."

"A boarding school? No, thanks. At least I'm part of something here."

"But if you're not happy . . ." I suggested.

"Who said I'm not happy? You can't judge a whole life in a couple of weeks."

"It's been six months, Caro."

"It's Cat, and I don't make judgments quickly." She glanced up, looking pointedly at my ring. "Maybe it's a learned thing."

"Do you want to talk alone?"

"Do you mind?" Caroline asked Matt. He smiled and shook his head. "Not in the least," he said.

We sat alone on one side of the aluminum booth, and I felt the struggle wrack her. She didn't say a word. I finally said, "I know it was hard on you, back when I first got sick. I also know that wasn't entirely my fault or my choice. You know that, too. But we have a whole future to change things between us. And it's going to be a much more stable future. . . ."

"How do you know, Mom? How do you know he won't leave you, too?"

I recoiled as if punched. "Caroline, I don't know. How do you know your father won't leave Joy?"

"They're happy, that's why. It's not all a show," she said venomously, but the tears were streaming now, "they're real. And he would never leave the babies."

"Rory was a baby."

"You always twist things, Mom! Always!" Caroline cried, leaping up. "You make it like it's all everyone else's fault!"

"Caroline, no. Forget what I said. It isn't about the past, it's about the future, and I want a future with you. I love you. You're my little girl."

"No, I'm not, Mom," Caroline said miserably. "I stopped being your little girl a long time ago."

Matt had to help me back to the car, and Caroline sat in the back, still hiccupping with her sobs. I tried to compose myself as we approached

Leo's house, taking wet wipes to my face and touching it up with powder. "That was a resounding success, huh? Welcome to the family," I told Matt, trying to plaster over his discomfort with apologetic small talk.

But he wasn't uncomfortable. "Julie, you two are under a terrible weight. It's obvious. The love. Yours and hers. But time has to pass for you two to figure out how that's going to play out. It hasn't been a daisy path every day for Kelly and me, either. Being a single parent is hard. But being a single parent's kid is even harder, maybe." I glanced in the rearview mirror and saw Cat give him a watery half smile.

Satisfied as a cat, too pleased even to be as miserable as I should have been, I thought, Hey, that's my guy.

As we turned up the lane, I saw Leo handing the little baby back through the screen door to a woman with a tumble of curls on her head, though I didn't catch a real glimpse of her. Caroline kissed me good-bye quickly and went inside. Leo sort of danced down the steps, then walked down to Matt's car with us. His cocky Leonine quality was back in place.

"Take good care of her, Lee. Our daughter's going through a hard patch."

"Adolescence."

"And a lot more. I think she needs me. Encourage her to come visit me."

"I'll try, Jules." He began to turn away, and then stopped. He swallowed. "Jules. Every blessing. I mean that."

"I know you do."

"I . . . never thought I'd lose you. Isn't that funny?"

"Funny. Yeah."

"You're a lucky guy, Mister MacDonald."

"MacDougall."

"Sorry."

"No matter. I know how lucky I am. I'm glad I got there in the nick of time. Before someone else snapped her up," Matt said.

"You mind if I kiss the bride?" Leo asked suddenly. Before Matt could react, Leo leaned over and put his cheek against mine for a long moment and then touched my lips with his. It's a cliché. They say this of drowning people: life flashes past you. That didn't happen, but I remembered these things: Leo in his black leather outside the rehearsal hall. Our wedding day—two skinny kids in that cavernous apartment, all dressed up as grown-ups under the flowered chuppah. Gabe's birth. Leo's triumphant roar as he glimpsed his son. His seeming to grow five inches in height when he handed over the deed for the cottage to his parents. A graduation gown, Leo's eyes seeking mine in the crowd. And then I stopped. Took my mind in my two hands and stepped back.

"Good luck, Lee," I said.

Caroline had come back outside, her hair brushed, her eyes clear. She slipped under Leo's arm. "I'll write you, honey bun."

She nodded.

"Be happy. Be careful."

"Oh, Mom," she said, herself again. "I'm not stupid. You take care of *yourself*."

Matt and I got into the car and began driving slowly down the narrow road. We heard the pounding on the gravel behind us before Caroline caught up.

"Mommy," she said, "will you tell Gabe that I'm sorry?"

I nodded.

She said, "He'll know what I mean."

We drove off then, while she stood there, hugging herself. I watched her until we turned the corner, and glimpsed her through the trees as we turned. She was watching us still, her eyes like a furnace. As long as I could strain to see her, she never moved.

THIRTY-FOUR

Gabe's Journal

So, Matt, he turned out to be a big guy who made big gestures, some of which worked out. I didn't mind him around. He came every weekend after they got engaged. I thought it was weird, given Mom's excellent experience with marriage, that she'd want to do it again, so soon. But she clearly wanted another whack at it, and I wasn't going to be around forever.

I didn't have to make it clear that I wasn't in the market for a daddy, but he wasn't easily discouraged. He figured out quickly I wasn't that into sports, and when we talked, it was movies and cars, books and music. I didn't encourage or discourage him. I didn't even know the guy. They were together only six months when they decided to go ahead with it. But, then, neither of them had that much time left, I guess. They were already, like, well over forty.

Just before they got married, we drove over to Gram and Gramp's. By then, I'd been accepted at UW-Milwaukee's program for, like, gifted eccentrics, and had survived the three-week stint in the wilderness that had been thrust on me by my mother.

Matt was curious about that. Apparently the woman he'd been with before Mom had been a hiker and a climber, and he'd done some of that, too.

"Try having to do push-ups for an extra pancake. Sitting out in the goddamned rain if you forgot to zip your tent. And, ah yes, biking. How about, oh, forty miles a day."

"Doesn't look like it did you any harm," he said.

I *had* bulked up. Every other doper and fatso on the first week stint had lost twenty pounds. I'd gained ten and grew three inches over that spring and summer. Mom said I looked like my grandfather Gillis. And it turned out that, once I was back, I was no longer able to make laziness into a sacrament. I got itchy if I didn't get out and run or stretch or ride my bike a few times a week. I'd also learned a couple of things about anger, which I wasn't about to share with Matthew.

The way it went was this. We all showed up, and they made us empty out our giant aluminum-mounted duffel bags of contraband, such as CD players or smokes or even a paperback book. You got a knife. You got a water bottle. You got some shirts and pants and shoes and a sleeping bag. Nothing that would inflate or cushion your skinny ass. You got dried vegetarian chili. You got hot Jell-O. On Sunday, you got pancakes for extra physical labor or service to others. Service to others could include helping someone get up a rock face or fixing someone's bike. Food for kindness. The most basic message of civilization. After the rest of the group of losers went back into their holes, I was out there for two goddamned weeks, making and breaking camps, with this guy, Leif, one of the leaders, who about came up to my waist and could have picked me up and thrown me ten feet no problem. I never saw a stronger guy. He was stingy with his history. So was I. But after a while, fuck, there was nothing to read, nothing to listen to but loons, and I asked him, "What the hell do you do this for?"

"A job," he said.

"I meant," I said patiently, "what the hell do you get from hiking around the same terrain with various screwed-up kids?"

"You get one, once in a while, who gets halfway unscrewed."

"What's the percentage?" I asked him.

"One in five. The rest, their parents just go back to spoiling them, buying them anything they want."

"That's me."

"Yours is a little different story."

"What's yours?"

"Well, I hated my father. He took off when I was seventeen."

"There's some common ground. Mine took off on me."

"That's about half the kids who come."

"And he left my mother with multiple sclerosis."

Leif peeled a stick and chewed on it. He was good with the long silences. Finally, he shook his head and clucked his tongue. "Mine died."

"He died?" I practically blew up. "You call that taking off on you?"

"Well, you never get a chance to say anything else. And it wasn't an accident."

"Oh," I said, thinking that my situation was infinitely preferable to having found Leo hanging from a rafter. "In my case, he made a cheerful choice."

"You think that?" Leif asked. "That he seemed like he was happy to leave you? Because even if he acted like he was, he wasn't."

"He was. Very."

"Yeah?"

"Yeah."

"You ever think about him, from when you were younger?"

I balled my fists. The first fucking thing that came to mind was the tree fort. "No," I said.

"That's bullshit," Leif said amiably.

"Don't we have to fall off a cliff or something now?"

"You don't like the tight spaces, huh, Gabe? Scared of what you might say?"

"I don't want to blow you off the mountain, to tell the truth. My father, my ex-father, is the lowest form of human life," I explained.

"I don't know the guy. But, man, you put a lot of energy into hating him. I looked at your so-called journals when everybody turned in their first entries last week. . . ." Journaling was mandatory. So was proving that you'd done it.

"You know I can't write well. Well, do handwriting."

"I don't mean how it looks. I mean it's all 'Leo left.' 'Leo screwed us over,'" he said.

"And?"

"Well, you're like a little kid. Your daddy left you and you can't get over it."

"You're about a mile wide of the target on that one," I told him, sneering. "Huh."

Another long fucking silence.

Then Leif asked, "You ever think of the power he still has over you?"

"That would be . . . none."

"No, the thing is, as long as you hate him, he's got you by the balls, Gabe. Look it up. The power you put into hating your dada for leaving poor Gabie all alone could light up Minneapolis. Whereas, if you forgive him, you're free. He has no influence over you anymore."

"That, and pardon me, is fucked up," I said.

"You're a kid. I didn't expect you to get it," he said. "Time to rappel now."

He left me alone for my isolation experience three days later. I wasn't about to jot down the yearnings of my soul in this tattered notebook they made me take. I tried to draw Tian. I gathered about a bushel of rose hips to bring my mother so she could make tea. And finally I pulled down some little branches off a sapling and made a dream weaver, or whatever they call them, for Rory. I used my old shoestrings—you had to bring six pairs—to make a pattern in the center. I slept for about fourteen hours, waking up when thunder struck a tree about two feet from me. I got my mummy bag and started trying to wring out the goddamned thing. It was like trying to wring out a phone book. I wrapped my poncho around my shoulders and sat out in the open so the lightning wouldn't kill me. I thought Leif would come for me then. But I was wrong about that. I had twenty of my forty-eight hours left, and he was going to make me live through it with a can of beans and a knife. Anyone would have started bawling. So I began to howl, timing my howls with the roars of thunder in case Leif should be within earshot. "Leo!" I screamed, "You fucking bastard! I forgive you, Leo! You're nothing to me! You're invisible! You're a jerk! You're a loser and a liar! You didn't give a shit about me!" By then, I was like Rory, so far gone in it, I thought I would throw up. And the howls kept coming. "Why'd you have me, Leo? Why? Did you have to prove you were a man? Or are you just nuts? Leo? Dad? Dad? Do you hear me? Dad? Why did you leave us, Dad? Why did you look at me like I was a bug? Why did you choose to talk Cat into coming with you, Dad? And not me? I fucking loved you. I fucking loved you. I thought you'd come back." I screamed until the rain stopped, and basically fell over sideways, exhausted. When I woke, Leo . . . no, Leif, had his arm around me.

"You did good, man," he said.

I hate that kind of shit.

When my mother flew up and drove to the lodge to get me, she looked all glowy and pink. I figured something was up.

But I never imagined how big it was.

The book thing would have been great on its own, but the guy . . . She was so, like, bubbly, she practically didn't even notice the difference in me. A beard (well, stubble) and the rest. She talked all the way home on the plane. She kept shaking me out of my stupor. She didn't seem to notice that something had transpired with me that wasn't physical, either. Maybe it hadn't. Maybe, or so I thought at the time, I was just worn out, or had that thing people get when they're held hostage. But I felt different, though I was not entirely sure in what sense. Or whether it would last.

I had priorities, though.

When I walked in the door, I kissed Rory, ate two large Tombstone pizzas, and fell into my bed.

He was there when I woke up.

Matt.

I sort of wanted to reenter my own life on my own. But he was an all right guy. I'd only met him before a few times. Now, I had to see him in this sort of bizarre new light. I knew from his having stayed overnight at our house—though they didn't sleep in the same bed; I could tell that from the laundry—that she was gooey about him. But I'd never figured her for the second-marriage type, given her complete loyalty to Leo, as-a-person-wise, which continues to this day. My grandparents had something for my mom, so he had to go over there. He asked me if I'd come. I shrugged. He kind of insisted. On the drive, after he asked me about the wilderness trip, Matt wondered out loud whether it was okay, his marrying Julie.

I said I didn't run her life.

But I thought it was borderline classy of him to do that.

We picked up what Gram wanted to give Mom, which was some laces made into a hat thing—they were hand-tatted by my grandmother's grandmother, and they were for my mom to wear with her cream lace suit. And I wasn't to tell Mom until the day before the ceremony.

On the way back, we stopped to get a sandwich, and Matt asked if I was going to school and if I would consider the East Coast. I said that right now, I wanted to stay by my grandparents. He didn't object.

When we walked in the door, my mom all of a sudden started to cry. She said, "You're as tall as Matthew."

I looked him in the eye. I was.

Matt stayed on the phone most of the time, making all these secret preparations for the wedding.

Then one day, we were driving to Connie's to borrow this little religious medal Connie wanted my mother to pin to her underwear. Again, Matt made me come along.

"How do you think your grandparents are taking this?" he asked me.

I told him the truth; how my grandparents felt about my mother marrying this guy was unreadable. They were understandably sad. Regretful, more like. They weren't losing her. But they were sort of sealing off this part of their lives, the part in which they were really any part of Julieanne's family, except through us. They would have to have whatever kind of link they could have with Leo. There hadn't been a divorce in the Steiner family in four hundred years. It made me fall silent, thinking that over.

"So car-wise, it's a beater," Matt said, totally out of nowhere. "Yours."

"Gets me where I have to go," I said. "You don't know what we went through to get that car. Well, what she went through."

"Dream car?"

"Real or like Testarossa?"

"Real.

"MXI. Four-banger with—"

"The Subaru, right?"

"You see it?"

"I mess with cars. I have the standard doctor car, the Explorer, because half the time I can't get out of my driveway and I have to get to the hospital on time. But if I played cars, that would be up there."

At Connie's condo, I hopped out, and she stood on her tiptoes to kiss me. She gave me the religious medal. "Now, all we need is something blue before you give her away," she said. This was a woman's joke, I gathered, and mentioned that I didn't see why they didn't just give her all the stuff themselves.

"I don't know myself," Matt said. "I think if they just shoved it at her before she walked down the aisle, it wouldn't be like, what do they call it, a trousseau. The woman's wedding stuff. Special stuff you only wear once."

"Speaking of aisles, where would that aisle be, Matt?" I asked.

"All in good time, Gabe," he said. "We have two weeks yet. You don't know what I have up my sleeve."

But I did.

I knew the big surprise was he was going to talk Cat into coming. She sent me letters, which I now occasionally answered with two lines. I was more or less happy she would be there because it would make my mother happy.

Three days before the wedding, Matt arrived from Boston with a suitcase the size of my bed. He opened it in the hall and started handing out airline tickets: Gram, Gramp, Cathy, Connie, extras for Stella and her husband. Then, brochures of the suites we had at the Bellagio Hotel in Las Vegas. The wedding chapel—he'd blacked out the cost, but I could still read it—that went for two large. "Okay, let's get organized. We leave tomorrow on the four o'clock plane."

I knew Cath had to have been in on it. What I didn't know was that half of fucking Sheboygan, even Klaus and Liesel, plus a dozen of Matt's friends and their wives, and his daughter, would be in attendance. It was almost humiliating.

Luke drove by in his beat-up paint truck—he was painting for the summer—and said, "What the hell is going on here, mon?" Luke hadn't gotten the athletic scholarship he wanted, partly because of his size and partly because he kept reinjuring his knee. I was going to college a year ahead of him. For the first time in our life, we were total equals.

There were trucks and junk in the driveway, the rental sign, the guy from the moving company with contracts on a clipboard.

"All this for one second marriage?"

"Massive undertaking, dude. Matt does things in a big way. They're getting married in Las Vegas."

"Not here?"

"Memories."

"He's from out east? Not there?"

"He's from Boston. But he's got this Vegas thing in his mind. I guess memories for him, too. He had a wife who died."

Luke nodded.

"I'll go there for part of the summer, then come back and stay with the grandparents until school. Come out. We can go to the Cape."

"I gotta work daily and weekends, mon. When's that?"

"What?"

"School."

"January, probably."

"You're going to live *in* Milwaukee?" Luke asked me now, in our soon-to-be-ex driveway. "The city?"

"No, here. At my grandparents' place. I don't think I could stand, uh, dorm life. Sounds so fun. Soap fights and panty raids."

"Are they ever going out there? The grandparents? To be near the short unit and you?"

"They're thinking on it. Maybe after a while. They're getting pretty Sequoia. It would be fairly disloyal to Leo, or at least they probably think so. And there's the cottage. They could still go there, though. For summers. They really love my mother."

"That's sweet. I mean that in a not really cynical way, dude. Way to go for the Julie."

"Yeah, he invited half the fucking town. Surprised you won't be there."

"I wouldn't mind. Excellent babes in Vegas."

Luke grinned. I grinned. He was still Luke, basically a goofy, good-hearted person. I was kind of glad, then, that we'd both be hanging around Wisconsin for a while. Like me, he was basically a C-minus kind of kid with no idea of what he wanted to do. And since he no longer had to certifiably avoid me in exchange for his stature within the dominant pack, I had no reason to resent him. So when we hung out, I didn't remind Luke of all the times in school when I'd been invisible to him. Bitterness does take a whole lot of energy, thank you, Leif. Pretty soon, we were just ordinary friends, like we'd been long ago, writing *Upper West Side Story* in my room.

Later that day, seeing the comings and goings, just as if Luke'd been staying over at my house every weekend, the way he did in seventh grade, Luke came back. Washed up, comb marks in his hair, with his mom. She hung on my mother's shoulder and said, "We're going to miss you so much. So much."

"Futures change, Peg," my mother said. "We have to adapt and change with them. I'm going to miss you, too. I'm going to miss a lot of things around here. The paper. Cathy—wow. And my in-laws. And I'm going to miss Luke like crazy. I'm glad he and Gabe are friends again." It was funny. Mom was her ordinary self, the way it had been when Peg dropped over all the time, even though Peg had basically seemed to lose her ability to see Mom on the street when Luke had become a sports hero and Mom a divorced crip. Futures change. You adapt. You give up what sucks because it takes too much out of you.

I had to admit it. My mother set a classy example.

That was when the WRX STI pulled into the driveway. I knew it was last year's model, but it was classic black, silver fleck, leather seats. A guy knocked on the door. "Gabe Gillis?" he asked when I answered. He had a clipboard and a shirt on with a patch from Mellony Motors.

"Sure," I said uncertainly.

"Uh-oh," said Luke. "What befalleth us?"

I turned and went back into the house.

"Listen, there's no way," I told Matt, who was on the phone with caterers and marriage-license guys and junk. "Really, man, get off the phone a minute." He said he'd get back in touch and faced me. "The bribe thing," I said. "You don't need to. She's the one you're marrying."

"What's the point, Gabe?" he asked. He took me by surprise.

"Of what?"

"The Man Without a Country act," Matt said. "You marry a woman, and you marry her whole family. That's the fact."

Luke followed me in. "That's a flat four-banger with a turbo charge. Listen, I'm basically willing for you to adopt me," he said to Matt.

"You can send it back or keep it," Matt said. "I got my daughter a classic Mustang. It's just a damn car."

"I'm not your son."

"No, you're *her* son. And that means I owe you. For taking care of her so long. But if you feel like it makes an ass out of you, I'll tell the guy to drive it back to the lot."

I thought it over. It was possible the car had strings attached, but there was no way I was going to get out of this without some obligation to Matt. I might as well enjoy it. "That is the ride of my dreams, Matt. Proud to welcome you to the family," I said. I shook his hand and he kind of half hugged me.

"And I as well," added Luke.

We drove all over the fucking town, until midnight. Even Luke's hair-teeth former buddies, sitting in their cars eating fries at the ice-cream place that used to be my grandparents' store, were blown back. It wasn't that bad.

The next morning was three-ring chaos.

My mother had packed for both of us. Sport coat. White shirt. Tie. Jeans. Swim trunks. She'd forgotten shoes. I got some out, red Converse high-tops. A small gesture, but important, I thought. I wondered what sort of getup Caro would wear. I tried to picture handwoven Hudson River goth. They were sure I had no clue. But I'd heard the whispered references to "her," and "her plane." I was prepared to suspend overt hostilities for the weekend, for the sake of Mom's tranquillity. Gram and Gramp showed up before nine in the morning, just to make sure they didn't miss anything. They sat there asking shouldn't we leave for the airport? Matt asked Mom, "Did you remember your shoes?"

"Go to hell," she said, like a little girl, sassing. They both cracked up. This was evidently a huge private joke.

Cath packed mother-and-daughter dresses for her and Abby Sun. With like, fifteen minutes before the limo came, Gram remembered she forgot her dental appliance.

"Leave it, Hannah," my grandfather grumbled.

"I'll have a migraine the whole weekend," she all but yelled at him.

I volunteered to get it. After all, I'd had the car only one night. We somehow dragged ourselves and our various traps onto the plane.

This hotel, it had fountains that danced to Frank Sinatra songs. The Eiffel Tower was across the goddamned street. "This place has changed," Matt marveled. "It's like Disneyland for adults."

"It's obscene," my mother said, staring around her with her bags at her feet, at a lobby that couldn't seem to decide whether it was an art museum, a waterfall, or a sculpture garden. "But in a kind of nuts, beautiful way."

"No, it's *garish*," Matt said. "That's an entirely different thing. *Garish* is okay."

"At least it's air-conditioned," my mother said, taking his arm. I could see her wilting, and wasn't sure whether she was having second thoughts—on the whole, at her age, not a bad idea—or simply needed to sleep. "I'm packing it in, party animals," she said. "I'm going upstairs."

And so instead of the spa haircut and massage she'd been gifted with by Matt, my mother slept away her wedding eve, not because she was sick but because, she later told me, sleep makes women over forty beautiful. But Matt and Cathy, along with Matt's thirty or so friends and my grandfather, who was shameless, played blackjack until two A.M. Gramp was out of his tree. He won two thousand bucks, and, being Grandpa Steiner, he saw this in terms of what it could buy him—a new pier for the cottage—and stopped. Everyone else was outraged.

Rory was bug-eyed, but I took her to watch the Cirque du Soleil show called *O,* in which nuts with the bodies of gods and goddesses dived and flipped and soared onto a stage that was, minute by minute, either covered with enough water to keep them from spinal damage or barely enough to wet the sole of a shoe. "Are they God?" Rory asked.

"Yes," I answered. We stood on the balcony and watched the fountains play "Singing in the Rain."

"Tired out, shortcake?" I asked her. We could feel the spray from where we sat on the balcony. I looked down. Rory was asleep with her head on the wrought-iron table. I picked her up and carried her, struggling to find my room card. Cathy tucked Rory in.

"Are you doing okay?" I asked.

"It's kind of much," Cathy said.

"I think it's what Matt wants. He's trying pretty hard."

"Yeah, and that's a good thing," Cathy said. "It's good for him to want to be over the top for her sake. And she knows how hard Matt tried to get Caroline to come, and as much as she's trying not to grieve about that, it's pulling her under. That's probably half of why she went to sleep." I nodded, with a half smile, knowing Matt usually got what he wanted. "At least, she has until three tomorrow to rest. What are you going to do? Matt wanted to see you. . . ."

I had been thinking of turning in with a movie.

"He asked me specifically to have you check in with him before you go to bed," said Cathy.

So let him have his surprise, I thought. I wandered down to the casino. Matt was in full roar, his shirt open at the neck, Gramp next to him, cheering him on. They were basically shit-faced. It was probably two in the morning. "Hey," I said, "what did you need?"

"I looked in on your mom," he said. "She's okay; she really is. Little overwhelmed. Sad about your sister."

"So Cathy said. It's cool. I was just up there. She's not used to noise, and, Jesus, this place would stun anybody, Matt," I told him. "I'm calling it a night. That's probably against the sword code of teenagers or something, but I'm whipped. Got to get my give-my-mother-away sleep." He checked his watch.

"You're not losing a mother, Gabe. You're gaining a nut. It should be okay by now," he said. He gave me another room key. "Listen. I got you a different room. With a view." Like he thought I *enjoyed* hearing the same Celine Dion song every forty-five minutes.

"It's okay. My stuff's already in the one room," I said.

"Indulge me." I remembered the Subaru, and shrugged. I took the key and struggled, half in a fog, up to the nineteenth floor. It finally came to me. It was my sister up there. I stood outside the door, bleary with lack of sleep, confused by the whole business, eager to get it over with. I inserted the key. And there she was. Perhaps an inch taller. Sitting on the bed, wearing jeans and a soft silk sweater, her eyes glued to the whirling, dancing fountains.

It was a room with a view all right.

Tian.

THIRTY-FIVE

Gabe's Journal

"I've only just come here, Gabe," she said, jumping up off the bed and up onto her toes. "You thought I would never be here again. And here I am. And look!" She threw open her closet. "My dress from our prom. It's still fit. I came in a limousine from the airport. All this Matt set up for me. I think he must want to make you happy."

But I was speechless. I held out my hand. She bypassed it and ran into my arms, kissing me with all the fervor I remembered from the year before last. It wasn't a gift, putting the two of us alone in a Las Vegas hotel room, because there was only so much we could do. Tian's father would expect me to treat her with respect; and I knew my mother would, but she wriggled like a goldfish on the bed, and, somehow, the sweater was off, and I saw and touched the tops of her breasts, and then the glory part, and then, thinking I would die, I put my mouth there. She reached inside my shirt and held my ribs closer to her. "I have missed you so much," she said.

"There's nothing else I've thought of, for months, no matter how bad it got," I whispered into her hair. "And it got lousy, Tian."

"I know. My poor Gabe."

"It's all okay now." Our mouths were raw by then; her chin looked like someone had buffed it with a Brillo. She was impossibly beautiful, her hair like a black glass ribbon twirled over her shoulder.

"But we have to get ready for the wedding," Tian said.

"Sure, you bet," I said. "How long will you stay?"

"Three days!" she trilled. I felt my stomach hit bottom. Three days? To keep in my hip pocket for the rest of my life.

"Okay," I said, and it was better than nothing.

I slept as though I'd been beaten, and woke to the phone. It was Cathy. "Your mom wants to see you." I thought, No, God, don't let her have had some rama-lama relapse. But Cathy said it wasn't that. She also said, "I saw Ben Affleck in the lobby." What this signified I couldn't imagine. "I just bought the little girls bridesmaid dresses. Matching green. With crowns. They were like two hundred bucks apiece. I couldn't resist. . . . Gabe, honey, were you surprised? By Tian?"

"It was like a dream," I told her. "And I don't say that easy."

"Did you . . . ?"

"No, Cath. Not that it's any—"

"Any of my business. I know you would have been responsible."

"Sheesh. Let's skip the lecture. Tian's father would have the Thai mafia murder me."

"But you're happy?" Cath went on.

"Nothing changed, Cathy. I don't feel any different. I love her."

"Maybe you'll never stop loving her, Gabe. But she lives in Asia, honey."

"She's going to Yale. A year from now."

"Oh, Gabe. You are the sweetest guy," Cathy said. "Now, you better come and see Mom."

"Honey," my mother said, reaching out for me, from where she sat in the blue chair. She pointed her finger at me like she was firing a pistol and then grinned. "Gotcha," she said, and grinned. Then, just as suddenly, she looked sort of young and sad. "Am I going to be able to do this?"

"Piece of cake," I said.

"Here's the weird thing," she said. "I'm so happy. I'm so happy. I just . . . feel like I'd be more happy if I could have had your sister here. And even more, and I know you're not going to get this . . . I wish Leo was here."

She was right. I didn't get it.

"I love your dad now like I love Janey. I don't want to live with him in his life. But I wish him well."

"Mom," I said, "you're something else."

Grandma and Connie came in then. They had one of those walkers with the rubber feet old ladies use.

"Get away from me with that thing!" my mother scolded. "Yesterday, I was just bushed from the heat and all. I'm *fine*. I'm really fine. There are just a lot of emotions, coming fast."

"I'll make it beautiful, Julieanne. Just in case. Better to be safe than sorry," said Grandma.

Tian came in. "Connie?" They hugged. Tian practically crawled onto my mother's lap. "You don't look sick! You look like a magazine model!" Tian looked at the walker. "Do you have to use this?" My mother shook her head.

"It's my mother-in-law's idea. She thinks I might need it, sweetie," my mom told her. "Tian, look at you! We missed you so much."

"And I miss you, Julie. I am sad for all your sadness. And very happy for your happy. I don't like to see you sick, though."

"Secret," said my mother. "I'm not as sick as they think. I was. But I'm not now. I think I'll make it down the aisle. Unless it's a mile long!"

I leaned over and gave her a kiss on the cheek. I thought twice about the red Converse shoes, and whether I was being disrespectful. But only briefly. It was, after all, a bizarre place. Then Cathy came in, all royal in this green suit with shoes dyed to match, which I pointed at, and Cathy actually blushed, and shooed us all out of the room. "No one can see the bride before the wedding. And she's got to get dressed now."

"Do you want to bring bad luck down on this?" Connie reprimanded us, slipping past with all these flowery things like pipe cleaners she started twisting around the walker.

"Connie!" I heard my mom yell as I shut the door. "Stop that! I feel like you're putting flowers on my grave! I don't need that!"

"Better safe than sorry," Connie told her.

Matt was out in the hall, pacing like a guy in old movies waiting for his baby to be born. "Kiddo," he said to me, "I'm forty-eight years old. You wouldn't think I'd get the willies, like a nervous groom."

I said, "I don't think getting married gets to be something you're blasé about. Unless you do it, like, eight times."

But Matt was still quite the wreck. "What's taking her so long?" he asked me. I was to learn that surgeons are all cowboys, used to telling 'em to head 'em up and move 'em out. And Matt was used to being around subservient, adoring nurses—such as on the *Good Ship Hospital,* or whatever the hell it was, that traveled to places like Guatemala and Vietnam to fix kids' faces. He could get impatient when things didn't go his way. This, I knew, was a red flag the size of Lambeau Field for Miss Julieanne Gillis, who was basically the same way.

I went into my room and, trying desperately not to wrinkle it with hands that suddenly felt like I had on catcher's mitts, put on my tux.

Then I knocked on Tian's door, and steered her and me into my room, where we made out on the bed with some idiot movie turned on loud, both of us keeping stiff as sticks so we didn't wreck my suit. It was after two when she said, "Gabe." And then louder, "*Gabe!* I have to dress now. And to put makeup on my chin."

I made my way back to my mom's room. Cathy peeked out and grinned. Matt was still pacing up and down again, but now in a black tux, with three sort of Matt-clone friends pacing up and down in identical tuxes. It looked like waiters in a parade. "Where have you been?" he said, but more softly than before.

"Take it easy, Matt. This is out of your hands," I said. I went into my room. The phone rang. It was Gram Steiner, from down the hall, asking how Mom was and saying Cat had called, would I please call her back? As a gesture to the fates, I did, and I got the goddamned answering machine. "We're out among the flowers," said the voice of Joyous, "but your call matters to us. Blessed be."

"Uh, this would be Gabe Gillis," I said quickly. "My sister, Caroline Steiner, aka Cat, called me here at the Bellagio in Las Vegas. I'll tell her mother that Cat's thinking about her. Later."

For the next forty-five minutes, I sat there trying not to sweat. It didn't work. I finally called my grandmother, who came rushing over in this cute little beaded old lady dress, with a hat and veil, and called one of the millions of minions at this place, which looked like a gangster's idea of a summer home, who steamed the wrinkles out of the tuxedo. Gram fixed the bow tie, which I had managed to fool with until it was vertical instead of horizontal, and dabbed some of the stuff she put on the bags under her eyes on my zits. "Gabe," she said, "I know you brush your hair straight down. But pardon me, you look like Hitler." So I put some water on it and messed it up a little. It was intended to be the Brad Pitt effect. But then Gram had to blow-dry the front of my shirt. By that point, I was about ready to sweat again, the volume of Hoover Dam. At the last minute, I took off the patent-leather pumps that came with the thing, and laced up my red Converse high-tops.

We all came out into the hall at more or less the same time. Matt was already downstairs, getting his troops in order. His best man was his partner in his practice, Louis. Lou's brother, Joe, was standing up, too. Mom's best ladies were Connie and Stella. Her ring carrier was Tian, and the little girls had on green dresses and little fake flower crowns on their heads. They kept twirling around so fast that Abby Sun finally fell over flat. It was the only time I ever heard Connie yell at her. She made her go sit on the floor.

Finally, Connie opened the door, and one of the bellmen from the hotel came running with this wheelchair.

And my mom sat down in the wheelchair. The look in her eyes, when she saw me, was bemused. "Looks like we aren't in Sheboygan anymore, Toto. This is a little baroque."

"Well, Mom, the guy just gave me a *car* for a party favor. And, you know, it's his wedding day," I said, surprising myself. "He's trying to give you a good old time. He doesn't know you'd rather have gone to City Hall." The fountains jumped then, in the sunlight, to the sound of "Memory." (My mom loves that song, but frankly, I could stand to hear it one more time, then never again for the rest of my life.) My mother smiled at me. The sun came out and hit the water as it leapt up, movie-style.

"No," she said, "this is all good. Isn't it, honey?" She burrowed in at me with her eyes.

"It's good, Mama," I said.

She gathered up her skirt around her legs so it wouldn't hit the rubber wheels of the wheelchair, and Grandma Steiner pinned the lace thing on the back of her hair, cockeyed. Connie reached over and straightened it, discreetly, and took the flower-covered walker. I took Abby's and Rory's hands, and down we all went, to the wedding chapel. The funny thing was, the sight of a wedding party, much less a wedding party with two Asian girls, one sixteen and one a tot, an old Jewish lady in a blue hat with veil, and a bride in a wheelchair, drew fewer stares than it would have in Sheboygan. I mean, people didn't look up from the craps table. We wheeled into the anteroom of the chapel, which was sort of under-the-sea decorated, and waited for whatever Matt had up his sleeve. There was an interval, where we all sort of stood there, while Stella's husband and everybody else sat down. It looked like a regular church, except up there at the front, on a side table with drapes and bows all over it was this wedding cake the size of the fake Eiffel Tower across the street. "Is this how people get married in America?" Tian whispered.

"Not usually," I said.

And then, he appeared.

It was, sweet Christ, Elvis.

On the whole, however, the serenade from the Elvis impersonator was not so bad. He was a guy in his twenties, with a dynamite voice, and he didn't schmaltz it up too bad. He was the leather-jacket Elvis, not the fat gold jumpsuit and sunglasses Elvis. And the song he sang, about fools rushing in, but being unable to help falling in love, had my mom holding her head back so that she wouldn't cry and make her makeup run down her face. I saw Matt's daughter, Kelly, this tall blonde girl with the body of a beach volleyball player, giving the come-over eye to the Elvis, who saw it, too. He hung around, when he would normally, pardon me for this, have left the building.

Then a recording came on, of the song Rory called "Taco Bell's Cannon." Grandma Steiner began to help my mother up.

But my mom put her hands on the arms of the wheelchair and gave me this look like Rory when she's done something smart but kind of mischievous. "Head fake!" she whispered. And she said to Grandma and Connie, "I just let you guys wheel me down here for grins. Thanks for the ride." She stood up, and, with raised eyebrows, she gently shoved the decorated walker behind a row of chairs. She reached out one hand for me. "Let's do it, Gabe," she said. And she took one step. She wobbled a little. "Don't worry," she said. "It's not being sick. It's just two-inch heels and nerves."

Then she put on the Gillis game face, pulled herself up, and held my arm tighter. And she walked right down that aisle like a racehorse, into Matt's arms.

That's the end of the novel. But it's not the end of the story.

THIRTY-SIX

Psalm 65

EXCESS BAGGAGE
By J. A. Gillis
Distributed by Panorama Media

Dear Reader,

It has been quite a few years now that we've spent together. That is why it's so difficult to say that now it's time for me to go. I have to say it quickly, or I'll take it back. It's so difficult for me to let go of this column, more so to give you up. You might think that the reason I've written this column was that I believed that I could help you. Well, certainly, I wanted to do that, and I was curious to see whether I could. But the truth is, the way it worked out, you helped me, immeasurably, to survive the worst passage of my life. When you wrote me, with problems that made my own seem small—my battles with multiple sclerosis, a deceitful and yet good-hearted ex-husband, and raising children alone as a disabled person—you helped me. You helped me go on, and to see that there was hope for me as long as I could breathe out and breathe in, love a song, listen to my child laugh. You were my lifeline. A version of this column is going to show up soon in a magazine once a month, and I hope you run

*across it. But if you don't, know this; I gave you advice, and, if
it helped, I'm grateful. But you gave me back my dignity.*

Sincerely,

Julieanne Gillis

It was Gabe's idea to combine our journals and massage them into a novel.

I had no idea about his journals, and how hard it must have been for him to concentrate on writing all that down. Of course, he'd read every word of mine.

You must think that we all lived happily ever after. No one does, though. Eventually, a version of that flower-bedecked walker sat in my closet, and there were times when I used it. There were times when I took ballet. There were times when I stayed in bed. There were times when I didn't dare drive Rory to school, and times when I felt I could have driven in the Indy. So far, I've never had a full-out relapse. But I've lost a tiny little bit of ground every year. And yet, my bones are strong, and I will fight this thing until it wrestles me to the ground. If it's up to me, that's going to take a long time.

Matt drank a little more than a little.

He wasn't a drunk.

His parents drank.

We had *that* in common, and there are two ways that can go. I didn't drink much. He drank whenever it was safe. He never drank anywhere close to his work, and he was a damned good surgeon.

But finally, I told him off about it. And instead of getting defensive, he got quiet for a while. Then he agreed that he was married now and a dad to Rory, so he toned down the big-football-road-trip stuff. These days, he has a full glass of Merlot when I have my half glass. He found out mighty quickly that I wasn't one of his nurses or interns and that he couldn't set up a plan for our life, or even our weekend, and outline my place in it. That led to some long and not-very-romantic nights, in which both of us got our Irish way too far up. It was natural. We didn't really know each other when we walked down that long aisle in Las Vegas. I didn't know that he hand-washed his wineglasses. He didn't know I flooded the floor of the bathroom when I washed my face.

And probably, we weren't in love when we got married.

I think Matt believed he was marrying the girl he'd always wanted, Little Miss Prep, Julieanne Gillis. I knew that I had stumbled on what was potentially a wonderful and safe thing. But for me, it was probably more a sense that we were well suited to each other than a grand passion. I thought we would be good companions. I would be safe. He would be, in public at least, proud.

Is that a terrible thing to say?

I'm way too far past wanting to gloss things over. It's the truth.

He became my mate. He came through. He came through when I tripped over something and took it out on him, and told him he was a sicko for wanting to be married to a woman who was a wax figure about three days of the month. His jaw set, but the next morning, he brought me a mug of coffee. And we clinked cups. We went on. If he got impatient on the days when I couldn't remember whether I wanted my laptop or my blow-dryer, he didn't show it. He used to throw all kinds of fancy-dress things. Now, we just do one, at Christmas, because they take too much out of me.

He thinks there are compensations for the hostess I might have been, in the confidante that I am. And you know what? He's right.

I've never spoken with Leo again, except through letters and e-mails.

When she was old enough, Rory went out there for a couple of weeks in the summer. She came back furious, saying Joy was bossy and mean to Caroline. This lacerated my heart, and I wrote Cat, begging her to come to us in Boston. But she had decided to go to New York, to try to take ballet seriously, to live with Joy's sister. She writes, and I have plans to visit her there next summer. I don't know how it will go. I know Caro never stopped loving me, but she's as bullheaded as I was at her age. It will be hard for her to admit that living with Leo, dearly as he loves her, was a bad idea.

I'm hopeful, because we can reach each other around dance.

We always could. I'm hopeful she'll let us help her along, and gradually, she'll slip in through the back door of this new family. So I'm going to praise my daughter the dancer and try to put my daughter, the defector, behind us. Caroline never grew taller than five feet two and I'd be surprised if she tops a hundred pounds. Her turnout was amazing from the time she was a little tiny kid, and her grand jeté startled Leah when she was small.

She could do it. She could make it.

It would be an ugly life. But it would be punctuated with great bursts of exaltation.

Which, as Gabe would say, is mostly like life, for anyone.

With a little bit of hurt pride, Gabe said after the wedding that I finally had my new life, so he wasn't going to be around that much. I knew Gabe well enough to know he protested too much. He started coming out the first summer, and now he and Matt are basically thick as thieves.

Matt wanted a child with me.

I told him that it was out of the question. We were both on the nether end of our forties by then, and adoption agencies weren't going begging for wobbly old mothers when there were legions of the young and strong variety available. One summer night, though, he brought home a picture of a two-year-old girl, who'd been born in Vietnam, the daughter of a prostitute, with a cleft palate that extended up into her nasal cavity. I put the picture facedown on my lap. But later that night, I picked it up. On the telephone with Cathy, we reached the mutual conclusion that the very thought of this was madness. I was ready to tell Matthew that the next morning, when, instead, I signed the papers.

Matt wouldn't work on his own daughter's face. But he scrubbed in, for eleven surgeries.

It was when I saw Matt come out of the operating room after her first surgery, his eyes red above the mask he quickly peeled off, the smile he valiantly tried to fake, the nod that signaled things had gone well, that I fell hard for him. Or I realized how much I'd cared, and prudently stored away, from the beginning. I let it rip after that.

And I remember thinking, with an inner gasp of panic, how horrible it would be if he were married to someone else. Just in time, I went nuts over my own husband. I began to invest, as he had, in the gestures of our marriage. It became more than Matt's being "a good man." Matt's being "a solid man."

He became my heart.

Our daughter is four now. We called her Pamela Lang, because Matt insisted we call her after me. The nuns at the orphanage hospital called her "Lang" as an endearment. In Vietnamese, it literally means "sweet potato." They used it to describe our daughter's nature, which was sunny despite the titanic challenges she faced. Now, she sings all day, and speaks English as if she'd grown up in Marin County. Rory would carry her around on a platter, and Lang would go for that. I'm certainly the oldest mother at the preschool—well, that's not entirely true, and I don't look as old as I really am. Oh, yeah, yeah, all is vanity, but it's true! Still, I'm definitely the only one with a cane.

Pamela is my real name.

Of course, you never like your real name.

Julieanne is just the prettiest name I could think of. For the book. This book.

We never lived in Sheboygan, Wisconsin. I've never even *been* in Sheboygan, Wisconsin. But we lived somewhere in the Midwest, where there was a smallish city with pine trees. Gabe's real name is Daniel. It suits him. He has the soul of a Daniel. We had to change all the names and places to protect the innocent, and as my Gabe (I'll call him Gabe here, for the sake of avoiding confusion) would say, not to flatter the guilty. I won't tell Caroline's real name. Someday, you might see her on a stage, and the pain between us, which may have healed by then, is too private.

None of the changes to names and places is to suggest that any of this isn't true. My father was a writer; my ex was a lawyer. There was that harrowing trip they took, which to this day I suspect I know of only in the edited version. It isn't fact. But it's true. All of it's true. It's possible, sometimes, and even necessary, to avoid the facts to tell the truth.

Cath is still my best friend. When Klaus died, and Liesel went to live in Europe, Cathy bought the old place. She's still on her own, but her practice is thriving. She had another psychologist working for her. I tell her that her success is all thanks to me, having lent her an in-house puzzle of family dysfunction to play with. Abby Sun has a little sister. I go to see them at least once a year, and within my limits, we have a big-girl party: Stella and Rory and Abby and the baby, Lang, and I. Cath and I go to class, which Leah *still* teaches, and more often than not, I can still get my leg up on that barre and my head down on that leg. And though I can't leap, or do an open pirouette anymore, I can still do a double that's good enough for government work.

The poetry book was sort of just what the agent said it would be, a greeting card for women who were pissed off, and bought to give to each other. The novel, because of its odd juxtaposition of authors and origins, had a modest success. When it was published, Gabe and I were on TV, on a morning show you would recognize, with a nice man whose name is a household word. We had a ball, waving at the people from our hometown outside the glass windows. That night, we went to see Brian Stokes Mitchell in *Man of La Mancha*. I took my shot, and spent the next two days in bed.

That's life.

I still have MS.

And Gabe still has learning disabilities.

He dropped out of college after the first semester in the achievement program. He was through. Kaput. Done. He felt as though they'd gone from treating him like pond scum to treating him as though he needed a seeing-eye dog. I got mad, and asked him what disgrace there would be in someone needing a seeing-eye dog. Or a walker, for example. He was contrite then. It was only that he was ashamed. After a year back home painting houses with Luke, living with my in-laws, he applied to journalism school at Columbia. That lasted one semester. Then he found this program in Boston for writers who have learning disabilities, a college within a college. It was pricey, but Matt encouraged him. Money doth have its privileges, and we hired a discreet full-time tutor, to supplement what the college provided. Gabe got along, and, with the help of a program that they normally use for little kids to organize the thought-hand process, he was soon flying along, putting down his ideas without burying the lead.

The following summer, Gabe got an internship at a newspaper in Connecticut. The second weekend he was there, after having moved into one room in the house of an old lady who had, Gabe said, either five or six golden retrievers, he drove up to Yale. He didn't know what he'd encounter. Except for a few notes, he hadn't heard from Tian since our wedding. My heart squeezed when I thought of what I was pretty sure he'd get for a greeting: Tian's joyous hail-fellow-well-met-American-boy-I-once-liked. I didn't hear from him the first day. I didn't hear from him the second day.

The mother hen in me finally won out, and I called and left a message on his cell phone.

When he called back, that night, my first words were, "What happened, Gabe?"

And he said, "Everything."

They're still together. Tian will finish college in a year, and so will Gabe. She has eight hard years of med school before her, and I'll be surprised if they make it. The intense purity of their love is dizzying to see. I think of a couple of kids whom I knew once, kids who couldn't wait. Perhaps they can.

Stranger things have happened. Against longer odds. I know that from experience. I got lucky. Maybe they'll get lucky. Gabe is the kind of guy I knew would fall utterly if he ever found the one. He found her when he was fourteen.

Myriad disconnections. A version of that phrase is what I called my book of so-called poetry for the pissed off. But it's a mirror of my life, or a metaphor for it. I had a life as neatly trimmed out as one of my Katharine Hepburn shirts tucked into my ever-so-nattily pressed trousers. Then, bit by bit, the way the sheath that protects the nerves ruptures and flakes in the body of a person who has multiple sclerosis, that life began to detach, parts from the whole, daughter and husband spinning off and away, function and form giving me chase, beyond my ability to catch up, until the whole was a collection, with parts in different places, no longer a tidy sum. And I thought, That's it, my life, my children's lives, would never add up again to more than a fraction of what had been.

But, slowly, bit by bit, more to the credit of Cathy and Gabe than to me, the parts again began to add up to something, then to something more. I'm not sure that the first life was in any sense a false life. It was not a failure, but it had a limited warranty. This is the one I have now, though, and I have to think it's better. It has the bouquet of longevity.

Not every woman who has this bastard disease will hold on to as much as I've been able to hold on to. I'm surrounded by medicine—with Kelly, Matt's daughter, in med school, with Tian, with my husband. There are many more than I who get dealt a harsher hand, and never draw a face card. That's what I speak about now, when I do speeches, the need for services and research and the need for grit—and also in favor of doing what Jennet told me, so long ago, getting up and getting a life. I'm only a person, but I have a big mouth. Maybe, as Leo said, I once was the duchess of smug, and I deserved a comeuppance. But no one deserves this kind of comeuppance. And no one *deserves* this good turn of fortune. It's all like Papa Steiner, bless his soul—he's still doing great—told Matt that weekend at the blackjack table. You win, and someone else goes bust. Next time, it might be you.

Some nights, when I've had a frustrating day, a day of garbled words and knocked-over chairs, and a creamer that overflows the coffee cup while I watch my disembodied hand go right on pouring it, when I've sent Lang to her room because I deserved it, or had to miss Rory's soccer game, I dream that I'm dancing. I dream the lights have come on, and I'm Odette, the swan princess. I fly onto that stage, and raise my arms, my ankle level with my forehead in grand battement. My fluttering leaps are effortlessness, in a way that they never really were in my waking life. My crossed hands, in the swan position, are poignancy in human form. I look out into the audience, and there is Leo, shaking his head in disgust when I can't unfurl myself from my bowed pose, shrugging on his jacket, leaving the hall without looking back. I wake, and my hands are fluttering, but it's because I tremor in the night, sometimes so much that I can't sleep.

Then I reach for Matt, and wake him, even if I know he has surgery in the morning. I shake him awake and ask him, "Are we still married?"

And he mumbles, "Yes, Julieanne. We're married. Go to sleep. We're still married. I'm here." If I'm lucky, I fall back into a kind of slumber, a sweaty and shuddering simulation of rest. I hold Matt's leg, to make sure he hasn't gone somewhere I can't go.

But when I wake, in the morning, I can smell the coffee brewing. He's still there. I'm still there. One more morning.

July 4, 2004
Cape Cod, Massachusetts